BOOKS B
CU00403999

LYNX

THE WILL SLATER SERIES BOOK FOUR

MATT ROGERS

1

Chocó
Colombia

Lying on his back in a puddle of sweat, Will Slater inhaled lungfuls of the thick jungle air and gave thanks he'd reclaimed his health.

He rolled over, onto his knees. Rivulets of perspiration ran down his forehead, along the bridge of his nose, and dripped to the floor of the training room. He focused all concentration on his breathing, and that took his mind off everything else. The lactic acid burning hot in his limbs began to subside. The aching dulled, second by second. More uncomfortable than he'd been in months, he allowed himself a smile.

Because he hadn't been certain whether he could work his way up to this level of physical fitness again.

And now he had. Another mental barrier shattered.

Now it was all muscle memory.

The mind body connection.

He was the monster he used to be.

He was sure of it.

He climbed to his feet, sweat glistening along his breast-bone. There wasn't a shred of body fat to be found. Two months ago his physical condition had been a different story entirely, but that was in the past.

He'd suffered a concussion, on the other side of the world, six long months ago.

He'd spent almost four months in bed, doing nothing in particular. Letting his brain recover. Letting his synapses heal. Letting his shattered mind repair itself, piece by miserable piece, willing it back to health with nothing but the strength of his own thoughts.

Four long, agonising months. No exercise. Nothing to do besides lie in bed, or pace around the room, or step outside for a brisk walk every now and then to breathe the winter air.

The Russian Far East hadn't been kind to him. Not in the slightest.

And then, day by day, he'd gotten better.

For a long time he thought he never would. He thought the headaches would be permanent, removing any hope of returning to the life he knew. Then one day he woke up feeling ever so slightly replenished. Nothing he could put his finger on. Something subtle, buried under the leviathan of his conscious thoughts.

But deep down in there, something had healed.

It probably wouldn't last forever. He knew that. Sooner or later the violence that had plagued his life for as long as he could remember would catch up to him, and he would succumb to the sinister effects of chronic traumatic encephalopathy. It was becoming a commonplace issue in the media now the medical industry had invented machines to test for it. Most notable in the NFL, popularised by damning reports. You could only take so many knocks to the head before your brain threw in the towel and gave up on any hope of a normal reality.

But so far, he hadn't experienced anything like that. And the reports didn't refute it. Everyone's brain is built differently, they said. Some can take more bumps than others.

Slater was built tough.

He fetched a white exercise towel, neatly folded on top of a pile situated in the far corner of the room. He returned to the stretch of marble floor where he conducted his morning calisthenics regime and wiped with vigour until all the puddles of sweat were absorbed. Then he turned and faced the tropical jungle river flowing past his compound and breathed in the humidity, allowing the stillness to close his pores and stop him perspiring.

It would take time.

Here in the bowels of Colombia, this far off the beaten track, the compound he'd purchased under a false name lay draped in ninety percent humidity twenty four hours a day, seven days a week.

It deterred most from venturing this deep into the country, even for a brief day trip. The humidity brought a level of discomfort few were capable of tolerating.

Not to mention the other threats.

Slater had yet to encounter any of the fabled *narcotraficantes* the region was infamous for. The jungles attracted all kinds of vermin that didn't want their business visible in the public eye. Slater had to concede he was following the same principles, but he put an imaginary line between his own past misgivings and the horrors associated with the Colombian cartels. They were out here — he knew it. He sensed their presence. There was darkness in the jungle — the canopy of trees hid an amalgamation of filth.

But he hadn't thrown himself into the line of fire.

Not yet.

So, he left the open-plan training area, his morning work completed. On the way to the bathroom he stepped up to a heavy bag swinging from the ceiling and delivered an earth-shattering uppercut into the damp leather, omitting a *crack* that spilled out onto the river and disappeared into the tropical air. A move chalked up to muscle memory more than anything else.

Just a nervous tic, to remind himself he was always ready.

At least that's what he told himself.

He showered fast, keeping the water cold as ice. In fact, he'd paid a handsome fee to install state-of-the-art pipes in the compound, ensuring he didn't have to wait long, agonising minutes for the temperature to adjust to how he preferred. The downpour, barely above freezing, chilled him to the core. The sweating ceased instantaneously as the sudden change in body temperature delivered a shock to his central nervous system. He shut the water off and towelled himself dry.

Skin tingling.

Brain firing on all cylinders.

Well and truly awake.

The routine had returned. Four months of inactivity had nearly rendered him useless, but he'd found the pain and discomfort of years past and tapped into it. As he dressed in simple chinos and a plain cotton tee, he glanced at himself in the enormous mirror and came away satisfied with what he saw for the first time in nearly half a year. He stood tall, his shoulders back, his chin held high, his body rippling with the kind of musculature that could only be forged after endless gruelling sessions. There were no personal trainers out here. No encouragement from friends or family. Just the heat of the jungle and the solitude of his own mind. He didn't want it any other way. The isolated compound eliminated excuses, and that was what he needed to return to the Will Slater of the past.

Maybe that's why he hadn't ventured out into the jungle yet.

He knew there was evil out there, and he knew it wouldn't take much effort to find it.

But he needed to bring the old guy back first.

He moved into the living area, another enormous high-ceilinged space resting directly adjacent to the training room. Both spaces had a wall missing, and both faced the river and the tree-lined bank opposite. The hum of insects infiltrated the air, rancid and incessant, but Slater had become so accustomed to the sound that it barely registered.

He started planning the rest of the day. He figured he would head into town for a meal, replenishing his muscles after the gruelling morning session. Then maybe a run in the jungle heat to assault his senses and increase his lung capacity. Then a few drinks. Then...

He didn't know. And that was the best part. He had no particular rush to get anywhere or do anything. In the port city of Vladivostok he'd sworn to continue confronting the worst of humankind, but he knew that wouldn't take much effort. They would find him before long. He wouldn't even have to try.

So he admired the view and soaked in the serenity for a few moments...

...and then a piercing squeal shattered the silence.

The doorbell.

He had an unannounced visitor.

2

Despite not having a clue as to what he might find, Slater knew it was nothing good. He'd yet to receive a visitor during the two months he'd spent in the finished construction, and he hadn't expected to receive one until Colombia grew stale and he disposed of the property as discreetly as possible.

So as he strode down the smooth modern hallway, made of glass and steel and concrete, a certain trepidation washed over him. But at the same time there was something more intoxicating, something primal and animalistic nagging at the recesses of his mind.

Because this might be threatening.

And Slater hadn't been threatened in quite some time.

In truth, he almost hoped he found confrontation. He couldn't deny the toxicity of the mindset. What if this was just lost travellers? He figured unnecessary hostility wasn't prudent.

So he opened the giant entrance door with a placid expression on his face.

Keeping things nonchalant. Acting unassuming, as best he could.

Then it all changed.

There were three men. None of them looked pleasant. Each was built like a praying mantis packed with lean, wiry muscle. All three were taller than Slater, ranging from six foot one to six foot six. The tallest of the three happened to be the heaviest, and he carried himself with a suitable confidence. It seeped from his pores, attempting to take command of the atmosphere before anyone had uttered a sentence. They were dressed in simple singlets and cargo shorts to alleviate the overbearing heat.

All three were sweating.

Slater started sweating, too. He tingled with anticipation. He held the giant wooden door in one hand, and kept the other low at his side, his fingers twitching. He assumed at least one of them noticed.

But they didn't understand what it meant.

He was ready to kill.

The tallest of the three smiled through a mouthful of teeth stained with artificial peroxide and said, 'No need to look so grumpy, hombré.'

Slater said, 'I'm fine.'

The shortest said, 'Nice place you got here.'

Slater said, 'Thanks.'

An uncomfortable pause. Slater didn't feel the need to advance the conversation, and he kept his gaze locked on the tallest man. He deduced the guy with the white teeth would be the first to lash out if it came to that. Unbridled tension supercharged the air around their heads.

'You're not going to invite us in?' the tallest man said.

'Why would I do that?'

'A friendly gesture, perhaps.'

'I'm not looking for friends.'

'How do you know that? The three of us are nice guys.'

'That's good to hear.'

'You don't even know our names. And we don't know yours.'

'Not interested.'

'Now, that's not very nice at all, friend.'

'We're not friends.'

'Don't you want to know my name?'

'Not particularly.'

'Usually people want to know my name.'

'I don't.'

'Usually people are nicer to me.'

'Sorry to disappoint.'

'If you knew who I was, you might be nicer.'

Slater swung the door a half foot towards the closed position. 'Do the three of you want anything? Or is this all to puff your chests out?'

'I am Bautista,' the tall man said.

'Good for you.'

He gestured to the shortest and said, 'This is Vicente.'

Vicente had the rabid energy of a naturally gifted athlete who knew he was fast, and powerful. Slater didn't find his type often, but when he did it set him on edge. The man didn't need to overcompensate for his limitations by packing on muscle — his frame was skinny, but noticeably strong. He was a bundle of fast twitch muscle fibres waiting to explode. He kept his sinewy arms crossed over his thin chest, exposing the veins in his biceps. He shifted back and forth on the balls of his feet, tensing his rippling calf muscles in turn.

The man's beady eyes drilled into Slater.

Maybe a consumer of the product these men no doubt

manufactured and packaged and funnelled through Colombia.

He was too jumpy to be sober.

Bautista gestured to the middle guy and said, 'This is Iván.'

Iván had little redeeming qualities — at least at surface level. He wasn't particularly well built and had none of the natural athleticism that Bautista and Vicente possessed. He was wholly unimpressive in Slater's eyes. It made Slater wonder what his strengths were. He must have an ace up his sleeve to have embedded himself with this ragtag group of undesirables.

'Lovely to meet you all,' Slater said. 'Is there anything I can do for you?'

Bautista stiffened and said, 'It is usually polite for the other party in the conversation to introduce themselves in turn.'

'Right,' Slater said, then followed up with, 'Is there anything I can do for you?' with the same sardonic tone.

'You can ask us who we are.'

'I couldn't care less who you are.'

'I think you should.'

'Narcos?' Slater said. 'Is that what you're getting at? I'm quaking.'

He said it dismissively, without a shred of interest in his tone. The trio picked up on it, and it set them on edge. Slater spotted them shifting a little faster on the balls of their feet. They weren't accustomed to a reaction like that. They were used to eliciting fear wherever they went. They were masters of intimidation.

Not here.

Not with Will Slater.

'On your way,' Slater said, dismissing them with a wave of the hand.

'Listen, you fucking—' Bautista started.

There was venom in his tone, and the instant Slater recognised it he burst into motion. He threw the door open with enough verve to startle all three of them, and he noticed Vicente and Iván backing up, reaching for leather appendix holsters tucked into their cargo shorts. Momentarily, he thought he'd made a mistake. He could die right here, right now — all because of his foolish recklessness. But he knew the specifics of human confrontation well enough to have faith in his ability to read people. And all three of the men in front of him knew he was clearly unarmed. Therefore any move to draw a weapon would seem like a horrendous overreaction, which would only serve to make whoever did it look like a weak idiot.

Slater was right.

The two men backed up, and their hands twitched imperceptibly, but they didn't wrench their pistols from their holsters and fire like morons.

Iván even let out a bout of nervous laughter, quickly cut off by Slater's subsequent tirade.

'You fucking *what?*' Slater hissed at Bautista, who hadn't stepped back, but had definitively jolted in place. Then he turned rapid-fire with his speech. 'Come on. You seem like you want to do something about it. You going to call me names all day or are you going to try something? I really, really want you to try something. Come on. Go for that gun at your waist. Do it. I'm on a tight schedule here, so either get straight to the point or turn around and fuck off back to where you came from and stop wasting my time.'

Bautista said nothing.

Clearly unsure how to respond.

He wasn't used to anyone standing up to him.

Let alone someone with Slater's confidence.

It wasn't easily replicable, even under the old "fake-it-until-you-make-it" adage.

It came from a decade of experience.

Bautista had come expecting a wealthy expat from some Western country with a silver spoon in his mouth and a whole lot of apologies for treading on the toes of the cartels inhabiting the area. Instead he got something wholly different. He got an African-American powerhouse with a psychotic glint in his eye who seemed more than capable of taking on a trio of lowly narco thugs.

And there wasn't a shred of fear or hesitation on Slater's face.

That's probably what deterred him the most.

So Bautista simply nodded, and backed up a step.

His mouth was a hard line.

'You get me?' Slater said, refusing to blink. 'You see my eyes?'

Bautista nodded.

'You think I'm scared of the three of you?'

Bautista paused for a long time, and then shook his head. 'I like you, friend.'

'We're not friends.'

Bautista leered and tapped the side of his head. 'You crazy. Loco. I like that.'

'You three want anything?'

'No.'

'Then get out of here. I know what you came here to do. You're not getting that from me.'

'What do you think we wanted?'

'I know what being friends means out here.'

'Thought you might have some spare cash lying around. We're always looking for donations, you know.'

Slater nodded. 'Yeah. I get it. Protection racket. I've got no spare cash. Fuck off.'

'You're not very nice.'

'That's rich coming from the three of you.'

'You don't know anything about us,' Bautista said, but he was smiling as he said it.

Menace dripped in his tone.

Slater thought he spotted a dry bloodstain on the shoulder of Bautista's singlet.

The wiry man gave a sickening smile, touched a hand to the butt of his sidearm reflexively, turned on his heel, and headed off back down the trail. Vicente and Iván followed in tow, flashing glances over their shoulders every few seconds to make sure Slater wasn't trying anything drastic.

He wasn't.

He stood in the giant doorway, leaving himself exposed in case any of them had a change of heart and tried to gun him down as he turned away. But he knew they wouldn't. His overly confrontational nature had disrupted their routine. They were used to getting their way, and now they hadn't. They did their best to hide it, but it rattled them.

When the trio disappeared from sight, ghosting back down the jungle trail, Slater mimicked Bautista's earlier movements. He reached back and touched a hand to the Glock 17 resting loosely in his waistband. He'd been unable to fetch his holster in time, but he didn't need it. If any of them had made a real move for their weapons he would have put a cylindrical hole in each of their heads in the space of a couple of seconds. With close to the fastest reaction speed on the planet, he had quiet confidence in his abilities to dismantle a few drug fiends.

He hoped he never saw them again.

Because he didn't feel like killing anyone today, and if they'd proven even slightly more aggressive he might have taken three lives in an instant.

He slammed the door closed, allowed the built-up adrenalin to subside, and resumed planning the rest of his day.

He knew Bautista, Vicente, and Iván were narcos, because they certainly weren't native. The majority of the population in the Chocó Department were Afro-Colombians, and the trio that had visited him didn't have the familiar dark skin that came with most of the region's occupants. They also hadn't carried themselves like locals. They didn't have the laidback, overly friendly gait of the men and women Slater had met during his time here.

So he felt reasonably comfortable with heading into town and avoiding any further interaction with the trio of scum.

Because he knew if he saw them again, he wouldn't be so kind.

He knew their type. The *narcotraficantes*. The fiends. The sociopathic vermin that inhabited dark swathes of the Colombian jungle, using slave labour to manufacture and package narcotics and ferry their product through the pre-established pipelines, taking it across the border and causing untold misery wherever their reign touched. The cartels were vicious, soulless beasts, and Slater figured he'd subconsciously come to Colombia to wage war against them. He knew he would work his way up to that reality eventually.

He simply wasn't ready yet.

He hadn't given himself time to switch gears.

He could have killed the three of them. Effortlessly. He could have wiped the smug expressions off their faces before they realised who he was. But he'd allowed them to sense his aura. He'd allowed them to understand what they'd be getting themselves into if they decided to fuck with him. And they'd made the right move, and retreated.

Thankfully.

But eventually he would come for them. He would hunt them down and tear them apart, and continue ravaging the jungle encampments until there was nothing left of the Colombian drug trade. But that would take years of warfare. Years of planning and tactical destruction. And he didn't want to go down that path just yet. Because it was a one way street. If he dipped so much as a toe into that world, he would never come out of it. The fire burning within him wanted nothing more than to tackle that particular challenge, but he knew he would be giving up every creature comfort imaginable.

He had to transition into what he used to be.

First, he wanted a few weeks off.

To drink. To laugh. To train.

So he waited until the trio were long gone and then left his compound behind, admiring the low structure as he trudged down the jungle path toward the small parking lot at the end of his patch of land. Before he made it to the semi-circle of gravel, enclosed by lush trees and vegetation and swamped in humidity, he prepared himself for what he might find.

If they'd slashed his tyres, or defaced his vehicle in any way, he might cut short his self-imposed downtime just for the hell of it.

Just to show them who the fuck they were messing with.

But the open-topped jeep he'd bought off a local auto dealer was unblemished. Well, it was rusting and rundown and looked set to fall apart at any moment, but the trio of narcos hadn't touched it.

Good, Slater thought.

Because he craved a beer after kicking the old primal instincts into gear.

It was cause for celebration, in some sick, twisted way.

He leapt into the driver's seat and fired up the engine, tasting the air flowing off the nearby river. The sounds of the jungle encompassed the clearing, complete with the shrills and hoots of exotic wildlife and the hum of mosquitoes.

He had no particular agenda. Nowhere to be. Nothing to do. Back in Vladivostok, cooped up in a small room above a bar for nigh on four months straight, he'd spent plenty of time dissecting the darkness inside his own mind. He hadn't been able to venture outside for the first phase, even if he wanted to, and the self-imposed exile had done him a world of good.

He'd come out the other side strangely calm. Strangely at peace with himself. He hadn't been alone, without conflict, for as long as he could remember. So now he felt no particular urge to leap back into the action. He knew it would come — that was inevitable. But until then he would resist the lure of confrontation. The old Slater would have beat those three narcos down where they stood. Probably killed them, too, given the fact that their mere existence created enough suffering on a global scale to justify their deaths.

But he hadn't reacted. He'd let them go, against his better judgment.

All in due time.

Right now, he wanted a drink.

He kept the top down and weaved through twisting jungle trails, heading for the nearest town. It was unnamed, small enough to serve as both a tourist trap and a local haunt. Slater had become intimately familiar with the grid of streets, considering it was the only source of clustered civilisation this deep in the Chocó Department. There was a bar there, too, and a damn good one.

Over time, he'd reluctantly admitted his problem.

In fact, he'd only recently started recognising it as a problem.

It didn't mean he was about to stop drinking.

He entered the town's outer limits and waved to a couple of familiar locals. As the days passed, he'd found his presence wholly ignored, and he welcomed it. As a black man he blended in just enough with the Afro-Colombians that populated the region to avoid standing out. And he kept a low profile, figuring there was no point ruining his few months of respite by flashing his wealth and encouraging every petty thief in the area to make an attempt on his life.

He understood the intricacies of encouraging violence, especially in these parts.

His compound by the river had enough extravagances within its walls to keep him occupied. When he'd recruited the only high-end construction firm in Quibdó to put the small fortress together discreetly, he'd spared no expense with materials. He'd ordered the best of everything, cutting no corners in the process.

But that was miles away from civilisation.

No-one — aside from the three narcos who had so rudely intruded on his privacy earlier that morning — knew about it. To the locals who knew him by facial recognition he was a simple man who drove an open-topped jeep and kept mostly to himself. He was generous with his money at the grocers, at the bars, at the hardware stores. He tipped well. And he seemed intent on continuing with his spartan existence for the foreseeable future. So they left him alone.

No-one poked.

No-one prodded.

He knew, eventually, that would change.

Someone would tip off one of the narcos, and the jungle would open its jaws and spit out a host of undesirables looking to intimidate the man who lived in the middle of nowhere. Anything foreign was a threat. And Slater had his first taste of that life now.

Bautista.

Vicente.

Iván.

They were the first.

Soon, the floodgates would open.

But not yet.

He parked in front of the same unnamed bar that had become a staple in his life, already teeming with occupants in the early afternoon. There were ample backpackers in town, flowing from the hostels littering the tiny village. Gentrification at its finest. Slater had heard tales of rural Colombia's renaissance — hence the uptick in young foreigners on a budget — but he figured most of the corruption and murder still lurked. It just kept to itself and left no witnesses.

The backpackers drifted to the best haunts like flies to

shit. The locals weren't immune from drowning their problems, either.

And Slater couldn't blame any of them.

Over a career — no, a lifetime — of the most brutal imaginings life had to offer, Slater had yet to find a better numbing agent than the bottom of a bottle. Maybe some found that sad. He certainly didn't. In fact it tantalised him. His life was a never-ending stream of relentless discipline.

He had one vice.

It wasn't his fault that he was so adept at satiating it.

It was a whole lot better than the drug-fuelled nightmare his life used to be.

He shut down the engine, twisted the key out of the ignition, and leapt over the driver's door that had long since rusted shut.

The bar beckoned.

H e selected a table at random. There was no order
to it. No reasoning. Maybe in the past he might
have conducted a rudimentary threat assess-
ment. Scoped out the darkest corners, put his back to the
wall, analysed every newcomer under the guise of a curious
alcoholic.

Now he didn't give a shit.

If they were going to come for him, they would come.

Who?

He didn't know. He didn't care. Often he wondered if the
concussion had changed him. He recalled every detail of the
altercation. The hulking giant of a man with blonde hair
and piercing blue eyes. Ruslan Mikhailov. The steel-toed
boot, slicing down through the air with over two hundred
pounds of bodyweight behind it. The sharp *crack* of sole
against skull. The blinding flash. The sound like a whip
lashing against his head. The loss of equilibrium. The
uncontrollable headaches. The disrupted vision.

The pain.

The endless pain...

He shook it off as a cold shiver ran down his spine. That was in the past. He'd spent four gruelling months recovering from that, shaking off the lingering symptoms, praying for a relief from the agony. And he'd found it.

Maybe that was why he was so reluctant to return to the carnage of the past.

Because it wouldn't take much effort for it to happen again. A glancing blow. A knuckle crashing against flesh in just the right place. Usually the soft patch of skin above and behind the ear worked well enough. He'd crippled countless men with the same technique. A looping right hook to the skull with hundreds of pounds of force behind it. Cracking bone. Splitting skin. Dropping the most intimidating men on the planet where they stood.

In the past, a voice in his head said.

He almost laughed out loud.

But that would have made him look insane, and although those effects lingered on the horizon, he wasn't about to give himself over to madness yet.

So he ordered a drink. Vodka, three fingers, straight up. No point making it any more pleasant than it needed it to be. He exchanged a subtle nod of recognition with the enormous, dreadlocked bartender, and took the tumbler filled with clear liquid to a table on the far side of the room.

He gulped it down.

Fast.

It burned, and that's what he relished.

Something extreme. His life was nothing more than one extreme sensation after the other. He never took anything easy. Even pleasure. He recalled his career in all its excesses.

Brutal, barbaric training — he trained harder than

anyone on the planet. He never took a moment's break. He pushed himself to the limits of what the human body was capable of, and then he kept pushing.

Then the operations themselves. Daring, violent, relentless. He never received an easy task. He threw himself at each mission in turn, putting his health on the line over and over again. More times than he could remember. It had all blurred into a seething mass of pain and fury. But he'd done good work. He'd lost count of how many people he'd saved. How many horrors he'd prevented. In Russia, a construction worker named Bogdan had said the world would be a worse place without Will Slater, and without seeming arrogant he had to admit he agreed.

And then there was the downtime. He'd treated that with the same intensity he brought to anything in life. Drink. Drugs. Women. All in excess. His entire life was one consecutive stream of excess.

He wouldn't have it any other way.

Which made the current downtime so uncomfortable. He was talented at many things, but none of them involved sitting around and thinking about life. Hence why the concussion recovery had proved so mind-altering.

Ironic.

To rewire his brain, he'd needed to scramble it first.

Disrupt the old patterns.

The old neural pathways.

And forge new ones.

But can you really change who you are?

He'd find out.

The bar was populated by a mixed crowd — some locals, some tourists, all in various states of intoxication. Some were further along that path than others. But the space was packed, seething with raucous laughter and raised voices and intense conversation. Slater felt right at home in the midst of it. Even though he was getting used to it, he didn't like to linger alone with his thoughts for any longer than necessary. He'd struck up conversations in this place with people from all walks of life.

Sometimes, a different perspective was exactly what he needed.

Someone bumped into him, slamming against his shoulder on their way past. He almost flinched, and then grimaced a moment later as warm alcohol spilled down the sleeve of his shirt. A feminine gasp floated over the atmosphere, and he turned in his seat to find a twenty-something Caucasian girl touching her fingers to his arm, her mouth agape in mock horror. He could see the warmth behind her eyes. She was suitably drunk, but holding it together well.

And as they made eye contact, her shock morphed into a smile.

'I'm sorry,' she said, almost purring.

American.

He took her hand off his shoulder. It required a little more effort than he anticipated. 'It's fine.'

She was cute, too. Dressed in tiny jean shorts that ended at the very top of her thighs, exposing legs honed through years of dedication to a Division I NCAA program. Volleyball, maybe. Her hair was light brown and straight, and it fell elegantly over slim shoulders. She carried herself well, too. She stood straight up. Her pronounced cheekbones moved effortlessly into the smile. No hint of shyness. Slater liked that.

'I'm not usually that clumsy,' she said. 'Sorry, again.'

This time, it seemed like she meant it. She seemed aware of the dangers of Colombia. The country was mostly pleasant at surface level, but everything had its cracks. Especially in South America. Every now and then, the darker side of humanity seeped through.

She'd likely learnt to be wary around strangers.

In direct contrast to his usual frame of mind, Slater hoped she wasn't alone.

'You with friends?' he said.

She nodded coyly. 'Up the front.'

'How long have you been here?'

'This bar?' she said. 'Or Colombia?'

'Both.'

'Two weeks in-country. And we've been around here for a couple of days.'

'Who are you with?'

'My boyfriend,' she said, and it seemed to bring her back to reality. Until that point she'd been staring at Slater for an uncomfortable length of time. Her blue eyes bored into him. Surprised to find a fellow countryman in these parts. And, on top of that, there was the fact he was travelling solo, in impeccable shape, and didn't seem to be a creep in the slightest. But now she realised what she was doing, and averted her gaze momentarily. 'And our friends.'

'How many of you?'

'Four.'

'You're looking out for each other, right?'

She smiled. Playfully.

'What are you, my dad?'

'I don't think I'm old enough for that.'

'No,' she said, and she returned to the prolonged eye contact, perhaps without even noticing. 'How old are you?'

'Old enough,' he said, and leant forward on both elbows, flashing a luring smile of his own.

Activating old tendencies.

'Look,' he said. 'Maybe your boyfriend wouldn't be happy you're talking to me.'

She flashed a glance over her shoulder, then turned back with something strange in her eyes. 'He can't see.'

'Doesn't sound like you care what he thinks.'

'Maybe I don't.'

'You should.'

'I can make my own choices.'

'You done anything like this before?'

She paused, once again sobering up to reality, and then said, 'No.'

And he believed her.

Because he knew he possessed a unique combination of characteristics. He'd lost the humility of ignoring the fact long ago. Ever since he'd first signed up to the secretive government division known as Black Force, womanising had been something that came to him as effortlessly as breathing. And he hadn't quite been able to put his finger on why until recently. Then he'd been forced to accept the truth — there was a certain subtle confidence that people like him possessed. Unseen, unheard, but resting there just under the surface.

He'd finally been able to pinpoint it.

It was the understanding that nothing in civilian life would ever compare to the indescribable burst of emotions that came with a life or death struggle. Slater had become particularly adept at those situations over the course of his life, and now all he could remember about his life was an endless string of adrenalin-pumping encounters. It made ordinary social settings effortless. He felt totally and utterly in control at all times, and it seeped out of him like a magnet. It attracted people.

Women included.

Even those that ordinarily didn't stray away from their partners.

The bar swelled in volume as a jovial song blared out of the surround sound speakers, injecting the atmosphere with additional life. Slater beckoned the girl closer.

'What's your name?' he said.

'Casey,' the girl said.

She stepped closer, following his commands.

'You should go back to your boyfriend, Casey.'

She paused, staring at him.

Then she nodded.

'Sorry,' she mumbled. 'Don't know what I was thinking.'

'Neither do I.'

'Actually,' she said, looking him up and down. 'Yes I do.'

She stroked a hand down his shoulder. He was sure the alcohol aided her confidence.

'You an athlete or something?' she said.

'"Or something."'

'I'll be up the front if you want to say hi.'

'In front of your boyfriend?'

'He won't bite.'

'You all from the same place?'

She nodded. 'Ohio. We're at college.'

'What are you doing all the way out here?'

'Having fun. You?'

'Same thing.'

'All by yourself?'

'I like being by myself.'

'I want to join you.'

'Where?'

'We could go to the bathrooms.'

Slater smirked. 'Go back to your boyfriend, Casey.'

And then she said the words that hammered a knot deep in Slater's gut, because he had enough life experience to know where that path led in a place like this.

She said, 'Do you know where we can get cocaine?'

5

Slater stared at her, unblinking, suddenly deadly serious.

He said, 'You don't want to buy cocaine around these parts.'

She rolled her eyes. 'Come on. It's Colombia.'

'I know. But you should have got it in a major city. It's not all fun and games out here.'

'You don't have any?'

He stared at her with newfound understanding. Less of a wild soul. More of a junkie. Especially if she was blatantly running her mouth about it.

'No,' he said. 'I don't have any.'

'You seem mad.'

'I'm not mad.'

'Are you against drugs?'

Slater almost laughed. 'You couldn't be more wrong.'

'Then what's the problem?'

He feigned ignorance. 'Nothing.'

'If you had some, would you sell it to me?'

'I'd give it to you for free if it meant you wouldn't go around asking anyone else for it.'

'Really? Why?'

Slater sighed. He had experience with all aspects of the human emotional spectrum. He understood personalities. Which meant he knew what would happen after their conversation came to an end, regardless of what he said. He set to work trying to find a way around the hard truth. Then he shrugged begrudgingly, reached out, and gripped her wrist. He pulled her closer to his table.

'Sit down,' he said.

'Why?'

'Just sit down.'

'Only because you're hot. Are those contacts or were you born with them?'

He tried not to roll his eyes, but he couldn't help himself.

'Sit,' he said.

She sat.

'No matter what I say,' he said. 'You're going to try and find drugs, aren't you?'

She stared at him sheepishly. She knew he knew.

'I'm going to tell you you shouldn't,' Slater said. 'Because of the location. And the people who live around these parts.'

'You know them?'

'Not well. But I've seen enough.'

'What have you seen?'

'Nothing here.'

'Then what's to worry about?'

He started recalling every dead, maimed, and mutilated body he'd found over the course of his life. He didn't have a chance at remembering them all.

'There's a lot to worry about,' he said.

'This is a lecture, isn't it? You're older than I thought you were.'

'Probably,' he said. 'But if you want the truth, I don't care if you die of an overdose. That's your choice to make. At least that'll be quick in comparison to ... look, just don't approach anyone weird. Okay?'

The blood started to drain from her face. 'You're really weird yourself. I'll let you drink on your own, then. Shame. This started so well...'

She started to kick the flimsy chair back. Slater snatched her wrist as subtly as he could, and planted her back in the seat.

'Casey,' he said. 'Go to the major cities and buy as much coke as you want. But not out here. You should have brought it with you.'

'Why?' she said with a sly smile. 'You want some? You scared to get it on your own?'

He almost snapped, but he reined in his anger. He glanced around the crowded bar, then shrugged to himself. Perhaps it was paranoia. Perhaps he was projecting what he'd seen in the past onto a situation that didn't warrant such an extreme reaction.

Then again, maybe not...

He held up his hands. 'Do what you gotta do.'

'You sure you don't want to go to the bathrooms?' she said.

Even to someone with his history, her overtness shocked him.

'You on anything right now?' he said.

She shook her head. 'Otherwise I wouldn't be trying to score, you idiot.'

'Just drinking, then?'

'Yeah.'

'The four of you all pretty wasted?'

'Yeah.'

'Stick to that for the rest of the day.'

'Whatever, grandpa.'

'I mean it.'

'So do I.'

'Get out of here.'

She kicked the chair back, albeit teasingly. There was a wry smile plastered across her face now. Her mood swings verged on bipolar. Before she left she bent down, curving at her wholly impressive waist, and whispered in his ear, 'I don't get rejected that often.'

'You're drunk.'

'So are you,' she said, indicating his empty glass.

He smiled. 'A lifetime of drinking. Takes a serious amount to get me feeling anything.'

'Then let us buy you a round.'

'For what?'

'I don't know,' she said. 'We're in Colombia. Having a good time. Does everything have to be so complicated?'

'Your boyfriend might not approve.'

'He'll love you.'

'Can I ask why?'

'You're full of questions, aren't you?'

'I'm a curious guy.'

'You don't seem that old. You're American. To them you'll seem cool as hell. And you look like an Olympian, babe. They'll love you.'

'Is that what this is all about?'

'You seemed like a cool guy. Before all the warning shit. But I'm willing to forget about it.'

'And why would I want to hang out with the four of you?'

She shrugged. 'Suit yourself. My friend's single.'

'I'm probably ten years older than her.'

'You're making things really hard for yourself, aren't you?'

'I'm not that drunk yet.'

'Even if you were, I still think you'd be a grump.'

'Yeah, well...' Slater said, recalling the madness of his past. 'People change.'

'So what about that drink? We haven't found a fellow countryman in days.'

'I'll take it. But I don't know what you're expecting from me.'

'The guys will think you're a living legend. You give off that vibe.'

'And if they knew what you'd offered?'

'Then they'd try to beat you up, probably.'

'I'd like to see that.'

'They're aggressive drunks.'

Slater said nothing. He just smiled.

'What?' Casey said.

'Probably best left unsaid.'

'You're mysterious,' she said. 'I like you.'

'So are we pretending this chat never happened?'

'If you know what's good for you.'

'I don't think I do,' Slater said, then he leant forward himself and whispered back in her ear. 'I almost accepted.'

She visibly bit her lip. 'How close were you?'

'Very.'

'What stopped you?'

'A memory.'

'Of what?'

'Let's save that for another time.'

'Because of the cocaine thing?'

He nodded. 'But not because of what you said. Because of something I saw. A while ago.'

'Don't want to talk about it?'

'Not in the slightest.'

'And it ruined our chances of a romp…?'

'I just … don't feel right anymore.'

'Another drink will fix that.'

'I take it neither of us should mention how forward you were around your boyfriend.'

'Don't know what you're talking about,' she said with a sly grin, and disappeared into the raucous crowd.

6

Casey's friends proved pleasant enough.

First came Jake, Casey's boyfriend. He was a big guy — a football player, probably — with the blonde locks and dashing good looks to match. Stereotypical enough, Slater noted. He greeted Slater with an over-the-top handshake and a beaming grin. His eyes were also muddied with the fog of alcohol. Slater figured the drinking had started long before the group had reached the bar.

Next came Harvey, a slightly less impressive kid with straight brown hair and a plain, unassuming build. But he made up in confidence what he lacked in physical characteristics. He leapt into conversation with Slater without restraint, and Slater decided to oblige them. The last of the group was Whitney, the supposedly single one Casey had talked up moments earlier. She was petite — no taller than five three — with striking green eyes and tanned skin. She attracted attention effortlessly — most of the men in the bar couldn't take their eyes off her. She shook Slater's hand politely as she introduced herself, and he noted the intensity of her grip. She lingered on him a little longer than what would be considered normal. Over her shoulder, Slater noticed Casey smiling at him.

He tipped back another glass of vodka Harvey fetched from the bartender, and immediately decided he wouldn't be trying anything today. A faint memory flared in his subconscious the second he considered seducing them. The memory of a woman in the Russian Far East.

Natasha.

He'd known her for less than a day before she disappeared. He'd razed Vladivostok to the ground searching for her. And he'd found her.

Far too late.

So he wasn't subjecting anyone else to the dark magnetic energy that seemingly plagued his existence. He hadn't set to work tearing it down yet. In fact, if his encounter with the trio of narcos earlier that morning symbolised anything, he was on the precipice of tumbling back into the madness. The Will Slater of old would have somehow talked Casey and Whitney back to his compound within the hour, but superstition nagged at him, and he decided to let it be.

Which meant he should go.

He maintained small talk, drinking and laughing and employing the guise of an ordinary traveller, but the discomfort of his past experiences sat there in his brain, gnawing at him, demanding that he take his miserable wretched bad luck and direct it somewhere else.

But he stayed.

Call it defiance. Call it a transformation. He was tired of running from normalcy. He was fed up with the pain he inadvertently brought to others, but he was more fed up with worrying about it.

He had to admit he was overanalysing every shred of data that reality was feeding him. Jake asked him something, and he shook himself back to the present as he realised he'd zoned out completely.

'Sorry,' he said, cradling a beer, deep in the throbbing bliss of alcohol. 'What was that?'

'I was saying, dude, what's the craziest shit you've ever done?'

Slater shrugged. 'I've been skydiving a few times.'

Jake's eyes widened. 'No way! I've always wanted to, bro. Never got around to it. Fuckin' terrifying, right?'

Slater recalled an endless stream of HALO jumps into hostile territories. The oxygen mask strapped to his face, his breathing laboured and rattling in his ears, his heavy gear strapped to his chest, the floor shaking, the light turning red, someone screaming *'Go, go, go!'*, the plunge into the abyss, the shaky landing, the wars on the ground, the blood-shed and death and fighting and beatings and murder and...

'Yeah,' he said. 'Pretty scary.'

'Where'd you do it?' Harvey said.

'All over the place.'

'Come on, man,' Jake said. 'You're not giving away anything, are you? You making this shit up, bro? You can tell us.'

'I wish I was.'

'You usually this quiet?'

'No. Not usually.'

'So what's up?'

'Don't know. In a mood, I guess.'

'Come on,' Jake said, gesturing at their surroundings with an over-the-top wave of his right arm. 'Look around. Everyone's having a great time. What are you stressing about?'

To reinforce the point, he tipped back the long-necked beer bottle and drained the last half of his drink in a consecutive string of gulps. He slammed the empty bottle down on the table, grinned, and glanced at the rest of the crew. 'Another round?'

Slater had managed to get away with small talk for the first stretch of conversation, but his capacity to put on a mask was rapidly deteriorating.

And, as he lifted his gaze off the chipped wood and made eye contact with Casey, he realised she knew. Maybe because of their prior chat. Maybe because she could read people well. But her brow furrowed and something awfully close to compassion crossed her features.

Slater shook his head imperceptibly, then wiped beads of sweat from the corners of his forehead.

I'm okay.

Then memories resurfaced in horrifying hallucinogenic montages of rage and pain.

7

He battled them back down as Jake and Harvey set off worming their way through the throng of sweaty patrons in search of the bartender.

Casey and Whitney edged closer around the table. Casey's focus had wavered, and now she was deep in muffled conversation with her friend. Slater gripped the edge of the table with slick palms, as subtly as he could manage. He didn't battle his demons often. But when they came, they came with fury.

Deep in his own mind, he barely noticed Jake and Harvey weaving back through the crowd. The pair had a freshly opened, ice cold beer in each hand — four total — and they planted them down on the table, accompanied by a loud collection of *thunk*s. In her drunken stupor, Whitney scrutinised the beers with narrowed eyes.

'The fifth?' she said.

Jake nodded. 'We've only got four hands. I'll be right back.'

He darted back to the other side of the room as Harvey

planted himself down in his seat. Slater took a beer and drained half of it, stilling his shaking hands.

An uneasy silence elapsed.

'Tell you what,' Harvey mumbled, his breath reeking of alcohol as it floated across the table. 'You've managed to avoid telling us a thing about yourself, bro.'

Slater feigned innocence, raised both eyebrows, and said, 'What?'

Harvey narrowed his eyes and pointed an accusing finger at Slater as both corners of his mouth turned upward. 'I'm onto you.'

'Don't know what you're talking about.'

Harvey turned to the two girls. 'See? See what I mean?'

Whitney laughed. 'I see. I see it clear.'

'Maybe he doesn't want to talk about it,' Casey said. 'Leave him.'

Cautiously.

Hesitantly.

She knew. Whether it had happened during their recent bout of eye contact or not, something had clicked. Maybe she'd pieced together why he was so insistent on looking for cocaine somewhere else. Maybe she asked herself what sort of life experience someone needed to know the dangers of rural Colombia. Maybe she finally realised someone might know more than her about what really goes on in the jungles, deep in the shadows where the ground is lawless and the ordinary folk don't venture. Maybe she started to extrapolate from there, wondering what might happen to a beautiful young American girl stumbling around looking for hard drugs. How effortlessly she might get enticed into coming to a back room, where she'd be drugged and beaten and carted off to who-knows-where to serve the needs of God-knows-who.

Or maybe she knew none of that.

But Slater did.

'Come on,' Harvey said, banging his fist on the table. He snatched up his fresh beer. Gulped a third of it down. Sent it clattering back to the table. He wiped his mouth with his sleeve and stifled a belch. Then he sniffed, blinked hard, opened his eyes wide. 'Damn. I'm wasted.'

'Tell me about it,' Slater said.

Harvey shot him a withering look. 'You're not wasted. Not in the slightest, bro. If you say you are then you're pretending. Your eyes are clear. I know the ... the signs...'

'Oh, really?' Slater said, and this time he didn't have to fake the smile. He found the kid's certainty somewhat endearing. 'And what would those signs be?'

Harvey squinted, suddenly confused. He hadn't been expecting to be asked to elaborate.

'I dunno,' he mumbled. 'But you've drunk more than me. And you're fine.'

'I'm used to it.'

'Damn. You an alcoholic?'

'Harvey,' Whitney snapped.

Slater held up a hand. 'It's fine. I probably am. Technically. I just like to have fun. And I think I'm good at having fun.'

He made brief eye contact with Casey, and she grinned. He shot her a look, as if to say, *Stop right there.*

'You travel a lot?' Whitney said.

'Yeah. But I've been here for a while. Guess I got sick of jumping from place to place every week.'

'Where were you before this?'

'Russia.'

'I've always wanted to go to Russia,' she said, almost

shouting with enthusiasm. 'Any recommendations? Did you have fun over there?'

Slater pondered how to respond for a long moment, before stating, 'Don't go to Russia.'

She paused. 'Oh. Why not?'

'I didn't have a good time.'

'Well, maybe you didn't go to the right places.'

Slater kept the past buried in the past. He sensed the memories stirring, but he didn't humour them. He stuffed them down, sealed them up, and threw away the psychological key.

'Maybe not,' he conceded.

Posing the question innocently enough, Casey said, 'Where the hell is Jake?'

And even though he had no physical signs that anything had gone awry, Slater found himself plagued by the suffocating sensation that his world was about to go mad.

8

On the verge of panicking, he latched onto the words, pivoting to look Casey in the eyes. 'Does he usually do this?'

She noticed his intensity. 'Do what?'

'Run off on you.'

'Sometimes. He's a bit of a loose cannon. We don't have him on a leash, if that's what you're asking.'

'That's not what I'm asking,' Slater said.

He wheeled around in his seat, scanning the entire length of the bar through the gyrating bodies populating the centre of the room. He caught brief flashes of movement from a wide range of patrons. None of them had the same build as Jake.

'He's probably taking a piss,' Harvey said. 'Relax.'

And despite the lackadaisical nature of the throwaway line, Slater relaxed. He swivelled back into a normal position, planted both elbows on the table, and brought his breathing back under control. He nodded. 'You're right. Probably taking a piss.'

The conversation faded out. Perhaps they noticed how strange he was acting. In fact, after only a few beats of silence, Harvey turned to Whitney and said, 'Buy you another round?'

She pointed to his beer. 'You haven't finished that yet.'

He drained it in a long, uninterrupted swig, and delicately returned the empty bottle to the tabletop, now wet with condensation. Then he cocked his head at her. 'Now?'

She nodded, seeming to get the gist in a hurry. He wanted to talk to her about Slater.

The pair disappeared, but not before Harvey threw a precautionary glance at Casey. She waved him away, shooing him off to the bar.

He raised an eyebrow.

'It's fine,' Casey hissed.

The pair disappeared.

She scooted her chair closer to Slater. Almost too close.

'You okay?' she whispered.

He nodded, staring at his calloused palms, watching the veins ripple along his forearms. 'Sorry if I'm acting strange.'

'It's completely fine. I get you probably don't want to talk about ... whatever's causing it.'

'I don't have the most savoury past,' he said. 'I don't want to scare you all away. I just need to tell someone the truth.'

She leant in close and muttered, 'I know. That's what makes you so mysterious.'

Despite everything, he managed a half smile. 'Adds to the aura, does it?'

'You could say that.'

'You're risking a lot by being like this.'

'Jake's a douchebag, anyway.'

Slater raised an eyebrow. 'Trouble in paradise?'

'You could say that.'

'Don't want to talk about it?'

She nodded. 'Same as you.'

He smiled. 'Not quite the same.'

'What did you used to do?'

'Nothing important.'

'Oh, yeah?'

Seeing right through it.

'You're good at this,' he said.

'You're not going to kill us, are you?'

'Are you being serious?'

She rolled her eyes. 'Lighten up. You think I'd still be here if I suspected that?'

'Well, you can't know for sure...'

'Yes I can.'

'Ever thought you don't know as much about the world as you think you do?'

She shrugged. 'I know you're not a bad guy. And you know that I know it. So you've just got to ask yourself how you think I know that.'

'Could be a wild guess.'

'Could be,' she said.

'So why are you with Jake, then?'

'He's not a bad guy either.'

'Then what's the trouble?'

'Every now and then he goes and does something stupid like...'

She trailed off, locking her gaze onto something over Slater's shoulder.

'Oh, fuck,' she said. 'Like that.'

Slater twisted in his seat as the music blaring out of the overhead speakers reached a pulsating crescendo. He spotted Jake moving through the throngs of swaying bodies towards their table, a broad grin on his face.

Concealed in his palm were four plastic baggies stuffed with fine white powder.

9

He tilted them into view, flaunting them to Casey and Slater. His teeth shone, white and unblemished, under the mood lighting. He made it to their table, planted himself victoriously on the stool between them, and tucked the baggies out of sight.

'Who's down to have some fun?' he said.

'Where'd you get those?' Slater said.

'Bunch of guys up the back. They were cool. Don't worry. Casey told me you're paranoid about that sort of thing. But they didn't suspect a thing.'

'Suspect?' Slater said. 'What the hell are they supposed to suspect in the first place?'

Instantly, he noticed the blood draining from Casey's cheeks.

'Oh, fuck,' she said again. 'Please tell me you got away with it.'

'Yeah, of course,' Jake said.

She backhanded him across the cheek, the sharp sound muffled by the din of their surroundings. 'You absolute moron. Why would you risk that?'

'We're short on cash. And it was your idea.'

'I was being *sarcastic*. I didn't think you'd actually go and do it. Do you ever stop and think for one fucking second about—?'

Slater gripped the back of Jake's stool and dragged it — with the two-hundred pound man on it — across the wood panelled floor of the bar, kicking up a fine layer of sawdust under the considerable weight. It was an inhuman feat of strength, but Slater had uncanny anger coursing through his veins. Jake's eyes nearly bogged out of their sockets when he realised he was in the process of being hauled along the floor.

Slater repositioned him on the other side of his own chair, so that he now formed a barrier between the two arguing parties.

That shut them both up in a hurry.

For good measure, he reached out and placed a hand on each of their shoulders, stressing the importance of what was to follow.

'Hey, man,' Jake said, reaching up and grabbing his hand. 'Get that shit off me.'

Slater seized the kid's trapezius muscle and squeezed tight. He was under no illusion as to the power of his grip. Jake opened his mouth wide and gasped, writhing on the spot in an attempt to get away from the sudden surge of agony. He hunched down, twisted away, and tried to lean out of range.

Slater squeezed tighter.

'Jake,' he said calmly. 'What the fuck did you do?'

'Nothing. Don't worry about it.'

'I'm worrying.'

'Why?'

'Did you buy the drugs off a group of three men?'

'No,' he said, then paused. 'Oh ... maybe. There were two of them, but the third guy in the background might have been with them too. I wasn't looking too closely.'

'You should have been.'

'What's with all this weird shit, man? Piss off.'

'They still here?'

'How am I supposed to know?'

'You did it just then?'

'Yeah. They won't work it out, though. Nothing to worry about.'

'Like I said, I'm worrying. Point them out.'

'What?'

'Point them out.'

'I don't want to look for them, bro. You're freaking me out now. I thought I could get away with it. I *did* get away with it.'

'Get away with what?'

'Fake bills. One of our college friends plays around with counterfeiting in his spare time. We brought a few over, more as a joke than anything else. Wondered if the locals might fall for it.'

'You gave fake bills to a Colombian drug dealer?'

'I thought you said there were three...'

Slater let go of the kid. He noticed Casey shooting Jake daggers over his shoulder.

'Idiot,' she muttered.

'You're going to need to point them out.'

'Why?'

'Because, believe it or not, I've had experience with this kind of thing.'

'You have? Experience with what?'

'Disappearances.'

'I don't—'

'You're not connecting the dots here.'

'I'm drunk.'

'I can see that.'

'I thought you were too.'

'I can compartmentalise. Where are your pals?'

'They're not my pals.'

'You're really testing my patience here.'

Jake swivelled in his seat, scanning the bar with eyes now wracked with fear. The sickly hot air and seething masses of customers aided his confidence — if the bar was less populated, he might have fainted from the stress of confronting the dealers.

'Why did you think that was a good idea?' Casey hissed.

'In case you weren't aware, we don't have any money left,' Jake said through gritted teeth. Then he lifted a finger and jabbed it across the room. 'There.'

He turned back to the table and put his head down, ashamed.

Slater squinted. 'Where?'

'I showed you.'

'Help me out here.'

'I'm not pointing again.'

'Oh, so now you're afraid?'

'I wasn't thinking at the time.'

'We should be fine,' Slater said. 'I'm probably paranoid. They won't know the bills are fake. They're not that smart.'

Reassuring himself more than anything else.

Then he spotted the trio across the room.

And they saw him.

Bautista.

Vicente.

Iván.

And they were all furious.

10

I t didn't take much effort to piece the situation together. Slater stared directly at the trio, noting the silent fury blazing in their eyes, recognising Bautista's hand floating toward his waistband where a weapon lay. He stared harder and made out the shape of the crumpled bills in Vicente's palm. The guy tightened his grip on the useless notes. He knew exactly what they were. If narcos had one field of expertise apart from handling product, it was cash.

It wasn't Slater's fault that Jake had no ability to figure things out for himself.

But it was his responsibility to make sure four dumb kids didn't wind up beaten to death in the humid backwaters of central Colombia.

Which meant he needed to act.

Right goddamn now.

Before he even had the chance to understand how radically his temporarily placid life was about to change, he twisted his head to the side and muttered, 'Stay where you are.'

'What?' Jake said.

The kid had barely heard Slater. His cheeks, previously red and flushed with the heat and the alcohol, were now pale and white. He couldn't strip his gaze away from the trio. Now they terrified him. His booze-induced confidence had rapidly subsided. Slater could see it in the kid's eyes. Jake understood the ramifications of his actions. He realised what an idiot he was. But it was far too late.

The four of them didn't deserve any harm to come their way. They were young and stupid and impressionable, but they meant no bad will by it. Jake probably figured a gang of drug dealers had more than enough cash to go around.

What's a few fake bills to add to the stash?

A hell of a lot, as it turns out.

'What?' Jake said again.

The uneasy stalemate settled across the room. Both parties were waiting for the other to make the first move. Neither quite knew how to react. The trio of narcos weren't ready to gun down four tourists in such a crowded location. They would do it without hesitation, obviously, but it would have to be somewhere quieter.

Slater knew he needed to give them the opportunity.

Or they'd target the weakest of the procession.

Bautista cocked his head when he recognised Slater. His hand froze on its way to his belt. Slater could almost see his brain scrambling for understanding in real time, trying to piece together how a bunch of dumb foreign college kids knew the strange guy who'd intimidated them at the front door of his compound earlier that day.

Slater didn't give the trio time to figure it out.

'What?' Jake said for a third time, refusing to take his eyes off the trio.

'I'm about to move,' Slater said, keeping his voice low and controlled. 'When I do, stay right where you are.'

'Where's Harvey and Whitney?'

'Coming back from the bar now. You see them?'

Jake nodded. 'What should I do?'

'When I go, these three will follow me. Then—'

'You sure?'

'Yes.'

'How are you so calm, man?'

'Experience.'

Casey let out a low breath.

Now, she understood.

'You a drug dealer?' Jake said.

'No, just a consumer.'

'What?'

No time to explain.

'Just stay where you are. When the coast is clear, take Harvey and Whitney and get the hell out of here. Where are you four staying?'

'The backpackers. Just down the road.'

'Which one?'

'Chocó Retreats.'

'Got it. I'll meet you there.'

'When?'

'Soon.'

'They're on the move.'

'I know. Ready?'

'I guess. What if they don't follow you?'

'Then I'll go to Plan B.'

'Which is?'

Bautista, Vicente, and Iván set off moving through the crowd ebbing and flowing around them. Bautista grumbled as a sweaty patron bumped into him and shoved the young man aside. His movements flared up as his body released adrenalin.

Slater stared him dead in the eyes and allowed mortal fear to pass over his own face.

Bautista hesitated.

Did Slater know something the three of them didn't?

Why was he so afraid now?

Slater didn't give them the opportunity to find out. He burst to his feet, kicking his chair back in a violent explosive movement. The rickety wooden contraption bounced off the side of the table with enough noise to drown out the surrounding racket. It certainly caught the attention of the three narcos. They all flinched simultaneously, their attention seized by Slater. He took off at a mad sprint, heading for the bar's open entranceway. On the way out he shouldered a couple of patrons aside, catching a string of profanities with each aggressive movement, and leapt down the short flight of stairs outside the bar in a single bound.

He landed hard, kicking up the fine layer of dust coating the lot outside the building as the soles of his boots slammed into the earth. He paused for only a moment then took off sprinting for the row of shopfronts across the potholed street. There was little activity on the grimy sidewalks, especially at this time of the afternoon. He quickened his pace, running like a man possessed.

He didn't bother to check if the three drug dealers were giving chase.

He knew they would be.

The mystery surrounding his appearance and involvement would be too tantalising an opportunity to pass up.

He ran all the way down the narrow alleyway wedged between two stores, passing wet trash and potholes flooded with garbage juices and the overwhelming stink of rot. He made it to a deserted dirt parking lot out the back of the general store, devoid of life, boxed in by jungle trimmed back to form a perimeter around the town.

He spun on his heel, put his back to the hot brick wall, and waited for the three men to catch up to him.

Allowing the fog of war to settle over him.

He loosened his joints and prepared to fight.

Will Slater, back in action once more.

11

None of them were prepared for what followed.

Vicente happened to draw the short straw, because he was the fastest of the bunch. He made it to the parking lot first and burst out into the open, deep in the process of arming himself with a Heckler & Koch pistol. He had it out of the holster, nearly ready for use. Slater caught a blur of movement and saw Vicente thumbing the safety off the weapon, preparing for an execution in the backstreets of the village.

They owned this town, it seemed.

Had all the locals in the palm of their hand.

Not anymore.

Lack of competition had made Vicente weak, overly confident, slow to react. Slater wondered when he'd last been in a genuine fight for his life. Experience had taught him that narcos relied on intimidation, and on the off chance they were forced to deal out suffering they did it quickly and ruthlessly, gunning their enemies down in the streets or overwhelming them with sheer manpower.

They were hard men, dangerous men, sociopathic men, but they weren't accustomed to adversity.

Slater bathed in it.

He burst into view like an unstoppable freight train and smashed a calloused fist into the delicate soft tissue of Vicente's throat. The man started to gasp for breath, and Slater jerked forward with manic intensity and headbutted him square in his lower row of teeth. The narco's jaw had fallen open in response to the first strike, so Slater's head-butt caught him clean, smashing three or four teeth loose and bloodying his gums. The guy started to crumple on the spot, barely able to slow himself down in time to regain his composure, and Slater hit him with a picture-perfect uppercut to the same debilitated jaw, lashing his broken row of teeth into the top row and knocking a few more loose. The impact lashed Vicente's brain against the roof of his skull, turning off the lights.

Now he really did crumple, his legs giving out from underneath him, sprawling forward in the aftermath of the horrific three-strike combination. On the way down his arms splayed, his grip slackening as unconsciousness took hold of him, and Slater simply plucked the Heckler & Koch semi-automatic pistol out of the guy's hands on the way down.

He sidestepped to avoid getting bowled over by the unconscious man, and caught Iván sprinting into the desolate lot a moment later.

The guy's eyes were widening, but he couldn't reverse his momentum in time. He started to bring his own identical sidearm up to aim at Slater's face, but Slater stopped it in its tracks with a stabbing front kick — boot against fingers, breaking a couple, ensnaring the mangled digits in the trigger guard of his weapon and preventing him from maintaining any kind of proper aim.

Iván went white, and Slater flicked a soft jab into his mouth, his knuckles crashing against the man's lips. It was a strange place to get hit, and it didn't feel good at all. Iván recoiled, experiencing a sensation akin to getting stung by ten bees on the mouth at once. Thankfully, the act of recoiling played directly into Slater's hand. It froze Iván in his tracks, which allowed Slater to load up with a twisting right hook that scythed through the air and—

Crack.

The punch floored Iván on the spot, ending his fight right then and there. He faceplanted the dirt without the help of his limbs to break his fall and lay flat on his stomach, probably sporting a broken nose from the impact. The whole ordeal — putting down Vicente, and then Iván in quick succession — had taken no more than four seconds. Two per man. Slater could barely comprehend the speed at which reality unfolded. It always felt like an eternity in the moment, but the rate at which he could floor his opposition never failed to demonstrate how fast he truly was.

He would never understand, unless it got captured on video.

Next came Bautista, but by then the translucent momentum that exists in the very heat of the moment had reversed. It wasn't anything perceptible, but to Slater it was everything. He'd demolished the first two, and that meant if he found himself on the receiving end of a lucky blow from Bautista he could recover, spin away, try to regain his senses before the man followed up with another punch. If one of them stunned him when it was three on one, he would never recover.

So the animal part of his brain took a seat.

He wasn't going to die here. He might face adversity, but Slater had never lost a one on one fight, and he didn't think he was about to.

You never know...

But fear of the unknown had put Bautista on a pedestal in Slater's mind. A pedestal the man didn't deserve to occupy. The wiry athletic narco threw a punch with serious weight behind it. If it had connected, it might have knocked him clean out. That would certainly shake things up. But instead it whistled past, because Slater sidestepped before Bautista even threw the limb, noticing the subtle tells in his musculature that revealed he was about to throw the left hand. The fist passed him by, the arm rippling with muscle, charged with kinetic energy, but wholly useless. Because it didn't connect. And therefore it meant nothing.

Slater caught the limb, hurled it further along its trajectory, searched for Bautista's chin, found it jutting straight up in the air, put an elbow into the lower part of his jaw, felt the vibration, heard the crack, followed through with a Muay Thai knee to the gut, felt the tight muscles shudder and protest, smashed the other elbow into Bautista's ear, recognised the third strike hadn't been necessary.

Stopped.

Like a record freezing.

Bautista collapsed. His jaw broken. His stomach bruised and battered. A swollen welt already forming on the side of his skull.

Three men. Seven seconds.

S later dusted himself off, admiring his handiwork. The three men lay squirming at his feet — usually feared and loathed throughout the Chocó Department, now reduced to traumatised wrecks. He quickly checked the distant mouth of the alleyway to make sure no-one from the bar had decided to follow, and as soon as he elected it safe to proceed he bent down and dragged Bautista up by the lapels of his shirt.

The narco wheezed, bleeding from the mouth. Sweat stained his face and seeped into his clothes. He reeked of fear.

'Listen,' Slater said, 'and listen closely.'

Bautista didn't respond.

He couldn't, even if he wanted to.

His jaw was broken.

'Against my better judgment I'm going to let the three of you live,' Slater said.

Bautista nodded, his silent eyes pleading.

Genuinely grateful.

'Anyone who sees this might think it's an overreaction, yes?'

Bautista nodded again.

'But I know how the world works and so do you, so thankfully I don't have to give a shit what anyone else thinks. I know your type. I know exactly what you were going to do to those four. And don't pretend like you weren't. You're a narco but you're not a good liar. I can already tell. You were going to make an example out of them, weren't you?'

A third nod.

'You knew that kid gave you fake currency. And ... actually, no, wait. You knew the bills weren't real before he gave them to you, didn't you? You handle cash every single day. You would have picked it up in no time. Right?'

A fourth nod.

'Right. So you went through with it anyway. You let him think he'd gotten away with it. For what?'

Bautista opened his mouth to try and speak, but before he could mumble a sentence Slater slammed him straight back into the dirt. The narco coughed and retched and fell silent. He'd learned his lesson.

'I talk,' Slater hissed.

A fifth nod.

'You thought you'd use him as a demonstration. Because the three of you are gods out here. You can do whatever you want because you have the cash that feeds the economy that pays the shopkeepers and the bartenders and gets the local police Christmas gifts for their kids. So why would they care if you made an example out of four foreigners? Right?'

A sixth nod.

Slater smirked. Nullifying a previously feared cartel

fiend and physically taking them apart piece by piece proved uncannily effective at making them compliant.

'And now you're confused. Your jaw's fucked. The pain is almost too much to handle. I can see it in those eyes ... yeah, there we go ... you're really feeling it now because I'm talking about it which makes it the only thing you can concentrate on, right?'

A seventh nod.

And something very close to a whimper.

Slater had unrivalled experience in this domain.

He knew which buttons to press.

He knew which levers to pull.

He knew what would burrow through into the recesses of Bautista's subconscious and stick there, lingering, making sure he never went anywhere near Jake or Casey or Whitney or Harvey. Because they were dumb kids, but stupidity wasn't deserving of torture and death at the hands of the cartels in the jungle.

'You don't like this very much, do you?' Slater said, now straddling Bautista, holding him in place with one hand pressed against his throat, half-choking him. 'Your friends are unconscious. There's no help. Strange, isn't it? You're really not used to this at all.'

Bautista shook his head.

And omitted something even closer to a whimper.

'It's not every day that you get fake bills from a dipshit college kid, is it? You knew the opportunity you had in front of you. In fact you probably had the whole encounter on camera. The bar's got CCTV. And everything's digital nowadays, isn't it? So you film yourselves killing the four of them in some facility you've got out there in the jungle, and you splice that together with the footage of them giving you the fake money, and you use it as a shining example to anyone who wanders into the area you control. And that way no-one fucks with you in future. That way you always get treated right. Like kings.'

A look of pure awe on Bautista's face. Because Slater had read his mind.

And then an eighth nod.

'Great,' Slater said. 'Now I should kill you. Because you're narcos, and every narco is a stubborn piece of shit. But I'm not going to do that, because I really don't feel like killing anyone today, as you found out this morning. So clean yourselves up and get back into the jungle and keep pumping out bricks of heroin and try to forget all about this. And don't go anywhere near those kids. Or I'll have to get involved.'

A ninth nod.

But this one was half-hearted.

And in that moment Slater had an impossible decision to make.

Bautista wasn't going to leave it alone. It wasn't in his DNA. He and Vicente and Iván would pick themselves up, dust themselves off, and then go straight back to their original plan. Like hell they were going to let the weird guy from the compound get the better of them. They were the kings out here, and the kings did as they pleased. Even though Slater had beat them into the dirt without batting an eyelid. They'd chalk it up to dumb luck. And they'd carry on doing what they wanted.

Because if they caved, even once, that was weakness. And weakness wasn't tolerated out here. It would fester and rot. It would seep into every other part of their lives. They knew that as well as Slater did.

From their perspective, the eyes of the world were on

them right now. Here in this desolate, decrepit parking lot, without a soul in sight. They were being judged by the masses, because if one person saw them surrender to Slater the news would spread like a virus. And if they lost their reputation they lost everything.

So, right then and there, Slater figured he either had to kill them or let them carry on with their crusade.

And he wasn't about to murder the three of them in cold blood.

Despite who they were.

Despite the horrors they'd no doubt taken part in.

Because Slater wasn't ready to be judge, jury, and executioner today.

He'd killed so many people in Russia that the very concept seemed like a foul disease.

He clambered off Bautista and stood above him. Staring down at the man. Slater paused to collect the three Heckler & Koch pistols that lay scattered around in the dust. They were VP40s, and they looked brand new. American guns. Slater wondered how the cartels had acquired them. They'd fallen off the back of a truck, perhaps.

He tucked the VP40s into his waistband, one by one, and cinched his belt tight against them, trapping them in place. No holster, so he had to make do with what he had.

He strode back over to Bautista and planted a boot on the narco's chest. Pressing down with most of his bodyweight. Nearly two hundred pounds crushing against Bautista's pectorals. The narco wheezed. Vicente and Iván were starting to wake up, scrabbling their limbs gently against the dirt. Wading through the mud of semi-consciousness, trying to find a ledge to snatch onto and pull themselves back up into reality. But they hadn't quite found it yet.

'Don't be stupid,' Slater said. 'Seriously. Don't do it.'

Bautista nodded.

Again, half-hearted.

Slater sighed, turned on his heel, and headed out of the lot.

The second he emerged into plain sight from between the two stores, Casey came sprinting across the road from the mouth of the bar, nearly getting hit by a passing pick-up truck in the process. A couple of locals swore at her, then wolf whistled when they noticed her build. She didn't even have time to turn and throw them a dark look. She pulled to a halt in front of Slater, panting for breath, and almost reached out for a hug. Then she stopped herself short.

Good idea, Slater thought.

'You okay?' she said.

He glanced down at himself. Did he have blood on his...?

No.

'Do I look okay?' he said.

'You look fine.'

'Then I'm okay.'

'What the hell just happened?'

'Nothing happened.'

'Where are—?'

She started forward, aiming to push past Slater. He gripped her by the shoulder, spun her around, and put her back on the right track.

'They ran off,' he said.

Together they floated toward the bar. She seemed to sense what his gesture indicated, and gave up trying to work out what had happened. Some things were better left unsaid.

'Don't you think I should know what really happened?' she said. 'Just in case?'

'No.'

'Why not?'

'Because my life is already a mess, and there's no point dragging you four down to my level. So stay blissfully oblivious, okay?'

'Okay.'

'You seem quieter than before.'

'I think I'm in shock. Did you...?'

'It doesn't matter what I did.'

'It kind of does.'

'No, it really doesn't. Where's Jake? Where's Harvey and Whitney?'

'Inside. At the table. Where you told them to wait.'

'Harvey and Whitney weren't there when I said that.'

'They came back.'

'From the bar?'

'Yes, of course. What difference does that make?'

'Just making sure,' Slater said.

They pulled up out the front of the long, low building, and all the raucous sounds of inebriation and the low vibration of bass-heavy speakers flowed out the open entranceway and rolled over them, encompassing them in its warm cocoon. Slater pulled to a halt in the dirt, and Casey stopped alongside him. A strange kind of purgatory settled over them. He could see the disbelief in her face, wondering if any of it had actually happened.

He put a hand on her shoulder.

'You're the toughest of the four. Mentally. I can see that.'

'I don't feel it.'

'Yeah, well, you're the best of a bad bunch then.'

She cast him a scornful look.

He smiled. 'Kidding. You've got your head screwed on straight. You worked out what I was before the others. I don't think any of them have quite figured out what I just prevented. Hopefully they never do.'

'Okay. So I know. What do I do?'

'Round them up. Go to the hostel. Pack your shit. And move on.'

'That's it?'

'That's it. Doesn't need to be any more complicated than that. You don't stop to talk to anyone and you hurry out of here. Get on a bus, catch a flight, pay a driver, whatever. Just get away from the territory.'

'I thought you said you handled it.'

'I never said that.'

'But you just took care of those three. I figured that much.'

'Yeah. And they're one speck of a larger cartel. You get me?'

She paled, and nodded. 'I get you.'

'Get moving.'

'Thank you.'

'Don't worry about it.'

'No, I mean it. We'd all be fucking dead if you weren't there. Jake would have given them those bills and...'

'Don't think about that.'

'It's the only thing I can think about.'

Slater shrugged. 'That's life.'

'You seem resigned to it.'

'I am.'

'You don't have to be.'

Despite everything he smirked. 'That's a conversation for another time, Casey.'

'Another time?' She almost looked hopeful.

'Metaphorical,' he said, somewhat regrettably. 'It's best for your physical and mental health if you never see me again.'

'If I'm never going to see you again, then can you tell me what exactly you are?'

'No.'

'Why not?'

'Because that's testing your luck.'

'Maybe I want to.'

'Maybe you don't,' Slater said, and started to walk away.

'Hey,' she called out. 'Where are you going?'

'Away.'

'Away to where?'

'I live nearby.'

'Can we stay with you?'

He stopped in his tracks to prevent moving too far away. 'Did you not hear a word I just said?'

'I know,' she said. 'But I don't feel safe anymore.'

'You shouldn't. You never should have. Not around here.'

'We're young and dumb.'

'Yeah.'

'I'm sure you were the same.'

'How old are you?'

'Twenty-two.'

Slater bit his tongue. At twenty-two, he'd been thrust into the secretive government programme that had altered the fabric of his reality. Life had shifted from boring monotonous routine to the very limits of the human spectrum. Endless pain and extreme experiences, compounding over time, creating something he couldn't really reflect on without falling into a pit inside his own mind.

No, he hadn't gone through the young and dumb phase.

For as long as he could remember he'd shouldered the responsibility of an entire country. All because of a genetic predisposition. All because he reacted faster than almost every single person on the planet. His brain fired at a rate his superiors hadn't seen before. Only a handful of supremely gifted individuals possessed the trait. And it meant they could get the jump on anyone standing across from them in a hostile environment. Which proved awfully useful in live combat situations. It meant he was thrust into war zones with nothing but the clothes on his back and a couple of weapons and forced to fend for himself in encounters that should have killed him a thousand times over.

But they didn't.

They never did.

And he might have become so used to it that death seemed a foreign concept. Even though he'd come close to it nearly every single day.

Strange.

A dichotomy.

So close, yet so far.

'Well?' Casey said. 'Is this it?'

'Of course this is it. It was never anything. You were in the wrong place at the wrong time and I was in the right place at the right time. And it all worked out. Get your friends and get the hell out of here.'

'Thank you, again.'

'Don't worry about it, again.'

And then he was gone.

14

He made it to the outskirts of the populated village centre, and then kicked the jeep's engine into overdrive, accelerating down the rural trails.

The sweat flowed from his pores as the alcohol he'd consumed that afternoon settled into a monotonous pounding in the back of his skull. Amidst all the madness he'd almost forgotten he was inebriated. It hadn't seemed to affect him in the fight — he'd kept all his fine motor skills intact — but he chalked that up to compartmentalisation.

When the time called for it he could lock away all his problems. In the past he'd managed to ignore severe concussions, broken bones, and grotesque bullet and knife wounds until he got the job done. What was a few drinks to impair his senses in comparison to that?

Every part of him knew keeping the narcos alive was a mistake. It went against everything he'd been taught, everything he'd been led to believe over a career in government operations that wouldn't even seem realistic if it was transferred to the big screen. Maybe that was half the reason he'd been able to fight the demons of his past for as long as he had. Sure, he could blame it on suppressing the memories with drinks and substances, but that only went so far. Many soldiers tried that and failed dismally. In fact, most just made their problems worse by trying to stifle them.

But perhaps Slater's past was so incredulous, so unbelievable, that he hadn't even managed to convince his brain that most of the things in his life had actually happened. And that made him float in this strange state of purgatory where nothing seemed genuine. He wasn't happy, per se, but he wasn't sad either.

He just was.

It didn't take him long to make it back to the compound. He parked in a screech of tyres, and he was through his front door less than five minutes after leaving the bar, coated in sweat but otherwise no worse for wear. The fight with the three narcos had taken skin off his elbows and nicked a couple of his knuckles, but in the grand scheme of things he was entirely unblemished.

He walked down the concrete hallway, fetched an ice-cold beer from the fridge, planted himself down on an authentic Hans Wegner armchair overlooking the steadily flowing river, and savoured some alone time to digest and process exactly what had happened.

He sipped the beer. Wiped a hand across his forehead. It came away filthy, coated in dirt and sweat and someone else's blood. With a sigh he heaved himself off the armchair, peeling himself out of comfort, and headed for the bathroom. He showered for an eternity, allowing the familiar sensation of muscle fatigue to creep into his limbs. Back in the deserted lot he'd tapped into the life or death strength stored deep within, and that took a toll on the central nervous system. No-one was a hundred percent after a fight. Slater was tough as nails, but he wasn't superhuman.

He killed the water, towelled off, changed into a fresh pair of jeans and a simple cotton tee that clung to his muscular frame, and returned to the armchair. The exhale that followed came out wrong, rattling in his throat instead of making a smooth exit. It wasn't fear. It was something else. Something he really didn't wish to think about.

But he had to.

Because it was resignation.

He'd never stepped into a situation like that and just walked away. No matter how hard he tried. Sure, he'd returned to the compound in an attempt to distance himself from the four college kids, but something told him their fates were now intertwined.

Because the cartel wouldn't leave it alone.

Slater had made a fool out of them, and they wouldn't take that lightly.

They weren't three men. They were much, much more than that.

Across the river, the jungle seemed to stir. The sun had started its descent hours ago, and now it tinged the canopy of treetops with a toxic orange, drenching everything in sight. Long shadows fell over the opposite riverbank, darkening the space between the trees, exacerbating the fear of the unknown. Slater cradled the beer with hunched shoulders and focused as best he could on recovery. The three Heckler & Koch sidearms rested on the glass coffee table in front of him. He eyed them warily. They might come in handy.

He had a feeling it was going to be a long night.

15

Deep in the Colombian jungle, wrapped in a protective blanket of vegetation, a cluster of concrete bunker-like buildings trickled into darkness as dusk fell. They were skewered into the earth in a tight grid, protected by a chain-link perimeter fence that weaved through the undergrowth in no particular pattern. Whoever constructed the place hadn't gone to the effort of uprooting the surrounding trees. Instead they'd worked around what already existed. It added a certain level of camouflage to the buildings, aiding their invisibility. Moss grew out of cracks in the concrete, and a couple of the overhanging trees had sunk low over the last few years, drooping their fronds across the bunkers.

Inside one of the buildings, Bautista, Vicente, and Iván stretched out on rudimentary camping mattresses, cradling their wounds. They'd been exiled to this fetid dump of a bunker on the outskirts of the compound as soon as they'd crawled back to the jungle with their tail between their legs.

The boss wasn't in yet.

But he would be.

Santiago had business to attend to during the daytime. Elsewhere. He ventured out into the wild, scouting nearby towns for signs of resistance, forming new supply routes, negotiating with third parties. Anything to streamline the process. Anything to lower the bottom line, and raise the profits.

Anything to win.

The three narcos had nowhere else to go. If they fled out of shame, it wouldn't take long to hunt them down. Santiago only had to put out the feelers and employ the services of every rival cartel. They would all sway their allegiances for the right price. Their boss could turn all of Colombia against them. And the surrounding countries, too. They wouldn't have a chance to make it out alive.

Before it was too late.

The door thundered inward, kicked open by a steel-toed boot. Bautista moved to lurch off the inflatable mattress — already stained with his blood — but a searing pain in his head sent him straight back to the soft material. He sunk into temporary comfort, cradling his injuries. No-one had treated them. No-one had cleaned them up. A couple of hired goons busy packing heroin had pointed them in the direction of the makeshift infirmary and told them in no uncertain terms to wait there or risk slow, painful death for their failure.

They'd probably still get that, anyway.

Now Santiago strode into the concrete room, his eyes as harsh and grey as the surroundings. He eyed Bautista, then drifted his gaze to Vicente and Iván. Neither of the other two had reacted. Bautista had been the only one to twitch involuntarily. And Santiago had noticed.

He was six-three, two hundred and thirty pounds. Considerable body fat coated his frame, but it lay draped over a dense slab of powerlifting muscle. It only added to his strength. His head was shaved bald, his eyes squashed and ugly, his pupils swelled with the tinge of a man who induced far too many hallucinogens, and his lips fat and red.

And he was always angry.

Bautista had only tested Santiago's strength once. He'd lost a brick of heroin on the way to an organised meet, and the boss had thought Bautista lifted the portion for his own personal gain. Santiago threw him through a wall, breaking three of his ribs and nearly rupturing a lung. Then a couple of hired guns had retraced Bautista's footsteps through the jungle and found the packaged brick lying in a ditch by the side of a trail. It had fallen off the back of the truck. Bautista had been telling the truth.

It had taken him two months to recover, and he'd been cautious to never do anything to displease Santiago again.

Now the big man stared at him with venom in his eyes.

'You three,' he said. 'Start talking.'

'There was a guy,' Bautista said, babbling too fast. He'd been preparing what to say for hours. 'We've never seen him before. He lives around here.'

'Where, exactly?'

'I can show you on the GPS.'

'Distance?'

'About twenty miles from us.'

'And he beat the shit out of all three of you?'

A trio of nods, in unison.

'How?'

'He was good,' Vicente said.

'That's not an explanation.'

'Better than good,' Bautista said.

'I'm still not satisfied.'

'That's all we can tell you. We're just as confused as you are.'

'I doubt that. Because you were there. And I'm trying to piece this all together from the sidelines. The three of you were armed?'

'Yes.'

'And you didn't think of using your guns?'

'We tried. He stripped us of our weapons.'

'One by one?'

'It all happened so quick.'

'Nothing happens that quick. Three on one, and you didn't have time to pull a gun? Not one of you?'

'I guess you had to be there.'

'I guess so. What's this I hear about a group of kids?'

'We sold one of them coke. At the bar Matias owns. The young guy paid us in fake U.S. dollars.'

'And you realised this after the fact?'

'Before.'

'And you did it anyway?'

'We were going to take them. Bring them back here. Make an example out of them.'

Santiago placed his beefy hands on his hips and twirled on the spot for dramatic effect, looking this way and that.

'I don't see them,' the big man said.

'We didn't have time to pick them up. We had to come straight back here and tell you about the newcomer. Because he's a problem.'

A deadly silence filled the air. Santiago's piercing glare infiltrated Bautista's soul, searching it for any sign of weakness.

And he found something.

Santiago surged forward, approaching the fetid air

mattress, and squatted low so he was face to face with Bautista.

'You reek of fear,' he said. 'And … you had time.'

'We didn't. I swear. These two will back me up.'

'I don't care if the Pope backs you up. You could have snatched those four. It wouldn't have taken any effort. What happened in town?'

'Nothing. We just got our shit kicked in.'

'That's not all.'

'It is.'

'No,' Santiago hissed. 'It isn't … did this black man tell you to leave them alone? And did you listen to him?'

'He didn't tell us shit.'

'I think he did.'

Bautista didn't respond.

Santiago said, 'In fact, I know he did. Your lip's quivering. What did he say?'

'To forget about the college kids.'

'And you listened to him.'

'No. Like I said, we weren't going to in the first place.'

'They gave you fake currency. And you let them. Why would you do that in the first place?'

'I don't know.'

'You planned to snatch them. And this guy scared you off. Made you run back here with your tail between your legs. You bent over backwards for him, and now you're here. Big mistake, my dumb friends.'

'You need us.'

Santiago raised an eyebrow. 'You think I will kill you?'

'We do your dirty work. We've done it for years. Who will you turn to without us?'

'It seems the three of you have reached your expiration date.'

Vicente and Iván visibly bristled on their mattresses, both discarded across the room. Bautista saw it over Santiago's shoulder.

The big man didn't even turn around. 'If either of you two even *think* about going for a gun, I'll make it as slow and painful as I possibly can. And all of you know how slow I can make it.'

'You're not going to kill us,' Bautista said.

'No,' Santiago said. 'But you've disgraced us. Matias has footage from the cameras. At the bar. People have seen the tape. You take false bills from the American kid. And those four are still waltzing around town. What kind of message does that send? What does that do to our reputation?'

'I'm sorry.'

'This man has put the fear of the devil in you.'

'Yes,' Bautista said.

He couldn't help but admit it.

'Well, then he is your responsibility.'

'I'm sorry?'

'He lives near here, yes? You said so yourself.'

'I don't want to go back there.'

Santiago's eyes flared with fury. 'You will never utter those words again. You sound like a snivelling child. You *are* a snivelling child. Pathetic. How were you so easily intimidated?'

'Vicente. Iván. Tell him what you saw.'

Neither of them said a word.

Bautista sent a withering glare in their direction.

It fell on blind eyes.

And his words fell on deaf ears.

'They don't seem too concerned,' Santiago said, his face now contorted into a manic grin.

'They're scared of you.'

'They should be.'

'We're hurt. We can't...'

'I know. That's your fault.'

'How do you expect us to—?'

Santiago reached out and slapped him on the top of the skull, shutting him up mid-sentence. The blow had little force behind it, more of a precursor to a beating than an actual attempt to hurt him, but the ripple effect seared down his temples and flooded through his mangled jaw. He moaned.

'I don't expect you to do anything but follow the orders I give you. That's our deal. That's why the three of you are out here making a fortune instead of slaving away at the maquiladoras back home. Do you understand?'

Bautista understood.

'You have nothing to bargain with,' Santiago said. 'The three of you are hurt, yes, but you will deal with your problem before you see a doctor. Take any of the men with you.'

'They're all useless.'

'I've never heard you voice these concerns before.'

'I've never encountered anyone like this guy before.'

'Then all the more reason to put an end to it.'

'And if I say no?'

'I think you know.'

Bautista knew.

He nodded grimly. 'Tonight?'

'Tonight. I will deal with the Americans.'

'Deal with them?'

'You planned to send a message. I still intend on sending that message.'

In the corner of the room, an old-school video camera

and a collection of blood-stained blunt objects ranging from baseball bats to wooden planks lay dormant.

Bautista eyed them warily. 'Isn't that a little … extreme?'

'Weren't you going to do the same?'

'Yes, but that was in the heat of the moment. I've had time to cool down.'

'Do you not understand what we do?' Santiago said. 'We cannot afford to cool down.'

'I know.'

'You don't seem to. Understand this. A single moment of weakness spirals into something uncontrollable. We can never compromise.'

'Yes.'

'They pay us with fake currency. We show the rest of the country how we respond to that. We set the example.'

'Yes.'

'Load up on painkillers. Take something extra, if you need. And then go finish it. You know where this guy lives?'

'Yes.'

'Hit it hard.'

'Always.'

Santiago disappeared. Moving to the next task. Relentlessly checking off his to-do list.

Bautista swallowed, tasted sweat and blood, and stuffed down the ball of fear lodged in his throat.

A sensation he couldn't remember the last time he'd experienced.

Why was he so afraid of this man?

He knew why.

He touched a finger gently to his jaw. Not broken like he originally thought, but close enough.

16

Deeply inebriated, Jake mumbled, 'I don't understand,' as Casey shoved him in the direction of the hostel at the end of the street. The sidewalk out the front of Chocó Retreats was deserted, with most of the backpackers either out exploring the hidden treasures of the region or drinking themselves into oblivion.

Casey studied her surroundings with a newfound apprehension.

Her heart raced in her chest, thudding beat after beat against her breast. She tried not to focus on it at risk of descending into an anxiety attack. She'd suffered one of those before, one night in college, grasping at her chest and gasping for air, convinced she was about to suffocate or suffer a heart attack. It had materialised in the midst of a particularly stressful revision week before exams. She'd been horrifically underprepared.

This was a hundred times worse.

It put the rest of her life's problems in perspective. She pictured a convoy of vehicles pulling up alongside them, stuffing the four of them into the cars, carting them off to the lawless depths of the jungle. She shivered despite the heat, and the sweat on the back of her neck turned cold.

Harvey said, 'This is bad, isn't it?'

Casey nodded.

'You fucking idiot, Jake,' Whitney said.

Jake shrugged, his eyes glazed over. 'I'm sorry. I didn't think.'

'The drinks are kicking in,' Harvey muttered to Casey.

She nodded again.

She searched for words, but found nothing.

Nothing could summarise the extent of their mutual idiocy.

'We'll be fine,' Whitney said. 'That guy dealt with them.'

'Who the hell was he?' Harvey said.

'Fuck if I know,' Jake mumbled. 'Did he beat them up?'

'Stop talking,' Casey said. 'Walk.'

'Don't tell me what to—'

Casey slapped him, hard. The crack resonated down the street, and it shocked the other three into stunned silence. None of them could believe it had happened — Jake most predominantly. He wheeled to her, almost losing his balance in the process. Fury laced his eyes. He started to formulate aggression when...

Casey launched into a tirade. 'You morons don't understand how close we just came to something really, really bad. We need to get to the hostel, pack our shit, and get the hell out of here. Next bus out. Got it?'

None of her friends could remember the last time her intensity had reached this level. It all hit them at once, and they nodded, suddenly scared and aware and on edge all at once.

'Okay,' Whitney said, throwing a paranoid glance over her shoulder.

'Now get moving,' Casey hissed.

They hurried toward the lobby.

17

Bautista, Vicente, and Iván nursed their wounds and felt awfully sorry for themselves. The atmosphere dripped with nervous anticipation. They completed rudimentary weapons checks and adjusted the ceramic vests compromising the entirety of their body armour. They looked at each other, silent the whole time, but deeply aware of how the other was feeling.

All three were terrified.

Bautista couldn't speak for Vicente and Iván, but he'd never experienced anything like this. For a brief, flashing moment he flirted with sympathy for the people he'd slaughtered over the last few years. Then that went away, because if he dove down that rabbit hole he would never resurface. So he locked the emotions away.

Because his life had been dominance. From start to finish. Constant acting and reacting, always getting his way, seizing a leg up over his competition. He'd never found himself in a position of true fear. No-one hammered an objective like he did. It was half the reason he'd been plucked from the slums and carted out here to the unforgiving jungles. The heat and the humidity and the discomfort hadn't deterred him, so how the hell could he expect to face any kind of resistance out here? He was an enforcer, through and through, and he'd made every part of his life revolve around being the best enforcer a man could be. He cut no corners. He fulfilled Santiago's every wish.

And now the boss was treating him like pond scum.

He hefted the Colt AR-15 into his right hand and tested its weight. It had been some time since he'd wielded this kind of firepower. In fact, the gun seemed foreign in his sweaty palm. It added to the unease. He gulped, wiped sweat off his face, and muttered something reassuring to himself.

'You're the fuckin' man,' he snarled under his breath.

Vicente looked across. 'What?'

'Nothing.'

But it wasn't nothing, and it was blatantly obvious. His friends had never seen him like this. And he hadn't seen them so scared either. They were a trio of hard, cruel men thrust into a dynamic they knew little about.

And none of them wanted to speak about it.

'The fuck are we doing here?' Vicente finally said.

Sweating too.

All three of them, sweating hard, tasting the foul air.

Bautista dropped the AR-15 to the rickety table in front of them. Stifled a curse. Breathed.

'I don't know.'

'Who is that guy?' Iván said. 'How'd we get like this?'

'I'm in so much fucking pain, man,' Vicente said.

Nursing his injuries.

'Get over it,' Bautista said. 'When we get this done we can relax.'

'*If.*'

'Shut your mouth.'

'Who's coming with us?'

'All of them.'

'All?'

'I'll do this shit for him,' Bautista said. 'But I'm not underestimating this motherfucker.'

'Are any of us?'

'What about the Americans?' Iván said. 'Who's picking them up?'

'Santiago.'

'Alone?'

'No. He's taking the help from Guatemala.'

'The hired guns?'

'Yeah. The brothers.'

'Christ. I almost feel sorry for the kids.'

Bautista fought down a knot of nerves in his gut. 'No you don't.'

18

The hostel corridors were, as usual, a raucous hive of activity. Drunk youths trundled from room to room, pausing in open doorways to converse with whoever lay in the bunks in each dormitory. Casey shoved a young guy with broad shoulders and absurdly enormous sunglasses aside. He sipped his beer and stared at her with disapproval sweeping over his expression.

'Hey,' he started.

She held up a hand to silence him for just long enough to get past, wheeling her suitcase behind her with manic intensity. The bag was stuffed to the brim. There'd been no time to pack with care. Jake shouldered past her, suddenly physical. She'd never seen him like this.

'You okay?' she said.

'Sorry,' he slurred. 'Did I hurt you?'

'No.'

'Uh, yeah, I'm okay.'

'Let's just get out of here.'

He nodded, staring at a fixed point at the end of the corridor, his trainers scuffing on the cheap carpet. He seemed to realise he'd overdone the day's drinking session, and it came at the most inopportune time.

'We'll be okay, right?' he said.

She nodded. 'We'll be fine. We just need to leave, right now.'

'No, I mean ... us.'

'Oh.'

'Casey?'

'Now's not the time. Let's go.'

She led him through the hostel's hallways, each indistinguishable from the last. She'd had a few too many to drink herself, and the obscene yellow paint on the walls swam before her eyes. The first day she'd walked into the hostel, dead sober, she'd found the attempt at seeming vibrant wholly distasteful. Now it was obscene. The toxic hue radiated outward, threatening to send her into a mad spiral if she wasn't careful about keeping her mind on the present moment.

'Relax,' she told herself.

She heard Harvey and Whitney tearing down the corridor behind them, and she quickened her pace in turn. She'd been waiting for them to catch up before putting the pedal to the metal. Now she hurried into the lobby, nodding once to the rotund receptionist with the awful combover. The man nodded back, his brow furrowed. She'd checked out the second they'd arrived, to make sure there was nothing left to do when their bags were packed.

They burst out onto the street, now strangely deserted. The surrounding buildings seemed akin to a fake town erected for a nuclear test site. Casey half-expected to see mannequins propped up at regular intervals, painted dizzying shades of neon to accentuate the illusion. Her head

swam. Her temples throbbed. She wheeled in circles —
where the hell had everyone gone?

Unless the cartels had more of an influence on the
region than she'd originally expected.

And why wouldn't they? she thought.

They've got the money.

Out here, they're gods.

A fuzzy black insect materialised at the edge of her
vision, roaring into full view of the hostel's entrance. It took
her a second longer than necessary to recognise it as a
moving vehicle. An SUV, to be specific, its windows blacked
out, its tyres screeching against the gravel underneath. Like
something out of a horror movie it jerked and jolted toward
them, almost in separate freeze frames. She briefly
wondered if someone had slipped something in one of her
drinks at the bar. Or, more realistically, the fear had leeched
into the effects of the alcohol and created something
horrifying.

Before she could even hope to react, the SUV skidded to
a halt in front of the four of them.

Casey.

Jake.

Harvey.

Whitney.

All frozen in place.

Unsure of how to react.

None of them moved. A dizzying wave of regret washed
over Casey, chilling her temples. Briefly, she figured she
deserved whatever was coming. How could anyone be so
stupid? She hadn't been the one to go through with the
deed, but merely associating with someone like Jake was
reason enough.

No.

This isn't your fault.

A man slipped out of the passenger seat, in no rush to intimidate them. In fact, he kept quiet. His appearance said everything. Built like a truck. Massive shoulders. Hands like bricks. A bald head. An ugly, squashed nose. An acne-ridden complexion. Fat, full lips. With a little beautification and some facial care he might have been able to clean up his aura, but it seemed he had no interest in such things.

He held a fat black pistol in his left hand. Casey knew nothing about guns. She couldn't identify the make, or the model. But she saw the man's finger around the trigger, and noted the fluidity with which he wielded the weapon. He knew how to use it.

She gulped.

He smiled through yellow teeth and said, 'You know what you did.'

They all nodded.

No-one was even remotely ready to put up an argument.

He gestured to the back seat. 'Get the fuck in the car.'

'No,' Jake said.

The expression on the man's face didn't change in the slightest, which was probably the most unnerving part of the entire ordeal. Keeping the false smile plastered on, he strode forward with far too much agility for his weight and smashed the butt of the gun into the bridge of Jake's nose.

The *crack* almost made Casey faint, but she held it together for the sake of Harvey and Whitney.

Jake crumpled, vomiting on the way down, the horrendous pain bringing the nausea of the day's drinking session to the surface. He spouted like a fire hose into the gutter, a sorry sight for any passersby.

But there were no passersby.

No doubt compliments of the man standing in front of them.

For good measure, the man kicked Jake in the ribs. He moaned and mopped his mouth with the sleeve of his outrageous floral shirt. The big man hauled Jake to his feet, dragged him over to the car, and threw him into the backseat. Casey caught a glimpse of Jake collapsing into the footwell, too uncomfortable to function.

'Anyone else want to say no?' the big man said.

Casey didn't react, and neither did Harvey or Whitney, but the hesitation lingered. She knew she was giving up her life if she got in the car. And it wouldn't be a quick death. The alcohol was keeping most of the awareness at bay, and the extent of her situation hadn't quite sunk in yet, but she knew she was making a fatal mistake if she complied.

But what choice did she have?

The big man sensed the resistance. He levelled the gun at Harvey's head.

The boy broke down in uncontrollable tears.

'Okay,' Casey said. 'We'll get in.'

'Good call,' the big man said, and smiled his sickly smile.

Casey headed for the back seat, trying not to gag.

Now the anxiety set in.

Truly.

Completely.

She focused on her breathing, trying to find a way out of this personal malevolent hell, and hoped with every part of her soul that the stranger from earlier that afternoon would find them.

But how would he?

A rare stroke of luck had protected them before.

And lightning, as far as she could tell, didn't strike twice.

19

Night fell. Thick, hot, overbearing.

The dark provided no relief from the humidity, or the stench.

The sweat flowed freely in the shadows.

The convoy ghosted through the jungle. Traversing the undergrowth, wading through the warm dark puddles coating the forest floor. Their faces blacked out. Their pulses racing from the Dexedrine pills they'd popped. Their grips slick and sizzling on the AR-15s in their hands. Considerable firepower, spread across a previously coordinated semi-circle. Closing in on a strange amalgamation of steel and glass and concrete slapped onto an otherwise deserted riverbank, way off the beaten track.

A prime target.

Bautista gnashed his teeth together as he closed in on the opposite riverbank. He knew he was foolish to be so scared. But maybe it was a blessing in disguise. Maybe this was the wake up call the three of them needed. The faceless goons around them would make effective cannon fodder, and then either himself or Vicente or Iván would fire the kill shot and that would be that. The devil in human form would be cut down, and they could return to lording over the Chocó Department.

Business as usual.

Christ, this scared him though.

What the fuck was he doing, sneaking around the jungle? The cartels didn't do this shit. They stormed in with their chins held high, obscenely confident. They ordered people around. They didn't sneak up on them with their tails tucked between their legs. That was weakness. And weakness just didn't cut it out here. If any of the rival factions caught wind of this particular escapade, there would be hell to pay. But Bautista didn't plan on letting anyone find out. They would execute the American, sweep him under the rug, and pretend he never existed.

Then they would go straight back to doing what they did best.

Winning.

But life is never that simple. It had been for quite some time, but Bautista was sorely aware he'd needed the pot stirred. The black man's speech resonated in his head. He couldn't shake the fact that he'd submitted to the guy. He might as well have bent over backwards and told him to take his time.

The soft trickle of flowing water filtered through the night. Passing between the trees. Tickling the edge of their hearing. The convoy stiffened, and Bautista glanced left and right to observe unfamiliar faces. Vicente and Iván were elsewhere in the procession, leaving him surrounded by drug-fuelled guns-for-hire. Nothing to ordinarily be wary of, but something about the nature of the operation made him pine for the reassurance of men he knew well.

Men he worked with.

Men he bled with.

Santiago paid well, but not enough to instil unwavering confidence. If the tide shifted, and the morale shattered, these men would run. They would value their own necks over the lives of their hired comrades.

Bautista grimaced, and approached the river.

He was overthinking it.

The plan was the same.

Put a bullet in the owner of the compound, and be on their way.

Simple as that.

20

S later awoke from the afternoon nap to find the sheets stained with perspiration and the sky outside darkening into dusk. He wiped a hand across his face, removing gunk from the corners of his eyes, and tested the waters of the hangover. He'd consumed far too much drink at the bar, and although he'd forced the inebriation aside as he beat down the narcos, he wasn't superhuman. He couldn't avoid the effects forever.

So he'd put his head on the pillow as soon as he got home and slept it off.

Now he stretched and shook off the same-day hangover symptoms, grateful that he'd handled the situation remarkably well. Gone were the days of all-out benders, complete with after-effects that almost made him prefer the battlefield. His muscles ached from the fight, and he sauntered straight into the training room and dipped straight into a gruelling vinyasa yoga routine to stretch out his tight hip flexors and loosen the knots bundled in his shoulders. It was daunting, exerting work, especially after such a whirlwind day. But he paid the routine no attention whatsoever, shifting into autopilot.

If he didn't think, instead relying on the automatic process of carefully refined habit, he barely had time to talk himself out of the vigorous exercise. He'd mastered the process of taming his mind over a decade ago. Not a day went by in his life where he didn't give thanks for that particular avenue of self-discipline.

Dressed in a pair of athletic shorts and nothing else, he continued through the maintenance work. By the time he clambered off the yoga mat — now damp with the sweat that had fallen off his hardened frame — he felt like a new man. He breathed life into his lungs, inhaling the air as best he could, and showered for a second time that day. He changed into a fresh pair of khakis and a simple white cotton tee and made for the living room.

Altogether he'd vanished for close to twenty minutes.

Shower, shave, dry, dress.

When he reached the hallway, about to step out into the open, he froze. All was not as it seemed. He heard all the familiar sounds, but they seemed hollow. Detached. Unreal. Call it a sixth sense. He knew it was a practice honed from spending years in the thick of combat.

There was a certain unseen electricity in the air. Crackling in the thick heat. Bringing the perspiration right back out of his pores. Firing neurons, activating circuits in the brain, channelling the devastation of years prior.

Still out of sight of the river and its opposing bank, he crossed to the chest of drawers in the hallway and wrenched the top left handle. The compartment spilled open, revealing the Glock 17. Slater touched a finger to the trigger, disengaging the safety. Veins rippled on his forearm as he wrapped a hand around the stock. He tested the weight, getting used to it, linking the gun to his own consciousness. Extending his psyche to encompass the firearm.

They were coming.

Movement in the training room.

Slater dropped without a hint of sound, flattening himself to the artificially cooled tiles like a snake. He crawled forward, inch by inch, breathing deep in his core. Stilling his nerves. It wasn't hard. His mind was at war, but his soul was at peace. He lived and breathed for these encounters. Strangely enough, they seemed more natural than the time he spent away from the line of fire.

That didn't bode well for his mental health down the line.

But he didn't need to think about down the line.

He needed to think about now.

A bulky silhouette appeared in the doorway.

Too easy.

Slater fired twice, blowing the back of the man's skull across the training room. Juxtaposed against the muted glow of the halogen lights overhead and the faint monotonous buzzing of insects outside, the gunshots exploded with twin roars. Slater would have flinched, had he not lived in this zone for most of his adult life. When he saw the gore spray he calculated the angles and leapt to his feet, using every part of the flexibility and dexterity he'd formed through daily yoga. He closed the gap between himself and the now-dead intruder in an uncanny burst of speed, still deathly silent as he ran. He screeched to a halt and caught the man by the front of his ceramic vest, freezing the guy in place before he could collapse. He noticed the two gaping holes in the man's forehead and admired his handiwork for half a second, then tightened his grip on the Glock as he held the corpse upright for just long enough to confuse the hell out of whoever else had deemed it necessary to intrude.

And there would be more.

There always was.

The positioning shielded him from view of the other hostiles. However many there were. He stood hunched over, concealed just inside the lip of the hallway. The intruder's frame filled the doorway. He was a big guy. Colombian, around six-three, with a giant frame to boot. All that muscle hadn't helped him one bit. A colossal mistake in a single moment in time and his life had ceased.

But that was the price you paid.

Already his eyes were glazed over. The milky film of death had developed in front of his pupils, awfully quick. Slater had lost count of the number of times he'd witnessed it up close, but it never got any stranger. He became oblivious to it, though.

Do anything enough and you can compartmentalise it.

So he held the corpse there without reacting. Not for long. A second or two. But it wasn't the natural way things developed. Usually gunfire resulted in chaos, one unsuppressed shot leading to a firestorm of bullets that shredded everything in sight and killed almost everyone on both sides of the firefight.

Not here.

If there was someone behind the first guy, he would see his friend's brains spurt out the back of his head. And then he would see the guy frozen in place, his view of Slater blocked by the big doorway.

Which would have rattled him even more.

All hypotheticals.

Now Slater put it to the test.

He timed the pause to perfection and shoved the corpse aside, clattering the body off one side of the doorway. It was an ugly sprawl. Limbs tangled and twisted and the dead guy went down in ungainly fashion.

The kind of brutal *thwack* and flailing tumble that seized attention, regardless of how well-trained you were. Your eyes darted to it. Because it was so strange.

Slater stepped into the doorway, now fully visible to the room, and his brain kicked into overdrive. He took in the sight of two men, both roughly the same size, spread across the room, clutching big chunky Colt AR-15s at the ready, their wide eyes focused on the body of their friend.

Surprised.

Not because of the presence of death.

They'd been expecting that, and no doubt hopped themselves up on stims to compensate for the trauma they were likely to experience up close.

No, it was because of the few seconds where the body seemed to levitate in place. Anything that strange demanded attention.

Shame.

Because putting attention in the wrong place in a situation like this, even for half a second, got you killed.

Slater shot the guy on the left in the forehead, then flicked his aim to the guy on the right and executed the exact same command.

Line up.

Trigger pull.

Done.

Thwack-thwack.

Two bodies hit the marble floor of the training room.

Slater heard it, but he didn't see it.

Because he was already out of sight, ducking back into the hallway.

A ghost in the wind.

Casey tried her hardest not to cry, but the endeavour proved useless.

The chassis of the big SUV rattled all around her as it jolted over potholes in the seedy darkness. They'd been driving for what seemed like hours, and she wasn't sure if it was a deliberate ploy to disorient the four of them so they had no chance of co-ordinating a rescue, even if they escaped. Looking out the window with misty eyes and a lump in her throat, she swore the terrain seemed familiar. She couldn't quite discern whether it was a coincidental bout of déjà vu, or if they were truly driving in circles.

But then the rural trails turned even more barebones, and the driver veered off into the real jungle and abandoned any shred of civilisation they'd been holding onto over the course of the evening. Night encompassed the vehicle, blackening the view outside. True night. The kind of uniform emptiness that removed all hope entirely. Casey stared into the blackness and considered leaping out of the moving car. At the speed they were travelling, almost reckless on the uneven terrain, she would probably break both her legs upon landing. But even that might be preferable to what fate had in store for them later that night.

No.

She didn't have the guts.

Because two men sat silently behind the middle row, taking up most of the space in the SUV's large trunk. They had guns — she'd seen the glint of metal as the big ugly man in the passenger seat had funnelled them into the car hours ago. They sat crammed shoulder-to-shoulder — Harvey, then Whitney, then Jake, then Casey. Neither the driver, nor the passenger who seemed to be in charge, nor the two men in the back had said a word the entire time. But the implicit threat was there. If Casey or any of her friends moved unnaturally, or reached for the door handle, or tried to call for help, they would catch a bullet in the back of the skull. And that terrified her endlessly, in a way she hadn't thought possible. She wasn't ready to die. Maybe the road ahead would involve torture and unimaginable pain, but it still came with a chance of survival. Getting all her senses cut off at once by a piece of lead pulverising her brain wasn't something she was willing to risk. No matter what.

She wasn't ready for that.

She wasn't ready for any of this.

Tears streamed silently down her face, and she caught a sob at the top of her throat. But a tiny fraction of sound followed it out. A guttural noise, making it startlingly obvious what she was trying to do.

The big man with the fat lips wheeled around in the passenger seat, fixing his beady eyes on her.

'Don't be scared,' he said.

'I'm not,' she muttered.

'We're not going to do anything unnecessary. We just need to send a message.'

'To who?'

Silence answered her. She returned her gaze to the darkness outside the window, watching the murky black outlines of tree trunks flash past. She wondered what she'd done to deserve this fate. Surely stupidity didn't cut it. She'd go back stateside and put her head down and never venture anywhere she wasn't welcome. She'd never be blissfully ignorant of a region's problems again. But to do any of that, she had to make it out of this alive. And with each passing second she found that a less likely outcome.

She shook her head from side to side, deriding herself for believing the promises of the big man for even a second.

He'd said it to calm her down until they got to their destination.

Some kind of jungle encampment?

Somewhere private, for sure.

Somewhere no-one would hear them.

She thought of the man from earlier that afternoon. Tall, dark, handsome. Radiating silent confidence. No wonder she'd made such a brazen move. She'd never cheated on Jake before, and never intended to, but something about the strain on their relationship and the mysterious aura of…

She hadn't even asked for his name.

He was lost to anonymity.

And she and her three closest friends were making a beeline for gruesome deaths.

She sobbed again.

The compound hadn't been designed for urban warfare. It was a long low structure with massive open sections leading right out onto the riverbank, allowing the hot air to flood into the rooms. Slater had deliberately constructed it that way, creating a permanent aura of discomfort that never allowed him to settle.

He'd been taught from an early age to fear the warmth of his bed.

All progress was made on the other side of resistance, so if he removed the possibility of an artificial atmosphere and instead drenched his body in the unbearable jungle air twenty four hours a day, seven days a week, he would return to his old self in no time.

And it had worked.

He'd lost the thirty pounds put on when he lay bedridden. Pounds stacked on through no fault of his own. He'd lost his Olympic-level conditioning, lost the uncanny power that enabled him to blast through human opposition like they were children's playthings. That kind of strength could only be forged in relentless discomfort. Hence the move to

Colombia after his brain had sifted itself out of the shit. Hence the gruelling daily workouts. Hence the pain on top of pain on top of pain.

It had all been for a reason.

He knew that now as he stalked down the hallway, feeling right at home in the madness. There were three dead bodies in the training room, and it meant nothing to him. He made it to the front door and tapped a series of commands on the digital control panel fixed into the entranceway. Darkness plunged over the compound. All the lights petered out at once, their auras vanishing, replacing the stark white glare with rapidly diminishing fields of view.

Without a sound, he slipped out the front door, cradling the Glock in his right hand. He stayed low and ghosted around the perimeter of the property, keeping his back to the thick concrete slab composing the entirety of the left wall. No windows here. No vantage points to use as a barricade, firing out through glass. Just concrete. And steel. He descended a low ditch packed with wet dirt and circled around to one side of the building.

And ran straight into a hostile.

Almost chest to chest.

The speed at which Slater was able to react meant he could have blasted the guy's nose apart before the man even knew what had hit him. But that would create a blaring report, which would resonate through the otherwise quiet jungle and reveal his position to everyone in the immediate vicinity. So instead he continued through the motions, not changing his trajectory in the slightest, which shocked the hell out of his adversary. Usually if two parties ran straight into each other in the dark there was the inevitable flinch, followed by a hasty scramble for weapons as each man took a backward step to try and make sense of what the hell had just happened. Instead Slater barrelled forward like a freight train, giving the other guy no time to react. He slammed his forehead into the lower part of the guy's jaw, probably knocking a few teeth loose and silencing any outcry the man could muster in the next couple of seconds.

Which was all the time he needed, anyway.

The headbutt had enough force behind it to stun the guy into taking pause. He knew why. Sneaking through the darkness, thinking you had control of the situation, then a rush of movement in front of you and a blinding fast burst of speed and a vicious crack on the lower half of your face and a flaring blitz of pain. It was enough to freeze anyone in place.

Bad news against a guy like Slater.

Slater went as far as dropping his weapon to free himself up for the couple of seconds he had to capitalise. There was no-one else around, and the nature of the terrain shielded him from catching a bullet from a distant hostile, so he deemed it safe. In ordinary combat it would be considered a suicide tactic. But Slater hadn't approached combat normally for as long as he could remember.

He immediately used his free hand to thunder a right hook into the side of the guy's head. Pinpoint accuracy. Uncanny power. Nothing had changed. It almost shut the guy off at the light switch but he kept his legs underneath him.

In fact, the AR-15 in his hands started a dangerous upward trajectory.

But it looped and wobbled as it did so. The punch to the temple had thrown his equilibrium out. The darkness didn't help. He was utterly disorientated. Slater snatched the gun and hurled it aside. It clattered off the wall. Inhuman strength. He elbowed the guy in the throat, destroying soft tissue, then loaded up the exact same right hook. It landed on the same patch of temple. It flipped the switch.

The guy went down.

But not all the way.

Because Slater caught him by the shoulders and threw his unconscious body into the concrete wall of the compound alongside them.

Head first.

Crunch.

He wouldn't be waking up anytime soon.

If at all.

No hard feelings.

Slater simply didn't want anyone recovering and sneaking up behind him. He had enough problems to deal with on his own.

For good measure he stomped down on the guy's head as he hit the dirt. It was dark, so the results were blurry. Probably a good thing. He knew it was bad from the way his boot crunched down against the man's skull.

Sorry, Slater thought.

You were about to kill me.

Now the hostile was unquestionably dead. Slater scooped up the AR-15 and checked the weapon in the lowlight. It came with a twenty-round box magazine. He ejected it and flashed a glance at the cartridges inside the clip. Fully loaded. No shots fired.

No shit.

He hadn't heard an assault rifle go off during the skirmish.

Wasted time.

Wasted opportunities.

Cursing himself, he took off up the side of the ditch.

He made it to the riverbank in a few seconds, spurred on

by adrenalin. Moving fast now. Four men dead. There wouldn't be many more. The three narcos from earlier that afternoon knew he was tough, but there was an extent to which their pride came into play. If they showed up with an army of twenty men to take on a single foreigner, it would bruise their egos. And cartel thugs had egos the size of buildings, and they wore them like suits of armour.

So he figured there would be one more, maximum, aside from the original three.

As fate would have it, he hadn't chanced upon them yet.

Unless they'd sent their minions to do the job for them.

No, Slater thought.

They weren't the head honchos. Which meant they'd be responsible for their own shortcomings. Which meant they'd come themselves. But they'd bring help. Hence the bodies riddled across the compound.

Slater vaulted onto the outside landing, which consisted of a vast concrete slab smoothed down and slapped into the earth, jutting out from the open-plan living area.

He pressed himself to his belly, and aimed down the AR-15's sights.

He needn't have bothered.

There were four of them.

Inside.

He recognised Bautista, Vicente, and Iván. The rough outlines of their shapes. He could still recall them from earlier in the afternoon. When he dealt with people in hand-to-hand combat he memorised body types. He was probably an expert in kinesiology without realising it. Practice makes perfect. So he knew instantly who they were. They moved awkwardly. They were injured. Beat down. They needed medical attention, but they were trying in vain to press forward and please their boss.

Whoever he was.

The fourth guy was an anonymous cartel thug. The menacing posture, the stooped shoulders, the frantic movements. Hopped up on stimulants, too. Probably Dexedrine, if Slater had any insight into the minds of narcos.

And Slater had caught all four of them with their pants down.

They'd been unnerved by the strange way the skirmish had unfolded. They'd expected a balls-to-the-wall gunfight. They'd game-planned accordingly. Maybe taken a few too many stimulants. Slater pictured their resting heart rates skyrocketing, their pulses pounding and their temples sweating and their nervous tics racing to the surface. They hadn't approached with a stealth mindset. They'd expected an assault, and now nothing was going according to plan. So they'd abandoned tactical reasoning and sprinted into the compound like the inexperienced morons they were.

All four of them had their backs to Slater. They were tearing across the living area. Weaving around designer furniture. Heading for the hallway where they'd last heard commotion. They'd be out of sight in a few seconds, and that would make things difficult.

There's no time like the present.

Slater killed the unknown narco with a headshot, spraying blood and brain matter across one of his favourite couches. The wet *thump* of the body hitting the leather upholstery froze the three familiar faces in places. Or, rather, familiar *bodies.* Bautista and Vicente and Iván. The ringleader in the middle. The other two manning either side like a guard of honour. Slater only needed one of them, and keeping all three alive would be too much to handle. So he shot Vicente in the neck, then figured he'd send a message with the last kill. He put six bullets in Iván, all in the centre of the man's chest as he turned to face the landing.

A deafening roar.

A body jerking like a marionette dangling from strings.

And a terrified last survivor, white as a ghost, his jaw swollen beyond comprehension from where Slater had broken it.

Bautista started to raise his own AR-15.

Bad move.

Should have dropped it.

Slater shot him in the gut.

23

S omething about the arrival at the encampment sent Casey into a downward spiral wracked with anxiety, terror, and above all helplessness.

She hyperventilated as they dragged her out of the SUV. Foreign hands on her flesh, pulling her arms, nearly wrenching her shoulders out of their sockets. She fell off the edge of her own mental clarity, and suddenly all the stifled emotions roared to the surface. She fought and clawed and bit and screamed, but her resistance was short-lived. There was no natural light to illuminate what was going on around her, and that compounded the terror. A hand shot out of the darkness and slapped her full in the face, firing nerve endings across her cheek and shocking her into temporary silence.

Before she could start screaming again, the big man with the fat lips rounded the passenger side of the SUV and crouched down by her shuddering form.

He leant in close.

'Listen,' he whispered, his breath disgusting. 'Can you hear that?'

Despite everything, she followed his commands. She said nothing, and listened.

She heard nothing.

She shook her head. 'No.'

'Exactly.'

She sobbed.

'Scream all you want. You're just wasting energy.'

'You said you weren't going to do anything unnecessary.'

'I wanted a pleasant car ride.'

She let out a guttural moan.

He slapped her again. 'I don't even know your name.'

'Casey,' she said instantly, as if her willingness to share might salvage the situation. 'It's Casey Hayes.'

He nodded, smiling a sick smile. 'Nice to meet you, Casey Hayes. I'm Santiago.'

'Nice to meet you too,' she mumbled through a split lip.

She stared up at him through bloodshot eyes.

He smiled wider. 'No. Don't lie.'

'What?'

'I hate liars.'

'What are you talking about?'

'It's definitely not nice to meet me.'

'I just want to go home.'

'Yeah, well...'

He gestured to his thugs, and they seized her by the armpits and dragged her away from the black SUV.

She didn't scream. She didn't even fight.

She lay there groggily, detached from reality, numb to the terror.

Her fear had reached its apex moments earlier, and now it had given way to a dead soul.

Now, the nihilism set in.

She didn't want to go home anymore.

She just wanted it to be over quick.

They hauled her wordlessly toward a concrete bunker.

Behind her, she heard the muffled protests of her three friends as they were led toward the same building.

24

B autista crumpled, bouncing off one of Slater's designer armchairs on the way down to the polished concrete floor. Even though the night was thick with humidity to the point where the air between them swam with shimmering heat, Slater would never forget the look in the narco's eyes as he went down.

Understanding.

Acceptance.

It was like he always knew he would lose.

Slater realised he'd done his job earlier that afternoon. He'd put mortal fear in this brutal, unforgiving cartel thug. Bautista had never wanted to come here. He seemed to have known the result was inevitable. But he needed to save face, because that was the nature of the cartels, and weakness wasn't tolerated in the slightest.

Slater almost felt bad for him, and then he remembered where he was.

He recalled the horrors he'd personally witnessed as a result of the drug cartels. There was nothing moral or even remotely human about these vermin. They were the scum of society. Irredeemable, at least in Slater's eyes.

Because they had the choice to walk away.

Child soldiers in Somalia and other undesirable parts of the Third World had no choice. Slater had witnessed that first-hand too. But there was no brainwashing here. These were grown men, who willingly put profit before humanity. He had no illusions as to the nature of the atrocities Bautista had committed.

So he switched off his moral compass for what came next.

He crossed the room, smashed a boot into Bautista's AR-15, watched the rifle skitter away across the concrete, and snatched the writhing narco by the collar of his shirt. He heaved the man to his feet, noting the dark red pool of blood forming underneath him, dripping down from his stomach.

'You don't have long left,' Slater snarled.

Bautista, white as a ghost, said, 'Please kill me.'

'No.'

'Please.'

'You took them, didn't you? Even though I told you not to.'

'No, no, we let them go...'

Slater heaved Bautista to his feet and slammed the man down on the leather couch.

On top of Vicente's corpse.

Bautista squirmed. Clearly uncomfortable. A sociopath, sure, but not all the way. Not devoid of any emotion whatsoever. The man underneath him had been a close ally. A person he could count on. And now he was dead, and Bautista was sitting on his body.

'Let me go,' he gasped.

Close to panic.

'You've got a choice to make,' Slater said.

'What?' Bautista snapped.

Now, he couldn't handle it. He needed a way out, fast. He would do anything Slater requested.

'I liked those four kids,' Slater said. 'They were stupid, but we're all stupid when we're that young. I know you took them. Maybe not you personally. Maybe your boss. Am I on the right track?'

'Yes, yes, you're on the right track. Take me off him, please...'

'You don't get to play the victim. Not here. Not now.'

'Please.'

'You took them back to your camp?'

'Yes.'

'You personally?'

'The boss.'

'Who's the boss?'

'Santiago. You don't want to mess with—'

Slater dragged the bleeding, dying man to his feet. 'Oh, but Bautista, I think I do. We're going for a drive.'

'No, please, just kill me here.'

'The four of them are at your camp?'

'Yes.'

'With the boss?'

'Yes.'

'To be executed? To have their deaths filmed?'

'Yes.'

'Then excuse me if I don't feel sorry for you.'

'Just kill me.'

'Then how would I know the way?'

'I can tell you.'

'I might get lost.'

'You won't get lost. It's a straight path through—'

Slater slapped him in the face, aggravating his damaged jaw. 'Good. But just to make sure, you can show me the way.'

He dragged Bautista out through the compound, not bothering to lock the front door or secure the property in any meaningful way. In truth, he'd never expected an assault before the trio of narcos had appeared earlier that morning.

That morning.

It felt like a month ago.

You're back in the system, a voice told him.

Back in the hell you tried to crawl out of.

He smirked to himself. No. He'd never tried to crawl out of it. He'd only been delaying the inevitable. And he was in shape. Damn good shape. Under the sweat-soaked shirt his muscles rippled, breathing life, tasting the all-out exertion of combat.

His mind was bulletproof. Six men dead in his territory, men he'd cut down with his own hand, and not even a shred of remorse had come to the surface. Maybe if he had less experience in this world ... maybe then the shock might have set in. Maybe then he would have considered the intruders human.

But they were linked to the cartel, and that entwined them in a world of malevolence. He'd long ago given up on trying to remain moral in a world like this.

Besides, he knew he was doing the right thing.

He didn't need to think about it too hard.

Armed intruder, right there. Shoot. Kill.

Simple as that.

He shoved Bautista toward the open-topped jeep. The big man bounced off the passenger door, and a *clang* echoed through the small clearing, choked by the oppressive night-time heat. He hit the dirt. He let out something close to a whimper. Slater wrenched the door open, pulled Bautista to his feet, and manhandled him into the seat. He put the seat-belt on, just in case they crashed en route to the encampment. He needed his tour guide conscious and functioning, not careening through the windshield.

Slater left him there. He walked back to the compound, strode boldly through the silent hallway, collected the AR-15s the narcos had dropped, ejected their magazines, shoved them into the deep pockets of his khakis.

Locked and loaded. Ready to go.

He left the building. Left the front door wide open. No-one would come. Not the cartel. They'd sent all the forces they were willing to expend. There wouldn't be more. If, by an impossible stroke of chance, a civilian happened upon the property, they would find a shocking crime scene and flee with their tail tucked between their legs.

Besides, if he wanted to lock up, he would need to find his keys.

And, quite frankly, he didn't have time.

Four college kids were somewhere out there in the jungle. Crying, sweating, shaking. Fearing for their lives.

They weren't used to this. Slater was.

So they needed him.

He returned to the jeep, and sure enough Bautista hadn't budged an inch. Slater eyed the man's lap, stained crimson, dripping onto the seat between his legs.

He wouldn't last long.

Slater got into the driver's seat and put the AR-15 down on the centre console. Normally an overwhelmingly foolish tactical manoeuvre. But the guy in the passenger seat was knocking on death's door, and Slater had enough faith in his reflexes to kill him with a single punch to the throat if he made any kind of move for the weapon.

But he really didn't want to do that.

Because Casey and Whitney and Jake and Harvey needed him.

You're dumb kids. But we all were.

He accelerated into the night.

25

They threw Casey down in a concrete room that stank of everything a human body could omit, from sweat to blood to faeces. She wiped a tear from under her eye and brought the same hand in front of her face, trying to scrutinise the dirt caked into her palm lines. She couldn't see a thing. It was too dark. The two men who'd dragged her here turned on their heels and left the room, sealing the door shut behind them.

She sat still in the darkness, her bones aching, her muscles cramping, her mind overwhelmed with possibility. Anxiety, multiplied by a hundred. Sensations she hadn't thought possible. Fear she hadn't thought imaginable. She sat hunched over with her back against the hard moss-ridden wall and wept.

Then a voice floated through the darkness, strangely close.

Weak and faint and soft.

Female.

'Hello?'

Casey reared up, eyes wide, but it didn't help. The room

stayed just as dark. Her surroundings seemed to grow more distant still. Like everything was tucked away behind a thin film. None of this felt real in the slightest.

'Who's that?' Casey whispered.

She tensed up, her whole body preparing in anticipation for what might come next. Fear of the unknown. Fear of the dark. The most primal human instinct. Cold goosebumps flared on her hot skin.

'I'm right here,' the voice came back. 'I'm on your side.'

Casey froze and said, 'What's my side?'

'You sound like you don't want to kill me. Therefore I'm on your side.'

The voice sounded scared. Underneath a brave front, it was shaking.

Casey said, 'Did they take you too?'

'Yes.'

'Who are you?'

'My name's Ruby.'

'I'm Casey.'

'Where'd they get you?'

'In town.'

'Same.'

'When?'

'Yesterday.'

'Why?'

'I don't know.'

'How old are you? Where are you from? You're American? You sound it...'

Too many questions, but Casey couldn't help herself. She needed to match some kind of identity to the floating voice. Attach some meaning to the talking darkness. She could just about handle the secret jungle encampment and the faceless narcos and the aura of dread draped over the entire place. She could almost handle the concept of a slow, laborious, painful death at the hands of people she didn't know, who would probably take a sickening amount of pleasure from the experience. She could almost handle the knowledge that her parents and entire extended family would never know what happened to her, or her three best friends.

But she couldn't handle anything more than that.

So she needed to know who this person was.

She needed an ally in her darkest hour.

Ruby said, 'I'm twenty-two. American, yes. From Maine.'

'You grew up there?'

'Yes.'

'You sound ... good. Ruby, you sound good.'

'Thank you, I guess?'

'You're holding yourself together.'

'I'm scared.'

'What are you doing here?'

'Like ... in this place?'

'In Colombia.'

'Seeing the world.'

'I didn't run into you in town.'

'I just got here.'

That was when her voice wavered. It was a soft voice, drenched in monotony, but the calmness was wholly enforced. When Ruby finished her sentence she sobbed, but it was a sob like nothing Casey had ever heard before. Nihilistic and forlorn and broken. The reality of the situation was dawning on her. Casey couldn't let that happen. Because then she would crack. She was trying to leech off the falsified strength Ruby was showing, and when she found nothing there she would break too.

They seemed to both know they were holding onto nothing.

But if they could both partake in the illusion, it might get them through the rest of their short lives with their sanity intact.

'Relax,' Casey said. 'Breathe. How long ago did you get here?'

'I just walked into town. This afternoon. I went to check into the backpackers' and they snatched me there.'

'How'd they do it?'

'Drove up next to me and acted friendly. Then told me to get in. Then I looked around for help and there was no-one there. And I think I started realising ... oh God ... how badly I'd fucked up.'

'Did you know the dangers? Before you came here?'

'I guess.'

'Didn't think about it?'

'No.'

'Me either.'

'You with anyone?'

'Friends.'

'How many?'

'Three.'

'Where?'

'Out there, somewhere.'

'What's happening to them?'

'I don't know.'

'Do you want to?'

'Probably not.'

They sat there in the dark, stewing on their circum-stances, unaware of what their companion looked like.

Then Casey said, 'I think it might be my fault you got taken.'

'Don't say that.'

'We fucked up. We made a bad call at the bar, and now they're punishing us for it. I think when they realised how easy it was to snatch tourists they might have got addicted to it. Just for one day. You know? Make hay while the sun shines. Because they won't be able to do things like this forever.'

'So what does that mean?' Ruby said. 'Does it mean that...?'

'I don't know. Don't think about it. Besides, there's a chance...'

'A chance of what?' Ruby spat, contemptuous, distrusting.

'I don't know ... I met this guy.'

'Boyfriend?'

'No ... no ... my boyfriend's out there somewhere.'

'You don't seem too concerned.'

'I'm just trying not to think about... look, this guy. He might come.'

'Who is he?'

'I don't know. He's American. He lives around here.'

In the darkness, Casey sensed Ruby stiffen. 'What if he just adds to all this? What if he joins in?'

'He won't.'

'You said he lives around here.'

'But he's different.'

'Different how?'

Casey said, 'Just different.'

26

S later hadn't felt this detached from civilisation in a long time.

An impressive feat, considering the last year of his life had seen visits to the Yemeni highlands and the barren corners of the Russian Far East.

But there was something palpable about the untouched jungle, especially at night. It lay in the unknown, in the impenetrable murky gloom that encompassed everything outside the range of his own headlights. Which was almost all of it.

The jeep's frame shuddered all around him, turning Bautista pale as a sheet from the pain of his wounds being disturbed. He proved no threat whatsoever. He barely even looked at the AR-15 resting between them. Slater had nowhere else to put it, besides his own footwell, and he wasn't willing to risk jamming the gun against one of the pedals and careening off the potholed trail into the overgrown vegetation. Then everything he'd worked for his entire life would have been for nothing. Stranded in the middle of nowhere, surrounded by nothing that didn't want to kill him and rip his eyes out, he would either succumb to dehydration or starvation or a gruelling combination of the two. Unless a jungle predator tore his head off first.

So the AR-15 rifle stayed on the centre console.

He wasn't about to let sheer bad luck lead to his own downfall.

'You know the stakes, right?' he said, raising his voice to be heard over the roar of the jeep's engine.

Bautista summed up all his energy and turned his head to look across the seat. 'What?'

'If you're leading me to the wrong place,' Slater said. 'You know what I'll do to you, right?'

Bautista didn't respond.

'I'll patch that bullet hole up.'

Despite everything, the man raised an eyebrow. 'You'll save my life?'

'If we don't find those kids in the next twenty minutes, you'll understand exactly why that's the worst thing you could hope for.'

Bautista didn't blink. A vain attempt to put on a brave face. But he knew.

He understood.

In his core.

'I'm not lying,' he said.

'Your best outcome here is death. You get that, right?'

Bautista nodded.

It took an ungodly amount of effort.

'I'll give it to you the quickest way,' Slater said. 'If you do what I say.'

'I'm doing what you say.'

'You could lead me into the middle of nowhere.'

'Why would I do that?'

'Because you're scared of your bosses.'

'Boss. Singular.'

'Doesn't matter.'

'I'm not scared of him. I'm a dead man.'

'But you're scared of what he would do to you if he killed me and kept you alive.'

Bautista paused, half dead but deep in thought. Then he blinked twice, swallowed hard, and took a deep breath.

Something was coming.

'Turn around,' he whispered.

Even paler than he was before.

Which Slater hadn't thought possible.

Slater said, 'What?'

'Turn around. We're going the wrong way.'

'I should kill you now.'

'But you won't. I'll take you to my boss. I swear. But...'

He trailed off, deep in thought. Slater knew what it was. The man was staring death in the face. His belief systems were collapsing. All of life seemed like a sick joke now. Nothing mattered. Except getting to the great beyond as quickly as possible. Whatever that encompassed.

'You should have done what I said from the start,' Slater said.

'Yeah, well, that's life. Just promise me one thing.'

'Maybe.'

'When we get there, shoot me in the head. Straight away. Deal?'

'Deal.'

'Thank you.'

'That doesn't scare you?'

'I don't give a shit about anything.'

Quite a farcical statement, but Slater knew what it meant. He had enough experience in this particular realm of existence. The closeness to death. The pain and suffering and anguish. This guy was done trying to defend anyone. In fact, it almost seemed like he was deep in the throes of an identity crisis.

Strange time to redeem yourself, Slater thought.

He turned and looked Bautista in the eyes. Just for a moment. Otherwise he might crash, and then his problems would amplify tenfold.

So he faced the rural trail again, stamping on the brakes and twisting the wheel and following through with a rudimentary five-point turn. Then he shot back the way they'd come. They must have missed a turn. Bautista would have glanced at it as they went past, debating whether to let Slater know, opting to keep it secret. Hoping he might bleed out before Slater discovered the truth.

But now he was telling the truth. Slater saw it in his eyes. Something was shifting in the man.

'What's going on?' Slater said, and the strange combination of darkness and blood and isolation seemed to encourage Bautista to speak.

'I don't like what I'm doing. Never have.'

'But you do it.'

'I would tell you I didn't have a choice, but I did.'

'So what's this discussion about?'

'I would be happy if you shot me when we got there.'

'What if I didn't? What if I patched you up and sent you on your way and you vowed to do as much good as you possibly could to make up for the first few decades you spent ruining people's lives?'

Bautista shook his head.

Decided.

His mind made up.

He said, 'No.'

'Why not?'

'I couldn't do enough good to make up for what I've done.'

Slater nodded.

Nothing more to be said.

'Okay.'

Bautista lifted a bloody finger. 'Here.'

Slater nodded again. He spotted the dark maw in the side of the trail, leading even deeper into uncharted territory, paving the way toward a section of the jungle even more lawless and deserted than their current location. If he had any less experience in the field it might have terrified him. Instead he gripped the wheel tighter. Worked his hands over the chipped, faded leather. Pumped up the veins in his forearms. Gnashed his teeth together in anticipation.

'How far in?' he said before they turned onto the trail.

'Not far. Less than a mile. I'd be ready if I were you.'

'Always ready,' Slater muttered.

'Remember what you promised.'

'You really don't want a second chance?'

'I don't deserve one.'

'Suit yourself.'

'Would you even give me one?'

Slater glanced at the man. 'Maybe. Maybe not.'

'Then it works better for both of us.'

'Why the change of heart?'

'Didn't happen in an instant. It's been building up for a while.'

'This morning. Were you supposed to rough me up if I didn't comply?'

'That was the suggestion. I told Vicente and Iván to pretend we did.'

'Why?'

'Like I said. Been building up for a while. I don't enjoy this life.'

'Did you ever?'

'At one point.'

'You ashamed of it?'

'Yeah.'

'Well, nice knowing you, I guess.'

It might have been a more poignant moment had Bautista not been on the verge of death in the first place. Instead, the pale man nodded once and gratefully slumped into a brief phase of unconsciousness. It wouldn't last long. He would come to in fits and bursts, wracked with pain, succumbing slowly to the gut shot. If he hadn't bled out by now, then it would take some time longer.

Unless Slater accelerated the process.

He twisted the wheel, sealing his own fate, turning into the narrow dirt trail. Sensing the towering jungle canopy flash past on either side of the jeep. Eyes dead ahead.

Focused.

Ignoring Bautista.

In hindsight, maybe a bad move.

Maybe he overestimated a cartel killer's capacity for decency.

Oh, shit, was all that flashed through his mind as two things happened at once.

The jungle encampment revealed itself at the end of the trail with a faint glow. Concrete buildings wedged into some sort of half-clearing, surrounded by dense vegetation and weeds and trees. A hive of activity in the middle of nowhere.

And Bautista came awake in an instant and lunged for the AR-15.

27

Casey almost became comfortable in the darkness. At least in here she wouldn't know what was coming. She hoped the door somehow opened without her realising, and the last thing she saw was a brief flash of gunmetal before the weapon fired and sent a round through her head. At least that would be quick. And then she could forget all about the terror of possibility and dip into an eternal slumber.

But, of course, that didn't happen.

She heard heavy thudding footsteps on the dirt outside. Ordinarily inaudible, but it was so silent in the concrete bunker that she could make out every morsel of sound across the encampment, filtering through the cracks in the big concrete door on the other side of the room. She thought she could hear a couple of people hyperventilating. Their breathing sounded masculine. Heavy. Laboured. Jake and Harvey, probably. Kept separate from the girls.

So where the hell's Whitney?

She didn't want to think about it. To her it felt like an eternity, but she knew they couldn't have arrived at the jungle camp more than half an hour ago. So the cartel gangsters were probably still co-ordinating, figuring out what exactly to do with the fresh stockpile of hostages they could have their way with. Maybe splitting up who was designated to which prisoner.

Maybe there were a couple of narcos out here in the jungle who swung both ways.

Who wanted Jake and Harvey all to themselves.

A shiver ran down Casey's spine. At that point she lost all hope. The guy from earlier that afternoon wasn't coming. He wouldn't know where to start. He wouldn't even know they were missing in the first place. She was out here, alone, burrowed in a bunker with a girl she didn't know, patiently awaiting her own demise. However that came.

She sobbed again.

Ruby said, 'It's not your fault.'

Remarkably composed.

'It is,' Casey said.

'Who's this guy you talked about?'

Prodding, again.

'I don't know,' she said, biting her lip hard enough to draw blood. It was all too much. 'I have no idea. There's no-one coming to help us. Just give up.'

'Casey...'

'Look, I'm sorry, but it's better if you just accept—'

Ruby burst into a sentence, about to cut Casey off, but both of them shut right up as the giant concrete door slid open. It ground against the floor of the bunker, scraping and whining. Ominous as all hell. The big man with the fat lips stepped into the room, backlit by the artificial lighting illuminating the clearing outside. Barely visible, just a silhouette looming over them.

And he seemed enraged.

'Who's your friend?' he barked at Casey.

In the lowlight, Casey flashed a glance at Ruby, seeing her for the first time. She almost did a double take. Ruby was stunningly beautiful. Amber eyes, tanned skin, straight brown hair. Draped in dirty, baggy clothes, with filth matted to the strands of hair hanging over her forehead. Thrown around by the cartel thugs, most likely. But Casey could see why they'd taken her. She was model material. Tall and slim and gorgeous. Briefly, Casey shook her head at the ridiculousness of it all. What was a girl like Ruby doing roaming around rural Colombia on her own?

And that made her more terrified for what was to follow.

Please, don't hurt her too bad, Casey thought.

She said, 'I don't know her.'

The big man snarled. 'Not her. Your other friend.'

'Oh.'

'Well?'

'I don't know anything about him.'

'Bullshit.'

'I'm telling the truth!' she screamed. 'Why would I lie to you?'

'I put up with your shit at the start,' he snarled. 'But not now. Not after this.'

'After what?' she said.

Growing increasingly desperate.

'There's been an incident.'

'Where?'

'I sent some of my men to take care of him.'

A surge of hope tickled the base of her spine. Barely perceptible. But there all the same. She found it, in the depths of her nihilism.

'And?'

'They didn't do so well. I can't contact any of them.'

'I don't know where he lives. I don't know anything about him. He just helped us.'

'Why?'

'I don't know.'

'Yes you do,' he said.

He dragged her to her feet by her hair, kicking and screaming.

Then he hauled her out of the bunker.

28

Before that evening, Slater hadn't seen combat in months.

Sure, he'd beat down the three narcos in the back lot of the general store earlier that afternoon, but there was a world of difference between fighting to send a message and fighting for your life. He'd been fighting for his life when the cartel thugs stormed his property, and as a result he'd killed seven people in a little over a minute. But he hadn't quite transitioned over yet. Hence the tendency to believe Bautista. To think that maybe a guy who had killed and raped and tortured for the unforgiving Colombian drug cartels might have the capacity to change. Because Slater didn't know the extent of the guy's issues. He didn't know anything about him. He was still reluctant to transition back to the hardened killer of his past.

Then he saw Bautista's fast-twitch muscle fibres firing, and saw the desperate lunge for the rifle, and saw the bared teeth and the wide eyes and the animalistic desperation...

...and he realised he never should have given the man a chance in the first place.

Not out here.

Not in the jungle.

Bautista was fast. Blindingly fast. He was an athletic man with no body fat, and he'd killed people before, so he was probably deeply familiar with that kind of desperation. Maybe this wasn't the first time his life had been on the line. So his fingers blurred as they shot through the air, coming down on the AR-15 before Slater could take his hands off the steering wheel. And there were those milliseconds of processing power firing in his brain, putting two and two together, realising, *Oh, everything this guy just told me was absolute bullshit.*

Making me drop my guard.

So Bautista got his hands on the gun.

But that was it.

Because as soon as Slater recognised what was happening he exploded off the mark.

And he was fast, too.

Faster.

He smashed his right elbow sideways, so quick and accurate that you'd think he'd locked onto the side of Bautista's temple with a laser-guided targeting device. He struck soft tissue and felt it crack under the rough, calloused skin of his elbow, and the thick bone underneath. Bautista flailed back, experiencing something akin to a bomb going off in his left ear, and Slater took his other hand off the wheel and brought it around in a looping bundle of nerves and strength. He kept his palm open, his fingers splayed, opting to disorient rather than try and put him out cold with a more accurate blow. He couldn't risk a closed fist whistling past, hitting thin air, leaving him horrendously exposed. Instead he slapped Bautista full in the face, palm to nose, fingers into eyes. But it was more of a detonation than a slap.

It broke the guy's nose and blinded him simultaneously, and the force behind it thrust him back into the soft leather of the seat, and now he was completely off-balance.

Slater wrestled the AR-15 out of his hands and spun it around and jammed the barrel into the man's throat, pinning him in the diagonal wedge between the seat and the passenger door.

He pulled the trigger.

Blood and gore sprayed but Slater barely saw it because he was reaching back for his own door handle, finding it, heaving it outward against the thick jungle wind buffeting the jeep like a slipstream. But he got it open and levered himself out of the driver's seat, and he glanced ahead and saw the encampment shockingly close, and he made out the wide eyes of a handful of perimeter guards recognising the fact that the oncoming vehicle wasn't slowing down.

The whole plan, the whole tactical approach, ruined before it had even begun.

Slater spotted commotion in the centre of the clearing. He squinted for a half-second — all he could afford, given the circumstances. He realised what he was looking at.

His eyes widened.

He adjusted the jeep's aim, shifting the wheel a couple of inches to the right. It probably wouldn't be enough, but he didn't have time for anything else.

He threw himself out of the moving vehicle, still clutching the rifle.

Plunging into the hot darkness.

29

The big man with the fat lips wrestled Casey out of the bunker, leaving Ruby with her head bowed and the manacles around her wrists locked tight. Casey caught a final glance of the slim girl and her overly baggy clothes. They locked eyes. The big man threw Casey over his shoulder, and she slapped at his enormous back to no avail. Ruby blinked once. Casey thought she saw tears.

Then they were out of the bunker, and Ruby disappeared from sight.

The big man heaved her across the clearing, throwing him clean off his shoulder with more force than necessary. She travelled a couple of feet in the air and then sprawled into the mud, hitting the clearing floor with a wet slap.

It hurt — everything hurt.

She stuck an open palm out in front of her body to break her fall, but it bent awkwardly at the elbow as she hit the mud. There was a *twang*, and a gasp, and a recoil as the pain hit, but she didn't think anything was broken. Not that she could tell. She could barely pay attention to it.

She tumbled onto her back and tried to get her feet

underneath her, regaining some semblance of balance, but before she could do anything the big man seized her by the hair and hauled her toward a thick smooth slab of concrete in the centre of the clearing.

It was a strange sight. She narrowed her gaze and focused on it, and her surroundings fell away. Tunnel vision. That was where she was headed, and it was all she could concentrate on. The laughing, leering, sadistic men all around her shrank to nothingness.

All she could see was the stone slab, like a crude version of an ancient Egyptian sarcophagus cut in half.

She realised it was some kind of giant meeting table, made from the same material the bunkers were constructed from. Leftovers, probably. Shaped and fashioned into a large rectangle and slapped in the centre of the clearing to please the narcos. Make them feel important. Make them feel like regular Italian dons. They could gather round something physical and huge, something that supercharged their testosterone. The big man with the fat lips probably felt like a king gathering his soldiers around the concrete, relaying orders, passing documents over the smooth stone.

Right now, it seemed to serve as the destination of Casey's last breath.

The big man picked her up off the ground, putting all his strength into the move. Nerve endings on her scalp screamed for relief — she was suspended solely by her sweaty hair, matted together in clumps and knots. She kicked and screamed. It achieved nothing. The big man regarded her with contempt, then seemed to decide that the act of executing her was beneath him.

So he passed it to an underling.

He threw Casey toward one of the narcos. A tall, thin man with rippling muscle and beady eyes and hollow cheekbones. His head was shaved bald. He wore a sweat-soaked singlet and cargo shorts. He caught Casey around the mid-section and threw her onto the table. She barely resisted. She sprawled out horizontally, and the next thing she knew the barrel of a pistol skewered into the side of her temple, pinning her head against the concrete. One shot and her brains would eject all over the stone.

'Please,' she whispered, mortally terrified.

The big man strode toward her and crouched down. 'Who is your friend?'

'I don't know, I swear.'

'Not a good answer.'

'You need me alive.'

The guy raised an eyebrow. 'Oh?'

'My ... friends. They know secrets about ... your enemies. They can tell you. But they won't unless ... I'm alive.'

The big man turned to stone, staring at her with genuine contempt, as if he couldn't quite believe what he was hearing. Then he laughed. Sarcastically. Mockingly. He wagged a finger in front of her face.

He said, 'You're not good at this.'

'Please.'

'The only thing keeping you alive is the fact that there's something in your head you can tell me about this stranger.'

'There's nothing.'

'Then you're worthless to me.'

He looked toward his underling — the guy pressing the pistol against her skull, wedging her in place.

The thin man's beady eyes lit up, and he nodded.

Almost salivating.

Casey risked everything by holding up a hand. The thin man jerked on the spot, recoiling involuntarily.

Hopped up on the prospect of murder, and accordingly reactionary.

The big man laughed. 'Bit nervous, hey?'

The thin man said nothing.

Still holding out her palm, Casey said, 'Wait.'

The big man said, 'You'd better have something good.'

'He seemed angry. When I spoke to him. I'd never met him before today.'

'Angry at who?'

'Everyone.'

'Psycho?'

'No.'

'Just angry?'

'Yes.'

'Well, that's not much help.'

'You should be on the defensive. That's what I'm saying.'

'He killed seven of my men in his own home. That must have been a gruelling war. He'll be in no state to play offence.'

'Are you sure?'

'Watch your tone.'

'I'm just saying ... how do you know that?'

'It's common sense.'

'I wouldn't use common sense with this guy.'

'Wishful thinking on your behalf. You want him to save you.'

'No, don't worry,' Casey said, eyes closed. 'I know he's not coming.'

No longer scared.

She'd reached the limits of her fear.

Now there was nothingness.

Tears ran from her eyes.

'Just do it,' she whispered.

The big man shrugged and backed away. He paused a few feet from the stone slab and nodded again to the thin man.

Final.

Unquestionable.

An unspoken command.

The skinny guy smiled and his beady eyes grew wider. He pushed the gun harder into the side of her head.

He was enjoying this.

Then an open-topped jeep containing nothing but a bloody corpse roared into the clearing and smashed into him from behind, pulverising his internal organs, throwing him several feet through the air like a rag doll, so loud and horrendous and overwhelming that Casey assumed the gun had gone off.

She blinked hard.

No.

She was still alive.

And a car had just barrelled through her peripheral vision, missing her by inches, scraping the side of the stone slab.

Heart thumping in her chest, almost paralysed by shock, she rolled away from the jeep — across the concrete — as all hell broke loose in the clearing.

30

S later did nothing.

He was at the edge of the narcos' awareness, enveloped in darkness, momentarily thanking fate for making him African-American. His skin wrapped into the night, turning him wholly invisible. He kept his mouth sealed in a hard line, so no-one caught a flash of brilliant white teeth. But they weren't looking. They were concentrating on the vehicular missile that blared into sight, coming seemingly out of nowhere. Its hood detonated across the back of the guy standing over Casey and sent him cartwheeling grotesquely through the air. He slapped the wet dirt and lay still.

Broken.

Irreparable.

Dead meat.

Slater did nothing.

Pandemonium broke out. A couple of trigger-happy narcos screamed profanities and unloaded their weapons at the empty vehicle, achieving nothing besides complicating the situation. The deafening racket of automatic gunfire destroyed the relative calm of the night, save for the aura of dread hanging over the encampment. Slater sensed it, even as he lay burrowed deep in the vegetation, with ferns and reeds and mud and brambles pressing in on him from all sides.

This was a place of immense cruelty, and suffering. Endless suffering. Nothing good came out of here. The assortment of bunkers lay shrouded in the long shadows created by the halogen floodlights. He'd made sure to select a tactical position on the perimeter of the camp, so that most of the floodlights were pointed away from him.

He raised the AR-15 and singled out Santiago.

It wasn't difficult. The guy exuded confidence and leadership — it was a subtle dynamic, but Slater could immediately tell he controlled things. He towered over the rest of the narcos, easily six two with room to spare, and his clothes bulged with a combination of muscle and fat. The kind of body professional strongmen possessed. People who trained their whole lives deadlifting incomprehensible weights, shovelling food into their mouths, transforming into literal cubes before their own eyes. Even from this distance Slater spotted the guy's enormous meaty hands. Fat fingers. Fat lips. An ugly contorted face. A nose like a pig. Squashed eyes.

Hideous.

And dangerous.

Slater quickly scanned the rest of the population and found nothing particularly threatening. They were all long and rail-thin and bony and unaccustomed to a situation like this. All wide-eyed consumers of their own product. The jungle heat had shredded their body fat. Slater could break them down in an instant.

But he didn't want to do that. He wanted this confrontation over before it got to close range. And if it did get in close, Santiago would prove a nightmare. So Slater lined up the sights with the AR-15 on the big man's barrel chest as he waved off the gunfire, ordering his men to calm down, his ugly eyes already scanning the perimeter like a watchful hawk.

And he spotted Slater.

Awareness dawned on his face.

Slater hesitated.

What? he thought.

Impossible.

Fucking impossible.

'There!' Santiago roared, pointing a beefy finger at the darkness.

Jesus Christ.

Slater abandoned all hope of eliminating the population discreetly. He was buried in undergrowth, as dark as the night around him, so Santiago either had X-ray vision or frighteningly good luck. But as the boss screamed a command the narcos twisted all the same, guns up, ready to roll.

Slater couldn't focus on Santiago anymore.

The big guy was unarmed.

And Slater's priorities had shifted monumentally.

Two assault rifles arced in his direction, close enough to hit him, even if they pulled the trigger and hoped for the best. Even if they fired blind.

Slater kicked into overdrive.

He whipped the barrel to focus on the closest man and pulled the trigger, blowing him away in a hail of gunfire. The guy took at least three rounds to the chest and went down like the sack of meat he was. Slater let go of the trigger and moved his aim to the second man and shot him in the mouth just as he was about to pull the trigger. The guy's jaw disappeared and he dropped the AR-15 and keeled forward, out of the fight, either close to death or already there.

Slater had no time to make sure of it.

He reeled in place, skewering himself down into the earth to compose his nerves and tighten his aim. He swept the clearing in a single move, tugging the barrel from left to right and scanning every dark corner for signs of resistance. It was confusing as hell, and he couldn't even make out how many narcos stewed in the shadows. Some were out in the open, but unarmed. Not an issue.

Any others armed?

Any other weapons?

There.

At the opposite edge of the clearing.

Oh, shit.

This guy had his aim locked on.

Already.

Slater fired.

He struck home. Two bullets to the throat, tearing across the clearing and pulverising flesh. The guy twisted and fell away.

But not before he got off a shot of his own, fired from a semi-automatic pistol. It was too dark to make out the weapon.

Twwaannggg.

The bullet grazed the top of Slater's head, and at that point all the training and reflexes and advantages fell away. He'd been hit before, but never anything like this. Not in terms of pain, but in terms of potential ramifications. He thought he was invincible, but the reality of how close he'd come to death froze him in place, like a deer in headlights. Warm blood ran in rivulets down his scalp. The tiny piece of lead had carved a thin line through the skin, almost pene-trating to the bone beneath.

Almost.

He froze, and a narco appeared. Another rail-thin man, but one charged with athleticism and explosiveness. Slater realised he'd misjudged the number of hostiles. This guy appeared from the darkness, unarmed, his fly undone. He'd been taking a leak. A couple of dozen feet to the left. No gun. No knife. Just a rampant death wish and an over-whelming urge to protect his boss.

He threw himself on top of Slater like a valiant soldier trying to smother a grenade.

Rabid and animalistic and intense.

His bodyweight pinned the AR-15 awkwardly to the dirt, ruining Slater's chances of using it at close range. He tried to throw an elbow upward, but the positioning was all off. He missed, and his limb whistled harmlessly past the guy's skull, weighed down by gravity. He preferred to throw down-ward, with gravity on his side, at all costs. Now he couldn't breathe, with a man's deadweight bearing down on his back, crushing his diaphragm into the wet mud, constricting his breathing, inducing a certain level of claustrophobia.

He pressed his face into the mud, cutting off his breathing.

But things had to get worse before they got better.

The compression gave him a few inches of space between the back of his skull and the face of the narco on top of him.

The guy lunged forward, sensing opportunity, thinking he'd knocked Slater unconscious with the manic tackle.

Slater sealed his mouth shut and wrenched his head back.

Skull against nose.

Crack.

All kinds of damage.

The narco fell off him, howling, clutching his face.

Slater reared up out of the mud.

A man possessed.

31

It was bedlam.

Slater levered his hips and tapped into reserves of strength and hauled the guy into the nearest tree. He scrabbled around in the mud, searching desperately for the AR-15.

Couldn't immediately find it.

Not enough time.

Reeling, pulse pounding, head swimming, he shot to his feet and timed the distance between them as the narco bounced off the thick trunk and stumbled back into range. The guy was seeing double, tears streaming from his eyes, blood streaming from his nose. All lined up for a single blow.

Slater gave it to him.

Elbow to throat.

A massive clothesline.

Taking him off his feet, destroying soft tissue in his neck, cutting off vital components of breathing. The guy gasped for breath as he went down into the mud, taking an amalgamation of vegetation with him. He kicked and writhed on the ground, manic in intensity, but nowhere near a respectable state to put up a fight. He would probably die from the collapsed throat wound.

Slater forgot about him.

Just like that.

Bigger threats to deal with.

He powered into the clearing, catching a glint of the AR-15 where it had tumbled out of reach into the mud. It was coated in the gunk. Slater got a finger inside the trigger guard, but it was all slick with mud and sweat and blood. He analysed what lay ahead. Santiago was nowhere to be found, vanishing into the ether. A ghost, by all accounts. Slater froze on the spot, momentarily puzzled. The big man hadn't been anywhere near cover.

Where the hell is he?

But he couldn't linger on that idea, because there were four narcos left, spaced out across the clearing, each in various states of distress. Two were powering toward the bunkers, no doubt in search of weapons.

Slater lined up his aim on one of them and let loose with a measured burst, dotting the guy's back with lead. He went down at full speed, with nothing to break his fall. Not pretty. Chest to mud, geysers of the gunk flying in a couple of directions at once.

Slater turned to the second man.

He lined up the sights.

He breathed out.

Calm settled over him, stilling his hands, making everything seem crystal clear, smooth and measured and composed despite the intensity of everything around him. It was vital for survival, especially in a world like this. Everyone in the vicinity wanted each other dead. There was something inherently primal about it. Slater didn't spend time thinking about that. He'd had all the time in the world to figure out the morality of it all years ago. Now he locked his aim on and tracked the guy across the clearing. He noted the bunker the man was headed for.

He started to depress the trigger.

Hot blood ran into his eyes — both at once — and he panicked. It was impossible not to. The thick viscous stuff hit both pupils at the same time, blinding him in an instant. It stung like all hell, searing his eyes. Instinctually, he took a hand off the AR-15 and wiped it across his face.

It worked well with water.

Not so much with blood.

He ended up smearing the crimson deeper into his eyes, under his eyelids, stinging and burning and searing. He grimaced and backtracked, now blind.

Well, not entirely blind.

Everything was still there, but he stared at it through a dark, blurry cling film, and any attempt to keep his eyes open for longer than a couple of seconds failed miserably. He blinked again and again, teeth clenched. Everything moved awfully fast. One second bled into the next, and he realised he was compromised.

Truly, deeply compromised.

Cursing his luck, he tried to find the perimeter of the encampment by touch alone. If he vanished into the jungle he could lay low, recuperate, spend time clearing his vision.

Not much chance of that.

Something hit him like a dump truck. In the side. Shoulder to ribcage. Like a defensive end smashing into him, crushing his mid-section, taking him off his feet. At the same time he felt an iron grip on the end of the assault rifle — he slid his good hand down the gunmetal and touched someone else's fingers. Desperately trying to wrench the AR-15 out of his grasp.

Slater still couldn't see a thing.

The guy who'd tackled him drove through with the move, disrupting Slater's equilibrium. Blind and hurting and panicked, he went down into the dirt, and almost lost his grip on the assault rifle. But that would have been game over. Right then and there. The second guy would have his hands on some serious firepower, and Slater would be defenceless. And then he would die slowly and painfully in the middle of nowhere, in the most brutal way imaginable.

So he kept a goddamn tight grip on the rifle.

Because it was his lifeline.

This is it.

The moment.

If he lost the tug of war, he would die.

He won it.

The rifle slipped out of the hostile's grip and Slater brought it down with him — not that it made things any better. He kept his arms wrapped tight around the AR-15 like a prized possession, but that left him exposed to the fall.

Pick your poison.

He was screwed regardless. Let go of the rifle and break his fall, and one of the narcos would snatch it up in a heartbeat. Clutch onto it for dear life, and risk concussion as the side of his head hit the earth.

He braced for impact.

The guy who'd tackled him drove harder into his ribs.

They both went down.

Impact.

Skull against dirt.

BANG.

32

But Slater rolled with it.

He knew he couldn't risk an impact to the skull. Even if he survived the all-out brawl, it would pose horrendous long-term consequences, considering the fragility of his freshly-healed state of mind. So he twisted at the waist, utilising the flexibility developed through gruelling yoga sessions, and rolled along the dirt across his upper back. There was a slight knock as the back of his head hit the earth, but the mud softened the blow.

Slater kicked free from the man's grasp, still blind, still terrified. He scrabbled like a madman, bucking and jerking, until he wriggled free. Then he scooted himself across the earth before either of them could pounce on him. He brought his sleeve up to his face and wiped it hard across his eyes, creating just enough of a gap in the crimson mask to make out his surroundings.

Two narcos.

Both the same — Colombian killers. Nothing more, nothing less.

Slater adjusted his grip on the AR-15 and shot each of them once in the forehead.

They shouldn't have given him a single second of opportunity.

They clearly hadn't understood who they were dealing with.

Slater rolled to his feet, bloody and dazed but reinvigorated.

He turned, as fast as he could. Now he was right out there in the open. Nowhere near cover. He had to act now, before...

Santiago loomed up out of nowhere, skirting around the stone slab he'd been cowering behind. Slater began to raise the gun, but the giant man caught it by the barrel and thundered a straight right into Slater's forehead.

Rattle.

A deadly sensation. It wasn't just the pain. His skull shaking, resonating from the force of the blow, sent chills down his spine. It brought nausea and hesitation and a certain distance to the reality all around him.

Head strikes were no joke.

The delicacy of the human brain could never be underestimated. Slater's grip slackened before his own eyes, and he was helpless to prevent it.

Santiago tore the gun away from him.

Game over.

The big man hit him in the stomach. He was a boxer — probably habits formed in his youth that never left — and if he competed professionally he would weigh in at heavyweight. Weight classes existed for a reason. Slater had seen his old colleague punch. Jason King was six foot three and two hundred and twenty pounds. He hit like a sledgehammer. Slater had power, but only relative to his size. He relied on speed, most of the time.

It all failed him here.

The shot to the gut crashed home, knuckles against flesh, almost paralysing Slater with pain. He gasped and retched, fighting the urge to vomit, and swung back.

Then he found out Santiago was fast, too.

The big man stepped back as if it was effortless, something Slater rarely saw and couldn't prepare for in such a compromised state. He was relying on instinct and reflex and automatic motor functions. He overcommitted to the swing. He missed. Santiago lined up the AR-15 — still holding it by the barrel — and swung it into Slater's forearm as it sailed past. There was no crack, but it knocked him off-balance, and he stumbled, and the blood ran back into his eyes, and now he was blind again.

He lost his footing.

Santiago hit him in the chest, crumpling him, folding him inward. The shock of the impact froze him up and he sprawled into the dirt.

He lay there, unmoving.

Santiago bent at the waist and squatted down. He pressed the barrel of the AR-15 to Slater's breast and held it there, like driving an imaginary stake through his chest.

'Wipe your eyes,' he said. 'I want you to see what's coming.'

Slater wiped his eyes. He took his time, breathing hard, the fight sapped out of him. The combination of blows to the stomach and chest had smashed the breath from his lungs. No matter how much he wanted to retaliate, there was simply nothing he could do. He could lunge at Santiago, but the big man would recognise the hostility instantly, and from there all it would take was a simple pull of the trigger to send a bullet directly through Slater's heart.

There were rounds left in the clip.

He was done.

Slater cleared the blood away and sighed, staring up at the night sky. The stars were out. Reality came back into focus. Santiago and the last remaining narco in the clearing stood over him, studying him like a lab experiment gone wrong.

Slater grimaced.

He'd come so close.

Two left, and the other guy would have been no problem at all. He was short and thin, with almost no fat on his frame, and not much muscle either. A single punch would have put him down for the count. Santiago would have proved a larger hurdle, but Slater figured he could have managed if the blood running from the top of his skull hadn't impeded his vision.

He gulped.

It had all come crashing down, here in the Colombian jungle. A lifetime of evading death. All to cease over a group of dumb college kids.

On that note, where...?

Slater stared across the clearing, and he forced himself not to react. There was Casey, cut and scratched and bruised but otherwise unharmed, with no significant injuries, stooped low and creeping across open ground. She had a small chrome object in her hand — the floodlights reflected off it.

A switchblade.

A rusting and blunt thing, but a weapon all the same.

Scavenged from nearby.

Slater's heartbeat caught in his throat. He pleaded his

body, his neurochemistry, not to give it away. She was his last lifeline, a final shred of hope in the darkness, the only thing separating both of them from an untimely demise. He stared straight into Santiago's eyes, his own eyes burning, refusing to let any kind of micro-expression cross his features.

It didn't work.

Santiago twisted on the spot and saw Casey approaching.

She was still a dozen feet away, at least.

'Get her,' he hissed.

His underling spotted the knife, and stared down at Santiago. Looking at the AR-15. Looking for backup.

'I'm not taking the gun off his chest,' Santiago said. 'He's too fast. Get her.'

'Just shoot him.'

'I want him to see it. He came for her.'

'Okay.'

The short thin man advanced toward her.

Slater watched.

Unblinking.

33

To her credit, Casey tried her best.

She'd obviously never used a knife in self-defence, and her adrenalin levels would be sky-high. Through the roof. Unquestionably.

In truth, Slater had never expected her to succeed.

Santiago kept his gaze locked tight on Slater's face. Watching him for any hint of rebellion. If Slater moved an arm, Santiago would pull the trigger, and that would be that.

'You should kill me,' Slater said quietly.

'No.'

'Why not?'

'You killed all my men. It'll be inconvenient to replace them.'

'So?'

'You need to pay for that.'

'What do you have in mind?'

The fat lips spread into a leering grin. 'Oh ... you have no idea.'

'I've seen worse, I'm sure.'

'No. You haven't.'

Spoken with supreme confidence. Santiago believed in his capacity to enact suffering in a way Slater had rarely seen before.

He couldn't help himself.

He gulped.

Tried to hide it.

Failed.

Santiago smiled again. 'You should be scared.'

'You'd better hope your friend is good enough.'

'He's good enough.'

'Want to see?'

Santiago didn't respond. He kept his gaze fixed. It didn't matter what was happening behind him. He wasn't budging with his grip on the AR-15.

Smart man, Slater thought.

Casey and the thin man were circling each other, waiting for the opportune moment to strike. He was hesitant because he had nothing to work with besides his own fists, which in an ordinary altercation against a knife-wielding hostile would spell disaster. But she'd never been in a violent confrontation in her life, and her hands were shaking from fear — certainly not the weather, because the heat drenched the atmosphere.

Slater's sweat mixed with the blood on his forehead.

His heart thudded in his chest.

Casey lunged.

She burst forward with a wild motion, swinging the knife too hard, too fast. She was too scared. The small man reacted impossibly fast, his nerves supercharged. He'd been anticipating the horizontal slash. He skirted around it and hit Casey so hard in the face with enclosed knuckles that she dropped the knife immediately, cowering into a ball and adopting the foetal position in the mud.

Her nose was probably broken.

Dread fell over Slater, but he pushed it aside. He didn't blame her. He would have achieved the same with no combat experience. This was another world entirely. A different beast. She never stood a chance.

On that note, where are the others?

It didn't matter.

Nothing mattered anymore.

Slater was going to die, right here in this humid clearing with the toxic air pressing down on him and his lungs burning and his eyes stinging and his stomach rippling with pain. He never imagined it would *actually* come to an end.

And here he was.

Santiago paused, studying the stranger lying on his back, staring up at the sky.

'You're something special, aren't you?' the big man said.

'I like to think so.'

'I'm serious. There's a look on your face. Like you never thought this would happen. Even though this should be a fluke, even for one of the best on the planet. Right? You killed seven of my men at your compound. And nearly that amount here. That should be impossible, and you should feel that. But it seems like you're angry. Angry that you got bested. You must do this regularly.'

'Regularly enough.'

'How?'

'Dumb luck.'

'No.'

'Hate to break it to you. That's about it.'

'No.'

'What do you want me to say?'

Santiago paused, taking the opportunity to survey the encampment, counting the dead. Tallying the damage. He kept the AR-15 skewered into Slater's pectorals. Any movement would be met with a quick trigger pull, and an equally quick departure from the land of the living. So Slater stayed put.

The big man's gaze wandered back to Slater. 'Can you be bought?'

'What?'

'Did someone send you here? Are you doing this for money?'

'No.'

'Then why?'

'I liked those kids you took. I didn't think they deserved what you were going to do to them.'

'That's not a motivation. That's an inconvenience. Why did you get yourself killed for them? There has to be something deeper, for that.'

'I'm just not fond of people like you.'

'Okay. But that doesn't answer my question. Can you be bought?'

'I don't know what you're saying.'

'Is there any world where you might work for me?'

Slater thought about going along with it. Doing his best to play the part of a sociopathic mercenary, pretending to negotiate a deal with the man looming over him. But he simply didn't have the mental fortitude. He was spent, completely. There was no use delaying the inevitable. At some point Santiago would see right through his lies and shoot him dead.

Might as well get it over and done with.

'No. Shoot me.'

But now Santiago was transfixed by the possibility. He

was staring at his fallen comrades, imagining how devastating a partnership would be for the other cartels.

They would rule Colombia, no doubt.

'You're going to work for me,' Santiago hissed, baring his teeth.

'And how do you propose to do that?'

'We'll keep you here. Long enough for you to come round.'

'You really think you can break me?'

'That happens to be my specialty.'

'Good luck.'

'I don't need it.'

'I wouldn't risk it if I were you.'

Santiago paused, contemplating, studying the man underneath him. Slater got the impression he was intimately familiar with the depths of the human soul. He wondered how many people Santiago had tortured. How many innocents. Slater doubted Casey and her friends were the first.

Whatever he was, he seemed to possess the capacity to read minds.

'You're thinking about how cruel of a bastard I am,' Santiago said.

'Basically.'

'I'm cruel.'

'I thought so.'

'Do I get points for embracing it?'

'No.'

'I have to be cruel.'

'You don't have to do this job.'

'Yeah, well, what else am I gonna do?'

He twisted on the spot, assessing how his underling was progressing. The small man had bound Casey's wrists and ankles with a coarse roll of duct tape he'd fetched from the back of one of the pick-up trucks the cartel used to bomb around the jungle. She was secure. Not going anywhere. Slater imagined the other three were tied up somewhere.

Game over.

Well and truly.

He closed his eyes.

'Open them,' Santiago said.

'No. Just shoot me.'

'Open them or I'll make you.'

'Whatever helps you sleep at night.'

Slater kept them shut. He wanted to infuriate the man. Get it over and done with. Better a quick shot to the chest than a drawn-out procedure. He knew they would make Casey suffer for longer. He wished none of this had ever happened. But there was no use wishing. Sooner or later he had to face reality.

Not right now.

He was tired. Forlorn. Worn down. Ready for an eternity of sleep. He'd done enough this life.

Onto the next, if there was such a thing.

Somehow, he managed to accept his own death.

Then Santiago bent down and forced an eyelid open. 'Keep them open or I'll make it more painful for the girl.'

Slater squirmed, then opened them. Everything came back into his field of vision, in all its depravity. 'Fine.'

Santiago seemed to sense something. He smiled. He relished the discomfort.

'You really don't like this, do you?'

'I've been held at gunpoint before.'

'No. You don't want to know what I'm going to do to your friends. Because that's what you do, isn't it? You protect them. This makes you squirm. This makes you *scared.*'

Slater said nothing.

Which said everything.

Santiago's smile widened. 'Thiago. Is she secure?'

The small man — Thiago, obviously — nodded. 'She's not going anywhere.'

'Get the other one.'

'Her friends?'

'No. The other girl. I want this guy to see I have another one. I want him to know how badly he failed.'

Thiago disappeared into one of the bunkers, and returned hauling a tall thin woman by her wrist.

Santiago put all his weight on the AR-15, driving it hard into Slater's chest.

Slater lost his breath.

Santiago leered. 'See? I'll have my way with her too.'

He bent down, staring into Slater's eyes, but Slater wasn't returning the gaze. He was looking past the big man, watching the girl. Her amber eyes jolted around the clearing, taking in her surroundings, noticing all the corpses riddling the encampment. He saw the genuine fear in her expression, and figured she was another casualty to add to the list. An unfortunate soul, caught in the wrong place at the wrong time. Beautiful, too.

Slater noticed her features, and dread fell over him. He didn't want to know what the two remaining men would do to her.

Santiago, and Thiago.

They would make it painful.

She'd just been released from her bindings. Raw skin ran rings around her wrists. Thiago must have unlocked her manacles in his haste to free her and present her to Slater. It didn't mean anything. She was defenceless against them.

Thiago was armed, and although she had a supple athletic frame, she was thin.

Then the fear on her face disappeared, replaced by dead calm and an icy awareness.

Slater froze.

34

W*hat the...?*

He'd never seen anything like it. An acting job for the ages. All her apprehension, all her tears and nerves.

All gone.

Right then and there.

Thiago wasn't looking at her face, and Santiago kept his gaze locked on Slater. Neither of them noticed.

In that moment, Slater understood.

She wasn't a prisoner.

She was here voluntarily.

For this.

She looked at Slater and smiled.

Something appeared in her palm, sliding down from the cuff of her baggy shirt. Something long and silver and shiny. Something resembling a stake. A cylindrical blade, without the hilt. She turned with muted resignation, twisting at the waist with dejection in her body language.

Thiago allowed it.

He faced her. Smiling. Salivating at the prospect of having his way with her.

Then she stared deep into his eyes and gently slid the blade into his throat.

He opened his mouth to scream, and she burst into motion. She wrenched her free hand out of his grasp and placed it firmly over his mouth, shutting him up on the spot. With her other hand, she took the blade out of his neck and put it in his stomach. Twisted it hard. Pulled it out again, and slashed it across his eyes. Killing him, and then blinding him for good measure.

Slater summed up all the willpower he had available and forced himself not to react.

This time, it worked.

Santiago tightened his grip on the trigger, oblivious to what was happening behind him.

35

No sound resonated across the clearing. She'd slaughtered Thiago with the utmost silence, lowering his corpse to the mud with enough strength and grace to indicate she had years of experience in this realm.

Slater couldn't believe his goddamn eyes.

Almost playfully, she touched a finger to her lips. Her eyes seemed to burn with a golden hue, charged with energy.

She crept up on Santiago from behind.

The big man, still staring at Slater, smiled again and said, 'How do you feel?'

Slater raised an eyebrow. 'What?'

'Knowing what I'm about to do to her. And your friends. Even the men. I go both ways, you know? I fancy myself both genders. If it makes you feel any better. I'm all about equality.'

'That's good to hear.'

'I'll make them suffer.'

'I don't think so.'

'You're confident for a man who's outnumbered.'

'I'm afraid you're outnumbered now, my friend.'

He sensed it. Right away. Slater couldn't hide his confidence any longer. Santiago reared up, tearing his gaze away, throwing a wild glance over his shoulder to check on how Thiago was faring. He spotted the woman, her hair draped over her face, now only feet away. Then the dilemma struck.

What was he to do?

Take the AR-15 off Slater's chest, and risk an instantaneous reaction from a man who had proven himself more than capable of decimating anyone in his path. Or keep the gun skewered in place and risk death at the hands of this strange woman. He hadn't seen her kill Thiago, and therefore he wasn't aware of her abilities, so from his perspective she'd landed a lucky blow and managed to capitalise on it. In his eyes, Slater was the far more dangerous party.

He had no idea.

But he still made the right call.

He took the rifle off Slater's chest, wheeling it around to face the girl.

Already too late.

He'd hesitated, and that was enough.

Slater could have exploded off the mark, launching up off his back and crash-tackling Santiago to the dirt. But he saw what was coming. He stayed in place. He didn't have any inclination to get in the way of this woman.

This force.

In truth, he had no idea what he'd stumbled into.

The AR-15 came round in a tight arc, and the woman caught it by the barrel. She wrapped spindly fingers around the gunmetal and aimed it away from her bulk. Santiago had half a second to pull the trigger and let loose with a volley of rounds. It would achieve nothing save from burning her palm, but it was all he had to work with.

Even that proved too difficult a task.

He was still in shock at how rapidly the situation had descended into anarchy.

As soon as she had control of the rifle she plunged the blade into his forearm and tugged downward, her own muscles rippling underneath the baggy shirt. She severed the lower half of Santiago's arm, tearing through flesh and muscle and bone without discriminating.

Santiago screamed.

She pulled on the AR-15, and it came toward her.

Because the hand attached to it no longer belonged to Santiago's body.

She didn't take hold of the weapon. She dropped it as Santiago took a knee, and followed up by plunging the stake into his chest.

Deliberately missing the heart.

He screamed again, a ghastly howl, and slumped to his knees. She cradled his face in both hands, and then delivered a colossal headbutt to the bridge of his nose. The fact that she weighed a hundred pounds less than him meant nothing. Sharp forehead to fragile nose. An equation that came out in favour of the forehead in every single altercation.

Slater heard the *snap,* and he winced.

Santiago screamed for a third time.

Blood pouring from his nose, he collapsed into the dirt, alone in the clearing.

Surrounded by his fallen comrades.

Now outnumbered.

He turned white as a sheet, and not from the pain.

Slater got his hands underneath him and backed away,

slithering through the mud, distancing himself from the horrifying spectacle before him.

The girl straddled Santiago's barrel chest, dropping a smooth tanned leg on either side of his bulk, flattening him to the dirt. She cupped his face again, holding his head in place. Her back stooped and she brought her face to within a foot of his.

Slater watched.

Fascinated.

Stunned.

'You like this?' she whispered.

American, Slater noted.

Crimson streamed from both Santiago's nostrils. His nose bent in a grotesquely misshapen fashion. Well and truly broken. Blood ran from his chest, too. His left arm ended in a grisly stump. It poured blood into the dirt. The night swallowed it up.

'W-what the hell,' the man stuttered. 'My arm...'

'What did you say you were going to do to me?' the woman said.

Her eyes glistened with rage.

'I...'

'What was that?'

'I wasn't going to... please.'

'Beg.'

'W-what?'

'Beg more. I like it.'

'Please. Stop the bleeding. I'm going to—'

She touched a finger to his lips. Almost seductively. He was paling now. Blood was pouring out of him, seemingly from everywhere at once.

'Jesus Christ,' Slater muttered under his breath.

'Russell Williams sends his regards,' the woman said.

She kissed Santiago on the forehead, leaving an imprint of her lipstick on the pale skin.

Like crosshairs.

Then she fetched the stake out of the dirt and shoved it through the mark.

Destroying his brain.

Santiago went limp.

She spat on his corpse, and climbed off it.

She looked at Slater and said, 'Less than he deserved.'

For the first time in his life, he was lost for words.

'Do you talk?' she said.

'Yes.'

'Then don't you agree? Less than he deserved?'

'That name,' Slater said.

'What name?'

'Russell Williams.'

She paused. 'You know it?'

'Yeah. I know it.'

'We shouldn't talk about that here.'

'Uh...'

He couldn't string a sentence together. It was all too much. She gracefully stepped over Santiago's corpse and approached him, offering a smooth palm to help him to his feet.

He took it.

'I'm Ruby,' she said, her eyes sparkling.

'I'm—' Slater said, and then he trailed off again.

He stared at Santiago's mutilated body.

He shook his head.

All he could think to say was, 'What the fuck is going on?'

36

Second by second, the tension in the clearing began to dissipate.

The cartel had been eradicated — at least, this portion of it. Every hostile man in the encampment had met their untimely demise. Slater stood on shaky legs, surrounded by devastation, trying to comprehend what the hell had just happened. He couldn't put it together. Not yet. But he didn't need to.

His sole priority was taking care of Casey and her friends, and Ruby made that clear.

She pulled him aside, stepping in close, making sure she could speak without Casey overhearing. The girl was still duct-taped, wrists and ankles bound, lying on her stomach in the mud with her face pressed into the hot earth.

She had her eyes closed.

She'd opted to ignore what was going on around her. It was for the best. It was all too much for Slater. He couldn't imagine what it would be like for someone unaccustomed to combat.

Still, he couldn't find the right words.

He stared at Ruby, analysing her, and he came away more confused than when he started. She was roughly five foot ten, all slim tanned muscle, with a face that could have easily graced the cover of an international magazine. Amber eyes, a pronounced jawline, smooth thin lips, straight brown hair. Gorgeous, from head to toe.

But beyond that there was something utterly encapsulating about her. She carried herself with the poise of a warrior. Like this was nothing out of the ordinary. And that directly contrasted with the terrified hostage Thiago had hauled out of the bunker.

She was a world-class actor, on top of everything else.

A chameleon.

Slater didn't know what to say.

She muttered to him, 'We need to get the kids out of this hole. They need relief. And counselling. Can you help me with that? The first part, I mean. I'll leave the professional advice to the shrinks.'

He paused. 'Yeah.'

'You're capable, aren't you?'

'I'm good enough.'

'Then it's good to have a friend out here.'

He paused again. 'Are you Black Force?'

'What?'

'Never mind.'

'Don't know what the hell you're talking about.'

He pressed a pair of fingers into his eyeballs. Just to make sure he wasn't dreaming. They came away, and she was still there. Staring up at him. Head cocked to one side. Eyes piercing into his.

He nodded again. 'Okay. Right. The college kids. Let's do it.'

'You're scared,' she noted. 'This can be overwhelming. I

get it. These are bad people around us. I don't blame you. You got a friend called Russell Williams or something?'

He froze. 'What?'

'I thought you knew my guy at the start. But it must just be a coincidence. You okay? You need some water?'

He steeled himself. 'I'm fine. The dead guys aren't what's worrying me.'

'Oh?'

'You're worrying me.'

Something tantalising flashed in her eyes. 'I like that. I like worrying people.'

'Who are you?'

'What happened to these guys? Who killed them?'

'I did.'

She paused. 'Ah. Maybe we do know the same Russell Williams, then.'

'I think we do.'

'Later,' she whispered. 'Let's deal with these kids first.'

'You keep calling them kids. But you look the same age as them. How old are you?'

'Twenty-one.'

'Jesus. We have a lot to discuss.'

'Age isn't always as straightforward as it seems,' she said, and planted a soft kiss on his cheek.

Then she danced across the clearing toward the bunkers, the stake in her hand.

Slater stood rooted to the spot, dazed.

She severed Casey's bindings and helped her to her feet. Slater ghosted forward a couple of steps, getting in range of the conversation. He was fairly certain both girls had materialised from the same bunker. Therefore Ruby would have been playing a part for Casey beforehand. He wanted to deduce how the conversation would go.

Casey said, 'What just happened?'

We're more similar than I thought, Slater thought.

Ruby said, 'I'm not who you think I am.'

'Clearly.'

'Let's get your friends.'

'Hold on,' Casey said, laying a hand on Ruby's chest. 'Who are you? You're with him?'

Ruby glanced at Slater. 'No. I'm not.'

'So is this just a massive coincidence?'

'I don't know what it is.'

'You'd better start explaining.'

Ruby cocked her head, and Slater sensed ice in her eyes.

'No,' she said. 'I don't think I will.'

Casey's eyes flared with rage. Maybe because of the circumstances. She was in a foreign country with nothing but the clothes on her back, only minutes separated from a fate worse than death. Slater pictured her adrenalin racing, her veins pumping, her vision wavering, her mind seeking answers that she'd never get.

'Who are you?' she demanded.

'It doesn't matter,' Ruby said. 'But you're the luckiest bitch on the planet. You and your friends fucked up many, many times. This guy helped you, obviously. And I just helped you now. Get out of rural Colombia and never wander into places you know you're not safe. Learn from this experience. You don't deserve to know who I am. Now let's go find your friends and you can babysit them into one of the larger towns and forget any of this ever happened. And if you need help dealing with it, see a psychologist. That's all I'll say on the matter. You got it?'

Casey didn't respond. She stared blankly at the girl in front of her, her entire perception shattered.

Then she mustered the capacity to respond with, 'Got it.'

Ruby nodded, her eyes ablaze with intensity. 'Good. Let's go find your friends.'

Slater sat down in the dirt and wondered how his life had taken such a drastic turn.

37

J ake, Harvey, and Whitney emerged from one of the low concrete buildings a couple of minutes later, led by Casey. She was in shock, but maintaining her composure remarkably well. She led her friends into the centre of the clearing, and for the first time they saw the devastation all around them. They spun in tight circles, wide-eyed and slack-jawed, acting out the stereotypes of traumatised college kids.

Slater didn't blame them.

He would react accordingly, if murder hadn't been part of his life for as long as he could remember.

The shock started to wear off. He relished the feeling.

It was indescribable how radically his viewpoint had shifted.

From thinking all hope was lost, beginning to accept his own grisly death as well as the rapes and murders of five innocent people, to a reversal of fortune he still couldn't quite believe. He stared at Ruby with palpable curiosity, assessing her every move. He came away with nothing.

She was a chameleon, alright.

Twenty-one years old, and unreadable.

Eventually he realised standing around gawking would achieve nothing, and opted to help as best he could.

He approached the five of them, meeting each of their gazes in turn, apart from Ruby's. He would figure her out later.

Casey said, 'Jesus, you're hurt.'

'You okay?' Slater said.

'We're fine.'

'No, you're not.'

'Seriously, we are. None of us are hurt. Slapped around a little, but that's it.'

Harvey stepped forward and said, 'We're okay, man. Thank you so much.'

'You feel okay now,' Slater said. 'You're ecstatic. As you should be. You feel on top of the world. But it'll hit you later on. Might be tomorrow, might be a few days from now. It's going to bring a range of emotions you probably haven't felt before. See psychologists, okay? If it gets bad. Promise me you will.'

Casey nodded. 'Promise.'

He could see it in her eyes. The look of a deer frozen in headlights. She seemed to have her wits about her, but all four of them were operating on autopilot, and it was no goddamn wonder. Slater couldn't recall a time in his life where he'd been without conflict, but if he could he never would have been able to handle a situation like this. Sure, they were young and foolish, but they held themselves together with remarkable composure, and for that he gave them credit.

'Come on,' he said, shepherding them toward one of the giant pick-up trucks scattered across the clearing.

Jake, Harvey, and Whitney piled into the backseat, and Casey slotted herself into the passenger seat.

Slater eyed Ruby warily.

She stood with her shoulders slumped, reclaiming the same innocence she'd possessed a few minutes earlier. A natural tendency, Slater figured. She must have spent days impersonating a terrified hostage. She wasn't able to shake the guise so effortlessly.

But her eyes said everything.

They were cold, and detached, yet somehow still ablaze with interest.

Slater cocked his head. 'What happens now?'

'You want to take responsibility for them?' she said.

He nodded. 'That's why I came here.'

'They're not my concern. Go for your life.'

'I want to speak to you. After this.'

'Maybe.'

'Humour me that, at least. There's a lot of things I need to know.'

'There's a lot of things I need to keep secret. I'm not telling you anything.'

'I know Russell Williams.'

'Could be bullshit.'

'Five-nine. Short brown hair with flecks of grey. Slate eyes. He's from Northern Maine. Looks a bit like George Clooney.'

Ruby said nothing for a long time. Silence fell over the clearing. Casey and her friends stirred restlessly in the truck. Slater stayed perched on the side step, awaiting a response. Ears perked. Eyebrows raised.

Finally, she said, 'Where are you taking them?'

'Quibdó.'

'The capital?'

'Safety in numbers. Especially as far as they're concerned.'

She nodded. 'Smart.'

'So?'

'I'll meet you there.'

'Where?'

'You said something about a force.'

'What?'

'A division. Of the government. I assume you work for them.'

'Used to.'

'So you're rich.'

'That's none of your business.'

He said it with a certain level of sarcasm.

Her mouth upturned into something resembling a half-smile.

'You're rich,' she said.

'Okay. Your point?'

'Find the most expensive hotel in Quibdó. Book the most expensive suite available. I'll find you.'

'That's not enough to go off.'

'Yes it is,' she said, and looked him deep in the eyes.

He saw capability there.

She would find him.

He nodded. 'Okay. But please find me. I need answers.'

'You sound desperate.'

'There's something forming in my mind. And I don't like it. I don't like it at all. I need reassurance.'

'What if I can't give you reassurance?'

'Then there'll be hell to pay.'

'You're not making it likely that I'll follow through with this.'

'Follow through with it. There's something in it for you.'

'And what might that be?'

'I'm good in bed.'

'You can't be serious.'

'We all need a release every now and then. Open invitation. Find out if you want.'

Then he swung into the cab and slammed the door closed, sealing Ruby off from the five of them.

He twisted the keys in the ignition, stamped on the accelerator, and floored it out of the clearing. Descending back into the hot oppressive night. Leaving the death and devastation behind. Forgetting the cartel ever existed.

There were dozens more out here, no doubt.

Cut the head off a snake, and two more take its place.

But it didn't matter. He had the college kids. They had their whole lives ahead of them. That was enough satisfaction for one day.

And he was tired as hell.

It was a couple of miles before he noticed Casey glaring at him. He looked across. 'What?'

'Really?' she said.

He rolled his eyes. 'It's a tactic. Maximise confusion. She couldn't possibly have been expecting that approach. And it's worked before. I guess there's something tantalising about me. It'll get her to Quibdó.'

'What were you banking on?'

'That she wouldn't anticipate me saying that.'

'And?'

'And it'd leave her confused. It'd put her on the back step. She'd be trying to break that down. Was there any hidden meaning behind it? Did it refer to something she's privy to? She'll be dissecting what I said for hours.'

Casey said nothing. Just stared straight ahead.

Slater muttered, 'Or it was just the truth.'

He barrelled deeper into the jungle, heading for the capital of the Chocó Department.

His whole life in turmoil.

38

He should have known they wouldn't conduct the journey in silence. Slater would have preferred that. He always favoured peace and quiet in the aftermath of brutal conflict.

He noted how insane his life must be if he had general principles of operating after murder.

Was it murder, though?

It sure felt like it.

He clammed up for the first portion of the journey, all his concentration on the inky blackness ahead of them. It was like something out of a video game. Their surroundings revealed themselves one miserable foot at a time, glowing bright, illuminated by the glare of the headlights, and then a moment later plunged back into darkness. It created a halo-like effect around the truck, swamping the rest of the jungle in mystery.

Slater didn't want to know what lay out there.

Aside from the obvious jungle predators, he knew Santiago's cartel wasn't an anomaly. He'd spent half his career wrapped up in this shit. These lawless territories in the dark heart of countries like Colombia stewed with gang wars, narco infighting, and obscene violence. He'd just experienced it first-hand, but he knew he was simply scratching the tip of the iceberg. He didn't want to venture any deeper. It would only lead to gridlock. There was too much devastation swept under the rug in this jungle, and he could spend his whole life on a rampage through the trees and only deal with half a percent of the narcos.

He knew that from personal experience.

He got on a main road — really, nothing more than a slightly wider dirt path, but in comparison to where they'd come from it felt close to the heart of a major metropolitan city. There were street lights interspersed every few hundred feet, all weak and flickering, some dead, but they indicated something resembling civilisation wasn't far off. The trees backed away, their tendrils sneaking into the gloom, exposing the night sky.

Slater buzzed the driver's window down a crack and breathed fresh air.

It was no different to the air deeper in the jungle, still hot and rancid.

But it comforted him all the same. Call it placebo. Call it whatever you wanted. He sensed a weight off his chest, a metaphorical cinderblock lifted. There was dry blood encrusted on his scalp and tremors in his hands and a dull throbbing ache in his gut, but he was alive, and the kids were safe.

He lapsed into silence, pulled a smartphone wrapped in a shock-resistant case from his pocket, and nodded with satisfaction at the absence of cracks in the screen. He drove with one hand and navigated to an offline maps application, setting the destination for Quibdó.

Casey noticed. The soft glow of the screen bathed the

interior of the truck in a small halo of light. She looked over and spotted where they were headed.

'You been there before?' she said.

Slater barely noticed her voice, entranced by the co-ordinates. They were four hours from the capital city if they kept their current pace. Surprisingly close. In another fifty miles the unkempt dirt road would merge with a highway and take them right up to the southern end of Quibdó's city limits. He breathed pure relief and tossed the phone on top of the dashboard, where it came to rest in a shallow groove. It would bark at him if he made a wrong turn. Not that there were any turns to make. Not out here.

'You got a signal?' Casey said, persevering even though she hadn't got an answer for the first question.

The darkness ahead became hypnotic. Slater stared at it, conjuring all kinds of demons that might stew in the night. Most of them from his own mind. He replayed the events of the night over and over again, like a VCR stuck on an incessant loop.

His eyelid twitched.

'Hey,' Casey said.

He looked across. 'What?'

'You don't talk anymore?'

'Adrenalin wore off.'

'You don't want to talk?'

'You must be a clairvoyant.'

She almost bit at the snark, then held her tongue and settled back in the seat. A poignant silence radiated from the back seats. Jake and Harvey and Whitney sat mute, squashed shoulder to shoulder, none of them so much as breathing heavy. Slater knew why. Instincts. They'd been fearing for their lives for the last half-day. That didn't fade easily. Not when it was their first time.

You always remember your first time.

Slater remembered his.

When the gangsters at the port took his mother, he was only thirteen. He stormed down there with a chip on his shoulder, cursing out men who had no business being cursed out, completely oblivious and mostly uncaring of the consequences. He even beat the shit out of one of the perimeter guards. No combat training — in fact, he'd never even thrown a punch in his life before that moment. But unbelievable natural athleticism and a genetic reaction speed nearly unrivalled in modern combat history counted for something. He almost killed the guy. The low-ranked thug hadn't been the one to put his mother on the boat and ship her to Saudi Arabia or wherever the hell they take women for sadistic purposes, but he might as well have been. By the end of it, his face resembled a swollen pumpkin.

Slater had planned to continue his rampage all the way up to the foot of the mob. But they'd caught him at the perimeter and shoved a gun under his chin and pulled the trigger and it jammed. Then they told him to fuck off back to the hole he lived in and not bother them again.

And to consider himself lucky for not joining his mother, wherever she was.

He'd followed their orders. Because nothing rivalled that first time.

The primitive part of his brain firing up, screaming, *Holy shit!*

Death's right there. Do whatever they say. Crawl away, apologise, do whatever you need to do to stay alive.

So he'd backed off. Retreated. Looked at the floor and said he was sorry. He let them hit him a few times too. To make up for what he did to their grunt. He took it in stride.

It cracked his nose real bad. And then he went back to his room and told his dad he'd got in a street fight. Not that the old man noticed. He was too busy grieving and drinking. He also knew who'd taken his wife. But he didn't have the spine to do anything about it.

Slater's father got a gun under his chin a couple of years later, too. But it was his own doing.

And it didn't jam.

Casey said, 'You okay?'

Slater wiped his eyes. There were no tears, but there might as well have been. He hated showing vulnerability. A natural instinct. He stuffed all the emotion back down inside. Deep inside.

'Fine,' he muttered, and kept driving.

39

T he monastic silence ended when Slater realised he would need to babysit the four of them out of the country.

They were two hours separated from the jungle encampment, and the shock was setting in. He noticed when Casey squared away, shrinking toward the passenger door and planting her chin to her chest. Her eyes glazed over and she stared at the dashboard, detached, replaying the memories of the evening. The same uneasy quiet resonated from the back seat, and Slater figured the three in the back had gone into shock the moment they left the clearing. They probably thought they were floating through a dream world, leaving their old lives firmly in the past. Emotions and sensations they hadn't considered feasible were now at the forefront of their minds.

Slater let them be for as long as he could. He'd needed that initial quiet to process the slaughter of a dozen narcos. It had been quite some time since he'd killed anyone.

But now he was fine.

Just another horrific memory to add to the bank.

He said, 'We're an hour out.'

Casey nodded.

No word from the back seat.

He said, 'El Caraño Airport is near Quibdó. You won't be taken in the city. Too busy. Too much room for error. They all prey on the small towns. You understand?'

Casey nodded again.

Still no word from the back seat.

'I have places to be,' he said. 'So I'll drop you off somewhere discreet and then you need to find your way home. Can you do that?'

'Here?' she said, her voice soft, her eyes widening.

She glanced out the window. Still nothing by desolation.

Slater shook his head. 'In Quibdó.'

'Places to be?' she said, almost mockingly.

'Don't know what you're implying.'

'This is a strange fucking world.'

'You're in shock.'

'How can you flirt with someone in the middle of all of that? Who was that girl? What the hell is going on?'

'I know as much as you do.'

'You were calm enough to flirt.'

'Is that a sin?'

'It's just weird.'

'You managed well enough at the bar.'

She shot him daggers, sideways, across the centre console.

From the back seat, Jake said, 'What?'

Slater threw a glance over his shoulder and saw him sitting there, shoulders hunched forward, white as a sheet. From the shock. Not from the accusation. Social gossip didn't mean anything anymore. Slater understood. Now their perspectives had shifted. Nothing mattered other than being alive.

Slater turned to Casey and said, 'It was normal for you. At the bar. Because you're comfortable in that setting. I just happen to be comfortable in settings like what you saw back there.'

'How?'

'You get used to everything.'

'That's not an explanation.'

'Yes it is.'

From the back seat, Harvey said, 'You do that all the time, man?'

'Frequently enough.'

'And you're still alive.'

'Yeah.'

'Lucky?'

'I like to think so.'

'Crazy shit, bro.'

'Yeah,' Slater muttered. 'Crazy shit.'

'I'm sorry we fucked up so bad,' Harvey said. 'I'm sorry for everything. For my part in it, at least. I can only speak for myself.'

Under her breath, Whitney mumbled, 'Sorry.'

She would be quiet for the next few days. Maybe weeks. And for good reason.

Jake said, 'I'm so sorry, man.'

'Don't apologise.'

'Why not? That's the least we can do.'

'I was your age once.'

'You were dumb like us?'

By then, Black Force had already recruited him.

'Yeah,' he lied. 'Happens to all of us.'

Except for a select few.

Like me.

'Just research where you're going next time,' Slater said.

'So that's it?' Casey said. 'This is the end of the road? We'll never see you again?'

'When we get to Quibdó,' Slater said. 'Then we'll part ways.'

'How can we repay you?'

'You can't.'

The truth.

She said, 'Do you need money? We can all transfer you. For the rest of our lives. We owe you that much, at least.'

Still young, still dumb, still foolish.

He said, 'I've got money.'

She said, 'I don't know what else we can offer.'

'Go and live good lives and do good for people,' he said. 'Sounds simple, but that's enough.'

'That can't be the only reason you pulled us out of that mess.'

'It's reason enough.'

'Why do you do it?'

'Habit. Probably.'

'Like you said before...?'

'You get used to everything.'

'Do you have a death wish?'

'Probably.'

The conversation petered out, mostly because Slater couldn't take his mind off the woman with the amber eyes.

Ruby.

What the hell was she?

A trained killer like him, and one of the best actresses he'd ever laid eyes on.

Russell Williams.

How did it all connect?

He floored the accelerator, stifling the questions running through his head, making himself concentrate like a hawk on the uneven road to ensure he didn't plunge off the trail and kill them all. It lifted him out of his thoughts. Casey protested, and there were mutters of disapproval from the back seat, but Slater ignored them completely.

His mind was far more dangerous than the road.

Because he couldn't stop thinking about a nine-year-old girl he'd left in the hands of Williams back in Macau, making the shadowy government figure swear to find her a decent home and give her some semblance of a normal life.

Had he?

Or had he done something else?

If there's any chance...

Slater pushed toward Quibdó, wondering if he'd crossed a bridge from which there was no going back.

40

He let them out on the outskirts of Quibdó, in a street that would ordinarily be considered dangerous for tourists, but paled in comparison to where they'd started.

Puddles swamped the muddy street, and two parallel ditches on either side of the main road created jagged miniature canyons that prevented any kind of foot traffic. But the rundown dilapidated houses had their porch lights on, creating a warm glow along the street, and a large group of foreigners milled around an open-walled building advertising itself as a luxury cab service.

Slater stopped the truck a few dozen feet from the procession, and pressed a crumpled wad of bills into Casey's sweaty palm.

'Use that to get a good cab,' he said. 'They'll cater to you if you have money. There's minimal risk of kidnap and extortion here. You'll be safe.'

'The airport,' she muttered. 'What was it called?'

'El Caraño.'

'That's where we arrived,' she said, nodding. 'A few days ago. Feels like years.'

'You're still in shock. You will be for a while. But it's better to get back to the States and then try to break down what happened. Take it slow. Piece by piece. It's not going to be easy. It never is.'

'Seems easy for you.'

'Like I said, I'm used to it.'

'What do I tell my parents?'

Jake, Harvey, and Whitney all murmured their agreements.

Slater said, 'Not the truth.'

'They'll know something happened.'

'I didn't say cover it up. Just ... don't be that specific. Say you were threatened. Say it scared the shit out of you. They'll believe you. They're protective, I'm sure.'

'You got parents like that?' Casey said.

Some kind of attempt at humour, given his seemingly personal relationship with avoiding death by a hair.

Slater's face turned to stone.

The replay of his childhood still ran fresh in his mind. Only recently conjured back up from the drive. Usually he would think nothing of it. Now he battled a rising surge of emotion.

Casey paused, understanding the silence.

'You three go,' she said, facing the back seat. 'Talk to the guy at reception. I'll catch up to you.'

Silent nods. Slater caught a flash of the gestures in the rear view mirror. Jake, Harvey, and Whitney shuffled silently out of the car, muttering half-hearted goodbyes as they stepped down into the mud. They weren't thinking about saying anything sentimental. They weren't thinking about saying anything at all. He didn't take anything they did or didn't say to heart, because he knew their brains were embroiled in a feedback loop, stuck on the same sensations.

Like fear and anxiety and terror all mashed together and then drip-fed a steady dose of steroids.

I remember my first time.

They closed the doors, already fading from Slater's memory, and he turned to Casey.

'I like you,' he said.

She seemed taken aback. 'What?'

'You've got your head on your shoulders. You're smart. You're handling this well. Don't blame yourself if it all goes downhill when you get back home. You're still in a different mode of being. You're travelling, backpacking, being wild. Or at least you were. So your brain's a little more adapted to experiencing new sensations. It'll be keeping most of it at bay. When you get back to your own bed you'll start to realise how close you came to dying. And it'll eat at you.'

'You're really doing a great job of reassuring me.'

'I'm preparing you. Better to know than be blissfully oblivious until it hits you.'

She nodded. 'I guess you're right.'

'Help your friends through it. Learn what not to do in future. That's all there is to it.'

She blinked twice, as if contemplating whether she was hallucinating all of this. 'So ... that's it?'

'What else is there?'

'I don't know. I still don't understand why you did it. Any of it. We deserved for you to let us die.'

'Don't talk like that.'

'It's the truth. You almost got yourself killed.'

'I basically did.'

'And then, that woman...'

'Did you speak to her? Before I showed up?'

'Yes.'

'Anything you can help me with?'

'In terms of what?'

'Did she give anything away?'

Casey paused, deep in pensive thought, chewing her bottom lip. Drawing into herself. The shoddy glow of the houses around them filtered through the windshield and bathed her in a warm light. Accentuating the sweat and dirt matted to her face. With specks of blood dotted all around like a sick accoutrement. She looked nothing like the quietly confident girl Slater had met earlier that afternoon.

She shook her head. 'I think — when I get back home — that's going to be the most puzzling thing for me.'

'What is?'

'You're like a god out here. This is your world. And even you're confused by her.'

'So she played the part well?'

'I believed she was a terrified hostage with every fibre of my being. I can't stress that enough.'

'So she's good.'

'There's something above good. Far, far above good. That's what she is.'

'Yeah.'

'You two used to work together?'

'No. But we know the same people.'

'You come from the same background?'

'Maybe. I'll find out.'

'Be careful.'

Slater smiled at the irony. 'Thanks. I knew I could count on you.'

She smirked. It took some serious effort, but she managed.

She looked around. 'Mad life, isn't it?'

'Mine's like this all the time.'

'You get used to everything,' she parroted.

He put a hand on her shoulder. 'Take care of yourself.'

'I just feel like ... this can't be it. Can it?'

'It'd be best for your health if you never saw me again.'

'I don't think so.'

'I attract trouble.'

'You don't know that.'

'Yes, I do.'

She shrugged. 'Fair enough. I'd tell you how much I owe you, but you already know how I feel. I'm sure you've pulled people out of situations like that in the past.'

'I have.'

'Does it feel good?'

'It doesn't feel like anything, if you want me to be honest. I just have to do it.'

'Why?'

'Because what else am I going to do?'

She left it at that. There was nothing more to be said. She opened the passenger door and hovered there for a beat, one palm on the handle, the other in the process of levering herself off the coarse leather. She froze in place and stared him in the eyes, as if searching for something. He gave her nothing. It would be best for her to forget he ever existed. Best to leave her the absolute minimum to remember.

She seemed to see right through that. 'You're a complicated guy. I hope you end up happy. Eventually.'

'I am happy.'

'You don't look it.'

'I put myself in so many situations like that, and I learned to suppress fear. Guess I suppressed every other emotion along with that. Just a byproduct.'

'You're truly happy?'

'I think so. It's complicated.'

'Then keep doing what you're doing.'

'I will.'

'Can I see you again? Even if it's years from now. I just ... I've never met anything like whatever the hell you are. I'm not coming onto you. It's just fascinating.'

'Do me a favour and pretend I never existed,' he said, accompanying it with a half-smile to let her know he wasn't being unnecessarily harsh. Then he leant across the centre console and gently guided her out of the car with an open palm. She stepped down into the mud, and looked at him again.

'I don't even know your name,' she said.

'Good,' he said, and pulled the passenger door closed from the inside.

41

He was two miles away before he realised they didn't have their passports.

All their luggage had either been destroyed or left outside the hostel when they were taken. Either way, it was gone. He paused with his foot on the brake, then figured they would have ample opportunities to contact an embassy or a consular service. So he pressed on. There was nothing he could do for them that they couldn't do for themselves.

He ditched the car at the next available opportunity. It didn't take much effort. Plastic containers of fuel ran along the edges of the truck's rear tray, held tight in place by thick straps and bindings. Slater eyed them in the rear view mirror and formulated a plan.

He trawled deeper into Quibdó, moving through what he guessed constituted the ghettos. He passed ramshackle dwellings and slightly larger houses with cracks running down the exterior and moss protruding from the walls. Passersby, most locals, barely threw him a second glance. His was just another indiscriminate filthy Toyota trundling the backwaters of this fetid city. He imagined the centre of town was a little more accomodating to satiate the tourists that trickled in through the airport.

Almost immediately, he forgot about the four college kids.

He'd found, through experience, that dwelling and speculating on the people he'd saved did him no good in the long run. It bogged him down in possibility, and he preferred an uncomplicated life. He simply helped when he saw it, and focused on maximising his own happiness in the interim.

Casey had probed deeper than she probably realised, and now he was forced to face those questions.

But he was happy.

His satisfaction just didn't reside on the ordinary spectrum.

He spotted a trio of locals positioned on a street corner at a deserted T-junction, in no man's land between the residential neighbourhood and the commercial district beyond. The commercial district sported hotels and convenience stores and a few skyscrapers dotted intermittently in the distance. This here was a desolate zone, devoid of life, inhabited by no-one except the three scrawny guys chain-smoking cigarettes and staring at nothing in particular.

They weren't talking much. Hard lines creased their faces, the cracks stained deep with dirt and muck. He could see it caked into their clothing. Workmen, probably pausing for a moment of stillness before returning to their homes after an obscenely long work day. Or getting up well before dawn. It was close to three in the morning — the strange hours where little happened and the shadows seemed to grow longer.

Slater made up his mind in an instant. He aimed for a sharp ditch a few dozen feet away from the three men, where weeds and vegetation grew thick, and put his seatbelt on. He slowed down at the last second, but the pick-up truck still pitched violently forward into the mud, its hood crumpling and twisting into the grime, mud spraying up and caking the windshield, seeping through a couple of cracks in the chassis.

Slater snatched up his phone, shoved it into his pocket, and got out of the driver's seat.

He tasted the night, pausing a beat to soak it all in.

This is really happening.

He fetched one of the dirty plastic containers, unscrewed the lid, and upended its contents across the truck's interior. The three men watched with placid expressions, likely amused but unwilling to share their emotions with this stranger. Then there was the language barrier to take into account.

Slater poured a second container across the rear tray and circled around the truck, now positioned at a grotesque diagonal angle.

He gestured to the closest man's cigarette, nothing more than a stub, hanging loosely from his mouth.

The guy stared at Slater like he was deranged, then shrugged and handed the butt across.

Slater tossed it on the car.

Flames seared, burning hot in the dark. Swallowing the atmosphere. Licking and torching and removing any trace of Slater's existence.

He nodded his thanks, and moved on.

He didn't pay attention to the trio as he sauntered past them. He heard them, though. One of them snickered, and that was the straw that broke the camel's back. The three of them devolved into raucous laughter, bemused by the ridiculousness of it all.

They finished their cigarettes and turned to admire the flaming wreckage.

Colombians certainly weren't easily deterred by the abnormal.

Slater patted himself down as he disappeared into the night.

Phone.

Wallet.

Passport.

Keys to the compound.

The four things he kept on him whenever he wasn't working out, to allow room for exactly the kind of behaviour he was currently exhibiting. The passport stood out as the strangest to maintain hold of at all times, but he never knew when he would be forced to abandon ship, in the kind of situation where the slightest hesitation would get him killed.

He walked off down the dirt road, alone with his thoughts and stripped of possessions.

And that suited him just fine.

42

H e took his time making his way into the centre of town. He kept the Atrato River to the west and used it as a reference point, zoning in on the rushing water as its sounds filtered through the streets. The night turned hot and oppressive, wrenching sweat out of his pores. He didn't think he could perspire any more than he already was.

That proved inaccurate.

The perspiration started coagulating with the dried blood all over his head — a disgusting combination. He paused in the shadows to locate a nearby tap and found one only a dozen feet away, a single metal pole spearing out of the ground and surrounded by overgrown weeds, caked with rust and grime.

But it worked.

He twisted the nozzle and a steady stream of water poured out into the dirt. He'd shot himself with every vaccination and immunisation under the sun before stepping foot in-country, so he had no qualms with scooping the water into his palms and drenching his face, his scalp, his neck. It burned in the wound across his scalp, but it was only superficial pain. There was no neurological damage. The bullet hadn't made it to his skull. It had only sliced a thin sliver of flesh off the top of his head. It would heal. Already the bleeding had stopped.

In the big picture, nothing to worry about.

Especially considering he'd taken on an entire cartel a few hours ago.

He removed all the dirt from his visible pores and carried on, allowing the night heat to dry him naturally. There were no passersby. No tourists. No pedestrians. It was too late for any of that. He was a ghost in the city, passing quaint dwellings with dilapidated walls and no fences separating the properties from their neighbours.

He sensed an air of community, even all the way out here, even under conditions that might classify as the worst kind of poverty to uninformed visitors.

He used the peace and quiet to think.

He hadn't been alone since the cartel narcos had stormed his compound, and he was accustomed to a lifetime of being alone. In fact, the excursion into the jungle had thoroughly disrupted his routine.

Driven him out of what he'd temporarily considered home.

Flipped his life on his head.

But there was no going back.

He found it effortless to hit the road — as he strolled through muddy streets he didn't know from the back of his hand, he sensed some kind of smug satisfaction, and he knew what it was.

This was his peak mode of operating. Leaving material possessions behind. Giving up the designer furniture and smooth floors and high ceilings for the open road. He had the clothes on his back, and that was it.

And somehow it felt more like home than the building he'd occupied for the last couple of months.

He'd always known it was a farce. Even when he'd hired the contractors, the architects, the builders, the laymen. Even when the plan he'd envisioned in his head came to reality. It was still a fixed physical location. Plenty of room for vulnerability. Maybe that was why he'd given up entirely on installing any kind of security system. They'd offered everything under the sun. Motion sensors, fortified windows, and everything in between.

And this was Colombia. Rural, deserted Colombia. They'd offered a hell of a lot more. Claymores and turrets and fully automatic machine guns.

He'd refused everything.

Because he knew none of it would matter, and it hadn't. In truth he'd been looking for an excuse to get the hell out of there.

He was worth four hundred million dollars — not that anyone knew. A strange and twisted detour in Macau had led to that. The funds had previously belonged to the triad, now secured in a private bank in Zurich, available at the tap of a button on his smartphone. He'd spent half a million building the compound, and it hadn't made a dent in his personal fortune. He accrued that amount in interest payments every couple of weeks.

So it doesn't matter.

The past left behind.

The future uncertain.

Just how I like it.

Then his mind turned to more pressing issues. Ruby. Twenty-two years old, and a true enigma. He figured he would never decipher her completely. He started down the mental rabbit hole, postulating where she might have come from and how she came into possession of the talents she displayed in the clearing.

Then he gave up, almost immediately.

He'd never allowed time for any of that.

He either knew something, or he didn't.

Speculating was utterly pointless, and a monumental waste of his life.

The lack of sleep caught up to him. Coming down from the violence, his limbs grew heavy and his mind stuttered, jumping from place to place as if ghosting through an illusion. Maybe it was the dehydration, maybe it was the stress, maybe it was the blood loss — or, more than likely, it was all those things wrapped up in a sinister package.

He barely comprehended the rest of the journey. The mud turned to blacktop and sidewalks formed — he was near the city centre. He aimed for the bright lights and hoped he was trekking in the right direction. He hoped he'd done a respectable job of cleaning himself up with the tap. The last thing he needed was to get turned away by the doorman at what would likely constitute the only luxury hotel in Quibdó.

He found it without much fanfare — a tall, unimpressive building on the outside, but according to his phone a respectable four-star establishment on the inside. A quick Google search revealed it as the only reasonably expensive place in the city.

There wasn't much going on in the Chocó Department.

Slater powered into the lobby, which sure enough revealed itself as architecturally well-designed and suitably well-furnished. He weaved through an array of chest-high pot plants meant to imitate the wide-ranging biomes of the

Colombian jungle. He didn't spend any time admiring their detail. He shuddered at the thought of any kind of flora. Right now, he wanted a cool climate and an absence of drug traffickers.

But a bed would suffice.

He crossed to the reception desk, manned by a young Afro-Colombian, probably in his early twenties with a thin frame and elegant posture. The guy sat straight up, no hint of a stoop, with his bony shoulders jutting wide on either side of his body. He took his job seriously, despite the late hour. He wanted to impress.

'After a room, sir?' he said.

Refusing to acknowledge the slivers of dried blood and dirt and sweat and overall wear and tear dotting Slater's frame.

A true professional.

Because they were frighteningly obvious.

Slater nodded. 'Is this the most expensive hotel in Quibdó?'

The guy barely paused.

Once again, a true professional.

'I assure you, sir, our prices are quite modest for the services we offer. We are quite simply the best.'

'Good. That's all I wanted to know. What's your most expensive room?'

The guy cocked his head.

Maybe not the most professional.

Slightly perturbed by the incessant focus on price.

'I'm not sure, sir. We have a two-bedroom on the...'

Slater held up a hand. 'You know what? Doesn't matter. Put me anywhere nice. I don't mind the price. But I'm expecting a visitor. Can you show her up to my room when she arrives?'

'Certainly, sir.'

Now, a sly smile.

Not professional at all.

Showing his age.

Slater smiled back. 'Make it a good choice, yeah? I'm trying to impress.'

The kid nodded. 'Yeah.'

Dropping the polite demeanour entirely.

Probably the same age as Ruby.

But a world apart.

That intrigued Slater all the more.

The guy asked for three hundred thousand Colombian pesos. Roughly the equivalent of one hundred U.S. dollars. To Slater, nothing. Out here, enough to support a family for a month. He fished his wallet out of his pocket and handed over the crumpled bills.

'Good selection?' he said.

The kid said, 'Best we have on offer,' and handed over a key.

43

S later couldn't remember the last time he'd been this desperate for a shower.

He burst into the room — nothing special, if he was being honest, but then again he'd tasted the absolute pinnacle of luxury in dozens of countries. Colombia had a beautiful culture, and a cheerful and warm population, but they weren't a country of interior designers. There was a nice bed and a clean carpet and a couple of polished side tables and a pair of curtains drawn across a window that looked out over Quibdó.

And not much else.

But that was all Slater needed.

He went straight to the bathroom and peeled off his bedraggled clothes, stained dark and deep with sweat and blood and mud and filth. He tossed them on the tiled floor and fired the shower up. The water was hot and clean. It was the little things that mattered in a city like Quibdó. Luxury was state-of-the-art water pipelines, good climate control, and the smaller amenities that people usually didn't pay attention to.

It all added up to a welcome escape from the humidity, and that felt better than a six-star penthouse in London.

He stood under the powerful jet for an eternity, refusing to get out from under its lure, intoxicated by the cleanliness. The cut on his head proved to be much less of a deal than he initially anticipated. It had already sealed itself shut, the blood clotting and forming a protective layer over the torn skin. He ran the water over his scalp to test it, and came away satisfied, barely in pain.

On a list of the injuries accumulated over a career to be reckoned with, it resided firmly near the bottom.

Out of habit, he yanked the handle to its coldest setting for the last minute of the shower.

Releasing stress chemicals, stimulating blood flow in his muscles, and providing enough of a shock to lend him a burst of energy despite the hurt and the fatigue and the lack of sleep.

He climbed out, cleansed and purified, and killed the water. Dripped dry for a couple of minutes, tasting the air, savouring it. He fetched a clean white towel off the rack and wiped the fog off the mirror. Studied his reflection for a beat. Checked his naked frame for any unseen injuries masked by adrenalin. It wouldn't surprise him if they were there. He'd once been shot in the upper arm and hadn't noticed until an hour later when the stress cocktail subsided.

But there was nothing.

No body fat. Just dripping muscle and sinew, tightly packaged, with veins running over his forearms like road maps. Nothing to scoff at. All the self-inflicted pain and discomfort had paid off. He stared at the pile of sweaty clothes he'd came in with and immediately refused to put them back on. He crossed to the wardrobe and fetched a thick robe made of terry cotton. He wrapped it around his body and tightened the knot.

All done.

He stared at the bed, strongly tempted to give up on waiting for Ruby. Fatigue hung heavy over him. He'd flirted with her in the heat of the moment, and it had been based on what he considered mutual respect and admiration. Nothing serious. They were on a level playing field, in some respects. Extreme violence seemed to be a commonality in both their lives.

Whoever she was.

The need for answers gnawed at him, but the need for sleep threatened to overpower it.

Sleep won.

He crossed to the large double bed, almost salivating at the thought of passing out for eight straight hours. He would wake at close to midday the following day, and then he could set to work deducing what to do with the rest of his life. Any attempt to weigh his options now would only lead to falling asleep on the spot.

He peeled back a corner of the duvet.

Someone knocked on the door.

It was a light rap, made with small knuckles, but there was strength behind the gesture. Slater sensed it immediately. For the first time in as long as his memory went back, a tremor of butterflies twisted his gut into a knot. It wasn't nervous anticipation — he'd lost track of the number of one-night-stands he'd had — and it wasn't fear of Ruby coming for sinister reasons. He figured he could dismantle her if it came to that.

They were both hardened killers, but he'd been in this business a long time, and probably outweighed her by fifty pounds.

No, it was something else.

It was the awareness that she was different.

He crossed the room and opened the door. There she was, appearing almost innocent in the soft light of the exterior hallway. Slater ushered her inside. She slipped gracefully past him, nearly tiptoeing, completely silent. She stepped into the room and twirled on the spot. Playfully.

There was something terrifying about it.

She stared at him with those tantalising amber eyes.

They didn't blink.

She wore the same clothes from earlier that night. Still stained with the blood of the cartel narcos. Still dirty from the jungle muck.

Slater said, 'You need a shower?'

She said, 'That would be good.'

She tiptoed into the bathroom and shut the door. He stood there, not quite knowing what to do with himself. The sound of running water filtered under the crack in the door frame, and a moment later it ceased, replaced by the faint scuffs and scratches of someone washing themselves hard. He imagined her scrubbing away at the filth of the evening until not a single morsel remained, symbolically shedding her skin. Just as he'd done.

He sat down on the bed.

Ten minutes past and then the door opened. She stood there, completely naked, her frame tanned and supple and lithe, her eyes glowing, her wet brown hair falling in streaks on either side of her face. Her lips were full and moist.

Slater sat still.

He didn't know what to do.

'I'm not getting back in those clothes,' she said.

Slater nodded. 'There's no spare robes. Sorry. You can have mine.'

'Got anything on underneath?'

'No.'

'You shy?'

'No.'

'I'll have yours then.'

He didn't hesitate. He stripped the thick cotton off his body and tossed the whole robe across the room. She caught it, one-handed, and gently lowered it to the floor.

'Not going to wear it?' he said.

'No need.'

'You sure? I'm quite a bit older.'

'How much older?'

'Maybe ten years. Give or take.'

She scoffed. 'We just slaughtered an encampment of drug traffickers and you're worried about that?'

He shrugged. 'Do I look worried?'

She stared. Looked from his face to his chest to ... lower.

The corners of her mouth turned upward. Ever so slightly. She couldn't hide her approval. She might be the best method actress in the world, but this was a different realm altogether.

'No,' she said. 'You look excited.'

He just smiled.

Rolled over and turned the bedside light out.

Plunged the room into darkness.

44

They writhed and jolted and moaned, tangled in the sheets, wrapped in each other's bodies, savouring every part of it, and when it was over Slater flashed a glance at the clock on the desk, its digits glowing in the gloom.

His eyes widened.

'Jesus,' he muttered, coated in a fresh layer of perspiration. 'That was ... longer than expected.'

Ruby half-chuckled, half-smiled, and rested her head on his heaving chest. Also sweating.

'Time flies when you're having fun,' she muttered. 'What was it? An hour? Two?'

'Nearly two. How'd I go?'

'You kidding?' she said. 'I'm exhausted.'

'Is that a good thing?'

'You bet.'

'I thought I might be rusty. Haven't been pursuing much lately.'

'If that was you rusty, I might need to hang around a bit longer.'

'You're not hanging around?'

'You want me to?'

'I have questions,' he muttered. 'So many questions.'

They lay there in the darkness, fatigued and exhausted and worn down but glowing with invigoration. Cradling each other's physiques, running hands over flesh, drinking in the hedonism.

It made sense, too.

They both operated in a world that revolved entirely around the physical. And usually the other end of the spectrum. Pain and violence and suffering.

Slater didn't blame himself for wanting the opposite when he wasn't clashing heads together.

He ran a hand down her back and it came to rest on her firm rear. He kissed her, hard, warming up for a second round.

She rolled on top of him.

'Wait,' he muttered. 'Let's talk.'

'We can do that later.'

'I don't think we can. I think you're using me for a thrill. And then I think you'll be gone.'

'Think what you like. I want you.'

She hunched over him, taking his ear in her mouth. Tasting it. Working her way down his neck.

He stifled a moan.

Took her by the hips.

Rolled her over.

Her silhouette reacted accordingly, two slender arms reaching up, fingers digging into his back.

'Listen,' she muttered. 'I've had a rough couple of days, and you're damn good in bed. I want round two. Either give it to me or tell me to leave.'

'Can you multitask?' he whispered in her ear.

'I might be able to oblige.'

They went slow, taking the polar opposite approach to the first time, which had been nothing more than a burst of uncontrolled energy and unbridled pleasure on both sides. Now they gyrated, moving their bodies together in a gentle rhythm, their faces only inches apart in the dark room.

Slater kissed her.

She kissed back.

He said, 'How do you know Russell Williams?'

In between a pair of gasps, she said, 'We work together.'

'Together?'

'He's my handler.'

'Should you be telling me this?'

'Probably not. But there were more men in that clearing than I was expecting. I probably wouldn't have been able to kill all of them if you hadn't picked off most of them first. So I owe you a debt. And you're doing good now. Really, really good. I'm in a giving mood.'

'Glad to hear.'

'But I really shouldn't be telling you this. Any of this. It'll get me killed.'

'You truly think?'

'I don't know.'

'What do you know?'

'Not much. Trust me. Less than you'd expect.'

'They keep you in the dark?'

'It's better for both of us, I figure.'

'You're fast as hell. And I thought you were a terrified hostage in that clearing. I bought it — hook, line, and sinker. And I can read people. Trust me. You said you're twenty-one?'

'I'm twenty-two tomorrow.'

'Happy birthday.'

'Thanks.'

'Did you celebrate?'

'No.'

'Why not?'

'Not part of the business.'

'What's the business?'

He sensed something building. He knew the underlying truth.

No-one could amass skills like that in three years. She didn't walk into a recruiting office at eighteen. Even if she was a prodigy, even if she was a stone-cold killer from birth, you couldn't teach that remorselessness, that lack of hesitation, that primal switch from hostage to hunter in the blink of an eye. Not in a few short years. That was a decade-long project. Just like Slater had been.

He said, 'When did you find Russell Williams?'

'I was twelve.'

'Fuck.'

'It's not what you think.'

'I'm not thinking about you.'

'Who are you thinking about?'

'What are you?' he said. 'You're not Black Force. You don't even know what it is. So you're something else.'

'I can't tell you that.'

'I'm retired. You don't have to worry about anything.'

'You seem angry. Under the surface. Like Williams took something from you. Some time ago.'

'I'm retired,' he said.

'You didn't look retired,' she said. 'Earlier tonight. You don't ... feel retired.'

He said, 'I'm retired.'

'Okay,' she whispered. 'I'm a protégé of the Lynx program.'

45

He didn't respond.

Maybe she was expecting him to. She paused for effect, letting the words sink in, but they meant nothing to Slater. He'd never heard of such a thing. And for good reason, too. For one of the most devastating solo operatives in black-ops history, he knew surprisingly little about the inner workings of the clandestine secret world. There were entire divisions tucked out of sight, shielded from prying eyes for legal and moral reasons. Men and women who had to go into bad places to do bad things for the greater good.

No judge, no jury.

Just a sea of executioners.

So it didn't surprise him when she mentioned an alternative program. In fact, it was the last thing on his mind. He was connecting other dots, formulating dark theories, hoping none of it was true.

'You were twelve,' Slater said.

'Yes. I'm not anymore, though. If that's what you're worried about.'

'Trust me, I'm aware of that.'

She gyrated underneath him, her hips moving faster. 'God, this is good.'

'Where are you from?'

'New York. Originally.'

'Originally?'

'Like I told you — I only lived at home until I was twelve.'

'And then?'

'I ran away. That part of my life is a blur. I try not to think about it. I hated my family. Hated them down to the core.'

'Most twelve-year-olds do.'

'Not like me.'

'Were they abusive?'

'No,' she said, almost offended. 'Not at all. We were just ... different.'

'Different how?'

'Do you care about my childhood, or do you care about Russell Williams? Pick one. I can't tell you my life story.'

'We could just talk for as long as this lasts.'

'That might be hours.'

'Then I deserve the story.'

She shrugged. Pulled him closer. Pressed her lips to his. 'Suits me.'

'Different how?' he repeated.

'Dad was ex-military. Strict as hell. Looking back on it I can see he meant well. We lived in Brooklyn. We had a good life. But he never took no for an answer. And neither did I. So we fought and fought and fought and eventually we were doing nothing other than fighting, eating, and sleeping. So I took off. Hated school, hated my friends, hated my sister. She bullied me, too. Figured I'd leave it all behind.'

'Do you regret it?'

'Somewhat, at the start. Not anymore. It made me what I am today.'

'And what exactly are you today?'

'You're probing deep.'

He raised an eyebrow.

And smirked.

She saw it in the gloom, and gave him a condescending frown. 'What are you, a teenager?'

'I didn't say anything.'

'Don't start.'

'Answer my question.'

'Now ... I'm an operative.'

'That's what they call you?'

'Are they not supposed to?'

'That's what they call me too.'

'What were you?'

'All kinds of things,' Slater said, and for a moment the memories emblazoned their trauma at the forefront of his mind. He pushed them away. 'Black Force was pioneered by a man named Lars Crawford.'

'*Was?*'

'I don't believe it exists anymore. At least not the way it was. By the end of his tenure, Lars was ... let's just say psychologically unstable. It's an unforgiving field.'

'What happened?'

'That's quite the tale.'

'We've got time.'

'Not that much time. That'd take days.'

'I can hang around. You're pretty good.'

'At talking, or...?'

'Both.'

'I don't have that much time,' Slater said.

'Got somewhere to be?'

'Probably. If my hunch is confirmed.'

'What's your hunch?'

'Tell me about the Lynx program.'

'First, what's Black Force?'

He sighed. 'A division of solo operatives. Lone wolves. Lars had a mountain of research on reaction speed and reflex capacity in the field and brought it to the Pentagon. They gave him the go ahead to start a new division. Off the books. Black funds straight from the Treasury. Basically, when Special Forces soldiers find themselves in a bad situation they have to rely on their instincts. If they test off the charts in reaction speed, they almost always win. Lars wanted to take these soldiers and hone them into something more. It was seen as taboo to send operatives out alone, until Black Force. He practically pioneered the concept of a one-man-army in something other than fiction.'

'How long did you work for them?'

'Nearly ten years.'

'And you survived? The whole time?'

'Like I said, I react fast.'

'And that makes you invincible?'

'Not quite.'

'It must be a damn good advantage. If you're still standing here. How many operations were you sent on?'

'Over a hundred.'

'How many people have you killed?'

'I lost count the first year.'

'You have bad dreams?'

'You don't know the half of it.'

'I'm starting to.'

'The Lynx program. What is it?'

'Black operations. Off the books. Funds straight from the Treasury. Same as you. But very, very different.'

'How so?'

'Were there any women in Black Force?'

'Not that I knew of. But I only ever met one other operative. There might have been.'

'Is this other operative still around?'

Slater paused. 'Not anymore.'

'How'd he die?'

'He's not dead. He's just … not around.'

She didn't push it. 'Lynx is all-female.'

'When you started, you said you were—'

'Twelve?'

'Yeah.'

'Most of us are. When we start. Some are younger.'

Fuck, Slater thought.

The perfect storm.

Where are you, Shien?

46

'Y'ou're sent out into the field at that age?' he said.

'Christ, no. But we're trained. The kind of training you can only get during youth. The kind that hardwires it into your brain. All I've ever known is espionage, stealth, combat, murder.'

'You like it?'

'I'm doing good work. It's the hardest job in the world, but the most satisfying. I'm doing alright.'

'Can you walk away?'

'I've never thought about it.'

'Why not?'

'What else would I do?'

'You ever thought about the fact that you don't know what a normal life is?'

'That's rich, coming from someone like you.'

'I walked into a recruitment office when I was of age. I was kicked from unit to unit until they finally made me the offer. I was over eighteen. They had my official consent. Your situation is—'

She shut him up with a kiss. 'I think you've had enough

experience to know that the secret world doesn't usually concern itself with anything black-and-white. We're in the grey zone, honey. Yeah, I've thought about it. I've been thinking about it for years. And I'm happy.'

'But if you don't know whether you can walk away...'

'Could you walk away? When you were employed?'

'I never asked. When I got fed up with it, I just disappeared.'

'You think I can't do that?'

He recalled her face in the clearing, as distraught as anyone he'd ever seen, tears pouring out of her eyes and pure terror contorting her features.

Then it had all vanished.

In the blink of an eye.

'I think you can,' he said. 'Whenever you want.'

'Good. Then it's settled.'

'Your training hasn't been the same as mine,' he said. 'I've never seen anyone put on a performance like what you did.'

'Honey, that was nothing. You should see me at my best.'

'You get acting training?'

'Years of it. Relentlessly. We all do in Lynx.'

'Why?'

'You ever seen a lynx?'

'Pictures. Nature documentaries. Not in the flesh.'

'They're stunning. Flawless. Beautiful and graceful and feminine. And then they snap, and their prey doesn't even know what the fuck hit them until it's far, far too late.'

'That's you?'

'That's us.'

Slater stared at the outline of her face in the gloom. He couldn't help but admit she was beautiful. She had the high cheekbones and pronounced jawline of an international model.

'Is that a criteria?' he said.

'We usually function for very specific purposes. We need to look good.'

'Dictators?' Slater said. 'Gangsters and bent billionaires and the shadow elite?'

She nodded. 'You're getting it.'

'The guys who throw cash at models like window dressing for their mega yachts? The models that are probably onboard when atrocities are being discussed? When slave trafficking and drug dealing and prostitution rings are being openly talked about? Because who's listening? Besides you.'

She nodded again. 'You got it.'

'That'd be efficient.'

'We go places no-one is allowed. We hear things no-one is supposed to hear. We look good and act drunk and act high and act oblivious. And then Command dissects what we overheard and we make the move. I've only been operational for three years and I've lost count of the human filth I've killed.'

'How do you get away with it?'

'Planning. Good preparation. And then most of the time it all goes to shit and I need to remove every witness anyway. And I never feel bad about it. Because everyone on those boats and in those villas and at those private parties knows what's going on. They know how their masters got their billions. They don't care.'

'How long has the program been running?'

'For years before I got there. And I imagine it'll continue long after I'm gone.'

'Williams has been running it the whole time?'

'It's his project. He dreamed it up like your guy dreamed up Black Force.'

'It's effective?'

'It's one of the most powerful programs in the United States government. I've been told that many times. I'm their best agent.'

'How many are there?'

'I don't know. Same deal as what you got. It's all kept very hush-hush.'

'You know the people you're killing are bad people?'

'The worst. Human scum. The things I've heard...'

'Do you have dreams?'

'Like I said, they're starting.'

'They'll get worse.'

'You get them?'

'It's an inevitable byproduct of the business.'

'I suppose you want to know what I was doing out here.'

Slater paused. 'There's too much on my mind. I hadn't even thought about it.'

'So you want the answer?'

'Keep it short. I have a few more questions.'

'Santiago Porras Zamora got some bad habits. The cartels are entrenched so deep in society and infrastructure out here that it's almost impossible for the government to go up against them. But this guy in particular just didn't know when to quit. He took five American girls in the last four months. Made a pattern out of it. We noticed, so they sent me into the hotspots to look good and play the role of the dumb bitch and wait to get abducted.'

'It worked?'

'They took me three days in.'

'They could have killed you long before you had the chance to retaliate.'

'Not immediately. That would be pointless. I knew they'd draw it out. Especially if I acted terrified. They like that. They seem to get off on it. I knew I only needed a narrow window and I took it when you showed up.'

'Now that's a coincidence.'

'A happy coincidence.'

'Don't know if I'd call it that.'

'I'm having a good time right now. That's all that matters, really, isn't it?'

'You've sure got your priorities sorted.'

'I know what I want from life.'

They settled into a steady rhythm, silent, both wrapped up in their own thoughts. They each had a lot to process. They let the physicality take over and descended into pleasure.

When it was over, the crack of dawn filtered through the curtains outside. They lay side by side, not shy about it, completely at ease with each other's presence. Slater sensed something in the atmosphere he hadn't felt in quite some time.

Camaraderie.

It wasn't just physical. It wasn't just sexual attraction. There was some undercurrent of connection between the two of them at a deeper level. Two people who knew what it was like to murder so freely, to put a blunt instrument through someone's head and strip them of everything that made them human. Who knew what it was like to watch that light go out, over and over and over again, and come away satisfied with what they'd done.

He lay there, thought about it for a couple of minutes, and then the fatigue overwhelmed him and he fell straight asleep.

47

W hen he came back, crawling out of the confusion that comes in the aftermath of a deep and undisturbed sleep, it took him some time to realise what had woken him up.

Ruby was dressed, wearing a simple floral shirt tucked into faded denim jeans that hung off her frame just right. She looked good. Better than good. Slater eyed her up and down, rubbed his eyes, cleared his head, and swung off the bed. Still naked.

He said, 'Where'd you get clothes from?'

'I went downstairs in the robe and convinced the receptionist to run and get supplies. He was more than happy to help.'

'I'm sure he was.'

'I got some for you, too.'

'You did?'

'Right here.'

She fetched a small bundle of neatly folded garments off the polished wooden table by the door and tossed them to him. Underwear, a short-sleeved tee — size XL — and faded denim jeans of his own. He pulled them on. They fit perfectly, the arms tight around his biceps, the abdominal region loose, the jeans snug on his bulky leg muscles. He stretched and moved around the hotel room for a minute or two, getting used to the fit, and then nodded his satisfaction.

'Perfect,' he said.

'Where did you put your belongings?'

'Sorry?'

'Your stuff. Are they keeping it downstairs for you?'

Slater pointed to the phone, wallet, and passport he'd fished out of his pockets the night before. He'd already tossed his keys in the trash. They served no purpose anymore. 'That's my stuff.'

'Nothing else?'

'Am I supposed to have anything else?'

'If you're travelling around Colombia, it's usually advisable to bring a suitcase. I guess this clothing incident has happened a few times, then? How do you change your clothes?'

'Like everyone else does. I have a wardrobe. Well, *had*.'

She paused. 'You live out here?'

'I did. Had a compound on the banks of a river. Right near that encampment you were taken to. Then the same cartel stormed the place because I pissed them off. I'll never be able to go back there. It won't be safe. And I've got bigger things on my mind than constantly feuding with the cartels for the rest of my existence.'

'Such as?'

'I met a girl,' Slater said, ruminating, trying to pick his words carefully, unsure how to put it.

'Am I supposed to be jealous?' Ruby said.

'She's nine years old. I saved her from a horrifying situation. I was in Macau. Eight or nine months ago. I stuck my nose where I shouldn't have. As I usually do. And I pulled her out of that filth and ... I guess I formed a connection with her. Maybe in another life I could have been her father.'

'Where was her own father?'

'Not around.'

'What happened to her?'

Slater paused again. Now deep in thought. Now wrenched back and forth with the possibility of what was to come. Because if he went through with it there would be no going back.

Not for a long time, at least.

He would have to do things that could be considered unconstitutional. Of course, most of his career fit in that category, but that had all been with the direct approval of the United States government. Under the table, of course. Now he would be going deep into that same labyrinth to save someone that meant everything to him. For the second time.

'Come back to bed,' he said. 'I need to talk to you about ... a lot.'

She shook her head. 'I was just leaving.'

He froze. 'What?'

'I can't stay. They think I'm still in the jungle, and I have to say this was a pleasant release from all the usual tension, but I need to go back stateside.'

'Let me come with you.'

'Not a chance. I've connected the dots. I see where this is headed. You're on your own.'

'Ruby...'

'I'm not some damsel in distress who's going to stay with you for no reason. I've got no reason to be here. I need to go.'

'I'm not going to force you to do anything.'

'Did I suggest you were going to?' she said, a spark in her eyes. The amber glowing hot. 'Besides, if you tried anything, I'd cut your throat.'

'You could try.'

'Let's not go down that path.'

He nodded. 'Suits me.'

'Then this is goodbye.'

'Wait.'

'I'm not helping you with this. Not a chance. In fact I should try and kill you right here. Because I know what you're going to do.'

'You don't even—'

'The answer is — I don't know.'

'What?'

'I'm a few steps ahead. You gave this little girl to Russell Williams. You thought he was the one point of normalcy in your life. You trusted him to find her a home and make sure she had a normal life because all you do is attract trouble and now you're worried he put her straight in the Lynx program. Because no-one would ever know otherwise. You gave him free reign to do what he wanted with her and you're just starting to realise you don't know him well enough to trust him.'

'Yeah.'

'And the answer is — I don't know. I don't know if she's in the program. I don't visit the facility anymore. I aged out of it. I'm operational now.'

'Is there any way you can—?'

'You know what I'm going to say.'

'I shouldn't bother asking?'

'I shouldn't even be talking to you right now. But you seem like you've got your head screwed on straight and I'm feeling generous after last night...'

'What time is it, by the way?'

'Almost midday.'

He nodded. 'That's enough sleep.'

'Yeah, well, I shouldn't saying a fucking thing. Because if it turns out she's in the program you'll probably raise hell to get her out of it. And I happen to hold that program dear to me. It forged me into what I am. Now I take no shit, I kill whoever I think is scum, and I love my life. And I'm not about to jeopardise the government's chance for other girls to do the same.'

In his head, Slater thought, *You're kids. You're all kids. It doesn't matter if it's girls or boys. You're raised not to know any better. I'm all for black operations but you have to choose to ingratiate yourself in this mad world when you've got a developed brain. If Shien's in this program, I'll tear the world apart to get her out of it. If she wants to be an operative when she turns eighteen, she can do it. But she's nine fucking years old. She doesn't know what's right and what's wrong. How dare you be complicit in your handler brainwashing her to be a hardened killer? You're brainwashed yourself.*

Out loud, he said, 'You're right. I'm sorry.'

Because, as much as he didn't want to admit it, he needed every scrap of information he could get before he set off. And he wouldn't get there by acting hostile. He estimated the gap between Ruby and the hotel door and contemplated doing it by force. She was a trained assassin, but there were no weapons in the room, and he outweighed her by fifty pounds. He powerlifted regularly, with a deadlift maximum a shade over six hundred pounds.

He could pin her down with ease.

He could get the information out of her, by any means necessary.

And then what? She would feed him bullshit under

duress, just as everyone did. He would accomplish nothing. She would probably send him to Slovenia in pursuit of a hidden facility he knew nothing about. She had him.

And she noticed him plotting.

A semi-automatic pistol appeared in her hands, practically out of thin air. She'd drawn it from the back of her waistband, but the Heckler & Koch SFP9 stared him right in the face with such speed that for a moment he reconsidered whether she was human or not. He looked down the barrel, contemplating whether he would even register the sight of the gun firing before the bullet blew his brain to shreds.

She said, 'Don't try a fucking thing.'

'Calm down,' he said, still seated on the edge of the bed.

'Don't tell me to calm down, you piece of shit. I can read you like a book.'

'Can you?'

'You need what's in my head. You're highly trained and highly motivated. I'm the only thing between you and this little girl. That'll twist your perception of things. You might think it's the right move to try and take me hostage. I'd advise you that's a terrible move, but you probably know that.'

'I'm not armed,' Slater said.

'It'd be dumb if you weren't.'

'Then I'm dumb. How'd you get that in here?'

'I've got an equipment stash in Quibdó. I went out to get it. When you were asleep. I assume you did the same while I was gone.'

'I slept.'

'Then you really are an idiot.'

'I told you. I'm retired. I don't do this shit anymore.'

'You should still have a vested interest in staying alive.'

'I do. I had the option. I chose not to take that avenue.'

'Then what is it?'

'I trust you.'

He stared at the gaping maw of death in the form of the SFP9. Not concerned. He'd looked down enough gun barrels for it to barely faze him anymore. He looked past it, to the woman holding the weapon. Her finger on the trigger. Ready to shoot without a moment's hesitation. Just like he would be, in her position. Cold and remorseless when the job required it.

She said, 'You shouldn't.'

'But I do.'

'You don't know anything about me.'

'I know enough.'

She lowered the gun.

48

'Five minutes,' she said. 'That's all I'll give you.'

'And I know my boundaries. I know you hold the Lynx program close to your chest. I know you don't want anyone to disrupt it. But right now there's a nine-year-old girl who might be in it, who didn't get there on her own. It's my fault she's in it, if she is. I handed her to the man who runs it.'

'Williams is a good man.'

'And sometimes good men do bad things for what they think are the right reasons.'

She paused. Breaking it down. Running it through her head. Weighing it up.

Paying it consideration that belied her age.

She was twenty-two going on fifty. Intellectually, at least. A smart strong girl who took no shit from anyone. And right now Slater was beyond vulnerable. His life was in her hands. All the standard precautions had run through his mind the moment he'd met her. He'd disregarded them. He figured in this case, it was better to sacrifice control.

He hoped like hell the gambit would pay off.

Because he was telling the truth.

There was no backup plan.

She said, 'I'm not giving you anything to do with the program. Or Williams. I assume you have no way of contacting him.'

'I just need to talk to him. Please.'

'No. He's like my real father. You understand? You'll never get that out of me.'

'Then tell me more about your biological father.'

'Why?'

Slater shrugged. 'I'm not going to get through to you. I can tell that already. Not a chance. Your mind's bulletproof. But you said I had five minutes. So humour me. You interest me. I want to know more about what makes you tick. Your background. Why it all went the way it did. Your dad. Who is he?'

'I should be gone.'

'Five minutes. You promised. I'm unarmed. You owe me that much.'

'Frank.'

'That's his name?'

'Frank Nazarian, if you want to be anal about it.'

'I didn't need the full name.'

'That's what I call him. His full name. Cause he's not my dad. He's just a guy that did a terrible job raising me.'

'Nazarian.' Slater rolled the surname over his tongue.

Ruby said, 'I'm Armenian.'

'I like it.'

'I don't like him. Why do you want to know about him?'

'You said five minutes. You didn't put a restriction on what I could ask. Apart from the Lynx program.'

'Fair enough.'

'What was so bad about him?'

'The typical ex-military type. Strict. Regimented. Took no shit. Didn't understand how to be a parent. And I was moody and hormonal and mad at life in general. Not a great mix.'

'You said he wasn't abusive.'

'No. Of course not.'

'I just fail to see...'

'I made a mistake, okay?' Ruby snapped. 'I shouldn't have left. I should have recognised what I had — a nice life in a nice suburb with a decent family, all things considered. But things got blown way out of proportion, as they always do when you're a teenager, and I ran away. Williams was my dad's old military buddy. Frank retired, and Williams kept climbing his way up through the ranks. I ran to him for counsel and he seemed to take my grievances seriously. I don't think he ever liked my dad all that much, either. Didn't think he was fit to be a parent. Williams said there was a retreat I could go to for a while, in...'

She cut herself off abruptly.

Slater raised an eyebrow.

'You almost got me,' she said, managing a wry smile. 'He said there was a retreat. I could stay a while. See how I liked it. Then I ended up liking it a lot, so I committed to the program. Signed myself up for life. What else was I going to do?'

'You *really* think you had a choice?' Slater said.

He didn't care about offending her now. He knew it was the most he would get out of her.

'Of course,' she said. 'I was old enough to make my own decisions.'

'Right. What about your dad?'

'He knows I'm alive. I get in touch every now and then. Let him know I'm doing well.'

'Does he know about—?'

'Of course not,' she snapped.

'Does he still talk to Williams?'

'Of course not.'

Falling on desperation, he said, 'Ruby, I'm going to need more than this.'

'No.'

'This little girl means more to me than you realise.'

'I realise. But that puts the program in danger, and I just won't do it.'

You're a twenty-two year old brainwashed minion, Slater thought.

He said, 'Okay.'

She cocked her head. 'That's it?'

'That's it.'

'Is this the part where I turn to leave and you try to tackle me into the doorframe?'

'No.'

'That's what I'd do, if I were you.'

'I'm not going to try anything.'

'There isn't much space between us. You could probably make it in time. You're fast enough. I saw you in the jungle. And you're powerful. You could probably take me right through the wall. Use me as a battering ram. Break a few of my bones along the way. Fuck me up real bad. Then I'd have to answer your questions. I'm sure you know "enhanced interrogation techniques." Everyone breaks after a while. I just want you to know that I know you're thinking about it. So please don't try it. Because I don't want to shoot you.'

'I'm not moving,' he said.

She lowered the gun. 'You're really telling the truth, aren't you?'

'As much as it might surprise you, I don't want to hurt you.'

'You think you could?'

'I'm not going down that line of conversation.'

'You probably could,' she admitted. 'If you set your mind to it. You've probably got ten years of experience on me.'

'I'm not moving,' he repeated. 'You're high on adrenalin. You're overthinking everything. Just leave.'

'Don't come after me.'

'I won't.'

'I'm sorry about this little girl. I hope she's in a foster home. But even if she's in the program, it might not be such a bad thing. Hell of a lot better than some of the homes I've heard of. She might go on to do great things.'

'Thanks for the input. Please leave.'

She paused. She hadn't been anticipating this kind of compliance. The gun quivered in her palm. She was more than ready to use it. She must have spent most of the morning talking herself into a sociopathic state, detaching her emotions as best she could. Firmly prepared to kill the only man who had everything in common with her. That took a unique subset of skills rarely found in the general population.

An emotionless assassin, struggling with her career choice.

And now she'd spent all that time postulating how she would put a bullet in him when he lunged at her. It wasn't happening. An anticlimax in every sense of the word.

She nodded, still unsure. 'I hope your retirement goes well.'

'I'm doing fine.'

'Okay.'

'Thanks for the evening.'

A half-smile crossed her lips. She blew him a kiss.

Then she disappeared through the open door.

49

H e didn't give chase.

What was the point?

He already had everything he needed.

He sat, and he thought long and hard about the direction his life was about to take. He considered the goodwill Russell Williams had shown in Macau, making the effort to seek him out and let him know the United States government was no longer interested in pursuing him for supposed crimes against his country.

He and his colleague Jason King had been cleared of all wrongdoing. No-one was hunting him. He no longer had to check over his shoulder every five seconds. He could get off the bed and resume something that constituted a normal life. He had four hundred million dollars in discrete funds and no responsibility whatsoever.

And by all accounts Williams was a good man. He'd acted quickly and decisively in Yemen to foil a biological terror plot, and Slater's judgment had told him to trust the man. With little alternatives in sight and the underlying knowledge that she couldn't stay with him, Slater had handed Shien over with the understanding she would be looked after.

But he remembered what he'd said to Ruby.

Sometimes good men do bad things for what they think are the right reasons.

Maybe Williams thought he was taking care of her. Training her for years, raising her in a secret government program, honing her mind and body to retaliate violently against anyone who wronged her. Maybe he thought that would shape her into a strong, powerful woman. Like it had for Ruby.

Maybe he thought, even if Slater found out about the Lynx program, he wouldn't find anything morally reprehensible about it at all.

Maybe he thought Slater would be happy for Shien.

It all made too much sense.

So Slater got off the bed. He waited a few minutes in silence to compensate for Ruby's paranoia. He knew she might loiter in the lobby or in the shadows of a nearby alleyway, her brain still convincing her the world was against her. He'd occupied a similar mindset earlier in his career. Back when everything was new and terrifying and overwhelming from a sensory standpoint.

Now, nothing meant anything.

The last night of his life — before the pleasant hedonistic detour — had been a horror show. At least from an objective standpoint. The jungle, the pain, the closeness to death, the wild array of sensations. But he'd already almost forgotten it.

That's what your life is.

He gave it enough time to make sure he wouldn't run into her and then left the room, tucking his phone, wallet, and passport into his pockets on his way out. He closed the door behind him and rode the elevator down to the lobby, deep in thought all the way to the ground floor. There were a couple of civilians in the cable car with him — tourists, by the look of it — but he barely paid them any attention. He briefly considered his lack of situational awareness, so he flashed a glance at them to make sure neither were planted by one of his numerous enemies to slit his throat on the way to the lobby. They both returned his stare, equally disinterested.

He faced forward, and went back to introspection.

He knew he would never see Ruby again. She would vanish into the labyrinth of the government underworld, a space so vast he knew he would never get to the bottom of it if he tried. Thankfully he'd never had issue with the secrecy during the time he was employed, but if he'd ever become stubborn about the lack of information they fed him he probably would have been locked in a room and provided with complimentary enhanced interrogation techniques until he became compliant again.

So he would never know how deep the rabbit hole went, and Ruby was just a single cog in a vastly larger machine. He gave up ever finding out more about her. She was a whirlwind, and it was best for both of them if they never crossed paths again.

But now he had a choice to make.

He had no way of contacting Russell Williams, who was practically a ghost. Black Force no longer existed, with that particular division disintegrating into parts swallowed up by the murky secret world. Positions would have changed, certain key staff would have remained behind, and all record of its existence would have been destroyed.

So that avenue was a dead end.

And he had no idea about the rest of it.

Which left him in a uniquely difficult position. He had certain skills and experiences imprinted on his brain, taught over a decade of involvement with state-of-the-art government training facilities, but they'd all been mobile outfits. They'd never surrounded him with tangible physical locations. Such was the nature of a Black Force operative. He'd been destined to do that forever until fate intervened when he'd been sent after Jason King in Corsica.

So that was that. No way to get in touch with his old superiors. He didn't even know who they were. Lars Crawford had handled the bulk of his operational career, and King had killed the man in Australia. All ties were severed. For good reason.

And now he needed to jump straight back in with both feet if he wanted to follow this to its conclusion.

He couldn't make the same call he'd made in Yemen. He was persona non grata to the U.S. government. They would shut him down faster than he could say his name. He no longer belonged to that outfit. His past mistakes were forgiven, and all knowledge of his existence had been eradicated.

An outcast in every sense of the word.

The elevator doors whispered open and he made his way over to a new worker manning the reception desk. He checked out of his room, thanked the middle-aged woman for his stay, and headed for the street, moving fast.

There was no sign of Ruby.

True to her word, she was gone.

He didn't quite know how to feel about it.

Who she was, and the division that had shaped her into what she was, occupied a complex moral grey zone he had no intention of diving into just yet. Whether the program was justified by the greater good was none of his concern.

He'd ducked out of the secret world for a reason. It posed these problems daily. He couldn't destabilise the entire government underworld on his own.

But he could rescue one little girl from its tendrils.

One girl he'd promised a bright future to.

One girl who had to make her own choices about where she wanted her life to go.

But he needed somewhere to start. If he stepped back and analysed the big picture it would overwhelm him.

First things first.

Find a way to reach Williams.

He pulled out his phone, navigated to an app, and booked a series of civilian flights that dumped him in the location he deemed prudent to start.

New York City.

50

Q uibdó to Medellin.

Medellin to New York.

After a lengthy wait at El Caraño and an extended layover in Medellin, he finally touched down on home soil on a dreary and grey morning at 8:05am local time. The plane rattled and shook in the turbulence when it bounced down onto one of John F. Kennedy International Airport's many runways. Slater opened his eyes when he sensed wheels on tarmac and tuned out the noise of a small child screaming three rows behind him.

He'd been retired for nearly a year now, but he still wasn't used to normality. The commercial flight was populated by the usual mix of solo travellers, businessmen, families, backpackers, and tourists from abroad. They all fussed over their plastic trays and complained about plane food and stressed over whether they'd be the first to get their luggage from the overhead compartments when the seatbelt signs flickered off. Even before the plane taxied to a halt, Slater sensed unrest in the cabin. Passengers were ready to burst out of their seats. There would be no holding back when the floodgates opened.

He sat completely still, his mind serene, at ease. One thing his violent past had taught him was perspective, and he considered it the most important concept in forging what he was today. Have one near-death experience and you realise almost nothing in life matters as much as you think.

Do it a couple of times, and your whole world tilts on its axis. What you considered important problems reveal themselves as the slight grievances they actually are.

Make a career out of it, and you end up almost monastic, calm and zen-like in every situation that doesn't involve fighting desperately and barbarically for your life.

Slater couldn't care less about when the plane reached the terminal. He closed his eyes and dipped back into rest. He'd planned the sequence of events as soon as Ruby left the hotel room in Quibdó, flying through the information available to him and dispensing with anything that wasn't absolutely necessary. Then there was nothing left to think about, so he took the time to detach from the world.

Years ago, he'd worked out the secret to keeping most of his traumatic memories at bay was deep and concentrated meditation. Sounds simple enough, but the first time he'd dispensed with every stray thought and focused entirely on the present moment, it had alleviated him of most of the stress and anxiety from past near-death encounters in an instant. Shocked, unnerved, he'd pressed on and made a habit out of it.

He had recent horrors in his mind, but he'd tamed them, subdued them, and now he was free.

His retirement had involved barbaric wars in Yemen, Macau, and Russia respectively. All extreme regions in every sense. Nothing commonplace. From one extreme to the next. Poverty in Yemen. Luxury in Macau. And desolation in the Russian Far East.

So an ordinary civilian flight landing in New York felt surreal. He'd never been one to blend in. He wasn't wired that way. The brain resting between his ears had been beaten and battered over years of hardship, and now sitting in a normal setting surrounded by normal people wasn't something he was accustomed to. He waited until the plane emptied, then walked down the deserted aisles. No luggage to collect from the baggage carousel, no carry-on to cart behind him.

Just the clothes on his back and the passport in his pocket.

But he didn't need anything else. Not in this day and age. Not with a phone, and a credit card set up in anonymity in Zurich. He navigated through the throngs of foot traffic, found a car rental service, booked a luxury sedan for a hefty fee that didn't matter in the slightest, and drove the Mercedes-Benz S-Class Coupé out of the airport's jurisdiction with the radio off and the smell of plush leather in the air.

He sat quietly in the driver's seat, calloused hands on the wheel, feeling the purr of German engineering under the hood. There was bumper to bumper traffic, but it barely fazed him. He waited it out and was rewarded with a smooth ride along North Conduit Avenue, heading fast for Brooklyn. He connected his phone to the car's audio system via Bluetooth and spoke into it, using voice command to dial a number he knew off by heart.

He knew of the stereotype — the ancient military veteran detached from technology — but it couldn't have been further from the truth.

He knew how to adapt to the times.

He was a man of supreme efficiency.

His earlier woes about being excommunicated from the secret government underworld didn't apply to ordinary administrative enquiries. He knew who to call to get what he wanted, and sometimes that involved slight breaches of privacy. Nothing the government wasn't accustomed to.

'Slater,' he said, as soon as the expensive speakers on either side of him indicated the call was connected.

'Confirm that,' a pleasant female voice said.

He rattled off a list of identification numbers provided to him at the very start of his career. He heard the woman tapping away at a keyboard. Probably trawling a database. She wouldn't find much. It would all be blacked out, and for good reason. But she'd understand his clearance level. She'd give him what he needed, as long as it wasn't too outrageous.

'Will Slater?'

'Yeah,' he said.

'We shouldn't be talking to you.'

'I thought I was cleared of wrongdoing.'

'You were put back in the database. That doesn't mean I should be helping you. Rumour is you're on shaky ground with us. And you've severed your ties with the upper echelon.'

'Yeah, well, shit happens. I don't need much.'

'Maybe I don't want to give you shit.'

There was a certain hostility in her voice he wasn't anticipating. Not on a professional level, either. And he thought he recognised the inflection, from years earlier. It reminded him of a drunken night in Washington.

'Enya?' he said.

'You're a real piece of shit, you know that?'

'Surely you're not still bitter about that.'

'I was young and dumb and drunk, but I still told you

how I felt. And you just disappeared. Never heard from you again until right now.'

'You still working for the same place?'

'Obviously. I know Black Force didn't give you much of a leash. But you were allowed to meet agents from surface-level divisions. Like intelligence gathering. Isn't that what you told me? I just remember being impressed at the time.'

'You knew about what I did, so you knew about why I disappeared. That was my life.'

'I'm not some dumb bitch who fell in love with you.'

'I know that. It was one night.'

'I just wanted an explanation.'

'I know. I'm sorry. I'm sure you can imagine the head-space I was in. If I remember correctly I told you quite a lot.'

'You over-shared, probably. Given your division's level of classification.'

'You knew about what we were. That was clearance enough. And I needed someone to talk to.'

'I thought you were opening up to me.'

'I did.'

'And then you left.'

'Sorry. I was fucked up back then.'

'Did you keep working for them?'

'For eight years.'

'So you're probably even more fucked up now?'

Slater paused. 'Depends how you look at it.'

'You did good work?'

'One of the best. Or so I'm told. I'm never one to brag.'

'Yeah, right…'

'Look, I need help.'

'So you're telling me you're out of the game and still expecting me to help you?'

'I need an address.'

'What — that's it?'

'He's ex-military, and he knew a guy named Russell Williams, so he's probably at enough of a classification level to have his personal details obscured in any of your standard search directories. That's why I'm coming to you.'

'Why should I help you?'

'Remember when I told you everything on that night? About my career, and the things I was doing in the service of Uncle Sam.'

'Yes. Vividly.'

'Even though it was a long time ago?'

'It stuck with me. I remember thinking I could never skirt death over and over again and make an occupation out of it. I thought you were insane. In a good way.'

'Okay, good. Think about that, and then think about whether I'd lie to you right now. I'm trying to help someone in need. I need the address for my own reasons. I don't want to share them with you because you'll be forced to tell your boss and it'll go all the way up the chain of command, and then it'll be game over.'

'What the hell are you talking about?'

'Just think about it. Am I a bad person?'

'You're a dick.'

'Am I a bad person?'

'No.'

'Frank Nazarian.'

'That's the name? Spell it for me.'

'F,' he said.

'I know how to spell Frank.'

'Oh, right.' He was distracted. Too busy thinking about a night almost nine years ago. He still remembered it too. He spelled out the last name, letter by letter. Then he said,

'Sorry, Enya. For walking out on you without an explanation. I mean it.'

'You doing okay, Will?' she said.

'Been better.'

'Why?'

'Trying to help a friend.'

'Lady friend?'

'Yeah, but not like that.'

'I'm sure.'

'She's nine.'

A pause. 'What have you got yourself into?'

'Trust me, you don't want to know.'

'It's our government that's doing this?'

'Maybe. I don't know anything for sure. That's what I'm trying to find out.'

She gave him the address.

51

It was nothing exciting. At least, as far as his relative experience was concerned. A quiet residential suburb on the outskirts of Brooklyn. Wide yards, old houses, old money. Plenty of room for kids to run around.

Ruby had called it a decent suburb, and she hadn't been lying.

Slater could imagine himself growing up here. Maybe that would have provided him with some semblance of an ordinary childhood. His reality had been far different from that. But he had enough experience to know it was usually the nicest looking homes that were the most broken. He could understand how a hard ex-military man might clash with his daughter on a frequent basis. No abuse, like she'd said, but enough constant conflict to breed resentment.

And if there was one thing about ex-military, it was that they didn't quit.

Maybe just an ordinary troubled childhood exacerbated by two different personality types. Arguments form habits, which form the entirety of daily life. They probably hated each other by the time she left.

Slater wondered how Frank Nazarian felt about it all now.

Maybe that was why he'd come here. If pressed, he wouldn't have been able to come up with a reason. Not one that made sense. But in discussion with Ruby, he'd sensed aspects of her father that mirrored Slater's own behaviour. He wanted to know more about the man who raised a government killer. One of the best on the planet, unless she'd been lying about that, but Slater didn't think so.

It wasn't something you boasted about unless you were supremely confident of the truth.

And he figured New York was the place to start on the quest to contact Williams. He probably wouldn't find it through Nazarian if Ruby had been telling the truth. It seemed like the pair had been out of contact for years, if not a decade. Nazarian likely didn't know it was Williams who took her daughter into the shadowy government under-world and never brought her back.

But it was as good a place to start as any.

And he figured he could find out more about the man who might have put a nine-year-old girl into a school for assassins.

From an old colleague.

Slater found the house he was looking for. One-storey, neat, squared away from the rest of the street. Nothing special about it, but a good home. A perfectly maintained lawn — the grass was cut short and radiated in colour. A bright, brilliant green. No doubt the handiwork of Nazarian. Ex-military. Meticulous in his neatness.

Old habits die hard.

The S-Class Coupé whispered to a halt on the other side of the avenue, and Slater killed the engine. He sat there with his hands on his thighs, back straight, staring at the dwelling. Unsure if he should follow through with it or not. He might be disrupting the equilibrium. A strange violent nomad wandering into a place he didn't belong. In all likelihood there was nothing for him here.

In fact, he was almost certain.

But he was ex-military of a different kind. He had habits that wouldn't go away quickly.

He saw everything through to its conclusion.

So he got out of the car. Tucked all his possessions in this world into his pockets and strolled across the smooth road and mounted the sidewalk and stepped through a gate in a white picket fence and made his way onto the porch and stopped in front of a thin screen door.

Ordinary civilisation.

Quintessentially American.

He felt like a distant stranger to this world. But he reached up and knocked on the door all the same. Three firm raps on the wire. The screen rattled in place. There was a doorbell, but Slater was old school in that regard. He stepped back and put his hands behind his back and waited.

Nazarian probably wasn't home. Slater figured he'd get the wife, or maybe one of Ruby's sisters. Maybe they would be able to help. Maybe not. He'd approached this in a cerebral manner. He hadn't prepared a speech. He hadn't chosen the words that would best suit the situation. Maybe he should have. This was important. This was information about a long-lost daughter.

A man opened the door. He was pushing fifty but still had all his hair, without a fleck of grey in it. Probably dyed. The jet black locks were pushed back off his forehead and held in place by some kind of subtle product. A good look, objectively. He was a handsome man with sharp features and slate blue eyes. Striking, was the first thing Slater thought. No wonder Ruby looked the way she did.

The guy said, 'Can I help you?'

Warily.

He probably sensed a threat. Slater was an imposing figure to anyone, and he was coming off months in the Colombian jungle. His face sported a couple of small welts from the cartel skirmish. The man stiffened, ready for a fight if it came to that. No hesitation.

Slater said, 'I've got information about your daughter. Can I come in?'

52

W hatever Frank Nazarian did, he did it well, and he was compensated for his skills.

Slater was no interior designer — hence the haphazard nature of his compound in Colombia, where he'd elected to import the most expensive furniture he could find and slap it all together in a grotesque amalgamation of luxury. Nazarian had a reasonable budget, especially given the squared-away nature of the house's exterior, but on top of that he had tact.

He came off as a man with obsessive compulsive tendencies.

As he ushered Slater into a comfortable entranceway, he paused to adjust an elegant vase on the hall table. Despite the news regarding his daughter, he still paid attention to the small touches. He nodded with satisfaction, stepped back to allow Slater to pass, and ushered him along an expensive handmade rug into a wide kitchen and dining area.

Slater nodded his thanks, and stepped through.

He found himself in a neat space with a cluster of faded

metal chairs arranged around a dining table that consisted of a giant slab of polished dark brown wood. Slater glanced at the setup, and immediately knew it was worth thousands. Both he and Nazarian were hesitant to discuss the subject of his daughter any further until they were seated, so in the meantime small talk would suffice.

Nazarian said, 'That's taken from an old shipwreck. Cost me a fortune.'

'You're doing well for yourself.'

He shrugged. 'It's not all about how good your kitchen table is.'

'No, of course not. Your wife—?'

'She's at work.'

'Do you work?'

'Why don't we sit down before we get into this stuff? Can I get you anything?'

'Just water. Thanks.'

'You drink?'

'Yes.'

'Then let's do that. I feel like the subject justifies it.'

Slater nodded, then paused behind one of the metal chairs. He placed both hands on the seat back and stared at Nazarian. 'Look, if you want me to leave, I will. I don't know how touchy this subject is. I can be out of your hair in seconds and you can pretend I never came knocking. If that's the way you want it to go.'

Nazarian just looked at him, those slate blue eyes piercing. 'You kidding?'

Slater sat down.

Nazarian fetched two chipped and faded whiskey tumblers down from a shelf above the sink and grabbed a bottle of Laphroaig from the minibar above the fridge. He poured a generous helping into each glass and brought them over to the massive wooden slab. He put one down in front of Slater, sat across from him on the corner of the table, and drank a hearty gulp.

He put the glass back down and interlocked his fingers. They were calloused, with dirt under the nails.

A hard man.

He said, 'Her name first, I guess. Just to make sure you're not here to scam me or anything.'

'Ruby.'

Nazarian nodded. 'Go on.'

Slater waited a beat, gathering his thoughts. He still had nothing prepared. He took a sip of the whiskey. It burned its way down his throat. The aroma wafted out of the glass, combining with the musk of the great wooden slab. He inhaled it all, and came away pleased with the combination. He picked Nazarian as a man who enjoyed cigars, straight liquor, and roaring log fireplaces.

He opened his mouth, then stared into the slate blue eyes and baulked. He tipped back the rest of the whiskey. Wiped his mouth. Bowed his head.

He said, 'Look, let's get things straight. I'm not here for goodwill. I'm here for myself, but I figure it could be a win-win for both of us. You get informed about what's happening, and I get the information I need.'

'What information do you need?'

'As much as you can give me. Hopefully over the course of this conversation I can stress that it's for the right reasons.'

Nazarian drained his own whiskey. 'You ex-military?'

'Yeah. You?'

'Yeah.'

'Where from?'

'I was a Green Beret.'

Slater nodded. It gelled with the picture he'd constructed in his head. Special Forces. Unforgiving, hard, cruel bastards when they needed to be. Which was almost always during their career. It probably bled over into parenting, even if that wasn't what you intended. When Slater had rescued Shien from the depths of a luxury casino in Macau, he'd developed a bond with her he hadn't anticipated. But, then again, he'd only been around her for a few days. Maybe the darker tendencies were exacerbated when you had to be around a kid seven days a week. Maybe that was why Slater had handed her over to Russell Williams in the first place. Because, deep down, he knew he wasn't fit to be a parent. He'd be too harsh. He'd expect too much.

Is that what you did? he asked himself.

Did you take the easy way out?

He didn't know.

That was a complicated enigma he wasn't ready to dive into.

He said, 'I figured.'

Nazarian said, 'What were you?'

'That's complicated.'

'You can tell me. I know most of the divisions.'

'Not mine.'

'You sure about that?'

'Very sure.'

Nazarian stared deep into his eyes. He must have found something there, because he nodded. 'Well, if you want my help, you're going to need to share some things you might not usually deem necessary to share.'

'Is that right? Didn't know you were dictating the rules here.'

'You need me. So you'd better open Pandora's box. Because I don't have much going on around here, so you can be damn sure I want to hear about secrets when they show up on my doorstep.'

'I could get up and walk out right now,' Slater said, encouraged by the burn of alcohol in his throat, soothing his nerves. 'You need what I've got just as much as I need what you've got. Otherwise you'll never find out about your daughter.'

Harsh.

But necessary.

Hurt flickered in Nazarian's eyes. Bitterness. He snatched the bottle of Laphroaig, poured another splash of liquid into his own glass, and gulped it back.

'Good,' he snarled. 'You think I give a shit? She walked out of my life ten years ago and she hasn't bothered to share one informative word with me since. She calls every now and then. Tells me she's still alive, and then hangs up. Why do you think I care what happens to her? Sure, she might have reacted emotionally when she was twelve, and that's understandable, but you don't think I'm judging her when she gets to eighteen and still decides I'm not worth her time? Since you seem to know her so well, why don't you get the fuck out of my house and go back to her? Wherever she is. Why don't the both of you live happily ever after and leave me here dwelling on what might have been?'

Tears in his eyes. The blue watering.

Slater said, 'There's good reason she hasn't contacted you.'

'Oh, I'm sure.'

'I used to work for an off-the-books regiment of the United States government handling solo black operations in places we certainly weren't welcome. Secret funds, secret ops, nothing on the record, all of it swept under the rug and buried. That division doesn't exist anymore. They nicknamed it Black Force to make things easier, but I'm sure it had an official name far more complicated on the dossiers. I never saw the dossiers. I was a live operative. I've probably killed a thousand men over the course of my life. They've all blurred into each other. I don't like talking about it because that makes me dream, and the dreams aren't good. In fact sometimes I think about putting a bullet in my head when I wake up in a cold sweat feeling panic like nothing I've ever felt before. Is that enough information for you?'

Nazarian twirled the empty tumbler in his calloused hands, looking deep into Slater's gaze. Studying him for any hint of deception.

He found nothing.

He nodded.

'I'm sorry I overreacted,' he said.

'Me too,' Slater said.

'What do you have to do with my daughter?'

'She works for a division very similar to my old unit.'

Nazarian said nothing.

A single tear rolled down his cheek.

53

After a silence that seemed to go on forever, Nazarian said, 'Why are you telling me this?'

His voice had lowered in both tone and confidence. There was none of the verve he'd shown earlier. It had all disintegrated in the face of Slater's words. Which Slater found odd. Usually such a ludicrous story would be met with apprehension. But Nazarian seemed to accept it instantaneously. He seemed quiet, reserved, squared away, just like his house.

He gazed at Slater and waited for the answer.

Slater didn't know what to say.

'What good does it do me?' Nazarian said, his voice shaking. 'To know this. Do you think I can change it?'

'I thought you might want to know.'

'Why?'

'I don't know, exactly. I thought if I was in your position … I'd want to know.'

'What can you tell me about it?'

'Not much. I don't know a whole lot. I only met her briefly.'

'What does she look like? I haven't seen a photo of her. For nearly ten years.'

'She's smart. And strong. And everything you'd hope for.'

'Apart from the black operations part.'

'Yeah,' Slater muttered. 'There's that.'

'Where did you meet her?'

'Colombia.'

'Some kind of covert underworld meet-up?'

'No. Coincidence.'

'Yeah, right.'

'It's the truth. And I've been thinking about it. A lot. I've had a lot of time to myself. Travelled here solo from Colombia. Just got in. Anyway, Ruby was in Colombia on a live op. Sent by Uncle Sam. I was there by chance. Retired around a year ago and I've been seeking out trouble ever since.'

'Why?'

'Habit.'

'Understood.'

Slater paused. He studied Nazarian's face. A knowing look passed over the blue eyes.

Slater said, 'When did you get out of the Green Berets?'

'A few years ago.'

'You been keeping busy?'

'This and that.'

'Apart from interior design, what do you do?'

'Nothing. I'm retired.'

'What does your wife do?'

'She's a nurse. She works in emergency. At Interfaith Medical Centre.'

'A noble endeavour. But that doesn't afford this furniture.'

'It's all cheap knockoffs.'

'No it's not.'

Nazarian shrugged. 'Okay. I pick up odd jobs.'

'I just shared something with you that would get me killed if certain parties knew about it. The least you could do is tell me the truth.'

'I have some skills. Not your level, but … enough.'

'What do you do?'

'I go where I'm needed. If I deem it the right work.'

'What's the right work for you?'

'Anything that catches my interest.'

'Tell me about your last job.'

'Poachers. In Africa. They slaughtered fifty elephants in a reserve. Sawed off the tusks and sold them at the markets. A couple of rich wildlife conservation types didn't like that. They put the feelers out. Found me. I went and dealt with the head poachers. In the middle of nowhere. On the plains. Could have got me killed. It paid well.'

'You killed them?'

'No. I'm not that guy. I just scare people. Rough them up a bit.'

'Sounds like we share a very similar mindset,' Slater said.

'You want to know what I did to them?'

'No.'

'Why not?'

'You expecting me to think you're a bad guy if you tell me the details?'

'Most would.'

'I happen to come from a line of work rather similar to yours. I understand that sort of morality. I understand why you do things like that. So no more questions. I get it now.'

'You have to do things like that. Every now and then.'

Slater thought of Ruby kissing Santiago on the forehead,

leaving her lipstick mark, then shoving the stake through the skull, into the brain.

Like crosshairs.

Slater said, 'I agree.'

Then he drew parallels between her and the man sitting across from him.

He said, 'Can you tell me more about why she left?'

Nazarian shrugged. Poured more whiskey into his glass, and ignored Slater's. 'She probably told you the truth.'

'You don't know what she said.'

'I'm sure she said there was fighting, and I was the worst guy on the planet, and it never ended, and eventually she got sick of it and left.'

'Something along those lines.'

'Yeah, well, it's mostly true.'

'The Green Berets?'

'I saw some stuff that fucked me up. I'm not going to pretend I didn't. I wasn't a good parent. I mean, I would never lay a hand on her, but I guess I was ... emotionally detached.'

'She didn't take that kindly?'

'I was dealing with my own demons. She just wanted a father. I couldn't be there for her.'

'I understand.'

'I blame myself.'

'You shouldn't. It's tricky.'

'We're never going to flesh this out in a single conversation.'

'I know. But we don't need to.'

Nazarian looked up from his glass, and saw that Slater knew all about battling internal demons. He nodded. 'Hopefully you understand.'

'We've both seen a lot, I'm sure.'

'You've probably seen more than me.'

'Yeah, well, I don't have a family.'

'By choice?'

'Hard to say.'

'Couldn't flesh it out in a single conversation?'

Slater nodded. 'Exactly.'

'But we don't need to.'

Slater paused. 'You regret having a family?'

Nazarian shook his head. 'Christ, no. I have another daughter, Abigail. We're close as anything. And my marriage is good. It's the only thing keeping me sane.'

'Do the three of you talk about what happened with Ruby?'

'Never.'

'Swept it under the rug?'

'Easier that way.'

There was a pause.

'How the hell did she wind up in a black ops program?' Nazarian said.

He put his head in his hands.

Maybe now it was all starting to hit him. The reality of the situation. It hadn't been explicitly stated, but he was slowly coming to terms with the fact his daughter was a killer. Sure, perhaps a noble one, but it was still a cold, cruel reality to face.

Especially considering Nazarian knew the intricacies of the trade.

He probably knew the look in a man's eyes when he passed away. Now he would imagine his daughter in those situations, far off in foreign countries, slaughtering brutal dictators and all manner of undesirables.

Not an easy concept to stomach.

Now Slater reached a crossroads.

Did he push on, and potentially destroy a family dynamic forever?

Who are you kidding? he thought. *It fell apart a decade ago.*

He said, 'Trust me, I'm only asking you this because I need urgent help. I wouldn't bring it up otherwise.'

Nazarian stared at him.

Slater said, 'Do you remember a man named Russell Williams?'

54

Nazarian didn't respond for almost a full minute.

Then he said, 'Did that motherfucker take her away without telling me?'

'I'm afraid so.'

'Why?' he said, exasperated, a vein protruding from the side of his temple. 'Why did she go to him?'

'Were the two of you close?'

'Back then, yes. He was a Green Beret, same as me. Back in the day. But when I got out, he went up. Straight up.'

'You remained friends?'

'For some time. I withdrew into myself when Ruby vanished. She ran away, obviously, but I couldn't accept it. I told myself she'd been kidnapped, maybe to assuage the guilt. So I stopped talking to anyone and everyone. Naturally I lost contact with Williams. And everyone else.'

'A blessing in disguise, for him.'

'I tried to get back in contact with him. A couple of years later. But he was a ghost. I couldn't find him in any database. No matter how much searching I did. And I was good at it. I had old contacts. But he was off the radar. Not in the way that a retired man is. I figured he kept going up until a shadow entity swallowed him. And then he was uncontactable. I assume that's what happened?'

Slater nodded. 'That's exactly what happened.'

'But when I was friends with him...'

'He must have already been involved with certain tendrils of the secret world,' Slater said. 'It would have all been kept hush-hush. He started a program in those days. Around the time Ruby disappeared, it took off. And with its success, he would have fallen out of the public eye. It would have taken him a couple of years to fall off the radar completely, but that's what happened.'

'What's the program?'

'It's called Lynx.'

'Lynx.'

Nazarian ran the word over his tongue. He didn't seem to like the sound of it.

'Feline. Dangerous. Silent killers.'

Slater nodded. 'Exactly.'

'They trained her? Ever since she ran away? She'd be — Christ — twenty-one now. Twenty-two in a few days.'

'Correct.'

'She'd be brainwashed.'

'She is.'

'Is she a monster?'

Slater shook his head. 'Far from it. But you can see the moral problems with the program. Probably more than most.'

Nazarian stared into the bottom of his glass for a long time, and then raised his head. 'What do you need from me?'

'There's a little girl who might be in—'

Nazarian held up a hand. 'I'm sure your reasons are justified. What do you need from me?'

'I need to talk to Williams, but—'

'I'm sure you got the hint during our chat.'

'You haven't spoken to him since Ruby left?'

'Not a word. If I could hand him over to you on a platter, I would.'

'You have no way of contacting him?'

'No.'

'Then I'm back at square one.'

'Can we talk about your demons?' Nazarian said.

Almost pleading.

Slater hesitated, taking into account the rapid change in direction.

He said, 'Now's not the time.'

'It's been a long time since I've been able to relate to anybody.'

'You don't have old military buddies?'

'No.'

'When this is all over, I'll be back,' Slater said. 'We'll have more whiskey. We'll talk.'

'I need to talk now.'

Slater weighed the heaviness in the air. For the first time he noticed the bags underneath Nazarian's eyes, the deep lines in his forehead, the twitching of his lip.

He said, 'What's wrong?'

'You think I would have let you in here if my life wasn't completely fucked?'

'What?'

'I think you were meant to come here.'

Slater tensed in the chair, sensing the hard metal under his rear. Had he misjudged Nazarian? Was the man mad? He certainly looked it right now. He sounded it.

'I'm in deep shit,' Nazarian said.

'How so?'

'We spoke about what I do on the side.'

'Is that relevant now?'

'Very.'

'Are we about to get assaulted by a pack of poachers from Cameroon?'

Nazarian managed a sad smile. 'Not quite.'

'What the hell is going on?'

'My wife's not at work. I sent her into Manhattan for a couple of days. She's staying at a hotel under a fake name. Abigail is with my wife's parents in Jersey.'

'What'd you do?'

'Pissed some people off.'

'The wrong people?'

'Yeah.'

'Should I be concerned?'

'Let's just say it was selfish of me not to turn you away at the door. I think I deliberately involved you so I wouldn't feel so alone. And now karma's catching up to me, it seems.'

'Why's that?'

'You didn't hear that car door?'

Slater got off the chair. He crossed silently to the entranceway, slunk across the rug, and glanced out one of the windows, peeking through the curtain. Nazarian stayed where he was, stooped low in his own chair, cradling his empty glass. Seemingly resigned to his fate.

Slater called out, 'I don't see anything.'

'The mob doesn't show themselves. I'm a dead man walking.'

'You sound awfully miserable for a Green Beret.'

'I'm one ex-military guy. That's nothing against them.'

'What'd you do?'

'Saw some bad shit happening. Interfered when I shouldn't have.'

'I do that all the time.'

'Something tells me we're a world apart experience-wise.'

'Not quite.'

'I've been drinking,' Nazarian admitted. 'Before you showed up here. I'm deep into this bottle. Very deep. My motor skills aren't there. I'm a dead man when they come through that door.'

'Where the fuck did all this come from?' Slater muttered to himself.

He crouched low, peering out the same window, staying away from the middle of the pane to avoid catching a bullet from anyone stationed across the street with an assault rifle. But he saw nothing besides a quiet residential street in Brooklyn with mown lawns and white picket fences and smooth asphalt.

From the sitting room beside the entranceway, he called out, 'Frank, I think you're paranoid.'

Then someone thundered a heavy boot into the front door and the lock snapped clean in two.

55

Thee New York City mob was not an organisation to underestimate, but at the same time, neither was Will Slater.

He had surprisingly little information to work with. He couldn't ascertain whether these men were showing up to simply teach Nazarian a lesson, or for something more sinister. The news about Ruby seemed to have distracted him for an adequate length of time, but eventually the facade had worn off, and Slater had stared into the eyes of what effectively constituted a dead man walking.

They're here to kill him.

That was his base instinct, and he reacted accordingly. As soon as the door thundered open he was there, taking up most of the space in the narrow crack, catching the giant wooden slab midway through its trajectory. The veins in his left forearm rippled as he seized the door by its frame, halting the momentum of the two men now charging into the entranceway. It created an awkward tangle of limbs that he utilised to its fullest advantage.

The guy taking the lead wasn't ready. He'd put a significant amount of effort into the kick to save looking like a fool and having to try twice. Although the house was old, the lock proved strong enough, and the result was a vibration through the man's boot, up his leg, rattling his hips and throwing off his equilibrium ever so slightly. He'd succeeded in smashing the door inward, but he was still in the process of recovering his stance.

Slater kicked him in the kneecap with the same amount of force the guy had applied to the door.

The man's leg hyperextended, still not skewered into the ground with enough support to protect him. Ligaments and muscle and bone crushed under the sole of Slater's boot and the guy's face seared with the kind of silent agony Slater had seen a hundred times before.

There was no outcry, no scream of rage or pain, just quiet acceptance and the blood draining from his cheeks and his mouth wincing and his eyes widening and his hands flying to his mangled leg.

He hadn't even hit the ground yet, but he was probably wondering whether he would ever walk again.

Slater used him as a step on the way down. He put his other boot on the small of the guy's back as he doubled over onto all fours, and leapt over him, colliding hard with the second guy. Chest to chest, awkward as hell, tangling their limbs in a manic flurry. There was a gun somewhere in the mix, but Slater ignored it.

He figured the pair hadn't been anticipating resistance like this in the slightest, and therefore wouldn't have been mentally prepared to execute Nazarian within the first couple of seconds of opening the door.

Therefore his finger probably wasn't in the trigger guard, to save accidentally shooting his buddy in the back on the way in.

He was right.

The guy didn't shoot him in the chaos. Slater grabbed the man's skull, one open palm on each ear, almost squashing his head in place. He kept his left hand there as a guidance accessory and surged forward into a massive elbow with his right arm, swapping the right palm for a pointed bone. He drilled the elbow into the soft tissue just above the guy's ear with the equivalent kinetic energy of a dozen punches in one.

Perfect placement.

It was almost obscene how much time he had.

The guy did his best impression of a newborn giraffe and staggered away from Slater, barely clutching onto consciousness. His knees wobbled in every direction at once and he managed to make it past his buddy, who was still down on his rear on the landing, clutching his broken leg with involuntary tears in his eyes.

Slater gave the guy he'd elbowed a gentle shove in the small of his back, aiming him in the direction of the house.

The man tripped over his friend, and kept staggering, straight through the open doorway.

Slater grabbed two handfuls of the other guy's jacket and hauled him to his feet. He shoved him toward the doorway and the guy tumbled and twisted and fell onto the rug just inside the entranceway, unable to keep his feet, with his left leg in enough pain to warrant fainting. Slater followed them in, ducking out of sight of the rest of the neighbourhood in case of nosy civilians. He barely broke stride. He slammed the door behind him, wedging it back in place despite the broken lock, and faced off with the first guy in the hallway, still semi-conscious, eyes almost rolled into the back of his head.

It wasn't even a fight. The outcome had been dictated moments earlier.

Over the guy's shoulder, Slater saw Nazarian materialise at the other end of the hallway, wide-eyed, in disbelief. Slater nodded a look of reassurance to him, then shot a stabbing Muay Thai front kick in the direction of the semi-conscious man. The guy had his hands halfway up in a pathetic display of self-defence, but the sole of Slater's boot shot through his guard like a knife through butter. The flat heel punched into the guy's nose, breaking it in a couple of places, the power of a brick with the speed of a whip. The rest of the boot hit him in the forehead and finished the fight, completing the requisite rattle of brain inside skull. Valuable neurons clashed off hard walls of bone and shut the lights off. The guy's legs gave out completely and he seemed to sink down vertically, limbs splayed.

The second guy, pale and sweating, reached for his leg. He'd come to rest seated on the rug with both legs extended straight in front of him, in too much pain to move.

Slater switched stances and lashed out and kicked him in the head and put him down for the count.

He adjusted his jeans. Tucked the black T-shirt into the front of his waistband. Gave himself the quick once-over for any freak injuries.

All clear. Just pumping muscles and a sweaty forehead and the breath rasping in his chest. All the usual signs of a fight.

No-one spoke.

In the movies, people knocked unconscious sleep like babies. In reality, they breathe in ragged and gasping fits and starts as they come to, drooling all over the floor. The pair of mob thugs did that, twitching on the rug.

Nazarian said, 'Yeah, you're definitely something else.'

'Had to be able to survive on my own,' Slater said. 'So they taught me to do things like that.'

'How?'

Slater put a hand on each of the unconscious guys' collars and hauled them through to the sitting room. 'By dedicating my entire life to it.'

56

Nazarian came back with a roll of duct tape, and Slater wrapped a quarter of it around the first guy's wrists, then did the same to his ankles, then repeated the process with the second guy. They weren't going anywhere. There would be no bold, daring escapes. They would lie on their stomachs with their limbs taped together and slowly come back to consciousness, weak and scared and surrounded by unfamiliarity. It would take them some time to even make the connection of where they were. And until they did that they would lie weak and placid. Then they would try to escape the restraints, to no avail. No-one had ever torn free from that amount of duct tape. It didn't matter how strong you were. It defied physics.

So Slater left them there, and guided Nazarian back into the kitchen.

He gestured to the table. 'Where were we?'

Nazarian stayed on his feet. He shook his head. 'We need to do something about that.'

'We will. First we need to talk.'

'I can't have them in my house like that.'

'What's the issue?'

Nazarian held out his hands, flabbergasted. 'I don't know. I'm not used to this.'

'I thought you used to be a Green Beret.'

'I did.'

'I thought you regularly go to rough people up for a living.'

'Yeah, but ... not like that.'

'You're a brawler?'

Nazarian nodded. 'Dirty. Sometimes I get hurt. Take one punch to give out two. I don't know anything else.'

'They're not going anywhere,' Slater said. 'Sit.'

'You sure?'

'Never been more sure.'

Nazarian sat.

'You think you could give me a few pointers some time?'

Slater raised an eyebrow. 'For fighting?'

'Yeah.'

'There's no pointers to be given.'

'Then how do you do it?'

'You want the truth?'

'Yeah.'

'I react faster than almost anyone on earth. Just genetic. On top of that I've spent well over ten thousand hours in modern MMA gyms, most of them built for me by the U.S. government. No kung-fu, no wushu, no bullshit. They call those places McDojos. They teach stuff that would never work in the real world. I've never stepped foot in one. All I've ever known is punching and kicking heavy bags and sparring partners and pads. I'm a black-belt in Brazilian jiu-jitsu, so—'

'I thought you said that stuff doesn't work in real life.'

Slater smiled. 'You don't know what jiu-jitsu is, do you?'

'I assume it's something taught at ... what did you call it? A McDojo?'

'Far from it. You can tear an elbow or a knee apart in a couple of seconds if you know what you're doing. It's all about torque and leverage, and it's awfully practical. If we tumble to the ground and I grab hold of you and rip every muscle in your arm to pieces with a kimura, you're not getting back up again. And even if you do, you'll be fighting with one arm. Simple as that.'

'A what?'

'A kimura. Look it up.'

'So that's it?'

'That's it. I hit harder than anyone my size and I don't get hit. Pretty simple.'

'And you can't teach that?'

'Go spend five years in a real gym. That'll give you some level of reflexes, even if they aren't there genetically. But I imagine by then you'll be too old to do this line of work.'

'I was already thinking about getting out of it.'

'Does your wife know about these ... expeditions?'

'The family thinks I'm independently contracted to a private security firm. So ... sort of.'

'They think you stand around and do nothing?'

'Basically.'

'When really you're out there knocking heads together.'

'Not really.'

'You know what I mean.'

'I don't quite operate on the level you do.'

'So you're a D-list enforcer.'

'Something like that. I only do what I think is right, though.'

'There's nobility in that.'

'It'll get me killed soon. That's why I'm getting out. I hope.'

'I'm finding it hard to accept that you had such a bad relationship with your daughter,' Slater mused. 'You seem the same.'

'Now, maybe. Back then she wasn't the wrecking ball you met.'

Slater nodded. 'Understood.'

'And there's no hope of rekindling it,' Nazarian said, bowing his head.

'You don't know that.'

'You said it yourself. She was bred to be an operative. You think she'll be able to have a normal relationship with me, or her mother? Even if she wanted to, she couldn't.'

'You haven't tried.'

'I'm sure she was trained to hate me.'

'Why?'

'Mitigate the risk of her running back.'

'You think Williams would stoop that low?'

'Ask yourself how low someone would stoop who conceived of a program like that in the first place.'

'You're adamant there's no way you can get in touch with him now?'

'Positive.'

'Could you track him down?'

'Wouldn't know where to start.'

Slater rested a palm flat on the table. He scratched at the wood intermittently. A nervous tic. Nazarian helped himself to a dash more whiskey.

'I'd cool it with that,' Slater said. 'Why were you en route to getting blackout drunk when you knew these guys were coming?'

Nazarian stared at him. Bloodshot streaks crept into the pale blue eyes.

'You haven't really grasped what's happening, have you?' he said. 'You think those two will be the first? I'm not you. I'm not some balls-to-the-wall one man army. I'm a guy who did some time in the Special Forces, but I can't wage war against the mob.'

'Why not?'

'I just can't.'

'What'd you do to get yourself here?'

'Acted like the kind of stubborn bastard that drove my daughter away in the first place.'

'Tell me.'

'It's a long story.'

Slater tipped the metal chair back, leaning on its rear legs. He balanced precariously in place to get a better angle down the hallway, catching sight of the two hostages on the sitting room floor. They stared back at him through foggy eyes, still swimming through the muck. He thumped the chair back down to earth.

'We've got time,' he said.

'I don't. They'll send more.'

Slater shook his head. 'Those guys were pros. If I hadn't caught them with their pants down it might have been a different story. They won't send more for a while. They'll give their men time to take care of business. The mob are loyal to their own to a fault.'

'How much do you know about them?'

'If you're talking about a specific crime family, not much. The mob in general — everything.'

'You spent much time around them?'

'I had a few operations in their midst.'

'How'd they go?'

'I'm still here.'

'You know about the Whelan family here in New York?'

'That's who's after you?'

'Yeah.'

'Never heard of them.'

'Then let me tell you a story.'

57

The two thugs in the sitting room eventually piped up, swearing and shouting as they became aware of where they were and what was happening to them. Their Irish accents were thick, and they started spewing depravity about what they might do to Nazarian's loved ones if he didn't set them free.

One of the voices seemed more nasal than the other — Slater figured it belonged to the guy with the broken nose. As soon as the volume reached an uncomfortable level, he leapt off the metal chair, fetched the nearly-finished roll of duct tape, and wound a final series of strips around both their mouths, making sure to leave gaps under their nostrils so they could breathe. Then he tossed the empty roll across the room and went straight back to the kitchen.

Nazarian watched his movements with unbridled fascination, like Slater was a gorilla at the zoo.

'What?' Slater said.

'You're very good at what you do.'

'I've done this a few times.'

'I can tell.'

'Gavin Whelan,' Nazarian said.

Slater paused, noting the abrupt change of direction. 'This the guy you pissed off?'

'My daughter did.'

'Ruby?'

'Abigail.'

'Of course.'

'She's a lawyer. Property law. So she's around folks from that industry all the time. You know how construction goes in this city...'

'Mob ties?'

'They'll never explicitly state it. But she's low-level at one of the major firms. Did well in college — very well, actually. Got offered an internship at one of the big players right off the bat. We were so excited for her. She's a real go-getter. They work her to death, but she's passionate about it. And that's all you can ask for, right?'

'Right.'

'But the firm isn't exactly savoury. They represent a few crooks. Nothing ever sticks to these guys, but they get the big deals, the big contracts. I don't know the details. Anyway, the Whelan family have deep connections to the unions. They're paying Abigail's firm millions to represent them. Big clients. So the extended family starts treating the place like home. The eldest kid, Gavin Whelan, starts to visit. He likes the look of Abigail. Talks to her endlessly. Never quits. She has a good head on her shoulders, so she's amicable, but she knows where he comes from and avoids his advances.'

'He doesn't like that.'

'Not one bit.'

'He gets more and more confrontational about it. He's not used to hearing "no."'

Nazarian paused. 'Seems like you know it better than I do.'

'It's a timeless tale.'

'It might not go the way you think it'll go.'

Slater shrugged. 'Did he cross the line and get too touchy one day? Maybe he cornered her in the office, spoke his mind, told her what would happen if she kept saying no to him. Did she tell you about it? Did you go find Gavin Whelan and give him the beating he deserved? Did Gavin run to his dad or uncle or whoever the hell sits at the head of the table in the family? Did they give you a beating of your own? Or maybe started following you everywhere, letting you know they're watching? Did you retaliate, because you used to be a Green Beret and it's the only thing you know how to do? Did you make a mess of it? Did you infuriate the family? Is that how you ended up here?'

Nazarian sat back, stewing, cradling his glass. 'Maybe.'

'Like I said, it's a timeless tale. I've seen a few iterations of it before.'

'What happens at the end of the story?'

'When I'm around? Only one thing, usually.'

Nazarian shook his head. 'I don't think that's the best idea here. You can do your work, and leave. And then I still have to pick up the pieces of a broken life. The Whelans are everywhere. They run a lot of shit under the surface. They have ties in everything. That's why I drink, and wait for them to show up. Because it'll be a never ending war. It'll only delay the inevitable. I realised that far too late. I never should have spoken up. Should have bowed my head and taken whatever came my way like the rest of them.'

'If they send guys like those two, I can deal with them.'

'What — forever? You going to sit here and be my guardian angel for the rest of my life?'

'No,' Slater said. 'I'm going to the Whelans.'

'Please don't,' Nazarian said, suddenly cold and deadly serious. 'You'll be ruining everything. If you were anyone else, I'd hit you if you tried anything.'

'That might not be such a good idea.'

'I put that together a few minutes ago.'

Slater got to his feet. 'I need to go to the Whelans, unfortunately. It's nothing to do with you.'

'What?'

'I assume they have ties with the cops.'

'No shit. They've bought half the city.'

'Good. Then they're exactly who I need.'

'I can't let you do this, man.' Then he paused, and furrowed his brow. 'I don't even know your name.'

'Will Slater.'

'You do this often, Will Slater?'

'I do it enough. And, trust me, it's a win-win.'

'How so?'

'Right now, getting in touch with Russell Williams is the most important thing in my life. It used to be a breeze, but the numbers I have access to no longer exist. Believe me, I've tried. So I need to do something radical. Something that gets his attention and makes him come to me. And you've got a problem that can't be addressed without a radical solution. You do the math. Pair them up. Make the most out of me while I'm here. Point me in the right direction and let me do what I do best.'

'And that is?'

Slater feigned delivering an elbow to a skull.

Nazarian thought about it hard, which was understandable, considering the future of his family rested on this crazed man pumped with energy who had materialised out of the blue in his time of greatest need. Then he said, 'I'll give you the address.'

'You sure?'

'Just don't fuck it up.'

'I never have. Not yet.'

'Don't let me be the first. Will you tell them I sent you?'

'Of course not. But you can be damn sure I'll deliver the message to leave you alone.'

'They won't listen.'

'I can be persuasive.'

Nazarian feigned raising his hands to his ears. 'I don't want to know. Just do what you need to do.'

'How much trouble do you think I have to cause for one of the Whelans to run word of what happened up the pipeline?'

'I couldn't fathom.'

Slater grinned, almost maniacal. 'I can.'

'You want the Don's address?'

'Who's the Don?'

'Tommy Whelan. The uncle.'

'You have his address?'

'It's in the system at Abigail's firm. I told her to steal it when I thought shit was about to hit the fan. I don't know what I was thinking. There's nothing I can do. It's a modern townhouse in Manhattan. Probably cost eight figures. Five or six storeys, or something ridiculous like that. The whole Whelan family goes in and out of it. He's a property mogul on the surface, but underneath...'

Slater grinned again. 'Oh, that's perfect.'

'You're insane, aren't you?'

'Maybe. Or maybe I'm just very, very good at getting things done.'

'I don't want to know about it. I'm going to pretend we never met.'

Slater nodded. 'Probably best for the both of us. This conversation never happened.'

'What about the two guys up front?'

Slater skirted around the giant slab of shipwreck and rested a hand on Nazarian's shoulder. 'I'll take care of that.'

'Don't kill them. Not in my house.'

Slater shook his head. 'I'm not that type.'

'Is this the part where you start to pretend you're noble?'

'Not in the slightest. I think we can agree my moral compass is skewed well off its axis. I like to think it's because of the things I've seen. It taught me there's times where violence is the answer. There's times where violence is good. But I don't kill people I've tied up.'

'So what's the answer?'

'I'll just make them forget.'

'Are you a wizard?'

Slater smirked, and took his hand off Nazarian's shoulder. 'Not quite.'

'Do I want to see this?'

'Depends. They were here to kill you. They had guns. Their safeties were off.'

'Then I want to see it.'

'It won't be pretty.'

Nazarian just looked at him.

Slater nodded. 'Right this way.'

58

The duct tape proved awfully effective at holding them in place. They lay flat on their stomachs, arms pinned behind their backs, legs bound together, chins pressed to the rug in the sitting room.

Slater and Nazarian stood over them.

Slater said, 'You think six months is enough punishment?'

Nazarian said, 'What?'

'I know these types. The Irish mob aren't exactly the most honourable. They were here to kill you, but they would have shot the whole family if they were home. That's the way it goes. Can't have witnesses, can we?'

Nazarian stared at the two writhing thugs with a new level of hostility. Slater sized them up for the first time, properly assessing their features.

They could have been brothers.

Twins, even.

They were both pale redheads with big stocky frames, probably six foot each. One had an uglier face than the other. That was about the only thing separating them. And their eyes were dead. Black and soulless. As they needed to be, serving as enforcers in the New York underworld. It was a sickening place to thrive.

Nazarian said, 'What do you mean, six months?'

Slater stomped on the first guy's head, putting all his weight into it, relying on technique forged in the fire of constant, relentless training. His boot crunched against skull, flattening the red hair and red face into the rug, knocking him out cold. Giving him a second concussion in the space of half an hour, this one far worse than the first.

The guy went completely unconscious under Slater's heel.

It stirred memories of a cold, dark wasteland.

He said, 'I had a similar injury in the Russian Far East. Only just now recovered from it. All the events around it are blurry, if I'm being honest. And my brain can take a beating. These boys aren't ready for that level of recovery. I'd give them six months until they're out of the woods, at least. And they won't remember me. That's for damn sure.'

Nazarian seemed barely fazed.

He just nodded.

'Sounds good to me,' he said.

Slater strode over to the second man and repeated the process. It didn't bring him joy. It didn't bring him anything. It was a practical necessity. No other option. He didn't find pleasure in the revenge, and he knew the moment he did he needed to walk away and exile himself to a tropical island for the rest of his life. Because then he would become something else entirely. Something that fuelled on vengeance, that drank it in. And he knew where that path would lead.

So it was with a grim face that he turned back to Nazarian and said, 'Can you take care of them?'

'What do you mean?'

'Put them in your car. Dump them somewhere. Cut the tape off. They'll figure out the rest.'

'What if they can't—?'

'Do you care?'

Silence.

Nazarian nodded. 'Understood.'

'It's your call.'

'No, you're right. I couldn't give a shit if they can't remember their way home. Like you said. I'd be dead.'

'So would Abigail. And your wife…?'

'Anastasia.'

'Anastasia. They would have shot both of them in the head.'

Another nod.

Nazarian said, 'You need Whelan's address?'

'Please.'

There was little left to say or do. Slater gathered up the pair of firearms previously possessed by the mob goons. Both identical sub-compact Sig Sauer P228s. Small sidearms, intended to get the job done and nothing else. Slater frisked both unconscious bodies for spare magazines, and came away empty. They clearly both had faith in their own abilities. They must not have anticipated much of a shootout. Perhaps they didn't know Nazarian's history in the Special Forces. Or they just thought he wouldn't dare retaliate. Not if he knew any better. If he fought back against them, wounding or killing one or both of them, the reaction would be unprecedented.

Slater understood his personal responsibility. He had to hit the Whelans hard, like nothing they'd ever experienced before, with enough force and shock to make them think twice about ever attempting to touch the Nazarians again. He knew what kind of pressure rested on his shoulders. He had to disrupt a mob family to its core. Rattle them in their comfortable throne. And if he didn't, they wouldn't hesitate to blow the brains out of Frank Nazarian and his entire extended family to get their revenge.

Slater knew the price of failure.

So did Nazarian.

The man rested a hand on Slater's shoulder, and the pale blue eyes bored into him.

'You understand, right?' Nazarian said.

'Of course.'

'You ever shouldered this kind of burden before?'

Slater almost laughed. He recalled a barbaric skirmish in the mountains of the Hadhramaut Valley, deep in the Yemeni highlands, fighting tooth and nail on a vast and dusty plateau to get his hands on a satellite radio and prevent one of the worst horrors of the twenty-first century from sweeping the streets of London. If he'd taken a few more seconds to achieve what he needed, hundreds of thousands of people would have died horrific deaths.

Even the memory of the Marburg virus sent shivers down his spine.

He said, 'Once or twice.'

'You sure you can do this?'

Slater shrugged the hand off his shoulder. 'You don't seem to understand. Usually I'm playing defence. It's a rare occasion where I need to play offence. And, I have to say, it's something to behold.'

'You sound awfully sure of yourself. Don't get yourself killed at the start.'

'Wouldn't dream of it.'

'Is there anything else you can tell me about my daughter?'

Slater mulled over it. Then he smiled.

'She seemed to take after you,' he said. 'For better or worse.'

'Will we ever see each other again?'

'Maybe. Maybe not.'

'Whatever you're about to do, do it well.'

'I'll try my best. You're a good man, Frank. You're like me. Stubborn and bone-headed to a fault. You see a problem and you do everything you can to fix it.'

'Something tells me you're a little better at it than I am.'

'I have a little more practice than you do.'

'I need to give you my thanks. You didn't just tell me about my daughter. You...'

He trailed off, his gaze sweeping from the empty kitchen to the entranceway to the sitting room. He shivered in the quiet, starting to realise what might have transpired if Slater hadn't arrived.

'You lost hope?' Slater said.

'What the hell was I thinking?'

'It happens.'

'Not like that. Not to me.'

'You saw a problem you couldn't fix. You caved. There's always times like that. It's human nature. As much as we want to run away from it. Even me.'

'Has it happened to you before? Have you ever given up?'

'I thought about it once.'

'Where?'

'Yemen.'

'What were you doing there?'

'Nothing in particular. Then it morphed into something I never saw coming.'

'What happened?'

'I had no-one to contact. I was excommunicated from my old division. I'd run away from them. I had to fight my way up a mountain of armed tribesmen to get to a satellite radio and somehow try and stop a bio-terror attack. Every way I looked at it, it was going to get me killed.'

'Did you prevent it?'

'Have hundreds of thousands of people died in a single incident in the last year?'

'Not that I heard of.'

'Then I'll leave that to your imagination.'

'But that overwhelming feeling ... when you can't see a way out, and you just sit down and wait for the end. You got it?'

'I got it.'

'And what did you do?'

'I didn't sit down.'

Slater fished an electronic key fob from the larger unconscious man's inside jacket pocket. It had a smooth *T* indented on the plastic. He shoved his fingers deeper into the pocket and came away with a wallet. It had a driver's license in it.

Michael Taylor.

Mickey, probably.

Couldn't find a more stereotypical Irish name if you tried.

He clapped Nazarian on the shoulder in a final gesture, and nodded a reassuring look to the man. There seemed to be a resurgence in the blue eyes. A spark of some kind. Fresh motivation. He was steadily climbing out of the nihilism that had threatened to consume him.

The law of unintended consequences.

Slater had shown up out of some strange sense of good-will, and had inadvertently saved a life.

He reminded himself that he would ruin that same life if he failed now.

Nazarian scrawled an address on a scrap piece of paper, folded it in half, and handed it over.

There was nothing left to be said.

Slater put the key, the wallet, and the paper into the pockets of his jeans and left quietly through the front door.

59

M anhattan proved as chaotic as Slater remembered it.

He'd left the Mercedes S-Coupé out the front of Nazarian's, preferring to drive a car that he wasn't responsible for to a siege. He sat in bumper-to-bumper traffic in a white Tesla, amused by the juxtaposition of a couple of burly Irish mafia goons driving around in a luxury electric vehicle. It was a Model S P100D, its make revealed on the enormous display screen that fired to life as he push-started the engine. Whisper quiet, the sedan barely purred as it coasted through the quiet Brooklyn streets en route to the madness that constituted inner New York City. Slater noted every feature of the car as he sat wrapped in the plush leather, using the smartphone in his lap to search for an accurate price. He came away with $180,000 for the base model, not including a smattering of customisable options.

So the Whelans are loaded to the gills.

The pair of Sig Sauer P228s rested in either side of his waistband, the belt threaded through his jeans cinched tight over their bulk. It would have to make do — he'd flown straight here from Colombia, and there'd been no time to stop and arm himself with appendix holsters and all the requisite safety gear.

The Whelan compound rested on the Upper East Side, which justified the obscene price tag Nazarian dropped on Slater earlier. It was a five-storey townhouse just off Park Avenue. No wonder it cost more than ten million. For a moment he wondered how the hell Tommy Whelan could justify living in such lavish luxury in plain sight, but it didn't take him long to figure out the life of a property mogul provided an awfully convenient cover story.

And half of it was probably true.

There was no doubt the family owned an amalgamation of commercial and residential properties in New York, which would provide a small fortune in rental income in its own right. Then there was the endless corruption and other more unsavoury dealings on top of that.

All in all leading to a bunch of wealthy brats who thought they could get away with anything.

Slater almost salivated at the thought.

It wasn't every day he received the task of causing as much chaos as humanly possible to a collection of scum.

He had Taylor's driver's licence in his left hand and the other resting on the steering wheel. He nosed forward, eyeing the skyscrapers dwarfing the street on either side. He'd already memorised the details. His mind entered a different mode of being, shifting from calm to wired. He analysed everything, sensing the stress chemicals building in his chest, just waiting to be released in an explosive burst. That would come, but not just yet.

He had a part to play first.

He found the townhouse easily enough. It stood out in stark contrast to its neighbouring buildings, five storeys of thick floor-to-ceiling glass with maximum tint. Like a modern work of art slapped between two ordinary brick and mortar structures.

There were two sentries posted in front of the entrance, at street level. Both pale redheads like the two men Slater had taken out in Brooklyn, each about six foot two with bulky frames under their leather jackets. Their faces showed disinterest, but the eyes never lied. They pierced everywhere they looked, searching for any sign of threats. To a passerby they might seem like a couple of big strong locals waiting to meet with a group of friends before a ball game, but to Slater they gave themselves away without much effort.

Still pressed up to the car in front of him, Slater finessed the brake pedal, eyeing a vacant parking spot a few dozen feet ahead seemingly reserved for one of Whelan's goons. It rested directly in front of the townhouse.

Perfect.

Slater had discovered, after years in the field, that most human interactions came down to confidence. The world of crime — the mob, particularly — was a complicated beast, most of it resting in the shadows with allegiances switching this way and that, and hired help utilised in almost all aspects when the family grew fat and lazy.

Slater had to hope Tommy Whelan didn't control the books with a painstaking eye to detail. That way, a newcomer would stand out. If there was even a shred of doubt in the sentries' minds, Slater was in the clear. He wasn't as talented as Ruby, but he could put on a game face when he needed to, and he'd spent enough time ingratiated with the vermin of society that he could do a pretty respectable job at it, too.

Before either of the sentries could put him on the back

foot, he seized a gap in traffic and shot the Tesla into the parking spot, screeching to a halt with enough precision to impress even the most critical of drivers. Still pumped up on false unrest, he made sure his T-shirt fell over the P228s before launching out of the car, levering himself up off the driver's seat and crossing the sidewalk in a few broad steps.

Five seconds, beginning to end.

He was face to face with the two redheads before either of them could get in the first word and put a moment of thought into the encounter.

'Nobody told me what I'm supposed to do with it,' he said, right to their faces.

He kept his voice short and clipped. His eyes bored into them, expectant. He jerked a finger back towards the Tesla. He raised both eyebrows, injecting as much urgency into his nervous tics as he could. Bringing them from a calm observational stance to a panicked response.

The first guy said, 'What?'

He had cheeks riddled with acne and a deep flush to his pale face. Black beady eyes rested in dark sockets. His hairline had started receding up his scalp years ago, even though he couldn't be far over twenty-five.

The second guy seemed far more confused. He was more handsome, with smooth skin and a straight hairline and a slightly more frantic nature. His eyes darted from Slater to the car, and from the car back to Slater. He seemed younger than the first guy. Newer. A fresher face. Not quite worn in yet. He'd withdrawn into himself at the first sign of confusion. He'd probably been taught to stand around and look scary and act intimidating if the situation demanded it. Now he didn't know what the hell to do.

Slater labelled them Guy One, and Guy Two, in order of the concern they might see through his ruse.

Guy One — the uglier one — repeated the question. 'What?'

Slater deliberately didn't answer, for the second time.

He put his hands behind his back, and crossed them together, and stared at the pair like they were the dumbest motherfuckers on the planet.

He said, 'You heard me the first time.'

Guy One said, 'I don't know who the fuck you are.'

But you haven't pulled a gun on me yet, Slater said. *So I've got your attention, haven't I?*

He said, 'Well, that's great, because I don't know who the fuck you are either. Look how much we have in common. It's a perfect match. Just make sure you take me out to dinner before you fuck me.'

Guy Two laughed.

Guy One looked past Slater, to the Tesla. 'I know the car.'

Slater threw his hands up in the air, in mock amazement. 'Holy shit. Incredible. Next you're gonna tell me you know Mickey.'

'Where's Mickey?'

'Don't ask me. Above my pay grade. I'm just the driver.'

'Why the hell did he tell you to bring it back here? It doesn't belong here. It belongs in the garage.'

'Did you miss the part where I said it's above my pay grade? All I heard was the job didn't go so well, so they're probably licking their wounds somewhere.'

'They're not supposed to do that.'

'They're probably not supposed to use cheap hookers either, but you know Mickey.'

Guy Two laughed again.

Good.

Guy One said, 'Alright, thanks.'

Slater said, 'Well?' and looked at the pair of them expectantly.

Guy One said, 'Job done. You brought the car back. Get lost.'

'Oh,' Slater said, as if realising something. He turned to Guy Two, the more susceptible of the pair. He jerked a thumb at Guy One. 'He doesn't know, does he?'

'Know what?' Guy Two said.

'I've got a message for Tommy.'

'Then you give it to me,' Guy One said.

Slater kept staring at Guy Two. 'Did you miss the part where I said the job didn't go well? Mickey has confidential information for Tommy. I've been told to bring it straight to him.'

'They invented phones a couple of decades ago,' Guy One said.

Slater turned to him. 'Alright, fuckface. Here's an idea. What if the job didn't go well because someone was lying in wait anticipating their arrival? And what if they're suspecting the phones are tapped, or something along those lines? It's a theoretical possibility, isn't it? I already told you I don't know the details. I was just given the order. So you can either let me in and I can deliver my message or I can walk away and you can deal with the consequences of that later. I really don't give a shit either way, so hurry up and make your mind up. I've got better places to be. Tick tock.'

If Slater had started with that particular train of conversation, his chances of success would have rested at close to zero percent. Right now, they weren't high, but at least he had the convincing act of believability to precede it. Guy One stared at him, a little crazed in the eye, and Slater realised he'd misjudged the man.

He certainly wasn't getting in through that avenue.

'I've never seen you before,' Guy One said. 'You haven't got that through your thick skull yet? You think we let anyone walk in here? Get the fuck out of here before I send you on your way myself.'

Slater flashed a glance at the guy's fists. They were tensed up. Every muscle in his body was probably tensed up. Ready for a fight at any moment. He had big hands, thick fingers, and calloused knuckles. A brawler, through and through. A man with endless experience in street fights. He might pose a considerable problem if it came to blows. Slater would need to get in hard, and get in fast.

He turned and looked at Guy Two's hands. Skinnier. Thinner fingers. Unblemished knuckles.

Again — not worn in.

Slater stared Guy Two in the eyes and said, 'Right. What's your name, kid? I'll let Taylor know who fucked with the messenger.'

Guy Two shifted from foot to foot. Glanced right, toward his buddy, but Guy One didn't return the favour. Guy One's eyes bored into Slater. Waiting for the first punch. He seemed to know it was coming.

Guy Two said, 'Come on, man. Just let him in.'

Guy One wheeled around, eyes wide. 'What'd you fuckin' say?'

'Let him in. I don't want to get on the wrong end of Mickey.'

'You ever seen this bastard before?'

'No, but—'

'You think he looks like a driver?'

'I don't fuckin' know. What's a driver supposed to—?'

But he didn't finish the sentence, because both of them had taken their eyes off Slater for a few seconds. That was all he needed. He had the smartphone out of his pocket and pressed to his ear before either of them could react. When they turned back, he was already deep in conversation.

'Yeah,' he said. 'Two redheads.'

They stared at him.

He paused, as if receiving bad news.

He said, 'I doubt Tommy will shoot them dead for this … you sure?'

Guy One lunged for Slater.

Guy Two lunged for the door.

60

Time slowed down.

Well, not exactly.

It was always a strange dichotomy. It slowed and sped up simultaneously — Slater's brain flooded with millions and millions of neural reactions, sizing up every angle and analysing every imperceptible movement. But reality played out in a lightning-fast blur, as if he was operating on autopilot. Those same reactions went down familiar pathways, creating solutions to problems in milliseconds, and commanding his limbs to react.

It went the same way every time.

A few seconds of shocking violence, and then nothing.

Guy One charged in with a short, sharp movement. His muscle fibres twitched, exploding into motion. He'd been ready for a fight for close to a minute now. But he didn't throw a punch with lethal intentions, which is what he should have done. Slater had one hand preoccupied with pressing the phone to his ear, and hadn't expected a reaction like that. Guy One probably could have hit him square on the chin with a lunging jab. Slater had uncanny reaction speed, but he wasn't inhuman.

Instead, Guy One went for a double-handed shove.

A power move. He probably had ten or twenty pounds on Slater, so he figured he could send him sprawling back into the Tesla, denting the metalwork as the kinetic energy took him off his feet. But this wasn't a game, and Slater hadn't taken part in a shoving match since he was a kid.

It was either all or nothing.

He dropped the phone and wrapped both hands around the back of Guy One's neck as he surged into range, locking the man's head in place. A standard Muay Thai clinch, infamous for obvious reasons, mostly because there was little the guy could do to break out of the hold apart from ducking face-first toward the ground. Which was exactly what Slater wanted him to do.

And he did it.

Still supercharged with adrenalin, the guy instinctively wanted away from Slater's fingers looping around the back of his neck. It was a strange sensation, especially in the heat of an all-out brawl. So he ducked forward, and Slater brought a knee up and smashed his face to pulp, breaking all manner of bones and rearranging his complexion in the process. He heard the sharp *crack* and felt the guy slacken in his grip, and then he let go, because there was no fight left in the man whatsoever.

Guy One went down like he'd been shot.

Two seconds since the craziness broke out.

No time at all for Guy Two, who wasn't used to combat. He'd probably been in a couple of hard sparring sessions at boxing gyms owned by the mob, but this was something completely different. He wanted away. He didn't understand how Slater slotted into the puzzle, and the outburst of movement had thrown him off his guard.

Slater waited a second or two, which in the heat of the moment felt like an eternity.

Just long enough for Guy Two to punch a four-digit code into a keypad and yank the lobby door open.

Perfect.

Slater kicked him in the back of the knee, hard.

The guy's leg buckled, and he stumbled on his way through the slim gap in the bulletproof glass door. Slater caught the door as it swung outward and kicked Guy Two in the back of the other knee, completely taking him off his feet. He hit the smooth concrete floor of the lobby on both knees, jolting in its intensity, and it took him a moment longer than usual to scrabble back to his feet.

He spun, wide eyed, reeling backward as if he thought that might enable him to get out of range of a forthcoming attack.

Slater unleashed a right hook and drilled it into the man's chin.

He didn't hold back.

Not one bit.

Jackpot.

Guy Two's neck muscles tensed in anticipation, but it was far too late. His chin whipped to the side and his entire body went round like it was on a rotating carnival ride and he splayed flat on the concrete floor on his stomach, unconscious before he hit the floor, which just made it worse when he came crashing down to earth. A grisly result, almost worse than Guy One.

They would both have headaches for weeks, if not months, to come.

And right now they were useless.

Slater stepped over Guy Two and drew both P228s from his waistband. It freed his movement, unclogging the front of his jeans. He'd checked them in the Tesla on the drive from Brooklyn to Manhattan and realised they were both fitted with aftermarket magazines, each holding fifteen rounds.

He wasn't planning a massacre, so he had no need for such firepower.

He just needed to send a message.

The lobby was entirely empty — a surprise indeed. It had a smooth concrete floor and plenty of natural light coming in through the front wall, which was nothing but a giant sheet of bulletproof glass. The furniture was minimal and modern, all hard edges and severe designs. There were a couple of leather couches bathed in daylight and an enormous statue of a warrior atop a warhorse in the middle of the space. It was a marble destrier, towering above the rest of the room.

Tommy Whelan was anything but subtle.

Slater crossed the empty lobby to a bank of elevators on the far wall. He checked every corner, every shadow, for signs of resistance. When he found nothing, it set him on edge. He had to remind himself this was a different world to what he was accustomed to. The cartels in Colombia and the tribesmen in Yemen were a different ball game entirely. This was opulent luxury in the heart of New York City, and you couldn't fortify the place to the nines without attracting suspicion. And the two sentries manning the door were likely more trained than Slater gave them credit for.

They were likely consummate professionals by industry standards.

Slater belonged to a different industry.

A darker industry.

Where he came from, the mob constituted a gang of schoolboys.

He called for an elevator — there was no key code on the controls. Just on the front door. A massive security error, but hubris is the killer of many men.

An elevator arrived with a gentle *ping* as soon as he pressed the button.

Someone was already on the way down.

Slater darted to the correct door and had both pistols pointed at the empty space before the metal doors whispered open.

A young guy, probably in his late twenties, almost walked straight into the barrels.

His eyes went wide and fear creased his face. He intuitively patted himself down for weapons, finding none. Probably a good thing. If he'd tried to pull out a sidearm of his own, Slater would have barely hesitated before shooting him in the forehead.

The guy had jet black hair — long on the top, shaved short on the sides. It was thick and hung in locks on either side of his face, naturally swept. He was blessed with good genetics. Full lips, a pronounced jawline, swirling green eyes. Pale skin, but that was to be expected if he was Irish. Clearly the son of an Irishman and a beautiful trophy wife.

'Gavin?' Slater said.

The kid's eyes lit up with recognition. 'Oh, thank God. You work for my dad, do you? I thought you were here to—'

Slater smashed the butt of the pistol in his right hand into Gavin Whelan's nose.

61

Blood sprayed, and Gavin backed across the elevator, hands flying to his face.

Slater followed him into the cable car and smacked the "close doors" button on the control panel with the bloody hilt of the P228. They whispered closed, just as quietly as they'd opened. Slater used the same butt to touch the emergency button, and the elevator froze in place.

They were alone in the small metal box.

Slater dropped one of the guns and kicked it behind him — he needed a hand free. He seized Gavin by the hair and shoved the barrel of the other Sig Sauer into his mouth. Two crimson streams ran out of the man's nostrils in equal measure, coating the top of the gun with a thin film. A couple of rivulets ran down either side of the black metal and dripped off the P228.

A grim sight.

Slater wasn't fazed in the slightest.

'You remember a girl named Abigail?' Slater said.

Tears in the eyes. Pain in the face. Terror in the expression.

A silent nod.

'Oh, that's good,' Slater said. 'She sure remembers you.'

Gavin mumbled something.

'What was that?' Slater said, and shoved the gun deeper into the guy's throat.

Gavin choked and spluttered on the barrel.

'What'd you do to her?' Slater said.

Silence.

'Answer me.'

Gavin started to mumble something, and Slater pushed the barrel deeper still between his teeth.

Gavin retched.

Slater said, 'Sorry. Thought you were insulting me.'

Slater extracted the barrel from the kid's mouth. It came out coated in saliva and blood from his nose. Not the prettiest sight in the world. Slater put it away, going so far as to re-engage the safety and tuck the weapon into the rear of his waistband.

Once again — no holster to satisfy standard safety requirements.

Slater frisked Gavin quick, but the kid was in shock, and in no way ready to resist. He came away empty-handed. It made sense. The Whelans had the confidence of a mob family ingratiated deep into society. They had connections everywhere. The sentries manning the door were probably just for show. They might as well have left their front door unlocked, inviting anyone to walk in off the street and test their might.

The warhorse statue seemed to speak for that.

Slater almost smiled at his good fortune, standing still in the stationary elevator, but he stifled the expression at risk of making Gavin Whelan relax. He needed the kid in a near-catatonic state for what would come next. The young

Whelan panted and wheezed and gasped for air as soon as Slater removed the gun from between his lips. He wasn't used to resistance. Maybe a dark look in the street every now and then, or a young woman named Abigail Nazarian swatting his advances away. But never would he imagine someone from New York trifling with the Whelans, showing them any resistance whatsoever. The repercussions would be immense.

Thankfully, Slater wasn't from New York.

And a family this confident, and this corrupt, was exactly what he needed to get to Russell Williams.

He slapped Gavin in the face, open palm, straight to the cheek. It would usually be considered a warning gesture, or an insult, but coming from Slater it was as good as a punch. The resulting *crack* seemed to echo off all four walls at once, and the roof, and the ceiling. Nerve endings exploded across Gavin's face, sending him down on all fours, accompanied by the sensation that half his face had burst. His cheek — and probably his eye socket — would swell in the coming hours.

Slater hauled the kid to his feet. 'That was fifty percent capacity. You want to test me?'

Gavin shook his head.

Paranoid now.

He couldn't contain the panic in his eyes.

He'd probably never even been on the receiving end of a verbal insult. Too much insulation, surrounded by a family that everyone knew ran the underbelly of the city. He probably had his way everywhere he went. Social expectations, and the undercurrent of fear. He'd probably never heard the word "no" until Abigail.

'You want to know who sent me?' Slater said.

Gavin shook his head again.

'Wrong answer.'

Slater slapped him again. Twice as hard. In the enclosed space, the equivalent to a bomb going off. Gavin crumpled, this time completely giving up. Slater could have made him eat a gun right then and there, if that was what he wanted, so shattered was the kid's morale. But he had other ideas in mind.

He wrenched Gavin to his feet once more. Already the left side of his face was starting to swell, ugly blotches forming on his cheek, above his eyebrow, his left eye beginning to seal shut.

'I hit hard, don't I?' Slater said.

Gavin nodded.

'Let's try that again. You want to know who sent me?'

This time, Gavin nodded.

Good, Slater thought. *I need my story to match up.*

He seized Gavin by the throat, backing him into the far wall of the elevator. They collided with the metal panelwork with a dull *thump.*

Slater said, 'You and your family have been bad boys, Gavin.'

Gavin nodded.

'So you admit it?'

Gavin shook his head.

Slater slapped him a third time.

And held him in place, pinned to the wall with a vice-like grip.

Gavin began to openly weep.

'I would have slapped you either way there,' Slater said. 'Just to let you know.'

'What do you want, man?' Gavin muttered, blood drooling from the corner of his lip where he'd bitten his tongue.

'I want to talk.'

'So talk to me. Stop fucking hitting me.'

'This is open palm. You don't want to see what a closed fist looks like.'

'I'll answer whatever you want.'

'That's the goal.'

'I swear, man, I will. What do you want to know?'

Satisfaction rippled through Slater. No more than half a minute, beginning to end, and he'd already broken the guy. Gavin Whelan didn't deserve to associate with a major crime family. As Slater had imagined, he was a spoilt brat who deserved nothing less than what he was receiving now.

'You've shamed the family by giving up so quick,' Slater said.

Testing the kid. Probing. Trying to find out if there was any morsel of resistance left inside Gavin that might make him falsify claims.

Gavin shook his head. 'Just leave me alone, man. Ask your questions and leave me alone.'

'Abigail,' Slater said.

Gavin nodded. 'Yeah. I was too pushy. I get it. Her dad already came for me, but a couple of my boys jumped him before he could get his hands on me. Not my fault. They were too harsh on him. I'm sorry.'

'What do you know about the hit?'

'What hit?'

'Okay,' Slater muttered. 'So you're just a young dumb dipshit. You're not involved.'

'Involved in what?'

'The family business.'

'They don't tell me everything, man. So I don't know much.'

'I figured. Now I'm going to tell you who sent me.'

'Okay.'

'A man named Russell Williams. Say it back to me.'

'Russell Williams.'

'My name is Will Slater. Say it back to me.'

'Will Slater.'

'Repeat both those names.'

'Russell Williams sent you. You're Will Slater.'

'Good. Now remember this.'

Slater backed up, and for a moment he felt a twinge of empathy for the young Whelan, but then he figured Abigail definitely wasn't the first, and she was probably the only one who had an ex-military father willing to do something about it. The kid hadn't heard the word "no" before, and he showed he picked his targets wisely, given the fact that he approached Abigail at a firm his family had their juicy paws all over.

So Slater lined up and kicked him square in the balls, and Gavin crumpled down onto all fours, and Slater kicked him in the ribs, breaking a couple of them.

Unbelievable pain. That was guaranteed.

Good.

Slater *needed* Gavin to remember this.

He needed the kid angry. Livid. Swearing revenge on anyone he could get his hands on.

He needed the young man running to every connection he could think of.

Passing it up the chain of command until it reached the top.

Slater left the kid there on all fours, retching and crying and gasping for breath, and he turned away from him and pressed the button for the fifth floor of the townhouse.

He hoped the rest of the family was home.

62

T hey were.

The elevator doors chimed open at the top floor, revealing a cavernous loft converted into a modern kitchen and dining room, and Slater had both guns up and aimed at the space beyond in case of emergency. Safeties off.

It proved unnecessary.

He marvelled at his luck — it was about time something went his way. He stared at a scene straight out of a Hollywood mafia movie, with seven burly men seated around an opulent table right near the glass windows looking out over the Upper East Side of Manhattan. The table was a big show-off thing, made of refurbished metal. The sunlight bathed them all in a soft glow.

They were deep in conversation, gesticulating back and forth about what Slater imagined were all kinds of important underworld issues.

Supply chains, and profit margins, and loyalty.

Probably.

They varied in size, with the smallest resting a shade

over five-eight and the rest somewhere between five-eleven and six-two. All big enough. They seemed to have overcompensated for their status by packing on muscle to look the part, but it made them tight and stiff in their undersized suit jackets, wholly unprepared for any kind of brawl that might unfold. Not that anything would happen up here, in their safe space, in what constituted their den.

Until Slater backed up and kicked Gavin Whelan in his broken ribs and sent him stumbling, screaming, crying, into the open space. Blood sprayed from the guy's mouth as he shouted for help.

It was sensory overload.

The very definition of it.

Perhaps in their wildest fantasies the Whelans expected to be interrupted by an aggravated intruder, whereupon they could make use of all the repetitions of bench presses they'd been doing in the gym, but they never would have expected their broken, mangled family member to stumble into one of their private meetings screaming bloody murder.

Slater had both P228s pointed at the table before any of them could wheel their shocked gazes around to take in the sight.

He screamed at the top of his lungs, 'If any of you move, I will shoot you in the head!'

Simple enough.

They got the message.

Slater knew it wouldn't be enough. There were seven of them, and one of him. Sooner or later one of them would muster the confidence to go for their weapons, if they had them in the first place. No way to tell from here. A marble kitchen island separated them from his line of sight — he could only see from their waists up.

He started rounding the island, moving toward them,

but he knew they would go for their guns in the next couple of seconds if they were going to at all.

He snapped his aim to one man and fired, one pull of each trigger, two enormous explosions of noise in the loft. He made sure the bullets passed by either side of the guy's face, leaving a few inches to spare on each side. The displaced air alone scared the shit out of him. The lead carried on and embedded itself in the sheet of bulletproof glass behind, creating spider-web cracks in the surface.

The guy flinched and ducked and probably came close to having a massive heart attack from shock alone.

Slater said, 'Sorry. Thought you went for a gun.'

Now they got the message.

Well and truly.

No-one moved a muscle.

Slater had proved himself a madman.

He made it to the other side of the kitchen island and came to a standstill, sweating through his tee from the sheer exertion of the last few altercations. He could feel the veins throbbing in his neck, racing blood around his body, but he didn't dare stop now. Gavin Whelan cowered behind him, out of his line of sight, but the kid was no threat. He lay balled up on the ground in the foetal position, hands on his ribs, wincing through the waves of pain coursing over his body, from cheek to throat to torso to genitals.

Slater regarded the seven men in front of him. All fit, all able, besides the eldest of the bunch, who sat at the head of the table.

Slater said, 'Tommy Whelan.'

The old man nodded. He had craggy weather-beaten skin, blotched red and white, and a tuft of blonde hair atop his head, so thin you could barely see it. His mouth was drawn in a hard line, and his eyes were narrow unforgiving slits in his sad face. It seemed he wished to break every bone in Slater's body, one by one, and then leave him to starve to death, for even daring to intrude on the meeting.

Little did he know it was about to get a whole lot worse.

Slater said, 'How are you related to Gavin Whelan?'

'He's my grandson,' Tommy said.

'Oh, good. I just fucked your grandson right up.'

'Is that him behind the kitchen island?'

'It is.'

'He sounds hurt. Gavin, my boy, you alright?'

A whimper floated across the loft.

'That's a no,' Slater said.

'Why'd you do that?'

'He pissed me off.'

'What'd he do to you?'

'He looked at me funny.'

Tommy Whelan shot Slater a thunderous look. It could have melted steel.

Slater found himself barely fazed. He'd dealt with a whole lot worse than an old cranky mob boss.

Tommy said, 'Better get to the point.'

'I don't think I will,' Slater said. 'I'm rather enjoying this. Watching all of you squirm. What a useless reputation the lot of you have built up. All cowering scum.'

Silent fury rippled through the ranks.

Slater shrugged, as if he was coming up with an impromptu plan. In reality, he'd forged the foundations of it on the drive over to Manhattan.

He said, 'Maybe I should give you all a chance to redeem yourselves.'

It seemed brash. Ludicrous, given the circumstances. But he'd done the calculations. He'd ran the hypotheticals in his head. He'd figured, if they were all Whelans, he could handle no more than eight. Seven slotted neatly into the upper end of the spectrum. Cumbersome, but manageable.

He said, 'Alright. All of you stand up. Right now.'

Chairs scraped back, and the procession of seven Whelans got to their feet.

Slater said, 'You should all think long and hard about this. If you come out on the losing side of this, your reputations will be ruined forever. I've tapped into the CCTV camera over my right shoulder and I'll have footage of this entire debacle. If it goes my way, you'll all be fucked. Forever. Imagine how humiliating this will be.'

'What?' Tommy spat.

Slater said, 'All of you lift up your jackets.'

They complied. Hands went to suit jackets and yanked the material skyward, revealing belts, revealing holsters.

Slater said, 'You. You. You. You. Guns out of your holsters. Two fingers, like pincers. If any of you even think about trying to use them you won't even know what hit you. You'll just be dead.'

They complied. They didn't even think about trying to beat him in a battle of reflexes. They'd seen how unnaturally fast he'd jerked in the direction of the first guy, firing the twin shots before any of them put it together. They weren't willing to chance it.

'Toss them over the kitchen island,' Slater said. 'Now.'

They threw them.

Thunk.

Thunk.

Thunk.

Thunk.

The guns clattered down on the marble floor, out of sight. Slater darted back in that direction, making sure Gavin didn't get his hands on one of the weapons by chance, but the kid was still curled up in a ball with his eyes squeezed shut, wracked with agony.

Slater sidestepped from pistol to pistol, punting them toward the open elevator doors. He scored four goals in a row, slotting each sidearm home. The four weapons skittered to a halt inside the cable car and spun softly on their axis'.

Slater jogged over to the elevator, reached inside to the control panel, and thumbed a random floor.

He ducked back out.

The doors whispered closed.

The Whelans watched the strange developments with an unfolding fascination.

Slater turned around, smiled, and tossed his own guns behind him. Flexed his open palms, exposing his vulnerability.

'Come on,' he said. 'Prove your reputation.'

63

Potentially the most foolish move in underworld history if he came out on the losing side of the equation. The stories would be told for generations about the moron that stormed into the Whelan compound without resistance, made it to the top floor, and threw everything away to get into a pissing match with the whole family.

But it was the way it needed to go.

Shooting six of them dead and leaving Tommy Whelan alive to deliver a message wouldn't have the intended effect. It might spread through a few degrees of separation, but it wouldn't get much further than that. He needed to utterly embarrass them, humiliate them beyond description, send them crawling to their connections with their tails between their legs, demanding swift and ruthless justice on the human vermin that dared to make them look so foolish.

That's what he needed.

And he would only get it this way.

The seven of them stood there awkwardly, unsure of what to do. They probably thought it was a cheap trick. The first one to step forward would receive a bullet to the head from a secret weapon Slater wrenched out from behind his back.

He lifted up his own T-shirt, and twirled on the spot.

A full three hundred and sixty degrees.

He smirked. 'I'm not bluffing.'

Tommy Whelan managed a laugh. He couldn't believe anyone could be so moronic. Seven men could overwhelm the toughest man on the planet through sheer bodyweight. They could all pile on and all the reaction speed in the world wouldn't mean a thing. It was the nature of physics.

But Slater had already put a mountain of thought into it.

He wouldn't fail.

Because in reality, it was six on one. Tommy Whelan wouldn't get his hands dirty. And Slater would make sure to beat the first guy so bad that the other five would doubt themselves, and then they'd be hesitant to step into range, because it would be like putting their hand voluntarily into a buzzsaw.

That's what he was relying on.

It all came down to the first exchange.

Slater thought of Shien. He pictured her big innocent eyes staring in awe at some training facility in the middle of nowhere. He pictured the humanity being stripped from her, piece by piece, as Williams fashioned her into a killing machine and ruined her chance of having a normal life before she had the ability and the wherewithal to decide for herself.

He saw flaming red, and his muscles supercharged.

There we go.

It all unfolded as he thought it would. It came down to the half-second gaps between actions, and he knew that's where he had the upper hand.

The first guy burst off the mark, clearly the most confident. Tommy Whelan's laughter had injected him with courage — he'd sensed the momentum shifting back in their favour. He regained his mojo first, and broke into a sprint, desperate to get his hands on Slater first. He likely figured this was an event that would go down in folklore, so he wanted all the bragging rights for future dick swinging contests.

Big mistake.

He came in way too fast, fists cocked, ready for the wildest swing of his life like it was a bar-room brawl. Slater met him with equal pace, throwing him off his game in every sense. He'd been anticipating a couple more feet of space before he needed to throw, but suddenly Slater was right there in his face.

Slater sliced an elbow upward, from floor to ceiling, a strange manoeuvre that required near-dislocation of the shoulder joint to pull it off. Thankfully, Slater had drilled the move thousands upon thousands of times, and it was etched into muscle memory. And he had all the burning rage and motivation of a nine-year-old girl's wellbeing in his mind, which added to the ferocity of the strike.

Not that he needed any additional power in the first place.

The elbow struck jaw and Slater's whole arm vibrated with the impact. One of the loudest cracks he'd ever heard echoed off the walls and the first guy's legs simply gave out underneath him. A mixture of shock, pain, and disbelief. Slater figured he must have shattered a few teeth, on top of breaking the guy's jaw. He pitched forward and Slater twisted into the right hook, dropping the elbow back and aiming to punch a hole right through the man's flesh. His calloused knuckles struck the side of the head and practically dumped the guy's body into one of the cabinets, breaking a couple of the cabinet doors off their hinges and sending the unconscious rag doll sprawling to the kitchen floor surrounded by wooden splinters.

Slater realised — amidst the crazed explosions of sight and sound — that he still had a couple of seconds to work with. The rest of the party were only now bursting into motion — they'd opted to observe their comrade's mad charge first before committing themselves. Slater stomped down on the first guy's elbow joint, producing another *snap* that rippled through the loft.

A couple of the Whelans visibly winced.

'Okay,' Slater said, trying not to pant from exertion. 'That was cute. Now you're unsure, aren't you? But you're not all going to stand there. That'd look awful — reputation-wise, I mean. Imagine that. There's five of you. One of me. And the CCTV's catching all of it. You going to let an unarmed man hold an entire esteemed crime family up by their balls?'

It had its intended effect.

Three charged at once.

Two held back.

Slater kicked the first guy in the stomach, stabbing with the ball of his foot, like a twenty-pound whip. It probably tore a couple of muscles, or broke a rib, but it didn't incapacitate him.

It didn't need to.

He froze in place, shocked to the core by the power with which Slater hit.

Good.

It put him on the back step.

Two to worry about.

Slater swung an elbow, left to right, with everything in

his system. Fast twitch muscle fibres firing, screaming with exertion. He landed. Right on the bridge of the next guy's nose. Practically punching it across his face.

Like walking into a buzzsaw.

Just as described.

The third guy hesitated, stunned by the devastation dealt out to the men alongside him, and that was all Slater needed. He thundered a boot into his groin, dropping him where he stood, and as he came down Slater brought the knee of the same leg up and smashed it into his jaw.

One-two.

Done.

The third guy crumpled, and Slater turned back to the first and kicked him in the exact same part of his stomach. Accurate to the inch. Bringing a whole new level of pain to the injury site. Now the guy lost his legs, and he went down puking onto the kitchen floor. Slater kicked him in the side of the head, turned back to the second guy, and headbutted him in his already-broken nose.

The second guy howled, and dropped, joining his friends on the floor.

Not unconscious.

But in too much pain to function.

Slater smirked. 'Would you look at that? Two left. I'm not counting you, Tommy, you geriatric fuck.'

That did it.

The last two Whelans charged.

64

S later feigned an elbow, and this time the pair were expecting it. They were the largest of the seven, opting to wait until last to demonstrate their superior fighting ability. One of them reacted fast, ducking back away from the elbow, but Slater hadn't even thrown it. By the time the guy realised what was happening, Slater wasn't there anymore.

He changed levels, ducking low and powering off both legs. With thighs like tree trunks, he had all the explosive athleticism he needed. He caught the first guy around the mid-section and heaved him off the floor, taking all his balance away, levering him into thin air and dumping him straight into his friend.

All three of them went to ground.

Slater thrived in controlled chaos.

Amidst scrabbling limbs and grunts of exertion, he found an unprotected face and smashed the same elbow three consecutive times into soft flesh. He broke a nose, an orbital bone, and a jaw on the same face. He rolled off that body and caught the last guy around the ankle as he attempted to surge to his feet. By that point the morale was shattered, and the last man seemed to be trying to make a beeline for the P228 sidearms Slater had discarded on the other side of the room.

Fat chance of—

The ankle whisked out of Slater's grasp, fast as a whip.

Too late, he realised his mistake.

He'd ended up on the far side of the room, close to the glass windows. The last Whelan had somehow, some way, managed to break free. Now he sprinted flat out for the bank of elevators, where the P228s lay on the floor.

Jesus Christ, Slater thought. *This can't be how it ends.*

He scrabbled to his feet and broke into an all-out sprint, almost turning his ankle twice in a row as he vaulted over unconscious Whelans en route to the elevators.

The last conscious Whelan made it there first, obviously.

He bent down to snatch up one of the Sig Sauers.

He got his hand on it.

He slipped a finger inside the trigger guard.

He brought it up level with...

Slater hit him with two hundred pounds of lean muscle in uncontrolled motion, a frantic football-esque crash tackle that sent them both careening into the wall between two elevator doors. They hit the plaster so hard that it caved in, spilling them both into the framework of the wall. Chunks of dust rained down on their heads.

Slater wrenched himself free of the debris, seized the gun with two hands, and hauled it away. He was operating on instinct now — the calm, calculated demeanour had gone out the window.

Reeling, battered and bruised from the impact, he waited for the last guy to peel himself out of the wall. His breath heaved in his chest. Pain wracked his insides. The mad tackle might have done more damage to Slater than his foe.

But it got the weapon out of the equation, which was all that mattered.

The last man somehow got his legs underneath him and levered himself out of the wall, tearing another chunk of plaster away from the crater. Slater let fly with another stabbing front kick, repeating the same action he'd thrown at half the Whelans, but this time he put his all into it. He needed to destroy the guy's face, preventing him from managing any kind of retaliation.

He missed.

He could chalk it up to the change of circumstances throwing him off his game, or the exertion he'd spent sprinting across the room tiring his limbs out, or the injuries sustained during the tackle, but no amount of excuses would change the reality of the situation, so he forgot about them.

His foot sailed past the last Whelan's face as the guy jerked to the right, missing his left cheek by inches. If it connected, it probably would have killed him right then and there, given the ferocity Slater threw it with. But it went spearing into the empty space through the plaster wall, throwing him off-balance. He stumbled and planted the foot down somewhere inside the wall, balancing on even ground. He wrenched it free.

The last Whelan went for a body shot.

Thank God.

He was trying to be smart about it. Trying to employ some kind of tactical prowess by targeting Slater's ribcage as he stood with one foot in the wall and one foot out. He'd probably seen all kinds of tapes — old boxers wearing their opponents out with perfectly timed jabs to the torso, taking their breath away piece by piece. Maybe he expected to dance around Slater like a court jester, demonstrating his superior fighting ability in the presence of Tommy Whelan. He might expect to earn a promotion while he was at it, and, of course, to be added to the folklore of this day that would go down in Whelan history.

But this wasn't boxing.

Slater stepped out of the wall as the jab landed against his obliques. He took it in stride, feeling the stabbing pain of aggravated muscle, mentally checking if the strike had impeded his movement. The last Whelan had thrown it with pinpoint accuracy and a fair amount of precision. Slater grimaced, but that was about it. It didn't break a rib. It didn't do anything to prevent him throwing everything but the kitchen sink at this poor hapless man.

And Slater could handle a bit of superficial pain.

So he allowed the punch to ricochet off his torso, tightening every muscle in his abdominal wall at once to absorb the force. Then he fired back with a giant looping haymaker of a right hand, sensing an opportunity he likely wouldn't have a second chance at. His fist whistled and arced and came down and landed.

This time, Slater couldn't miss.

He might as well have hit the guy with a brick. Everything shut down at once and the young man's eyes glazed over. Unconscious, not dead. Slater didn't care either way. The guy had gone for the gun, and that meant he didn't need to hold back, or show mercy. Not that he would have in the first place.

He stood still, breathing hard, soaking up the burning pain in his shoulders as the lactic acid built up. He'd thrown over a dozen kicks and punches like his life depended on it, full power, draining the central nervous system like nothing else. He was familiar with the feeling. It wasn't pleasant. But he was feeling a whole lot better than the six Whelans sprawled across the loft, either flat out unconscious or in a weeping, moaning state of semi-consciousness.

Tommy Whelan stood frozen in place, white as a sheet.

Slater smiled. 'You're going to remember this, aren't you?'

65

A poignant silence hung over the space. Slater retrieved the P228s, double-checked to make sure there were no firearms in sight, and commanded the eldest Whelan to sit back down at the head of the table.

Tommy Whelan shuffled over to the chair and lowered himself into it.

Tentative.

Withdrawn.

Awfully meek for a mob boss.

Slater sat down at the other end, over a dozen feet away from the old man, but it provided him with a sweeping view of the loft, and a direct line of sight to the elevators. If anyone arrived, he'd be ready. But he didn't figure that was likely. He assumed he'd dismantled most of the family on the Upper East Side. These men weren't all Whelans. Some were either hired muscle or, more likely, the upper management in charge of certain jurisdictions. Not related by blood, but close enough. He figured he'd flatlined half the command.

At least, judging by the look on Tommy Whelan's face.

Slater said, 'I've been sent by a covert division deep in the government. You've never heard of it. We're not very happy with you.'

'Why's that?'

'The men and women you pay off in law enforcement, and in the courts, and in low-level government. You're over-stepping your boundaries.'

'We do everything the right way. We honour all the traditions. We've never skimped or saved on anything. We are very generous to the right parties. Isn't that the way it's always worked?'

'Not anymore.'

'Well you could have fucking told me like a man. Instead of coming here and kicking the shit out of anyone and everyone just to send a message. Man, who the hell are you anyway? Some kind of executioner?'

'Something like that,' Slater said. 'I'm here to tell you how it's going to work in future.'

'Like hell you are.'

'Watch your tongue. Or I'll do to you what I did to these boys.'

'I'd rather you just put a bullet in my head and get it over with.'

'No. You're my bitch now. You're the property of my division. And my boss is going to be more than happy to get his fingers in all your pies.'

'This is the man that sent you?'

Slater almost smirked. *It's all too easy.*

'Sure is,' he said.

'I take it you're not going to tell me his name.'

'Why wouldn't I?'

'To protect him.'

Slater laughed, harsh and guttural. It rang through the

cavernous space. 'You think we're afraid of an operation as shit as yours? His name is Russell Williams. Remember it. He owns you now.'

'Does he?'

'Yes, and as a matter of fact, as soon as I'm out of here you're going to go to every contact you have in law enforcement and tell them they no longer serve you, by order of the same Russell Williams. Or I'll come back here and use bullets instead of my fists. Understood?'

'You've got a big mouth for someone who hasn't killed any of us yet.'

'Don't get confident in front of me. You'll be mopping up parts of your family for the next few hours. This is a warning. A demonstration, if you will.'

'It almost didn't work,' Tommy Whelan said with the hint of a smirk.

Good, Slater thought. *Get that confidence back, old man. You'll need it.*

Slater nodded, shrugging, raising his open arms on either side in a platonic gesture. 'Fair. That guy almost had me. Who is he?'

'My son.'

'And how'd that end up working out for him?'

They both turned their heads to check on the wellbeing of the last Whelan standing.

Slater had left him in a motionless crumpled heap on the kitchen tile, but now the scene was even worse. The man had reared out of unconsciousness with the energy of a crazed bull, but his brain hadn't yet begun to function at the same level as his body. He ended up twitching and drooling on his side, eyes wide and rabid, swimming through air in an attempt to reconnect vital synapses between his temples. Slater knew from experience the guy would be fine in roughly ten to twenty minutes, and the headache would dissipate after a few weeks of rest, but to Tommy Whelan, it must have looked like his son was in the process of succumbing to a gruesome death.

As Slater suspected, the old man sent his grunts out to do the dirty work on the streets. To intimidate and blackmail and exploit. He sat up here in his bulletproof townhouse, planning his every move. He didn't see the grisly details.

Maybe he'd been privy to beatings and rapes and killings up close in the past.

But that was a long, long time ago.

So the violence all around him started to seep in. Slater saw the shock setting in, taking over his every movement. His gaze flicked from man to man, reeling at the physical consequences, lingering on the blood dripping from nostrils and lips, coating the floor in crimson.

Tommy Whelan flapped his own lips like a dying fish.

Slater slammed his elbows down on the table, seizing the old man's attention once more.

'I told you this was a warning,' Slater said. 'Next time I'll keep you all alive again, but the trauma will be even worse. I'll pick my shots selectively. Third time I'll use a gun.'

Tommy nodded, white as a sheet, and for a moment Slater feared he'd gone too far.

He needed that spark back.

He said, 'How does it feel to bend over backwards for us?'

Tommy shrugged.

'Because that's what you'll be doing. Crawling around on all fours, looking over your shoulder for who Russell Williams is going to send next. All your manpower in the force and in office is going to be useless. Understand?'

A gentle nod.

More resistance.

Ideas forming.

There we go.

Slater got to his feet, strode along the length of the table, and put a hand on Tommy's shoulder.

'You going to be a good boy?' Slater said.

A vein protruded from the side of Tommy's temple. He probably hadn't been insulted or degraded in three decades. He didn't know how to handle it.

Slater knew how he would handle it. And it would sure get the attention of the man he was looking for.

Slater said, 'Was I too quiet?'

'I heard you.'

'You going to be a good boy?'

'Yes.'

'Good. Now, just to make sure...'

Slater took Tommy Whelan's old craggy nose between two of his fingers, in a pincer-like grip, and snapped it to the left.

66

He stepped back out into the crisp afternoon air with a fresh lease on life.

He made sure to have the P228s at the ready in case either of the sentries had recovered their senses enough to mount resistance. But he found them sitting idle in the corner of the lobby, tucked away in the shadows, unarmed, with their knees brought up to their chests and their eyes directed at the floor.

When the elevator arrived, they lifted their gazes, exposing bloodied swollen faces, and Slater had one of his barrels aimed at them before they could blink.

He'd been around hundreds of set-ups in the past.

At this point, nothing would surprise him.

But they weren't faking their dejection. They turned their gazes straight back to the floor, averting their eyes from Slater. It gave him a near-mythical aura. Right then and there he knew he wouldn't have any issues staying in New York for a few days. They wouldn't put out a direct hit on him. The morale was shattered, and they had very little information to work with.

The whole compound lay in a shroud of misery, opened up and rattled and torn apart by a lone individual.

If they talked about it in public too often, the more embarrassing details would come to the surface.

Slater walked straight past the broken sentries and breathed in the scent of the Upper East Side. It didn't have the usual stink of rotting trash and open sewers that a large portion of New York City sported these days. He kept both guns hidden from any passing civilians by tucking them under his T-shirt, and he dropped one of them in a trash can almost immediately. A single Sig Sauer would suffice, and he didn't expect to meet much resistance in the next few days.

Now, the waiting game began.

And he certainly needed it.

His muscles began to cramp. Every second that passed brought new knots, new bruises and bumps and disrupted fascia. He could knock a man dead with a barrage of punches, no thanks to a decade of relentlessly honing his ability, but he wasn't Superman. That kind of exertion — especially at the level he'd dished out — wasn't sustainable. He needed a shower and a bed and a long rest.

He found the Four Seasons only a few blocks over and paid mid-five figures for a five-night stay in the Royal Suite, which the concierge confirmed as available after a few minutes of tapping away at his keyboard. Slater barely glanced at the price before handing over a credit card. They must have assumed he was either a New Age tech billionaire or an oil tycoon from a more traditional region of the world.

Either way, they didn't seem to care in the slightest.

The direct opposite of a low profile.

Exactly what he was going for.

'Will Slater,' he said when they asked for his name.

He made sure they entered it in the system.

Then he made them check again.

He confirmed the spelling.

They handed over his room key and he headed for the elevators.

The rest of the afternoon was a blur. He went through the same familiar routine he'd seen a thousand times over — elevator, carpeted hallway, dark brown door, lavish suite. The views over Central Park from the suite were astonishing, breathtaking, captivating — and he barely looked. He'd seen it all before. A career like his had tasted the highest of highs and the lowest of lows. He'd dropped the inordinate sum of cash more to attract attention than to purchase luxury. He needed his location easily identifiable.

He stripped off his clothes — stained with sweat, but no dirt or blood — and showered for close to an hour. He needed it. His body was already starting to shut down on itself, his arms growing heavy and his knees growing weak.

Only in the movies could a hero brutalise his enemies with his bare hands without slowing down for days on end. Slater had dumped his energy reserves, used up every ounce of adrenalin in his body, and burnt out his entire central nervous system over the course of the day.

He shut the water off, sauntered to the phone, and ordered room service — nearly everything on the menu. It arrived in impressively fast fashion, and he wolfed down close to two thousand calories to replenish his system. Steak, eggs, pasta, salad, bread. A massive serving of each. Gourmet, too. Packed with micronutrients, especially the salad — a blend of kale and spinach and avocado. A world away from the plane food he'd been forced to stomach en route to New York. He didn't want to know how much it would set him back.

His stomach fit to burst, he went to the bed and climbed straight in.

Surrounded by opulence. Provided with one of the most desirable views on the planet. He tuned it all out.

He closed his eyes.

He slept.

67

He came awake in the early hours of the morning, almost entirely revitalised.

It was still dark outside.

The trauma he put his body through on a regular basis back in Colombia paid dividends now. He'd always known it would. Otherwise he wouldn't have had the mental fortitude to go through with it. But back in the thick jungle of the Chocó Department, he'd risen each day with the determination to push his body slighter further than he had the day before, setting off a compound effect with his physique that had slowly, piece by piece, created the shape he was in today.

He rolled out of bed, showered again for good measure, and dressed in the same clothes from earlier that day. He headed for the balcony overlooking Central Park and Manhattan, and leant on the railing for what could have been an hour, deep in his own head. He couldn't shake the incessant thoughts, and couldn't hope to decipher them. So many strains competed for his attention that eventually he gave up and zoned into the view, admiring the bustling night lights and the dark swathe of Central Park, forcing everything else out of his head.

It certainly wasn't easy to abandon a life at the drop of a hat, no matter how much he'd grown used to the road. Now he had no fixed abode. He wondered how long it would take for the cartels or a group of savvy locals to dismantle the lavish compound he'd left behind on the banks of the river. There would be endless value in the raw materials. Maybe they would be carted off into the jungle to build a new, better encampment to replace the clearing he'd emptied of life.

The wheels keep turning.

People keep snorting and injecting and swallowing.

The demand grows.

The cartels provide.

He shivered at the helplessness of it all. He couldn't hope to make a dent in the industry. In any industry. Even the mob. Sure, he'd decimated a townhouse of what were reportedly the toughest sons of bitches in Manhattan, but there would always be more to take their place.

He couldn't concern himself with that.

What he could focus on were the isolated incidents. The ordinary people he encountered, the people he could communicate with face-to-face, the people that actually mattered.

Like Shien.

He forced all those thoughts away. He had to. It could be days before the web of chaos he'd created ran its course, and he wasn't sure what form the outcome would take. Until then it would serve him no purpose to speculate about what could be. It would only waste mental energy. If all went well, Russell Williams would reveal he'd put Shien in a respectable foster home and Slater could be done with that train of thought forever.

It was a mad game to play — not knowing if anything he was doing had a purpose — but he figured he'd made the world a slightly better place in the process regardless. A cartel in Colombia, and a mob family in New York. Neither of which had anything to do with Slater, or the girl.

Just rare strokes of happenstance leading to violence.

That practically summed up his life.

He must have dwelled in a near-limbo state for far longer than he expected, for the pale blue light of dawn seeped into the sky before his eyes. He shook himself out of the trance and gave himself the once-over, shocked that hours had passed. His elbows had turned raw, leaving pale red wounds in place of his usual dark black skin tone, and he winced as he bent his arms back and forth to test them. Whatever injuries he sported, he figured those on the receiving end of the blows had it a thousand times worse.

He wondered how the Whelans were coping with the complete disruption of their lives. Most of the men Slater had encountered wouldn't be getting out of bed for weeks, which would leave a sparse workforce to deal with the ramifications. Tommy Whelan would have to take certain matters into his own hands.

And right now, he would be seething with fury.

He might have already made the necessary calls.

Word would be travelling up the pipeline, minute by minute...

Slater stepped inside. *There's no use speculating*, he reminded himself for what felt like the hundredth time. He figured he might as well get to work, and stay busy for the rest of the day. The calmness of solitude was no stranger to him, and he would be perfectly content sitting alone in his hotel room for as long as it took for the next phase of his plan to take place, but there were too many thoughts vying for attention.

He needed something in front of him.

He found a Brazilian jiu-jitsu gym on his smartphone, only a few blocks away, and his eyes widened as he noted the esteemed lineage the founders held. He had no way to prove the black belt he'd earned during his years of secret training in Black Force, but he figured actions spoke louder than words. It had been quite some time since he'd put on the *gi* and stepped foot on the mats.

He made a mental note to buy a fresh wardrobe, left the Royal Suite behind, and headed for the street.

Wholly unperturbed by the fact that there was likely an entire crime family hunting for his head.

68

His intuition proved accurate enough.

He didn't run into anyone. He found no confrontation. He didn't even catch a dark look from a passerby. Everything took time, and Tommy Whelan would still be in the process of scrambling for reinforcements.

He loaded up on designer clothing, including activewear and jeans and shirts and jackets, spending close to ten thousand dollars on a few outfits for the sole reason that the outlet rested neatly between the Four Seasons and the jiu-jitsu gym. Ever since Macau, money had ceased to mean anything to Slater. He no longer looked at price tags. He went where he wanted, and did what he wanted. Black Force had ensured his every need was met during his time in active service, but four hundred million dollars of triad funds put him in a whole new ballpark.

It had taken some time to get accustomed to, but as Slater had come to learn about everything in life, habits develop quick.

He found the gym, paid the entry fee, and bought a traditional *gi* from reception. The staff stared at him, smug in their disdain, likely under the impression he was a tourist with a fat wallet and no knowledge of Brazilian jiu-jitsu. They thought they could bleed him dry on private coaching sessions and a smattering of optional extras. As soon as he was on the mats, he sought out a cluster of men in their late thirties with rough hands and thick, calloused fingers. There were black belts around their waists. As he expected, they ran the joint.

He explained his predicament.

They didn't believe him.

He spent three consecutive hours proving his worth.

There was a certain indescribable flow to a jiu-jitsu rolling session that Slater couldn't put into words, but it achieved exactly what he was going for. He thought nothing of what his future might hold — given the fact he might have to go up against the entire government, he figured he was handling the impending crisis well.

Intense physical exertion stripped you of all other concerns.

He twisted and levered his frame across the mats, grappling with all comers, giving every black belt in the gym enough competition to stun them. He tapped purple and brown belts with ease, and they quickly learned not to underestimate him. After only a few minutes of cranking arm-bars and diving for leg locks, the inexperienced members of the gym backed right off.

Then the black belts fought back. Slater got his knee caught in a precarious position, and the man he was rolling with pounced on it like a pit viper. Slater tapped immediately, aware that any attempt to try and tough it out would be met with a crank of the submission. He didn't fancy getting his knee torn apart before what might constitute the most vital few days of his life.

After a final gruelling roll with the gym's chief operator, the most elite black belt in the whole place, Slater collapsed onto his back as the man finally called the session to a halt. They both lay there, side by side, drenched in sweat, chests heaving, grateful for the opportunity to test their mettle against such ruthless competition.

The wizened veteran rolled into a seated position with the dexterity of a cat, wrapping his arms around his knees and observing the rest of the mats.

Slater clambered upright, nowhere near as graceful.

He said, 'Thank you.'

The man looked at him with a hard lined face and said, 'Who gave you your black belt?'

Slater paused. 'I can't actually tell you that.'

'I believe you have it. You proved yourself. You don't need to be secretive about it.'

'Yes, I do.'

'Would I know the man who gave it to you?'

Slater nodded. 'Probably. He's esteemed. Held in high regard. You'd know him.'

'But you can't tell me?'

Slater got to his feet, put both hands on the guy's shoulders, and jokingly pushed him back to the mats. 'He signed an NDA before he started training me. If you know one of BJJ's elite who disappeared off the map about eight years ago, and then resurfaced back out of nowhere ... that's because he was training me.'

The man's eyes widened. 'Wait...?'

Slater nodded. 'Yeah.'

He deemed it prudent to get the hell out of there before he revealed anything else. The trainer in question had dedicated two years of his life to bringing Slater into the realm of the elite jiu-jitsu practitioners in the world nearly a decade ago, during the foundations of his career. The government had paid hand over fist for his commitment. He'd been instructed to never speak a word of it.

And Slater had practically revealed all to the guy seated next to him, a guy he'd never met before today. But bonds were formed on the mats, deep in the sweat and exertion and pain.

Brazilian jiu-jitsu was a brotherhood.

And Slater was proud to belong to it.

So he knew the information wouldn't travel far. Black belts had a cunning and an intellect rarely found in the general population. After all, they had dedicated years of their lives, day after day, to honing themselves into human anacondas. They had steadily learned to deploy patience and calmness above all. This man wouldn't react foolishly with the information. He'd mull over it, consider the circumstances, and determine that it probably wasn't worth pursuing the matter any further.

In fact, he already seemed to be figuring that out.

Slater nodded farewell, and used the bathroom to change into a new pair of jeans, a crisp white shirt, and a dark leather jacket that cost him what most would consider a month's salary. He slung the rest of his gear over his shoulder and bid the staff goodbye with a brief wave, heading past them fast. They stared at him with undisguised interest — the reception counter had a direct view of the mats, so they must have seen him prove his prowess.

He found a fairly nondescript brunch spot and loaded up on eggs, bacon, avocado, spinach, chorizo, and a small mountain of bread. He hadn't eaten since the night before, and burning over a thousand calories on the jiu-jitsu mats depleted him like nothing else. But he'd conditioned himself to experience that kind of output day over day, so the food fuelled him right back up, supercharging his energy. He ordered a couple of jumbo styrofoam cups of long black coffee to go, and downed them en route back to the Four Seasons.

Fatigued by an enormous meal and a gruelling training session, he crashed again as soon as he made it up to the Royal Suite. The old military adage — *sleep when you can, not when you need to* — was burned into him from long ago, and he didn't take it lightly. He didn't know how much he'd be able to sleep over the coming days, if at all. So he drew the curtains and climbed into bed and turned the lights out with the touch of a panel above the headboard. The lavish space plunged into darkness, and he breathed deep, in and out through his nose, and then he was asleep.

A knock at the door woke him hours later.

69

He came awake in an instant. None of the grogginess, none of the hesitation, none of the murky confusion. Just a lightning-fast flash of ice, searing his temples, revitalising him.

Telling him, *This is it.*

There was no other reason for the knock. Ordinary civilians weren't allowed up to these floors, and he'd hung a *Do Not Disturb* sign on the door, so it couldn't be hotel staff. He snatched the Sig Sauer off the nightstand and thumbed the safety off, ready to shoot and kill if the situation deemed it necessary. He couldn't find an ounce of hesitation within him. That had been drilled into him nearly a decade ago.

You pause, you die.

He gave the Royal Suite the once-over. He had no idea which way the coin would roll when he opened that door. He prepared to abandon everything. Still dressed in the same clothes he'd changed into earlier that morning, he shoved his wallet, phone, and passport into the pockets of his jeans, and gave the Dolce & Gabbana shopping bag a final glance.

Unnecessary. Deadweight.

He left it where it was.

The price tags still on the gear.

He was ready. It couldn't have been more than ten seconds since the first knock, but his brain flipped into overdrive. He ducked low in case a preliminary gunshot blasted through the wood. He crossed the room, skirting around armchairs and rugs, reaching the keyhole and peering into it with bated breath, ready for an onslaught of the deepest, darkest operatives the United States had to offer. The men and women pulled out of the depths of the secret world, sent to put a rogue asset in check, and most likely eliminate him.

What he saw through the keyhole made his heart skip a beat.

No.

Really?

Holy shit.

He realised he'd built castles in his head that weren't there. There was no need to have been paranoid. If Ruby hadn't talked, then he was supposedly on good terms with most of the covert world.

She clearly hadn't talked.

Not a word.

Silently, Slater thanked her.

Then he put the Sig Sauer behind his back and re-engaged the safety, tucking it comfortably into his jeans. He squared up, took a breath, and opened the door.

Russell Williams said, 'What the fuck do you think you're doing throwing my name around like that?'

He stood there on his own, unarmed, dressed in dark grey pants and an open-necked shirt and a thick black winter coat. He had a five o'clock shadow the colour of salt and pepper across his jaw, and short dark brown hair flecked with grey. His eyes were brooding, piercing, yet open. Slater had only met him once — back in Macau — but Williams had evidently made such a fatherly impression that Slater had ended up trusting him with the life of a nine-year-old girl with nowhere to go and a lifetime of hardship to look back on.

It might have been his biggest mistake yet.

Slater ushered the man inside, gesturing into the Royal Suite. 'Please.'

Williams barrelled past, clearly in a furore. 'You've been busy.'

'I had to.'

'Why?'

'To get in touch with you.'

'You couldn't have called?'

'You're uncontactable, remember? You shut down my old avenues of communication.'

'I'm sure there's other ways to get hold of me than making it look like I picked an esteemed mob family up and dumped them on their head. Do you have any idea how much of a shit-storm you just caused?'

'I needed you here. In the flesh. I needed an urgent response. And ... I had to target the Whelans anyway. For other reasons.'

Williams eyed him warily. 'Should I have brought back-up?'

'For what?'

'Exactly. I trust you. I thought we were on good terms. Was that a mistake?'

'Not at all.'

'I'd say it's good to see you, but what the hell are these circumstances?'

Slater stepped back, ever so slightly. Putting just enough distance between them to prevent a wild rabid lunge on Williams' part. As far as he was concerned the man had no combat experience — hence his position as handler — but one could never be too careful. Slater made sure to inject a lackadaisical nature into all his movements. And he kept a hint of unrest on his face, screwing his eyes slightly shut, as if something was bothering him. It added to his own mystery, drawing Williams away from the simple fact that they were in a hotel room together, alone.

Slater said, 'You can say it. It's good to see you, old friend.'

'I wouldn't go that far.'

'Maybe. Maybe not. You don't have to know someone for long to know you can trust them.'

That seemed to bring Williams' guard down. He kicked his coat back and dropped into one of the armchairs. 'What the hell have you been up to, Will? I'm hearing my name in places it should *never* be spoken.'

Slater sat down on the edge of the bed, distinctly aware of the P228 nudging against the small of his back.

'That was the point,' he said. 'I told you — I needed a fast response. I needed you here. No backup.'

'For what?'

Williams eyed the door. Slater knew he didn't have long. Williams hadn't been expecting this. He was running through the hypotheticals now, wondering how he could have been so stupid to drop everything and track down Slater on a whim.

Now he was realising he should have employed more caution against ex-operatives — people he'd forged uneasy alliances with, but little more than that.

Slater said, 'I need to ask you a question.'

'Sounding awfully sinister now, Will.'

'Yeah, well...'

'What?'

'Desperate times.'

'What the hell are you talking about?'

'I've been contemplating how to do this for the last few days, but in reality there's no way to get you to talk without—'

He drew the Sig Sauer, making sure it was in full view of Williams when he thumbed the safety off. He aimed the barrel square at the man's head.

Williams' brooding eyes turned dark and cloudy. 'Oh, you really don't want to be doing that, Will.'

'I think I do.'

'You'd better choose your next words very fucking carefully.'

'Okay,' Slater said. 'Not a problem. Did you put Shien in the Lynx program?'

70

S ilence.

Deafening silence.

You could hear a pin drop.

They stared at each other across the room, both locked in a battle of stares that neither man was willing to break. Slater knew Williams was fighting the urge to display a single nervous tic — trying not to twitch his lip, or blink, or flare his nostrils. He fought so hard to control his poker face that Slater knew immediately the next words to come out of his mouth would be egregious lies.

'What's the Lynx program?' Williams said, deadbeat.

'Wouldn't have a clue. I heard a rumour.'

'From where?'

'An undisclosed source.'

'You'd better get to the point so I can discredit whoever the hell is feeding you this bullshit.'

'What bullshit?'

'What the hell is the Lynx program?'

'Where's Shien?'

'Safe.'

'Where?'

'You want the truth?'

'Always.'

'She's in a foster home, Will. I did exactly what you told me to do. But I made sure to take her off all government records, so no-one can ever track down where she's being raised. It'd ruin her childhood. I protected her even from you. I didn't want a shred of danger following her anywhere. Even if you thought you made the wrong decision in the moment, and wanted to reunite with her, and thought the only way to do that was to latch onto the first bad rumour you heard and run with it all the way to this hotel room. Is that right? Are you delusional?'

'I'd like to be.'

'I don't know what else to tell you.'

'The truth.'

'That is the truth.'

'And I might have bought it. It was awfully convincing. Great job on that. Do you teach them to act yourself? Do you take the weekly classes?'

'I don't know what the hell you're talking about, and I suggest you either start making sense or put a bullet in me, because either way you're fucked.'

'Am I?'

'Point that gun at me for another five seconds and I might not be so kind when we sort this out.'

'Who says we're sorting this out?'

'You don't know what you're getting yourself into, Will. You don't know the world I belong to.'

'Yes I do. I belonged to it for ten years.'

'You think you did. You belonged to the outskirts of it. You don't know a thing about how the internals work, and for good reason. It's a dark beast inside that cage, Will. You understand the resources I have access to, right? You know what I could do to your life if you made an enemy out of me?'

'Not much you can do six feet under.'

'Empty threats. Either shoot me or put the gun down. Your call.'

'I think I'll keep it right here.'

'I told you — you don't know what you're talking about. I came here on my own because of the work you did for your country. You practically dedicated your life to it. And we've lost track of the number of times you almost died. It's all in the files, buried deep down under a mountain of encryption. Every operation you undertook. Sometimes I dive in, for light reading. Just to see what kind of a man you are.'

'And...?

'And as far as I can tell, you're a good one. Which is why I came. It's why I came in Macau, too. I wouldn't go on my own for anyone else. But I read your file extensively before I associated myself with you, and I trust you.'

'I like what you're doing,' Slater said with a smirk. 'Manipulation tactics at their finest.'

'What?' Williams said, his eyes searing with cold. Then he said, 'Actually, you know what, I don't give a shit. Put that gun down or this conversation is over.'

'You must not have read my file as extensively as you thought.'

'Trust me, I did.'

'Then you *never* would have come alone, and you *never* would have lied to me.'

'I haven't lied. And I'm about done with defending myself.'

'That's a shame to hear. Because I can't say I've read your file, and—'

'I don't have one.'

Slater raised an eyebrow. 'Well, there you go. You can talk all you want about the grave danger I've got myself in, but really all you can do if you walk out of this room alive is make a few calls and send a few of your minions running around searching for me. I'm sure they're well-trained, and I'm sure they're ruthless, but I'm big-headed enough to put myself in both those categories, too. I'm sure "the file" spells that out in as many words.'

'It also says you're a decent man. Which is why I'm surprised—'

'I am. I care about the wellbeing of a little girl I rescued from hell.'

'As you should. But you have nothing to—'

With a manic glint in his eye, Slater said, 'In fact, I'd be willing to wage war against the entire fucking government if it meant pulling her out of hell again.'

71

Williams stirred icily in his chair. He gripped the armrests with white knuckles, clearly hoping Slater didn't see.

Slater saw everything.

Williams said, 'You have nothing to worry about. I swear to you. You're hearing fairytales.'

'You didn't even ask me where I heard it.'

'I'm not interested in who's feeding you bullshit. Is it King? Because he doesn't know a thing.'

Slater smirked. 'No. King is in the past. He's done with this life. But I'm not. Which doesn't bode well for you.'

'Then who did you hear it from? An excommunicated outcast? I assume those are the only types you have contact with these days.'

'I don't have contact with anyone, as a matter of fact. It was a chance encounter. A run-in.'

'Now you're the one making things up, Will. Come back to reality. Please. Shien is counting on it. Leave her be.'

'Is she? She's counting on it?'

'Yes.'

'That's interesting.'

'Come on. You know me. Would I do anything to piss you off? Do you honestly think that? I've read your file, like I said.'

'And I think the file showed I'm brash. And reckless. And prone to outbursts of impulsiveness. Most of the time it's what gets the job done. But in Macau it made me leave a little girl with a man I hardly knew. And now I'm starting to think you weren't really there to tell me I'd been cleared of wrongdoing. I think you know exactly why you were there.'

'You're psychotic, Will. You don't know what you're talking about.'

'How'd you know I was with her? CCTV live feeds? I'm sure you were telling the truth about the deep dark secret world. I believe that. I've seen enough on the outskirts, as you said. Were you watching me in Macau? Were you keeping a close eye on the girl? Running background checks? Understanding she's a ghost? Plotting to snatch her out of my hands?'

'You gave her over to me. And, besides, she's safe.'

'I almost died in Macau. I complied a list of injuries so extensive it took me months to recover. That seems to be a reoccurring pattern over the last year. But that casino broke me. It chewed me up and spat me out. And you knew that. You knew I'd hand her over. You knew I was at my breaking point, and needed to be alone. You knew I'd trust you.'

'Once again, you're delusional.'

'I don't think so. Want to know where I was three days ago?'

'Not particularly.'

'I think you do.'

'Okay, go on. Will you take the gun out of my face?'

'No. I was deep in the Chocó Department, in rural Colombia.'

Briefly, a shadow of recognition crossed his face.

He noticed the same time as Slater.

They both knew he couldn't take it back.

With resignation, Williams said, 'Christ. What the hell were you doing there?'

'Living out there. For such a fearsome know-it-all, you certainly weren't keeping tabs on me.'

'You're bluffing.'

'Wish I was. It's a tough place to live. But the humidity and the atmosphere cultivate discipline. I had to put myself through the ringer. I had a certain kind of injury a few months ago. It set me back, physically and mentally. I had to reshape myself into what I used to be.'

'Did you?'

'Take a look at me.'

'You've never lacked self-confidence, have you?'

'Is that in my file too?'

'In between the lines. You could assume that.'

Slater smirked. 'Never had a problem with that. I know what discipline gives you. I can recognise my strengths.'

'And they are?'

'When I put my mind to something I make sure it gets done. Fairly simple, when you put it into basic terms like that. But most people don't understand what that really means. It means you can get almost anything you want from life if you're willing to put in what's required. So when I tell you to take care of a young girl with no family and a horrific past, I make sure it gets done. No matter what that takes. Are we on the same page?'

With one final burst of resistance, Williams said, 'I don't know what you're talking about.'

'That wasn't your operative in the Chocó jungles? Must have been someone else who just happened to drop your name, then...?'

Williams glared. 'What did you do to her?'

Now Slater was the one to hesitate. 'Nothing. Why?'

'Have the decency to tell me where you buried her. She was a good operative. One of our best. Don't you fucking dare try and pretend you let her walk away. I played your games until the truth came out, but now we might as well get on the same level. My program is my business. You handed Shien over to me, and you didn't put a thing in writing. You technically kidnapped her, if you want to get specific about it. Therefore I was free to do whatever the hell I wanted with her. And I did what was best. But if you have the gall to think you can lambast me about her wellbeing when you put one of my very best talents in the ground, then you have another thing coming.'

'I didn't touch Ruby Nazarian,' Slater said, then shrugged. 'Actually, I did, but only what she wanted me to do. Not my fault you lost her after she walked out on me. You never know — maybe she had a change of heart about the program. But thanks for the clarification. Now, the pair of us are going on a trip.'

'Where?'

'The facility. Wherever it is.'

'What makes you think I'd take you there? You of all people.'

'Is this the part where you try to convince me you're thick-skinned?'

'Maybe I haven't seen combat,' Williams said. 'But don't take me for a pushover. I'll die before I give away information that confidential.'

Slater smiled. He got off the bed, crossed to the

armchair, and crouched down. Right in front of Williams' face. He jammed the barrel of the Sig Sauer into the man's throat. Not hard. Gently, letting him feel the texture of the barrel against the soft tissue of his neck.

'You see, that's where we differ in opinion,' Slater said.

Williams sat still as stone. Trying to give nothing away. But the eyes never lied.

'I don't think you're ready to die,' Slater said. 'I think you're a very careful and patient man. And I think you're smart. You say you've read my file, but now's the time where we really see if that's true or not. I'm sure you think you're doing the right thing with the Lynx program. And you have the backing of the government. It's a mad world out there, and lines need to be crossed. I get it. Maybe you're approaching it from a utilitarian perspective. Sure, you're ruining a few childhoods, but the assassins you're forging are priceless. You're reducing far more suffering than you're creating. By an overwhelming amount. It's a bitch of an issue to grapple with. I'm not interested in that. You know I'm single-minded, and you know I'm reckless, and you know I'm determined. So, ask yourself, is it really worth getting your brains blown out across this room just to spite me? Think about the life you've spent so long cultivating. Do you really want to throw it away?'

'Yes, if it means destroying all the work I've done.'

'I won't touch your work. I disagree with it, but those days are past me. I just want Shien to have a normal life. At least until she's old enough to decide for herself. Understand?'

'I see where you're coming from,' Williams said.

'And?'

'And it's not as simple as that.'

'Why not?'

'You've already crossed a line. Several lines, in fact. The second you pointed that gun at me everything changed. I'm not going to help you with a thing.'

'You don't need to help me. You just need to point me in the right direction.'

'The North Maine Woods.'

Slater studied the man's face. He found no hint of deception — then again, Williams actively managed a top-secret division specialising in deceit. Slater didn't trust him for a second.

'I think I believe you,' Slater said.

'Go find out for yourself.'

'I'm bringing you along.'

'You shouldn't do that.'

'You're not in a position to argue.'

'Will, I promise you — if you take this any further, your life is over. You know it just as well as I do.'

'You're confirming you have her in the program?'

'It was the right thing to do.'

'Then off we go.'

He stood up from the crouch, and seized hold of the shoulder of Williams' coat. Maintaining a strict power-lifting regime in Colombia had its advantages in times like these. He threw the man out of the chair like he weighed nothing, sending him stumbling across the room. Midway through the off-balance stagger, Williams wheeled around and made a snatch for the Sig Sauer. He almost got his hands on it too. For the equivalent of a desk jockey on steroids, he sure had a mean game face. One of his stubby fingers glanced off the barrel of the P228, nearly bumping it out of Slater's hands. He'd seen the move coming, but Williams had speed and dexterity that belied his status as a handler.

Slater lunged back, lightning fast, and Williams carried on past.

Slater smashed a fist into his ear as he went by, disrupting his equilibrium, disorienting him.

Immediately, he knew Russell Williams had never been hit in his life.

The man might have a smattering of training, passed down by all the covert instructors that honed black operations soldiers into hardened killers. Slater doubted it would cost much to the government to employ their services for an extra few hours each time, making sure all the off-the-books intelligence officers had a basic grip on combat for when they found themselves in situations exactly like this.

But that didn't correlate with experience.

Williams clearly knew how to move fast, with purpose, utilising his adrenalin. That had been drilled into him. But he'd never taken a punch, or an elbow, or any kind of strike that shattered bone and tore muscle tissue and came with a myriad of dire consequences.

He went down on the plush carpet, not knocked unconscious, but pale as a sheet.

Stunned.

Slater smirked, shoved the barrel of the Sig Sauer in the man's ear, and shoved him toward the doorway.

'To Maine,' he muttered.

72

They stepped out onto the street, surrounded by rush hour traffic and an onslaught of pedestrians and the cacophony of sound that accompanied this time of evening in New York City.

Slater wore Williams' coat, with one hand in the pocket and the barrel of the Sig Sauer aimed squarely at the man's bulk at all times. Williams shivered in his button-up shirt, taking the lead. He had broad shoulders and a fast-paced, get-shit-done gait. Much more refined than the meek intel officer Slater had originally chalked him up as. The few times Slater had met the man, he'd kept his physique hidden under a few layers of expensive clothing.

But it was all show muscle. He'd never been hit. Slater let the thought spur him on as he focused on making one consecutive move after the other. If he slowed down, he'd realise what he was getting himself into, and he'd give up.

He said, 'Walk.'

Williams glanced over his shoulder. 'Where are we going?'

'Wherever I say. If you've got eyes on us right now, and

you're thinking of reciting a couple of subtle gestures you rehearsed in a training room somewhere — keep in mind that I'll recognise them. I'd advise doing nothing. I've got a finger touching the trigger, so if you've got a man ready to take me out from a distance you'll almost certainly kill yourself in the crossfire. And you're not ready to die.'

'There's no-one. I came alone. I trusted you.'

'And I trusted you.'

'I did the right thing.'

'We'll have all the time in the world to talk about it on the drive.'

They headed north, mingling with the swarms of civilians heading home from work, or out to dinner, or to a ball game, or to the theatre, or anywhere entertaining in the greater metropolitan region of New York City. Slater sensed an undercurrent of camaraderie in the air, and for a moment he regretted the fact that he'd never known a normal life. There was something simplistic and welcoming about heading out for the evening after putting in your eight hours at the office. He'd never known that.

He'd known pain and death and accomplishment.

That was all.

Slater caught Williams glancing to the left at a particularly busy intersection.

'Russell,' he snarled in the man's ear. 'I'm right here.'

Williams cocked his head, shrugging off the thought of escape. Slater saw a visible shiver run down the man's spine. He knew how close he'd come to catching a bullet in the spine. An unpleasant concept, especially to a man who'd never been in a fistfight. He'd no doubt sent men off to die, and trained child killers to slaughter dictators, but he hadn't experienced the visceral reality of it. Not up close, in the flesh. Now he could picture the lead puncturing his vertebrae, paralysing him, leaving him to bleed out with his face squashed against the grimy pavement of a New York sidewalk, blood mixing with saliva and dirt around his lips and eyes as he faded into—

From that moment onward, Williams complied.

'You really came on your own?' Slater said after a prolonged silence.

Astonished by the stupidity.

'I thought you were better than this,' Williams said. 'It never crossed my mind.'

'Well, I'm not.'

'I won't be alone for long.'

'I imagine there's strict protocol in place. If you don't contact certain parties in a certain timeframe, then...'

The back of Williams' head nodded. 'You'll be running from a storm. You won't outrun it forever.'

'I'll take my chances,' Slater said. 'You lot hunted me before. You'll just have to do it again.'

'We called it off. Because we thought you would put your head down and live a normal life.'

'Fat chance that was ever going to happen,' Slater said. 'Stop. Right here.'

Williams stopped in his tracks, so abruptly that Slater almost ran into him. The sidewalks were mostly deserted. They'd reached the Upper East Side. It was that time of the evening where the neighbourhood's residents ducked into private limousines or town cars to head to their social functions.

They certainly didn't walk.

And as a result there was no-one around.

At least, not for a short while.

Slater had maybe half a minute.

So he pulled the Sig Sauer out of his pocket, seized

Williams around the throat with a looping forearm, and pressed the gun to the man's temple with enough force to get his attention.

'Through that door,' Slater snarled.

'Right here?'

'Yeah.'

'It's locked.'

'Knock.'

'A certain number of times, or...?'

'Just knock.'

Williams knocked. A few seconds later a pair of silhouettes appeared behind the milky glass, stalling, maybe checking security cameras. Slater thought he heard someone curse out loud. Then the door swung open, and Slater came face-to-face with the same two sentries he'd brutalised the day before.

Guy One and Guy Two, with Heckler & Koch pistols in their hands and horrific welts and bruises on their faces.

73

S later smiled. 'Bet you're happy to see me again.'

Two gun barrels raised to his face.

Slater yanked Williams in front of him, keeping the Sig Sauer pressed to his temple. He was distinctly aware that everyone in the vicinity wanted his head on the chopping block.

He said, 'Don't do anything stupid, boys. How are your injuries?'

'Get out of here,' Guy One said.

It came out all mangled, no thanks to his broken nose and swollen cheeks and uneven jaw. It seemed they'd yet to receive medical attention. Guy Two had no swelling, but he'd been brutally knocked out the previous day, and he didn't seem to be operating on the same level of reality as his colleague. He had a glassy look in his eyes and pale clammy skin. He could barely stand. Slater took one glance at his knees and noted they'd both swelled to the size of pumpkins.

He said, 'The big boss hasn't sent you to the hospital yet?'

'Punishment,' Guy One mumbled. 'For letting you get past. Now fuck off before I bring all the Whelans down on your head.'

'Because that worked so well last time.'

'Just get lost, man.'

'Soon. You know who this is?'

Slater jerked the Sig Sauer against Williams' head.

Guy Two shook his head. 'No.'

'It's Tommy's accountant. You know what that means, right?'

They had no reason to believe otherwise.

Guy One shrugged. 'Not our business.'

Slater said, 'He and the big boss have a good thing going. I pull the trigger right now and a *lot* of pipelines go belly-up. The cash flow stops. Your empire crumbles. You really want to be the ones responsible for that?'

Guy Two muttered, 'How the fuck does he do this shit?'

Guy One said nothing for a long time, then he glanced toward the ceiling. A subtle tell. Indicating separation from the top. Isolation. The sentries were outcasts as far as the upper echelon of the Whelan family was concerned.

He said, 'What the hell do you want, man?'

'A car.'

'What — that's it?'

'I thought you'd be hesitant to give it up.'

'Take our fucking car, man. Take our money, too, if you want. Just don't come back.'

Slater twitched. Clearly he'd generated more fear than he first thought. He nodded.

'You got the keys on you?'

'Yeah.'

'The car's here? Behind me?'

'Yeah. It's the Ford. The big one.'

'You're not going to report it missing, are you?'

'It's stolen, and the plates have been swapped. We're a mob family, you fucking idiot. You really think I'm going to the cops about this?'

Slater smiled. 'Pleasure doing business with you.'

No-one said anything.

Slater said, 'The keys.'

Guy One reached for his back pocket. Slater sensed a blast of adrenalin in his temples like an injection to the brain. If the situation demanded it, he would take the P228 off Williams' head, shoot both sentries dead, and have the barrel back against his skull only a second or two after taking it away.

Hot and steaming, freshly used.

But Guy One came out with a bunch of keys, as promised. There was no need for alarm. He held them out, looking at the floor.

Defeated.

Slater took his left arm off Williams' throat, grabbed the keys, and slotted them neatly into his back pocket. Then he returned his arm to the choke hold.

'One more thing.'

'What?'

'A roll of duct tape.'

'You serious?'

'Dead serious. You got one lying around?'

'There's one in the back room.'

'If you even fucking think about picking up a phone and warning your family, I'll shoot the accountant, I'll shoot your friend, then I'll come in there and shoot you. And then the rest of them, too, for good measure. I've got nothing to lose. You got it?'

Guy One nodded. He put his weapon on the floor. Guy

Two mirrored the action, even though he hadn't been instructed.

Utterly defeated.

'Be right back,' Guy One muttered.

He strode away, disappearing into the darkness of the lobby, and Slater stiffened. Now was the moment. It could all come crashing down around his head in an instant. If Guy One fetched help, it would be over. Williams would escape in the carnage, or get killed in the crossfire, and that would be that.

But defeat hung thick in the air.

Guy One returned in less than a minute, wielding three thick rolls of heavy duty duct tape. He passed them across. Slater slotted them into coat pockets.

'Thanks,' Slater said. 'Close the door now. If I see it open again, I'll shoot you both dead. I mean it.'

'I believe you,' Guy One said.

He closed the door.

The silhouettes disappeared.

Slater shoved Williams toward the only Ford in the vicinity — a giant Raptor pick-up truck — and hurried after him.

74

They drove in silence until they were out of the city limits.

Slater racked the seat back and set himself up in a comfortable position. He couldn't say the same for Williams. He'd used all three rolls of duct tape. The man was bound so tight to the passenger seat that he had no hope of budging an inch. Wrapped in a grey cocoon, he stewed silently in place, bolt upright, his jaw clenched and his gaze fixed out the window, staring at nothing in particular. Wondering how these circumstances transpired.

'I need to piss,' he muttered.

'No you don't,' Slater said. 'And if you really need to, then go right there. You think I care?'

'It'll smell.'

'Clearly the files didn't make my past experiences clear enough. Where I've been. What I've seen.'

'Oh, I can imagine.'

'Then shut up and tell me where to go. The only way you come out of this alive is taking me to Shien. Anything else and I'll put a bullet in you.'

'I don't think you will.'

Slater glanced across the cabin. 'Want to test it?'

'How do you see this going?' Williams said, suddenly hostile. 'What's your best-case scenario here? You get her, and then what? You can't travel anywhere. We'll have a photo of your face at every airport in the country. We'll be looking for her, too, under the guise of a missing persons campaign. We'll have the both of you on every major news network in the country within hours. You're making a huge mistake.'

'I'll cross that bridge when I come to it.'

'You're a fool.'

'And yet, here I am. Still kicking.'

'Think about the alternatives,' Williams said. 'Really think. Your best bet is to let me out of this car and forget any of this ever happened. I'll chalk it up to a manic episode and never come looking for you again. We can both pretend the other doesn't exist. That's your best outcome.'

Slater didn't respond.

Williams said, 'It's understandable. What I saw in your file ... that'd fuck anyone up. A whole career of it. We can write it off. Post-traumatic stress. You lost the plot for a brief spell, but we'll sweep it under the rug. Because of what you did for your country.'

'Where in North Maine?'

'Christ, Slater.'

'We're in for a drive. Better you give it up now than spend the whole drive stewing over whether it's worth your life.'

Williams bowed his head. 'Okay. If this is the way it's going to go, then okay. Have it your way. I'll take you to the facility. You promise you just want the girl?'

'Promise.'

'You won't interfere with my operation?'

'Wouldn't dream of it.'

'Why do I sense you're lying?'

'Why do you think you're in a position to do anything? You're discussing ramifications that aren't relevant. Right now all your brainpower should be focused on giving me the location or accepting a quick death.'

'Your file says it all. You've never killed anyone without being provoked or forced into a situation. This would be a new low. Slaughtering an intelligence officer in cold blood. A man who never laid a finger on you. I don't think you'd do it.'

Slater lowered his tone, putting his emotions on his sleeve, and said, 'If you don't give me the location, Shien stays in the program. She grows up. She's brainwashed. You're killing that little girl's chance of a normal life, without her consent, and therefore you're killing her. She'll never be normal. I saw what you did to Ruby. I saw what she is. I'm a special type of monster, but I can detach from it, and I made the choice myself. You put Ruby Nazarian in the program at a young enough age to completely wipe out any hopes of her being able to distance herself from the life of a killer. And if the same's going to happen to Shien, then I'll take that very seriously. And I'll shoot you in the head. I'll dump your body somewhere in North America and they'll never find you. If you think I'm bluffing, try me.'

Now Williams didn't respond.

Slater said, 'Fucking try me.'

Williams said, 'It's near the Allagash Wilderness Waterway.'

Slater said, 'Good decision.'

'Can't say the same for what you're doing.'

'I'll be okay.'

'I don't know about that.'

'When were you supposed to check in?'

'A few hours ago.'

'What'll be happening now?'

'Not a whole lot. But it'll ramp up exponentially as the time passes. Trust me — you'll have all law enforcement in Maine on you soon enough.'

Slater stared across the cabin, read Williams' face, and stamped on the accelerator, surging up I-95. He overtook a semi-trailer and a couple of trundling passenger vans and found a stretch of open highway. He gunned the engine, and the Ford screamed in protest.

'The Allagash Wilderness,' he said. 'How far's that from here?'

'If you don't stop — maybe eight or nine hours.'

'I can do that.'

He accelerated harder.

Williams slumped down in his duct tape tomb and closed his eyes.

75

Three hours into the drive, Slater almost fell asleep at the wheel.

The monotony got to him, and his body entered autopilot as it recharged his energy reserves. He was well-rested, but the stress of the situation drained on him, and the next thing he knew the world went dark.

He closed his eyes for a moment, and suddenly he was two lanes across, on a direct collision course with a massive oil tanker. He jerked awake, wrenched the wheel, and repositioned himself in the centre lane. A sedan behind him blared the horn. He stuck a hand out the window in a wave of apology.

Williams allowed a smirk to creep across his face. 'Getting tired?'

'I'm fine.'

'You sure? You know what you're going to be walking into? You'd best be prepared.'

'Nothing's going to happen, because I'll have you at gunpoint. You'll do everything you can to keep the situation under control. You'll lead me to Shien, and that'll be that. The both of us will disappear.'

'And then we'll hunt you.'

'Maybe I'll kill you. And everyone in command there. It won't take much. All I'll need is the provocation. Just the slightest bit.'

I-95 stretched on into the darkness, endless and flat. They were past Boston, fast approaching Portsmouth. Night fell thick over their surroundings, masking everything but the interstate.

Slater said, 'You don't want to change the location, do you? I'll give you one chance.'

Williams said, 'What?'

'If you're leading me into the middle of nowhere in hopes of breaking free, I'd strongly advise you against it.'

Williams did his best to shrug, but the thick layers of duct tape prevented any upper body movement. He settled for a cocking of the head. 'You think more of me than you should.'

'You're admitting weakness?'

'I'm admitting common sense. You're not going away easily. The file states that in no uncertain terms. Best to give you what you want and attempt to pick up the pieces later.'

'Why'd you do it?' Slater said, suddenly hot with anger. 'You couldn't have given her a normal fucking life? Was that too much to ask after I rescued her from that darkness?'

Another half-hearted attempt at a shrug. 'You've got a narrow-minded view of the world. You have to. We send you from operation to operation, and we did it for a decade. All you focus on is what's in front of you. Like right now. You can't look at the big picture. You can't look at anything from the top down. But that's the most important part of intel. It's why I started Lynx in the first place. Like you said. Utilitarian. But it's so much more than that. We're getting things done you couldn't dream of.'

'Or maybe I'm not just a mindless minion,' Slater said. 'Maybe I *have* thought about it. And maybe I realised a long time ago that looking at anything from the big picture is a recipe for disaster.'

'How so?'

'Nothing changes. Zoom out on anything and it shows you how bleak things are. All you can focus on is isolated incidents. Or you'll go mad. I'm sure it happens more often than not in your profession. You said it best — my career was singular. One focus. One mission. Over and over and over again. You, on the other hand, have to grapple with the morality of it all. And I don't envy you. It leads you down dark paths. It's only natural. I don't blame you for what you're doing. All I care about is a promise you made.'

'The girl is better off in my facility.'

'We'll have to agree to disagree.'

'You're naive if you refuse to look at the big picture. You're a piece of shit. You can't handle the grey zone, and you don't belong in this world. You should get out before you ruin more lives.'

'Get off your high horse,' Slater snarled. 'You're brain-washing kids.'

'Ten years from now, there'll be a horde of dictators, sex slavers, guerrillas, drug barons, cartel thugs, and sadistic psychos who all get away with their crimes. They'll profit massively, live full wholesome lives, get everything they ever wanted, and then die peacefully in their sleep of old age. All because you pulled a young kid out of a facility in North Maine. You're the hero of your tale, Slater. The righteous knight rescuing the girl from the bad man. But have you ever thought you're the villain of someone else's?'

An uneasy silence descended over the cabin as the Ford carried on up I-95.

Williams said, 'You said it yourself. The world goes on. That's human nature. Ten years from now there'll be a kid, and her parents will be on the receiving end of some injustice. Maybe they're journalists in Mexico. Maybe they're tortured and flayed and beheaded by the cartels for daring to give them bad press. Maybe that kid will wonder what could have been done to save her entire family from being mutilated. And maybe they could have been. Maybe, in another life, a young girl named Shien kept training in the North Maine Woods. She grew up to be one of the most effective killers in the government's arsenal and slipped her way into the upper echelon of the cartel under the guise of a prostitute. Then she proceeded to tear the whole beast apart from the inside, as ruthless as she is, and the happy family carried on with their normal life instead of dying a disgusting death in the slums. Surrounded by filth. Not a pleasant way to go out. You're the villain of that story, Slater.'

'Stop talking,' Slater said.

He hated the secret life.

He hated the secret world.

He hated everything in it.

Sometimes all you could focus on was the small picture, to prevent yourself going mad.

76

They entered Maine without fanfare.

The drive took longer than expected. Traffic built up as they flew past Boston and slowed their progress to an uncomfortable crawl. Slater made a point of eyeing the rear view mirrors every few seconds, more of a nervous tic than anything else. Williams noticed. He smirked and squirmed in his seat, to no avail, and when the confidence wore off he settled back and closed his eyes and tried not to think about his predicament.

As they trickled along the interstate Slater gave silent thanks that the Ford's windows were tinted to the maximum. Often they stopped right alongside ordinary civilian vehicles, and Slater had a man duct-taped to the passenger seat. In any other setting, it might have looked hilarious. Now his heart hammered in his throat every time an unassuming guy or girl glanced over in traffic.

But no-one saw anything.

Except their own reflections, staring back at them.

No alarms were raised.

And the duct tape held tight, as it was designed to do.

Williams wasn't going anywhere in a hurry.

The traffic dispersed as most took turn-offs, heading home after a long workday, and the hours ticked by. It passed midnight, then one a.m., then two a.m. After the first involuntary nap Slater managed to figure out the trickier details of monotony, and there were no further incidents. He kept his eyes on the road and his mind sharp and alert. There would be no more adrenalin dumps, no more crashes. Now was the time to recharge the batteries. He had no idea what he might find in the woods of North Maine.

Williams didn't provide any help.

Slater said, 'Describe the facility.'

'What do you want to know?'

'Everything.'

'I thought you just wanted the girl.'

'I do. But I don't want to run into any surprises on the way in.'

'You're going to, no matter what. I assume you can deal with them. It's heavily guarded.'

'By who?'

'Private contractors. There's a staggering market for vets with nothing to do and an arsenal of skills to utilise. Usually that takes place in more unsavoury locations, and we turn a blind eye, even though we know it happens. But sometimes we can put those skills to use.'

'You've got a bunch of old guys holding down the fort?'

Williams shook his head, without the use of his shoulders. 'The word "veteran" doesn't mean what you assume. There's a stereotype around it. We take killers. Ex-Green Berets and Rangers and other, more secretive positions who've retired from active service and are looking for a better dollar.'

'The types who'd go to mines in Africa, or oil reserves in the Middle East?'

'Yes, those types. There's always a narrow band of outliers. Better *we* employ them than the alternative.'

'How many are there?'

'More than necessary. We've spared no expense. Specifically for situations like this.'

'Stand them down.'

'And where would they go?'

'Just do it. Get them away from the facility until I can pull Shien out.'

'How am I supposed to do that? You think I have all their numbers in a little book?'

'You can get hold of them. Don't play the village idiot.'

'You smashed my phone back in New York.'

'Use mine.'

'I can't dial.'

'You can speak.'

Williams sighed. 'Fine.'

Slater hesitated, and looked across. 'You're not going to raise the alarm, are you? I'm sure there's protocol for situations like this. Certain words you can use that tip your colleagues off. I wouldn't do that if I were you.'

'How will you know if I do?'

'Because we'll get to the compound and it'll be fortified to the gills and I'll turn around and shoot you in the head the second I realise you weren't true to your word.'

'I've heard a lot of empty talk,' Williams said. 'Not much action. You keep threatening me with everything under the sun. Sooner or later it starts to get old.'

Slater made sure there was no traffic in the vicinity. He was doing eighty miles an hour, surrounded by the cold desolation of Maine, trundling upward toward the Canadian border. Flecks of rain lashed the windshield, and the drudgery of the region lay over everything in sight. The darkness was impenetrable. There was a lorry a few hundred feet behind him, and nothing ahead. Deserted.

Good.

He reached down with one hand and pulled the Sig Sauer free from his belt, palming the black polymer of the grip. He disengaged the safety, leant over the centre console, and aimed at Williams' left foot.

'You've been pointing a gun at me over and over again for hours,' Williams said. 'That's getting old, too. Either—'

Slater shot him through the top of the foot, taking a couple of toes off.

The muzzle flare lit up the cabin and the sound deafened both of them, exploding in the confined space with all the furore of a dirty bomb. Slater flinched and worked his jaw, opening and closing it in a half-hearted attempt to get his hearing back. He couldn't hear Williams screaming in pain. He focused on the road ahead and waited for everything to return to normal. Sound crept back in, first the thumping bass of the car and the shouting and the writhing — all low percussive thrums. Next came the trebles, the high notes.

Everything steadily crept back to normalcy, and he heard Williams' shouts and moans of despair in all their glory.

'Shut up,' Slater said.

'I'm going to bleed out, you—'

'No you won't.'

Slater set the Ford to cruise control and snatched Williams' thick winter coat off the back seat, dragging it into the front compartment. He reached over and ducked low and wrapped the bulky item around the man's mangled foot. The wound gushed blood into the footwell, but Slater cut it off with an effective knot, pinning the sleeve against the ragged flesh. It stifled most of the flow, but Williams grunted through gritted teeth from the accompanying pain.

Slater said, 'What was that about bluffing?'

White as a ghost, Williams slumped back in the duct tape encasing and sealed his lips tight.

The cab descended into silence.

77

Almost eleven hours after setting off from the centre of New York City, the Ford arrived at the border of the North Maine Woods.

Slater leant pressure on the accelerator, spurred forward by the milestone achievement. Midway through the journey up the East Coast his motivation had faltered, right after shooting Williams through the foot. That had shut the man's trap for the rest of the journey as he drew inward into an uneasy unconsciousness, fading in and out of reality, accompanied by cold sweats and pale skin, clammy to the touch. Slater made sure to check Williams' vitals every couple dozen miles, but there was never any issue. He shivered and shook and gasped for breath when he came to, but Slater had seen the familiar signs of shock a thousand times before. It did little to unnerve him.

But the silence did.

He was left alone with his thoughts, and with nothing noteworthy happening outside the vehicle, they were all he could focus on. His mind wandered to endless possibilities of how the next day might unfold, and this time he couldn't force them out. Williams was right. What the hell was he to do next?

He stewed deep in the recesses of his own head until the fingers of dawn crept into the sky and the woods wrapped around the pick-up truck like snow-dusted shadows.

Slater buzzed his window down an inch as the clock on the dashboard struck six in the morning. Icy air rushed in, lowering the temperature inside the cabin in a frenzy. The chill stirred Williams out of his slumber, and he came awake with heavy bags under his eyes and bloodshot tendrils sneaking out of his tear ducts, red spreading across the white.

'Sleep well?' Slater said.

'Fuck you.'

'We've just got one more stop to make.'

'And where might that be?'

'Right here.'

Slater spotted what he was looking for and veered off State Route 11 into a giant mall outlet. He trundled through the empty lots as pale blue light filtered across the sky above. It didn't take him long to locate a warehouse-sized military surplus store, open twenty-four-seven to accomodate a broad customer base, halogen lights glowing outward from within. He pulled to a halt on the bitumen, parking a few dozen feet away from the entrance to reduce the chance of nosy onlookers spotting Williams. He got out, slammed the door closed, and locked the car — not that it was necessary. He could leave all four doors wide open and Williams wouldn't be going anywhere in a hurry. There was nobody in sight, and the duct tape was impenetrable without a sharp instrument.

Slater headed straight into the endless aisles of cold weather gear and loaded up on winter camouflage khakis, heavy-duty all-terrain boots, a black compression long-sleeve, a bulletproof vest and a giant overcoat. The cashier, a young guy with oily black hair who looked half-asleep, loaded all the gear onto the conveyor belt and gave Slater a quizzical look.

'Planning a siege?' he joked.

Slater laughed as if it was the funniest thing in the world.

Then he looked at the kid, noting the unfocused eyes, and said, 'You know what? I need some other things, too.'

'What kind of things?'

'Food. Water. And ... something else. Let's talk.'

78

Back in the Raptor, with all the gear stashed safely across the back seat, Slater turned out onto the interstate and continued north, always north.

They passed Eagle Lake as the sun soared over the horizon, casting an amber glow over the still water. It flashed by on the right, and then it was straight back to endless rows of snowy alpine trees. The gorgeous sunlight didn't last long — soon enough, it plunged behind cloud and a dreary grey draped thick over everything. The clouds only intensified as they pressed further north, one hour blending into the next. Slater followed the GPS on his phone, turning left at Fort Kent, right at the very precipice of the border. Then it was a long straight shot down State Route 161, which according to the digital display would terminate at Allagash.

From there, it was anyone's guess.

'You've got just under an hour to get specific about the details,' Slater said, disrupting the silence. 'Or I'll blow your other foot off. This time all the toes.'

Silence.

'Then I'll start on your fingers.'

'You really think you're the good guy, don't you?' Williams cackled, close to delirium. 'You're dead, Will. Dead as dead can be. You'll get Shien out, and then you'll be stranded in the middle of nowhere. You'll be a child abductor to anyone with a television, or a smartphone. How do you think that's going to work out for you?'

'I'm figuring that out as I go along.'

'Good luck with that.'

Slater waited another beat, then wrenched the Sig Sauer free. 'Okay. You did this to yourself.'

He flicked cruise control on, dropped an elbow on the centre console, and stuck the barrel down in the passenger footwell. Aiming at a fresh appendage.

Williams shouted, '*No, no, no!*' at the top of his lungs.

Slater's finger froze on the trigger.

'Details,' Williams gasped, close to hyperventilating. 'Christ, okay, details. I never refused. I wasn't trying to stall.'

'Yes you were.'

'I—'

'Two seconds.'

'What?'

'One.'

'I'll give you the co-ordinates,' Williams hissed through gritted teeth. 'Christ's sake.'

'And if there's nothing there?'

'What do you mean? Of course the facility's there.'

'If you give me the wrong location.'

'I won't.'

'Hypothetically. Let's say you do.'

Silence.

'I'll tell you what'll happen. I'll go back to that same surplus store and buy pliers. And then we'll get to work on your fingernails and toenails. And then the real fun will start.'

'You're psychotic.'

'I'm single-minded. Like you said. I promised a young kid a normal life. I'm going to deliver her that.'

'Fat chance of that with what'll happen afterwards.'

'I'm sure we'll come to an arrangement.'

'It has nothing to do with me. This program is greater than me. You've already made an enemy of the entire government.'

'I don't see them anywhere.'

'You won't have far to run. Soon. Very soon.'

'Not soon enough, in your case.'

Williams fed him a set of co-ordinates, latitude and longitude, and Slater punched them into an app he down-loaded on the fly, tapping away at the smartphone like his life depended on it. It punched a dart deep into the woods beyond the Allagash River, to the east of Falls Brook Lake. Only traversable by foot, with no roads in sight — at least not on traditional GPS. He didn't underestimate the desolation of the region. It was a far cry from the highlands of Yemen, but it might as well be the same. The perfect location for an off-the-books compound bankrolled by black funds sent directly from the Treasury. Slater knew enough about the secret world to put the pieces together.

'It has to be accessible by vehicle,' he said.

Williams nodded, reluctantly. 'You don't want to go that way.'

'Why not?'

'Why do you think? There's tripwires and motion sensors and cameras and guardhouses. And artificial road-blocks, too. Trees we draped across the trail that lift up when we need them to. Anything to prevent travellers stumbling across it. Look, I'm trying to help you out here. Okay? My stance has changed. I'll get you the girl however I can. I just need out of this goddamn tape. My foot hurts like hell. I need a hospital.'

'You need a cup of concrete.'

Williams looked at him, flabbergasted. 'What?'

Slater smirked. 'I was in Australia many years ago. For Black Force. A guy I ran into gave me the same prescription.'

'What does it mean?'

'Harden the fuck up.'

'Here,' Williams said.

Slater screeched the Ford to a halt. It had served him well. The beast had covered hundreds of miles without any issue, finally bringing them to a deserted parking lot caked thick with ice and snow on the cusp of the teeming Allagash River. The icy water flowed and frothed past the riverbanks, cutting a twisting serpent-like line through the forest. Slater had no chains to drape over the tyres, but he didn't need them. He was abandoning the truck right here — he figured whatever lay ahead, there would be ample opportunity to steal a vehicle.

Williams stared down at the gaping wound in his shiny bespoke dress shoe. 'How the hell do you expect me to walk all that way? We need to go off the trail here. There's a checkpoint only a few miles across the river. We need to go inland. But I can't. You'll have to leave me here.'

'That's not happening.'

'You see another solution?'

'I negotiated with the cashier at the surplus store,' Slater said. 'Picked up a few extras that aren't usually available over the counter.'

'Such as?'

Slater didn't respond. He forced the door open and leapt out into the chill, tasting the alpine air. A distinct aroma wafted from the woods, frosty and inviting.

In another life Slater might have raced to the nearest slopes and rented a snowboard, but he was stuck with this life, so he skirted around to the passenger side and ripped the thick barrier of duct tape apart by slashing at it with the Raptor's optional ignition key.

It took a couple of minutes, but finally he wrenched the tape down and outward, creating enough of a gap for Williams to fall forward and stagger precariously out onto the asphalt. He barely managed, and Slater realised aiming a gun at him would prove futile. He wasn't going anywhere in a hurry, and even at full health Slater had already established the existence of the reflex gap between them.

And now Williams was compromised to the extreme.

As white as the snow around him, his hair seemingly twice as grey as when Slater had first met him at the Four Seasons, Williams staggered a couple of steps in the cold before collapsing against the side of the Ford. Stress lines etched deep in his face, and the falling rain droplets lashed his hair, plastering it down across his forehead. The overcoat formed a makeshift moon boot around his right ankle, but it wouldn't hold up for long.

He was running on an intoxicating cocktail of stress chemicals and forward momentum, but eventually he would crash, as all men did.

'Need something for the pain?' Slater said.

'No,' Williams said, a vain attempt to mask weakness.

'Too bad.'

Slater changed right there, shivering in the abandoned lot as the cloudy sky grew infinitesimally brighter. He pulled on the khakis and tugged the compression long-sleeve over his barrel chest. Then he slipped into the vest and shrugged on the giant winter coat. He fetched the Sig Sauer out of the driver's seat. It had an aftermarket fifteen-round capacity, and he'd already fired one bullet into Williams' foot, but the lack of spare magazines didn't faze him as much as it should have. He figured sooner or later he'd come across one of the mercenaries Williams had recruited to guard the compound, and if all went according to plan he would put the guy down and strip him of his firearms before he knew what hit him.

Slater held the weapon at the ready and pointed to a narrow bridge that ran across the Allagash River, barely wide enough to fit a single vehicle.

'Walk,' he said.

'What about the extras you mentioned?' Williams protested.

'Oh. Right. Something for the pain.'

Slater pulled a packet of OxyContin out of his pocket, siphoned off the kid at the surplus store for twenty bucks above asking price, and tossed one of the strips to Williams. He regretted taking advantage of the opioid epidemic, but he had little choice. 'Take four.'

'Won't that put me in a trance?'

'That's the goal. As little resistance from you as possible.'

'I don't want four.'

'Take four or I'll shoot you four times.'

Williams nodded. He put the tablets in his mouth. He mumbled something.

Slater snapped a plastic bottle of water off a six-pack in

the back seat and tossed it underhand. Williams caught and drank.

'Hungry?' Slater said.

The man nodded. Slater couldn't help but agree. His last meal had come the day before at the brunch spot. For good measure, he waited ten minutes silently in the cold, tapping the Sig Sauer against his leg, watching Williams like a hawk. Without any food in his stomach, the pills hit like a truck, and Slater saw the man's eyes glaze over.

Williams faltered, resting against the side of the cabin, and started sliding down the Ford's chassis. Slater propped him up, slapped him on the shoulder to kickstart his processing capabilities, and handed him one of five ration packs Slater had scooped up at the surplus store. Williams flapped his lips together, a dull smile plastering his vacant face, and tore at the cardboard packaging.

Slater fetched two MREs of his own.

They tucked into Italian chicken and instant noodles and muesli, each serving as dull as the last. But it was food, and it filled the void in their bellies all the same. Slater checked the coast was clear before handing Williams his second pack. The man ate it groggily, openly salivating, spit drooling from the corner of his mouth. Slater helped himself to the final ration pack, unsure when he would eat next.

Recharged by the nutrients, no matter how poor they tasted, he levered himself off the back seat and dropped down into the snow alongside Williams.

'Ready?' he said.

Near a state of delirium, Williams nodded, but this time his smile wasn't as open.

It was sinister instead.

Slater put everything together. The drugs were hitting

hard, and they wore away any hint of deception. Slater should have fed them to him earlier.

Now he said, 'You'd better tell me what's up.'

'Too late,' Williams mumbled.

Slater came up with the gun, ready to shove it into the man's ear and make him squirm with fear, but before he could do that the cool touch of a blade pressed hard into the artery in his neck, only ounces of pressure away from opening his lifeblood up to drain out into the snow. It startled him with such ferocity that he almost shot Williams through the chest from fright alone, but he managed to refrain with milliseconds to spare. His heart rate skyrocketed, thumping so hard in his chest he thought it might burst.

Ruby Nazarian whispered in his ear, 'Bet no-one's ever snuck up on you like that.'

80

S later stood bolt upright, rigid, unmoving, like a sick mirror image of a soldier standing at attention.

Gently, he muttered, 'What would you like me to do?'

'Let go of that weapon, for starters.'

He dropped the gun without hesitation. He had no other choice. The slightest hint of unwanted movement in any direction would set Ruby off. He knew it with absolute certainty. He'd seen the way she'd slaughtered the men in Colombia. Graceful, with no wasted movement. His death might even look artistic. A quick line across the neck, barely noticeable in the moment, and his fate would be sealed.

It'd take less than half a second.

As fast as he was, nothing trumped her speed. So he let the Sig Sauer clatter to the earth and stood palms out, fingers splayed.

Ruby shot a foot out and kicked the gun a dozen feet away across the slick concrete, where it came to rest in a miniature snowbank. Well out of range.

Russell Williams watched in a groggy stupor, eyes hazy and unfocused, but satisfied all the same.

'Where the hell did you come from?' Slater muttered through clenched teeth.

'Shhhh,' she breathed in his earlobe, so close he shivered from sheer unrest. 'Quiet now. That's it. You got anything else on you?'

'No.'

'He's telling the truth,' Williams mumbled.

The man took another bite of his instant noodles. Grinned through a mouth full of food.

'He could have deceived you,' Ruby said.

'He's not that smart. He thought you never returned to duty. He actually believed me.'

Ruby purred. 'How could he think such a thing? I would never...'

'What happens now?' Slater said.

'Just give me the word,' Ruby said.

'Wait,' Williams mumbled. 'I'm thinking.'

'You're high as a kite. Let's get this over with.'

'Wait.'

'How many pills did he give you?'

'Four.'

'That's not too bad...'

'They're strong,' Slater said. 'Evidently.'

'I can see that,' she hissed, her voice intoxicating. 'Not another word from you, you beautiful man. You're not in charge here.'

'I'm in charge,' Williams said.

Slurring his words.

'Not as much as you might think,' Ruby said. 'You're on cloud nine.'

'But ... you still answer ... to me.'

Oh boy, Slater thought. *They're kicking in now. All those opioids, straight to the brain.*

Williams swayed on the spot.

'Okay, well, you're persona non grata,' Ruby said. 'I'll count you out.'

She gripped Slater's throat tight, pushing the blade an ounce or two harder. She drew blood. It ran hot and crimson down his neck.

She pressed her full lips right up to his ear, grinning, probably flashing the same pearly white teeth Slater remembered from a hotel room in Quibdó.

'I quite liked you,' she whispered. 'It's a shame.'

He didn't move a muscle. He couldn't afford to.

'Couple. More. Seconds,' she said.

Her breath came soft and deadly into his ear canal.

'There we go,' she said.

Practically erotic.

Williams said, 'Wait.'

Practically yelling.

Ruby sighed, and it sounded like thunderclouds in Slater's ear.

She said, 'What?'

'He came all this way. Shouldn't we show him around?'

'He's not worth the risk. You're high. Don't be an idiot.'

'As far as I'm concerned ... I'm still in charge here...'

'I'm overruling you. You're not fit to do your job.'

'Don't you dare cut his throat.'

Slater tilted his head to the left as much as he dared, which constituted only a few millimetres. But now his voice had no chance of getting caught by the wind.

He was nearly face-to-face with Ruby.

He said, 'Did it hurt that Abigail was better than you at everything?'

She jolted a millimetre. Stunned.

His intuition proved accurate.

Wherever she'd come from, she didn't know Slater had paid her family a visit. It stunned her into a split second's hesitation, and her grip slackened, just enough to create the tiniest of spaces between the blade and Slater's torn skin.

He whipped the side of his skull into the bridge of her nose, shattering something important.

She recoiled — a forgivable offence in the big picture.

It was human nature. There was no resisting that sort of response. Unavoidable. No matter how much training you had. Slater would have reacted the same.

She jerked with the knife, blinded by a hot flash of pain but determined to cut Slater's throat regardless. But the recoil, coupled with her grip slackening, gave enough space to sidestep away from her. Slater cut it close, but the same could be said for anything in his life, and he figured by this point he had an unquestionable knack for escaping death by a hair's breadth. He felt the displaced air wash cold and dangerous over his throat, the blade coming so close to his flesh he could hear the gentle *whistle* of steel through freezing alpine air.

He nearly gasped from the terror alone.

But then he was out, twisting away from Ruby's lithe frame, and for the first time he saw her. She wore an expensive tracksuit sculpted to her body, probably worth a few hundred dollars alone, designed to keep the cold out and keep the heat in.

Her hair was pinned tight behind her skull, revealing the Southern European bone structure shared by Frank Nazarian. The same tight jawline and high cheekbones and glowing eyes. Beautiful, in any other setting.

Like a supermodel.

But now the eyes were closed, and the blade slashed at thin air, and her nose streamed blood, twisted at a grotesque angle. Slater recalled exactly how fast she'd moved in the clearing in Colombia, and he knew he wouldn't stand a chance with his bare hands — her with a knife and him ... without.

The pain still seared in her head, hot and recent, and he knew he'd only get one attempt at a strike before she cleared the cobwebs and came back with composure and precision. So instead of maintaining his outward trajectory and going for the Sig Sauer on the ground, he backtracked inward and twisted into a side kick.

There was nothing artistic or graceful about it. It was technical, of course, but the nature of the Muay Thai arsenal relied almost entirely on brute power, on drilling a certain move over and over and over again until it seared into the brain and became muscle memory. You see combat on the big screen, with villains performing beautiful spinning attacks derived from capoeira and other performance martial arts, but in reality most attacks in that vein are fundamentally useless. Slater had nothing impressive in his repertoire besides ten years of unlocking his hips and kicking the shit out of a leather bag until his shins bled and his lungs burned in his chest. And, piece by piece, he got more powerful. He hit harder. He knocked the bag a little further. He began to twist so fast and kick so hard that it was a wonder he didn't tear the leather clean in two.

That was all it came down to. Musculature, and power, and speed, and ferocity.

He hit Ruby in the ribcage with all four.

He didn't hold back.

In his compromised state, Williams flinched and ducked low as the *slap* of shin against abdomen ricocheted off the impact site and rang through the empty parking lot. The man probably thought he'd been shot.

Ruby crumpled, dealing with all kinds of internal injuries Slater couldn't hope to list, and the knife spilled from her spindly fingers. He kicked it away, neither as graceful or as poised as she'd done to his own weapon, but with ten times the power. It sailed through the air like a fastball and disappeared into the rapids a few dozen yards away.

Slater grimaced — he'd caught himself in the heat of the moment. He could have used that switchblade for what lay ahead.

Oh, well.

A gun will suffice.

'That was my favourite knife,' she breathed.

Then she shut up.

Because the pain overwhelmed her.

She squeezed her eyes shut, curled into a ball, and rocked back and forth, bleeding from the corner of her mouth as well as her nose.

Slater said, 'Sorry. You did just try to kill me.'

He fetched the gun, half-expecting Ruby to rise to her feet like something out of a demonic nightmare, but nothing happened. Williams stood rooted to the spot, visibly aghast at the change in circumstances. His tiny pupils, shrinking from the effects on the parasympathetic nervous system, darted from Ruby to Slater, and back to Ruby.

He screwed up his face.

'Damn,' he said. 'That sucks.'

Almost comical.

Four pills deep.

Slater picked up the Sig Sauer, strode right back to Williams, and snatched him by the collar. He thrust him forward, in the direction of the bridge, and the man began a series of staggering lunges in that direction, barely keeping his feet underneath him.

Slater crouched down in front of Ruby.

Now they were alone.

He pointed the gun at her head, just in case.

She opened her eyes. The amber seared into him.

Accusatory. Inflamed. Enraged.

'I probably broke a few of your ribs with that kick,' he said. 'You're not doing anything in a hurry. All that grace and dexterity — out the window. Damn shame. I should kill you now. You'd do it to me. But maybe that's the difference between us. Because you lost all your free will when they brainwashed a twelve-year-old. You don't know anything but the mission and the objective. You don't know anything else at all. You'll never change allegiances, no matter how much evidence you get shown. I can do that if I understand I'm wrong. Maybe because I walked into a recruitment office as an adult, when I was old enough to decide for myself.

Maybe that's why I'm leaving you alive right now. It's not the smart thing to do, is it? You could probably take some painkillers. Get up and find your knife in the river and come hunting for my head. Maybe you will. But I'll take that risk. Just like how I'm risking everything for a little girl I barely know. You know how easy it would be to walk away right now?'

She just looked at him.

He got to his feet.

'I'll say goodbye now, because I doubt I'll ever see you again. You're not sneaking up on me again like that with broken ribs. If I see you again, I'll kill you. Make no mistake about it.'

She kept looking at him.

'But you don't deserve to die.'

The amber eyes glowed.

'Ask yourself if I'm really such a bad guy. Ask yourself if I'm really the monster they told you I was.'

She said, 'Thank you.'

Barely audible over the wind howling out of the forest.

He didn't say anything.

He walked around her and headed straight for the wilderness.

A gun in his hand, a vest over his shoulders, and not a clue as to what he might find in the forest.

He crossed the bridge, following Williams' lucid stumbling, and a dark thought struck him as the trees wrapped around them and they stepped off the trail.

He thought, *What if Shien doesn't want to leave?*

82

It didn't matter.

He cared about her more than she knew, and he was prepared to seem like the devil to her if it meant giving her a normal existence. If she felt right at home in the Lynx program, learning deception and espionage and fifty different ways to kill a dictator, then when she turned eighteen she could head straight back to the military and weave her way back into a government program at her own discretion. Slater wouldn't be around to judge her then. She could do whatever the hell she wanted.

As he kept a hand on the back of Williams' neck and listened to his dreary mumblings and directed the man through a shadowy army of alpine trees, he wondered what the hell had kept him motivated through this whole ordeal.

Was this a futile attempt at being a father?

He shrugged it all off, and focused on the dark gloom ahead.

Winter had seized hold of the region, harsh and brutal in its intensity, covering the treetops in a thick dusting of snow, blocking the cloudy light from filtering through to the forest floor. They walked through the shadows, almost ethereal in nature, heading for nowhere in particular, with no plan in particular to rely on.

Slater didn't care.

He was accustomed to this.

Lowering his voice to compensate for the sudden quiet, he said, 'We're getting closer. If you haven't given me an accurate layout of the facility by the time we reach it, I'll announce my arrival by shooting you in the back of the head.'

Williams believed him. He craned his neck, head drooping left and right, trying to look Slater in the eyes. Slater touched the barrel of the Sig Sauer to the man's brow.

'Speak,' he said.

'It looks like a ski lodge,' Williams mumbled, the OxyContin reducing his vocabulary to grade school level. 'There's a big long basement underneath, where all the training takes place. They live upstairs. In nice rooms. Bunk beds. Uh ... two guardhouses. Wait, no, three. I don't come out here much. Just normal booths. Nothing special. All the good stuff is around the compound. All those tripwires on the trail. Motion sensors. They'll know you're coming.'

'Motion sensors everywhere?' Slater said. 'Even in the woods?'

'Mmhmm,' Williams mumbled.

His eyes drooped closed.

'Thanks for letting me know,' Slater hissed through gritted teeth. 'Anything else you're not telling me about?'

'My foot hurts.'

'How close are we?'

'Close.'

'Give me your best guess.'

'A hundred yards. Very close. Can I sit down when we get there?'

'You can sit down now.'

Slater gently lowered the man into a seated position at the base of one of the pine trees. Williams rested his head against the bark and smacked his lips together, a dull smile on his face. Grateful for the respite. Slater slid the packet of OxyContin from his back pocket and pressed one more tablet onto Williams' tongue, for good measure. He forced the man to swallow it dry.

Williams gulped it down without hesitation.

Slater said, 'You'll remember what I'm about to tell you. You let yourself go blind for the sake of progress. You spoke to me about being single-minded, but you didn't consider the PR shit-storm if this goes public. You threatened me up and down in the car. You said you'd have my face at every airport, and Shien's face on a missing persons alert. But you're not going to do that. Because the second I get the sense that I'm wanted, I'll go to every major newspaper in the country and feed them everything. You've seen the new world we live in. There's an anonymous op-ed every other day. You think they won't publish it? I'll give them *everything*. And you don't want that. So you won't touch me, or her. You'll let us live our lives, wherever we choose to do so. You'll go back to your job and forget any of this ever happened. And you'll have a deep understanding about where you went wrong.'

He took the Sig Sauer in a double-handed grip, skirted around the tree, and crept forward.

The wind picked up, rattling the branches above his head, dusting him in a light coating of snow.

Unperturbed, he carried onward.

Ready for war.

83

He broke into a sprint.

His eyes wide and manic.

Like a nightmare swelling up out of the woods.

He abandoned any hope of a stealthy approach. Ruby might have disagreed, but that had never been his style of approach, and he wasn't about to start working on his weaknesses.

Not here.

Not now.

He pushed himself faster, kicking up snow as he ran, the boots doing an adequate job at keeping the cold out. Thankfully genetics and patient plyometric training had blessed him with the athleticism of a professional athlete. Where others might have stumbled and fallen in the uneven snow, he surged faster. He covered a hundred yards in roughly fifteen seconds, despite the sloping terrain and the maze of trees and the falling snow, and suddenly the compound was right there, looming up out of the woods.

Tucked away from civilisation.

He almost ran straight into one of the guard booths.

Everything happened at an astonishing speed.

He spotted two silhouettes huddled in the guard booth, barely visible through the foggy glass, and he raised his Sig Sauer to shoot them dead but they pounced back from the line of sight with uncanny quickness. At the same time he realised the glass was likely bulletproof, so he ducked low as he maintained as much pace as he could. In five massive strides he made it from the tree line to the chipped wood, arranged in the style of a log cabin. He knew there was a thick layer of metal on the other side of the artificial exterior, preventing the men in the guard booth from enemy fire. Slater took a deep breath, in and out, then leapt through the snow like a panther, diving to the left and clearing the side of the booth with his face and arms extended first. He twisted in mid-air, coming down on his side, gun up, and caught one of the guards in a precarious position. The guy was halfway out the narrow doorway, an orifice that hadn't been converted to make room for the giant slab of muscle trying to squeeze through.

He was stepping out sideways — ordinarily not a big deal, but in a game of milliseconds and millimetres, all the difference in the world.

Slater took one look into the cold and soulless eyes, and saw the Heckler & Koch HK416 rifle with attached red dot sight and vertical fore grip heading straight for his own body, and he shot the man between the eyes.

A quick stab of guilt. Maybe the guy didn't know the extent of what he was involved in. Ignoring the fact he was a mercenary for hire, offering his combat services to the highest bidder, there was a slight possibility the man hadn't a clue regarding what he was protecting. But that was bullshit. He spent all day, every day out here. There was no-one else around. And the kids weren't kept in cages underground. They patrolled the lodge, and therefore had to be let outside for fresh air every now and then.

Of course, there was the consideration of blissful ignorance — it was a government program, so the guy was simply going along with the herd.

Then again, so were most of the Nazis.

Slater rocketed to his feet, snatched the HK416 off the ground, testing its sizeable bulk, and swung it up to put it to use.

He crashed straight into the second man.

Again, everything happened horrifically fast.

The second guy had an identical high-powered assault rifle and he thrust it forward like a bayonet, hoping to feel the jolt as the tip of the barrel hit the meaty flesh of Slater's torso. Then he could simply squeeze the trigger and put ten consecutive rounds through his mid-section and tear out most of his insides. Instead he overcompensated with the lunge and Slater jerked like a marionette on strings at the last second and the barrel sliced through the space between his arm and ribcage. He pinned it against his underarm and the guy squeezed the trigger regardless. The rifle jerked and jolted against Slater's jacket, and the sound threatened to deafen him, but he held tight, and the bullets fired into the woods behind him.

He headbutted the man full in the face, missing his nose, striking forehead. Thick skull against thick skull. Practically concussing both of them. They recoiled at the same time, each arcing backwards, mushroom clouds going off in both their heads.

Slater couldn't see or hear.

But if he had one talent on this godforsaken earth, it was to recover fast from punishment.

Faster than anyone.

Seeing stars, seeing double, seeing triple, then seeing nothing at all, he lunged forward, barely fazed. The HK416 he'd stripped off the first guy was nowhere to be found. He'd lost it at some point. His outstretched fingers found a uniform, and he wrenched with all his might. Still barely able to see. He bounced a skull off bulletproof glass, accompanied by a sickening *crack,* and then he rotated the momentum back in the other direction and hauled the guy *up,* then *across,* then *down.* Putting technique into it, faint archaic echoes of judo practice imprinted on his memory. Putting his hips into it. The guy weighed less than him, so he was helpless to resist, especially with his limbs slackening from the impact against the glass.

Up, then across, then down.

Straight on his head.

Silence.

Slater's vision came back, along with an ear-splitting headache, nearly the equivalent of a migraine. Working his jaw left to right, he stumbled out of the tiny guard booth, grabbed two handfuls of the first guy's uniform, and dragged him into the cabin, moving fast.

He looked down at the uniforms.

Froze in place.

Thought hard.

And got straight to work.

They were nearly identical to the gear he was dressed in. At least from a distance. He eyed the room and found a full face military helmet with a visor. Old school, for winter combat. He grabbed it, shoved it onto his head, and put the visor half down, so the shadow would conceal the rest of his face anyway. But he needed his voice to make it out of the helmet. He checked himself over, put his hands behind his back to hide the fact he was black, and sauntered out onto the small landing like nothing at all was wrong.

Roughly six seconds after dumping the last guy on his head.

A single second later, four guards materialised from either side of the giant lodge in the centre of the snow-covered clearing.

Two per side, running at full pelt, breathless, weapons at the ready.

Two had helmets on.

They screeched to a halt in their tracks, spotting what appeared to be a colleague just outside the booth. Slater nodded from a distance, keeping his hands behind his back, tilting his face toward the floor. He adjusted his position, covering the murky puddle of blood on the landing, freshly drained from the exit wound in the first man's skull.

The four of them looked to him expectantly. He stared at four automatic assault rifles, held at the ready.

If it had come to a firefight, he wouldn't have survived. Not out here. Not with a complete lack of cover, besides a guard booth so small he could touch both walls at the same time by standing inside and holding his arms out straight.

Slater shot a sideways glance at the bodies inside the cabin, mulled over it for an instant, and then took a wild-ass guess.

'False alarm, boys,' he yelled in a muffled mixture of every accent in the continental United States, hoping they would each interpret it in their own way. 'Thought I saw a buck.'

'Are you kidding?!' one of them yelled back.

'No. It scared the shit out of us. Sorry again. A little jumpy today.'

'Don't ever discharge your weapon again without good

reason to, you dumb fuck. You're both fresh faces but you should know the goddamn rules.'

And then the barrels came down, and they dispersed, grumbling to themselves, with a hint of embarrassment that they'd come ready for war.

Slater stood panting on the top step, and he swallowed raw fear as they headed back for their booths on the opposite side of the lodge.

84

H e stayed where he was for a beat, and then strode straight back into the booth.

He took a deep breath. Put his hands on his thighs. Bent down and recovered. He was still off-balance from the clash of heads, and now that he was alone the terror returned in all its grandeur. He pictured his brain, every part of it, infinitesimally tiny, every neuron rattled and displaced and thrown off-kilter by the clash. He could see it there with its own consciousness, furious at the surrounding body, in disbelief that someone as idiotic as Will Slater would disrupt the frail parts of it so soon after recovering from the worst concussion of his life.

'Relax,' he breathed, his voice rattling around inside the helmet. 'You're fine. You're fine. Relax...'

His heartbeat settled, descending into monotony, and he breathed in and out again.

'You're okay,' he said. 'You're okay.'

A black operations warrior reduced to a nervous wreck.

The frailty of the human mind, he thought to himself.

And he *was* okay. He recalled the patches of missing

time from the Russian Far East, and shivered involuntarily. Nothing could be worse than that. He'd knocked his skull around, but the brain was a fickle thing, and sometimes everything was fine. He had a headache, and nothing else. No blackouts. No nausea. No stutter-like effect on his reality.

He grasped the hilt of the HK416 in a sweaty palm. Steeled himself.

Not long to go.

And then what?

Don't think about that.

He dropped the visor all the way down, plunging the world outside into a murky filter. Something about helmets unnerved him. Like he was playing a video game. Like none of this was real. He stepped out of the guard booth, slinging the assault rifle over his shoulder as casually as he could. The lodge was too far away, and there were too many windows across the two storeys. He couldn't tell if there were eyes on him.

He coughed, straightened up, and headed for the building, stepping down into the snow. His boots sunk into the fine powder, wrapping around his ankles. He lifted one out, and put it down. Like wading toward a war zone in a hazmat suit. But it was the only way to conceal his identity.

Quite frankly, he couldn't believe the ploy had worked in the first place.

But that was why Black Force existed. Split second reactions. Spur of the moment decisions. Abnormal processing power, computing the best possible outcome, putting it into effect without fear or hesitation.

Actually, that wasn't true.

There was always fear.

Endless fear.

But Slater had never let fear dictate what he did and didn't do.

His breath clouded the inside of the visor, fogging it up, superheating it in comparison to the outside chill. An ordinary problem for civilians across the world. Usually no issue. Stop, clear the visor, put it back down, continue. But Slater couldn't do that. He cursed the flimsy nature of the plan. He pressed on. Wading through quicksand. Trudging through no man's land. He couldn't see the windows. He couldn't make out any features of the building itself, apart from the fact that it was a gorgeous log cabin with awnings jutting out over the windows and giant snakes of snow built up on the roof ruts.

Sweat trickled down his forehead, running over his nose, continuing to heat the inside of the helmet.

He kept going.

He pulled up to the door and knocked on it three times, a loud *bang-bang-bang* with the side of his fist with all the impatience he could muster. But he took care not to inject aggression into the tone. Just a disgruntled guard in one of the booths looking for an answer sooner rather than later so he could get back into the warmth of his hut.

The door opened.

Almost immediately.

Slater could barely see.

85

A female voice said, 'Want to explain why the fuck you were shooting into the woods when the kids are having breakfast?'

'False alarm, ma'am. Nothing to worry about.'

'What are you doing here?'

Slater didn't respond.

The voice said, 'Get back to your shack. You're not welcome here. Not during breakfast hours. And especially not now, after that shit you just pulled.'

Slater opened his mouth, then closed it again.

The helmet fogged even more.

The voice said, 'Do you not understand the rules?'

Slater said, 'It's urgent.'

'Do you think I care what's urgent and what's not? The rules trump whatever's urgent.'

'This trumps the rules.'

'What is it?'

'Above your pay grade.'

The woman snorted with derision. 'Then it's sure as hell above yours.'

'Lady, this is serious. Williams called me directly. Ruby Nazarian is compromised.'

'What? She just went out to deal with the threat...'

'Is that what she told you?'

'She said she needed to go. Immediately. She didn't explain much.'

'There was no threat. We think she's defected.'

'You can't be serious. You're a perimeter guard. Why's Williams interacting with you? And take that helmet off, for Christ's sake.'

Slater froze, unsure how to respond. If he ignored the direct request, it would be immediately apparent what was happening.

He needed the upper hand, somehow.

But he had to oblige.

So he stepped inside, one giant gesture, planting his foot down inside the lodge's entranceway and shoving past the mystery woman at the same time. It was aggressive enough of a gesture to warrant a reaction, but he reached up and grabbed his helmet with both hands to try and dissipate the tension. If she saw he was following her commands, she might relax.

She didn't.

She stepped into him, trying to force him away from the door frame with her own body. It hadn't come to blows yet, but a couple of seconds more resistance and it might. She was trying to shut the door. He sensed her straining, pushing the big wooden slab back into place. It hit his shoulder and stayed there.

He kept going.

He forced his way inside, shoving straight past her. From the brief physical interaction he sensed characteristics. She was somewhere around five-ten, tall for a woman, with a strong frame. She had no extra weight that didn't need to be there. As soon as he made it past he darted another step into the empty room, yanking the helmet off in the same breath.

She slammed the door closed, and stood there, only a couple of feet away from him, staring at his face. She was in her thirties with a severe expression and piercing black eyes. Black as night. Like a praying mantis, like a beetle in human form. Half-Asian, if Slater had to guess. Maybe half-Latino, too. A strange mix of ethnicities. She wore a plain grey short-sleeved shirt tucked into a pair of black khakis, exposing thin arms laced with muscle and sinew. A hard woman. Used to ordering people around. Probably very good at it, too.

She said, 'You're not one of them.'

Slater said, 'No.'

He tightened his grip on the HK416, testing the weight of the fearsome rifle.

He said, 'How's this going to go?'

She stayed with her back to the closed door, still dangerously close, within striking distance. But Slater figured with an automatic weapon in his hands and an obscene size advantage, he could more than hold his own.

She said, 'There are young kids here. At least a dozen.'

'I know.'

'Are you here to kill them?'

'No.'

'What are you here for?'

'A girl named Shien.'

The woman pursed her lips. 'I see.'

'Do you know her?'

'Of course I know her. I'm raising her. She's one of our best pupils.'

'You're their carer?'

'I'm Mother.'

She said it like a first name, like a title.

'Right,' Slater said.

'You're not welcome here.'

'I didn't expect to be.'

'And yet, here you are, all the same.'

She spoke with a strange dialect, like she had no accent at all. And her conversational timing was way off. She left jagged gaps between sentences, and he got the impression she didn't communicate with adults much. The whole vibe of the lodge threw him off. It was shockingly quiet in here. He felt the walls might crumble if he used the rifle. Like a strange fantasy land where no one followed cultural or social norms.

Which it had to be. If it was raising killers.

She said, 'You're not going to shoot that in here, are you?'

'I hope not.'

'Hope?'

'I just want the girl. And then I'm out of here.'

A long pause.

She said, 'Do you, now?'

Everything shifted. The atmosphere, the silence, the temperature. Slater noted the heat for the first time, and he took in his surroundings. The floor was hard linoleum, designed to hold water and snow on its surface rather than letting it sink into the material. Apart from a thin wooden bench running along opposite walls, the space was devoid of furniture. There were dozens of metal hooks along the walls to hang cold weather gear off, to drip dry. The artificial heating ran thick in the air. Everything echoed in here. Their voices off the walls. The steady *drip-drip-drip* as the snow melted on Slater's overcoat and ran down his sides in rivulets, plinking against the hard floor underfoot.

'Let's not make a scene of this,' he said.

'You don't want to shoot me,' she said, and she smiled.

And she was right.

If there was the off chance Shien had acclimatised to the Lynx program, then Slater murdering her carer in cold blood would devastate the bond they'd formed in the past. She would see him as a monster for the rest of her days. Taking her out of the lodge would have the same effect as kidnapping her. He needed to remove her from the premises as gently and uneventfully as possible, and then he could get to work deciphering what they'd done to her.

If she was brainwashed.

If not, it didn't matter.

But he wasn't willing to risk it.

He put that all together, and at the same time Mother dived to the floor and rolled straight into his shins.

86

At first he thought she was insane, and then it all became abhorrently clear, far too late.

And he couldn't do a thing to prevent it.

She preceded the manoeuvre with flailing arms and legs, like a wild animal, obviously designed to make her appear insane. Which Slater bought — hook, line, and sinker. A spectator wouldn't have been able to tell, but he froze up for just long enough, and Mother seized hold of his right ankle with both hands. He could have jerked the leg out of the way as soon as he sensed movement, but the confusion worked, and now she had hold of him.

He wrenched his leg back with all his might, but she held tight, and a half-second later her legs darted through the air like twin vipers, folding over her body like a closing book, and she wrapped them tight around his knee. Now she'd manoeuvred herself upside-down in the air, latching onto his right leg with a speed that defied logic. For a moment he couldn't believe what was happening, and that was all she needed. She twisted hard and he stumbled back a step, taking him off-balance, and that was when it all struck him with a sharp explosion of terror.

She's going to tear my heel off the bone.

In jiu-jitsu, it was known as "Imanari roll to inside heel hook."

A complicated series of movements that had to be drilled relentlessly to have any chance of success.

But when it worked…

It made him cold, but he couldn't do anything to resist. As he fell backward, she jammed the top of his foot into her underarm with the expertise of a seasoned Brazilian jiu-jitsu practitioner. He'd underestimated her. He shivered as he hit the floor across his upper back, and lunged rabidly for the limb, but it was too late. Aided by the weight of his chunky outdoor boot — a luxury not usually afforded on the mats — she levered her whole body onto the foot, twisting it at a grotesque angle, tearing muscle in the first second, breaking the bone in the next.

Slater nearly passed out from the pain.

Mother seemed satisfied by the damage she'd caused. She slackened her grip, the limb now rendered useless. He wrenched it away from her, his foot practically dangling from his ankle, hanging at an awkward angle.

Trying not to think about the consequences, he used most of his athleticism to get his good foot underneath him, and sprang up on one leg.

She couldn't compute. She'd just torn his whole foot to pieces, and somehow he was upright before she was. She seemed a little slower to react — a dangerous game to play around Slater. She got to her feet and he let fly with an elbow, and it struck her in the forehead, and she went down surrounded by the percussive *boom* of bone against bone, ringing off the walls over and over again.

He cocked his right fist, ready to drop a staggering right hook onto her chin as she lay prone, but he loosened when he realised she lay unconscious. Her eyes stared vacantly up at the ceiling, her mouth twisted into a sick smile, the expression frozen on the moment her brain thudded back and forth around the walls of her skull.

She'd won.

'What the hell are you supposed to do now?' he said.

Ordinarily not one to talk to himself, but white-hot pain can change your personality awfully quick.

Sweat pooled around his temples, but not from the heat.

Shock started setting in.

The pain was wholly unlike anything he could remember. He'd been shot, and stabbed, and beaten to a pulp, but whatever damage Mother had done to his ankle was in a league of its own. He wondered whether he would ever walk properly again. Then he scolded himself, because that was nowhere near as important as figuring out how on earth he was going to get back on State Route 161 if he couldn't move. He hadn't a hope of putting weight on his right leg, no matter how tough he thought he was. It simply wasn't physically possible.

As a test, he touched his right heel to the linoleum, and an endless detonation of nerves seared up his leg, through his torso, into his brain.

He bent over, fought the urge to vomit, and breathed in and out through his nose in deep, rasping breaths.

He hopped on his left leg, and still the right flared with pain.

But he could deal with that.

He turned back to Mother's unconscious corpse and considered putting a bullet in her for good measure. An efficient operative would. But that was half the reason he'd fled

Black Force. He wasn't prepared to gun down anyone in sight to achieve the objective. He'd done it for years. Now was a different time. A different life. He could have murdered every Whelan in New York City if he'd deemed it necessary. He could have killed Williams, Ruby ... the list went on.

The smart thing to do.

But Slater had long ago decided to leave the ruthless amoral decisions to others.

He hopped across the floor and made it to the carpeted hallway just past the drying room. From there it was a short trip to a set of stairs that ascended into a communal central room connecting what appeared to be nearly a dozen separate dormitories. There was no-one in sight. Slater put a flat palm between the corridor's walls, and helped himself along with the aid of his upper body. He grimaced, and noted his faults. The HK416 swung on its strap around his shoulder, but there was no way to have it at the ready and walk at the same time. He would have to make do with what he could feasibly accomplish.

He made it to the foot of the stairs. They took a sharp right turn upward, and he rotated his body to get ready for the short journey. He would have to leap from step to step on his left leg.

He lowered himself into position.

A dark shape passed across the opening at the top of the stairs.

Slater looked up, reaching for the gun.

He froze.

The shape froze.

He locked eyes with the little girl he'd travelled halfway across the world to find.

87

No one spoke.

Slater couldn't find words. Pain thrummed dull and horrid in the back of his head, but it all fell away when he saw her.

Shien stood four and a half feet tall, small and frail, with the same wide gentle eyes and straight black hair that fell gracefully on either side of her head. She stood clad in a pair of tracksuit pants tucked into fluffy socks and a long-sleeved white shirt, rolled up around her slender wrists.

She barely reacted. Processing it internally. Eyeing the man at the bottom of the stairs that had single-handedly pulled her out of hell in Macau.

Are you the enemy now, Will? Slater thought.

Is that what she's thinking?

Is that what she's been trained to believe?

He didn't say anything. He let her make up her own mind. He was hesitant to pressure her into anything.

She stifled a sob. Caught it on its way out, and stuffed it back in. Sealed her lips tight. Her eyes turned wet.

She smiled.

And suddenly everything was still possible.

'Hey, kid,' he said, as loud as he dared, barely more than a whisper in the silent lodge.

She hurtled down the steps, taking them two at a time, and threw herself into his arms. He took all her weight on his left leg and hugged her tight, sensing her heart pounding a million miles an hour, feeling the sheer relief in the air. She still hadn't said a thing, but he could tell she didn't hate or despise him, and a ball of happiness built in his chest so full and so complete he wasn't sure there was any feeling in the world better than this.

In its own unique way, it made him want to give fatherhood a shot.

He set her down on the second step, so they were nearly eye level. Tears streamed down her face, but she didn't cry. She kept the sobs at bay, quiet as a mouse.

Looking out for both of them.

'Will,' she said, small and timid.

He paused, his breath catching in his throat, and he got the sense she'd been preparing a speech like this every chance she had a moment to herself.

She said, 'I know you work with these people, but I don't like them, Will. And I don't want to be here. Please don't hurt me for saying that. I know maybe you think I should be here, but I don't want to be. I don't like it. I really don't, Will. I'm not mad that you put me here, I'm just ... I want to go somewhere. Anywhere. Not home — I know I don't have that. But I just want to start again. Please, Will. Please.'

Music to his goddamn ears.

He leant in and said, 'I didn't put you here, Shien.'

'You gave me to that man.'

'He promised me something different. Something very,

very different to this. And then he lied to me and put you here.'

Her face lit up with an ecstasy he hadn't considered humanly possible. 'You're ... you're not with them?'

'No.'

'Can you get me out of here?'

'Nothing would make me happier.'

She launched at him again, arms around his abdomen, squeezing as tight as she could. The meaning wasn't lost on him. He sensed every morsel of pure energy in the hold, her tiny forearms trying to disperse the elation wracking her body, doing anything she could not to cry out with joy. When she pulled away, the tears streamed harder down her face.

Slater flashed a glance back down the hallway, catching a sliver of the drying room.

There was no sign of Mother's slumped, unconscious form.

He froze, and out of the corner of his mouth said, 'Shien.'

She looked up at him expectantly.

He said, 'The woman. The one who looks after you in this place.'

She drew into herself, her lips sealing into a hard line, her tears turning from joy to terror. 'What about her?'

'What's she like?'

'Please don't ever let me see her again, Will.'

'Why's that?'

'She hurts me.'

'What does she do?'

'It started as bruises. She's so strong. She grips my arm, really hard. The guards say she's not supposed to hurt the students but she does it anyway. In places they can't see. But now it's getting worse. Because she can tell most of us don't want to be here. There's ... what's that word? Unrest. There's unrest in the house. I guess I'm probably causing most of it. I keep telling them they don't have to be there.'

'Mother doesn't like that?'

'She knows I've been through a lot. And I know what happens when you don't speak up. Because of Macau. So I speak up, even when she tells me not to.'

'What does she do, Shien?'

He spotted a shadow against the door frame. Too far away to hear the sound of feet scuffing against flooring, and too far for the stalker to hear their conversation.

But close enough for concern.

'Nothing yet,' Shien muttered. 'But she says bad things. Horrible things. She keeps saying if we don't start behaving she's going to put things inside us.'

'Inside?'

'You know ... in our parts.'

'That's not very nice of her.'

'No,' Shien agreed. 'It's not. Where is she, Will? She scares me. She's ... so strong.'

'I know.'

She looked down. Saw him balancing on one leg. 'You're hurt. Oh my God ... your foot.'

'Stay right there, Shien.'

He kept his eyes trained on the door frame.

She said, 'Did Mother do that?'

Slater said, 'You said it yourself. She's very strong.'

'Don't let her get her hands on you. Her grip is so strong.'

'I won't.'

The shadow moved.

'Close your eyes, Shien.'

She obliged.

The shadow lunged.

Mother appeared in the doorway, a massive swollen lump already forming on her forehead, a Beretta M9 in her hand. She looked like she knew how to use it. She didn't get the chance.

Slater blew her face open with two rounds from the HK416, perfectly placed.

Bang-bang.

Forehead, eye socket.

The noise of the gunshots was horrendous in the lodge, ripping through both storeys at once, spearing through the whole building, unmistakeable. At the source of the gunfire, it was deafening.

Shien shrieked.

Slater watched Mother sprawl to the linoleum, narrowly missing the carpeted hallway. Her head hit the floor with a wet *thwack.*

He said, 'Hard for her to grip anything now.'

Shien said, 'How are you going to get out of here on one foot?'

Pale and cold, Slater said, 'I might need your help with that.'

88

Screams rose throughout the building, unnerving in their intensity. All children. All scared. Some more than others.

Some were just frightened by the noise.

Maybe they're further along in the program, Slater thought.

A sharp voice called from a far-off room, 'You can't be in here! Get out of here! No shooting in here! This is our space!'

Followed by discordant wailing.

Like something out of a horror film.

Shien tensed up, hunching her shoulders.

Slater looked at her.

'We're taught rules,' Shien said. 'Some of the kids have been here for years. They don't know anything else. Mother is very strict on the rules. No guns in the house is one of them. The girls aren't going to stop screaming. Until they put the place on lockdown.'

'They're going to raise hell?'

Shien had clearly never heard the expression before, but she nodded. 'We should go.'

'I agree.'

'Where are we going?'

'Haven't figured that out yet.'

'Will...'

'Work with me here, Shien. It wasn't easy getting here.'

'You need a vehicle.'

'Yes.'

'They're all locked up.'

'There's a garage?'

'Around the other side of the lodge. Underneath it.'

'How do we get in?'

'We can't. Locked doors. They're metal or steel or ... something. There's codes.'

'Who knows them?'

'Mother.'

'Who else?'

Shien simply stared at him.

Slater nodded. 'Right.'

Already he could picture the four remaining guards huddling together outside, scolding themselves for not taking the situation seriously, forming a plan to storm the lodge from all sides at once, or together in a tight cluster. He put himself in their shoes. They'd heard gunshots in a distant booth, and then they'd all had a strange interaction with one of the guards, who they now realised hadn't been one of the guards at all, and now they'd heard gunshots in the lodge itself.

Slater would be thoroughly unnerved, if he was them.

Which favoured sticking together. Splitting up might prove more efficient. Slater certainly preferred it that way. He could maybe deal with them one on one, four consecutive times. A coin toss either way. The damage inflicted to his right foot was steadily hammering home. He was starting to understand the bleakness of his situation. It was awfully difficult to do anything on one leg.

He sat down on the first step, breathing hard.

'What?' Shien said, leaning over him, placing her hands on his shoulders.

'Quiet,' he hissed.

He listened, hard. Rifle at the ready. He extended his right leg straight out, and when the mangled foot touched the carpet his whole body screamed a protest in unison. He ignored it, tasting cold sweat that ran down his nose, over his upper lip, into his mouth.

He wasn't doing so well.

'You okay?' Shien said.

'Yeah.'

Torn muscles. A broken bone. Maybe two. He forgot about it.

'How are we getting out of here?' she said.

'I'm going to have to kill all the guards, Shien.'

She stiffened. 'Can't we sneak away?'

'Not with my foot. It's just not possible.'

'I can hear them coming.'

'You can?'

Perhaps the unsuppressed gunshots had affected his hearing more than he thought. He twisted around to face her. 'Where?'

'Front door,' she said, meekly.

She backed away, scaling a couple of steps.

'Stay there,' he said, quiet as he could.

He slumped down off the first step, now seated on his rear on the carpet. He had a direct line of sight to the giant wooden door set in the far wall of the drying room.

He brought the red dot sight up to shoulder height.

'Shien,' he said. 'Do you know if this lodge has crutches?'

'There might be some in the storage room.'

'Where is that?'

'Downstairs. In the basement.'

'How many ways are there into the basement?'

'Only one. Except...' Then she shook her head. 'No, that's blocked. Only one.'

'Go down there now. See if you can find them.'

'I don't like the basement, Will.'

'Why? Does Mother have helpers?'

'No. It's just her.'

'So the basement's empty?'

'Yes.'

'You're going to have to do this for me. Or I'll be dead. That's how serious it is.'

She nodded, solemn, reserved.

'Okay,' she said. 'I'll be right back.'

She leapt off the third step, directly over him, landing like a cat on the other side of the hallway, and took off running in the other direction. He kept his gaze locked firmly on the front door, ready to empty the magazine as soon as it burst inward. Behind him he heard a sliding door rolling on its tracks, and then the soft *pitter-patter* of footsteps descending down into darkness.

Williams' words rang in his ears.

What's your best-case scenario here?

You get her, and then what?

He didn't know.

One step at a time.

One problem at a time.

First, the guards.

The front door shot open, its lock snapped clean in two.

89

It swung on its hinges and bounced off the opposite wall, and Slater instinctively fired a three-round burst through the doorway, before he even knew what was there.

The lead sailed straight out into the forest, lost to the woods.

Hitting nothing.

Finding no targets.

There was no-one there.

Slater froze, still seated. He went through the same acrobatic manoeuvre, getting his left foot jammed tight against his rear, then levering upright. Balanced precariously on one leg, he kept the HK416 aimed tight at the open doorway and tensed his finger against the trigger.

A soft sound.

Boots on snow.

Someone moving, close by.

Then something sailed through the doorway. A small blunt object, about the size of a tin can. It clattered to the linoleum, making a racket, and skittered into the carpeted hallway in a stroke of bad luck.

An M84 stun grenade.

Slater processed it all at warp speed, and realised he had a decision to make.

Surrendering now, or surrendering later.

Either way, he was going to lose.

But surrendering later wasn't a definite guarantee. And Slater was a born and bred fighter. So without considering the consequences he lunged forward on his left leg — the only possible action. The stun grenade had lost its momentum a few feet away from Slater. He could reach it with one massive hop, and punt it with the other foot. It was a case of picking his poison. Either put all his weight on the shattered ankle, or use the appendage to kick the grenade.

Either way, he was in for a world of hurt.

His athleticism assisted him, allowing him to close the gap in a bounding stride, all his leg muscles tensing at once, a hard explosive bundle of fast twitch fibres. He sealed his lips and prepared himself as best he could and thundered his broken foot into the grenade.

He nearly passed out from the pain.

But he hit it right where he needed to. It shot back toward the doorway like a dart, a tiny black capsule that spelled disaster for whoever was in the vicinity when it went off.

Which, unfortunately, was Slater.

The stun grenade sailed halfway across the drying room, then exploded in mid-air. Slater had meant to turn his whole body away from the room the instant he kicked the grenade away, but the horrifying pain rippling through his foot froze him like a deer in headlights.

For a half-second, his brain refused to compute — enough to seal your fate in a game like this.

He had his eyes on the grenade when it went off, and the accompanying blinding flare of light ruined his vision.

He'd already been off balance, and the disorientation finished the job.

He went down hard, temporarily deaf and blind, almost landing on the wrong side, with his good foot crushing the bad one. But he rolled at the last instant and landed on his stomach, squashing his face into the carpet, mouth wide open, sucking in deep ragged breaths. He lifted a hand to his face and pawed at his eyes — he was no stranger to the sensation of a stun grenade, but it didn't make it any easier to deal with.

He blinked fast, three or four times, and rolled to his back, bringing the rifle up to aim at where he thought the doorway lay.

Still blind.

Still deaf.

Panic hit him like a truck. He threw caution to the wind and fired, pulling the trigger, feeling the HK416 vibrate in his hands. He didn't hear the reports, or see where he was aiming.

Then he stopped immediately, because he had no idea if or when Shien would return from the basement. He pictured her racing to the top of the steps, brandishing crutches, cut down in the carnage.

He let go of the trigger.

He couldn't run that risk.

He would sooner die than put her in harm's way.

His vision came back, piece by piece...

He made out dull shapes looming up in a glowing white rectangle.

The doorway...
Then the bullet hit him in the shoulder.

90

I t tore a chunk of flesh off his deltoid muscle, and all the pain followed immediately after. His brain barely knew how to deal with itself, focusing back and forth between the grisly foot injury and the fresh destruction of nerve endings in his right shoulder.

He gasped, still deaf, mostly blind.

He moved to re-adjust his position and get the bulky HK416 aimed at the silhouettes in the door frame, but his right arm refused to move.

He tried again.

One last time.

Nothing. His vision seemed to get worse, and he heard nothing but the dull *thrum-thrum-thrum* of everything at once. No discernible sounds. No ability to raise his arms.

He knew when he was defeated.

He screamed, 'I yield,' at the top of his lungs. His own voice rattled in his head, but he couldn't hear anything that came out of his mouth.

He let go of the gun, letting it cascade to the floor. He

stretched out on his back and put his hands above his head, fingers out, palms open. He stared up at the ceiling. Barely seeing it. Barely aware of what was going on around him. He felt a *squelch* under his right shoulder, and sensed blood soaking into the carpet. As he lay back he dragged his right heel across the ground, and the torn muscles gnashed together.

He groaned.

And then they were all standing over him, four of them, and he could make out their features a little clearer. They all had their helmets on now. Slater wondered if the material was bulletproof. One of them crouched over him as the other three aimed rifle barrels at his chest. The guard flipped up his visor, and Slater stared into green eyes burning hot with rage.

The guy had the square head and weather-beaten complexion of a stereotypical Marine. Or, ex-Marine, if Russell Williams was to be believed. A get-shit-done type. He couldn't have been much older than thirty. Close to Slater's age, but even if he'd had a career for the ages he would still rest a world apart in experience.

Experience did Slater little good now.

The guy reached down and shook Slater by the collar of his jacket, deliberately aggravating his shoulder wound.

A fresh torrent of blood poured out of the torn jacket.

Slater moaned.

'You really thought you could do this?' the guy said.

'Figured it was worth a shot.'

'Who sent you?'

'No one sent me.'

'We'll get it out of you.'

'I'm terrified,' Slater said. 'Listen, guys, can we all agree that any attempt to beat information out of me is only going to lead to me feeding you false intel? Can we come to a mutual understanding?'

'Why would you want to convince us of that?'

'Better a quick death. Get it over with.'

The guy shrugged. 'Probably. But you're not dying on us. You'll lose consciousness, maybe. But not until...'

He looked up at the faceless guards around him.

They all nodded in unison.

The guy bent down and gripped the back of Slater's skull with a meaty hand, lifting it off the carpet. He growled, 'You're not as smart as you think. We've got surveillance access in the booths. We saw what you were doing.'

'Oh,' Slater said.

'Where is she?'

'I told her to run off.'

'You told her where to go.'

'I've never been in this building before. You think I know all the hiding spots?'

One of the faceless guards screamed, 'Roll call!'

A cacophony of high-pitched responses drifted down the stairwell, piercing into what little hearing Slater had left. He grimaced. In response, the three guards in helmets hustled up to the communal dormitory area. He heard them split up, checking the rooms, sweeping them for any sign of Shien. A couple of the kids floated innocent questions, which were all met with harsh single-syllable responses.

Now was not the time for explanation, evidently.

The first guy with the green eyes took a Beretta M9 out of an appendix holster at his waist and jammed it into Slater's throat, pinning him against the carpet. He wasn't going anywhere.

'Looked like you were here to rescue her,' the man muttered. 'You her father or something?'

'Do I look like her father?'

A pause. Studying skin tone. 'No, you don't.'

'How'd you figure that one out? Are you a Mensa member?'

The man slapped him in the face, producing a wet *crack*.

Slater groaned.

The guy said, 'I think she's in the basement.'

'What makes you think that?'

'Seems the logical place to go. It's a maze down there. She could hide for hours.'

'Why don't you go find out?'

'I think I'll take you with me. I'm not in the mood for hide and seek. Seems like you mean a lot to her. I wonder if she'll stay quiet when I shoot you in the head in front of her.'

'You're going to traumatise her like that?'

'That's the least I can do. I'll make her suffer afterwards.'

'Aren't you here to guard these kids?'

'I don't like your friend one fucking bit. She's the rebel of the group — that little runt. I've told Command time and time again that the whole program would be better off without her. But her test results are phenomenal, apparently. So they're keeping her around — even after all the trouble she's caused.'

'Sounds like you've got a whole host of your own issues to deal with if you're getting this worked up over a kid.'

The green eyes sparked, and the guy smiled. 'Of course I do. Why else would I be all the way out here?'

He hauled Slater to his feet — it wasn't an easy process. First he tried to lever him upright with all the weight on his shattered foot, and Slater pitched violently to the left to avoid that result, which sent him tumbling straight back to the carpet. He flailed around on the floor like a lifelong alcoholic deep in a bender, willing himself to retaliate, trying to figure out how to disarm the guard without the use of his right arm or leg. One side of his body, effectively shut down.

He couldn't do anything to resist.

The guard got him balanced on his left foot, and then touched the Beretta's barrel to the back of his head.

'Walk,' he said. 'Basement.'

'I can't walk.'

'Then hop.'

Slater forced himself to concentrate, to fight through the whirlwind, to try and find some way to seize the upper hand. This was the only chance he had. One on one, despite the circumstances, despite the disadvantages. He would have to find some way to get it done. Most of the firepower was upstairs, clearing rooms, securing the lodge.

But then the first man called out, 'Get down here!'

And the other three guards thundered down the steps, filling the hallway with their bulk, brandishing their rifles at the ready.

Slater stood still, his head throbbing, his heart racing, his blood turning cold.

One of them said, 'All clear.'

'Good,' the first guy said. 'Basement.'

They all nodded.

One on four.

With no right arm, and no right leg.

Against fully automatic assault rifles wielded by men who knew how to use them.

Impossible.

Slater bowed his head, defeated, and jolted across the carpet, hopping on his left foot, heading for the sliding door.

Descending down into darkness, with the cool touch of a Beretta against the back of his skull.

He fought the urge to vomit and pulled the door along its tracks, staring down into murky blackness.

'Basement,' he said.

'Let's go find your favourite kid,' the first guy hissed, something sadistic in his tone.

Slater didn't like this one bit.

He leapt down onto the first step.

91

He tried to take his time, but they wouldn't let him. He fought tooth and nail for any chance to compose himself, to unscramble the wild array of thoughts tumbling end over end through his head. He paused on the second step, pretending to wince, feigning some kind of disruption to his left ankle. The guard with the green eyes shoved him forward by forcing the barrel harder into his head, nearly sending him toppling head over heels to the bottom of the staircase. He fought for balance and took the next three steps fast to avoid a similar fate. By the time he realised what the guard was doing, it was too late.

They were already halfway down the stairs.

They reached the basement, and the guard looped a muscular forearm around Slater's throat and held tight. He switched the Beretta from the back of Slater's head to the soft patch of skin above his right ear, jamming the gun in tight.

Smart.

In an attempt to disarm the guy, Slater had to lunge across his chest with his left arm, an awkward manoeuvre that gave the man plenty of time to see what was coming and squeeze the trigger. The bullet might exit Slater's head and enter the guard's forearm, but it seemed to be a risk he was willing to take.

They stepped out into a long low space with weak flickering bulbs every few yards along the concrete ceiling. The walls were concrete, too, and the floor. It was like a dungeon, with all the floor space taken up by rows of rusting metal shelving. The shelves sported fight gear and knives of all kinds and regular lumber and building supplies to patch up any discrepancies in the lodge.

Like a nuclear fallout bunker, only larger.

The guard screamed into the darkness, 'Shien!'

Silence.

'I'm going to kill your friend!'

Silence.

'Three seconds, Shien. Don't make this any harder than it needs to be.'

Slater sensed the man's finger against the trigger, unbearably close to pulling it. He reflected on his life, and determined it had been a good one. He didn't see it flash before his eyes. None of that sentimental crap. Just a rudimentary analysis, followed by acceptance, followed by a single thought.

Well, if this is it…

He closed his eyes.

'Okay, Shien, it's your call! You did this. Ready? This is the sound of your friend getting his brains sprayed across the room. I might make you clean it up. That's your punishment for playing hide and seek.'

Silence.

'Damn,' the guard whispered in Slater's ear. 'I was going to do it anyway. But I really wanted her to see it.'

He started to put downward pressure on the trigger.

And then he stopped.

He grunted in disapproval.

Slater felt him turning on the spot, looking over his shoulder, searching for his three buddies.

The man said, 'Fuck this. She needs to see this. I didn't keep him alive for nothing. Go find her and drag her here, and then I'll shoot this guy in the head. Maybe some of his brains will hit her. That'll teach her to play games.'

Even the stern-faced guards grimaced at that.

'Go,' the first man urged.

'They're thinking you're a sick, sick puppy,' Slater said.

'Maybe I am. How's this for a bit of excitement? God, I hate that booth. Nothing to do all day. You've got to spice things up every now and then.'

The three other guards shouldered past Slater and the green-eyed man, pushing deep into the basement. The weak light cast long shadows off their helmets. Slater felt the burn in his broken foot and the coagulation of blood pooling around the sleeve of his torn jacket, and he waited for the end to come.

He couldn't fight it.

One guard took the lead, impatient, wanting it over and done with, likely frustrated at the commotion caused. Mother was dead, and that would mean an upheaval of the routine as Command scrambled for replacements.

Anything to keep the wheels moving, the cogs turning.

Slater sensed the sickness and psychotic nature of everything around him and figured this was what happened when men and women in the upper echelon of the government failed to do their due diligence. Williams might have started this whole thing with pure intentions, but it had clearly descended into some kind of freak show. Almost cult-like. The isolation, coupled with the job stress. No doubt it twisted minds into something darker. Hence Mother, and the green-eyed guard, and the surreal nature of the entire setup.

The first guard made it a few more feet, and then a silhouette reared up out of the darkness, and there was a flash of movement, and the *punch* of a broken visor and the *squelch* of a sharp implement being thrust through flesh, and then the silhouette vanished as quickly as it had appeared, and the guard stood on his feet for another couple of seconds, as if in denial of the fact that he was already dead, and then he toppled back with the front of his helmet shattered and a metal stake driven through his eye socket, already pouring blood onto the dusty concrete.

The other pair froze, limbs locking, eyes widening, hearts pounding.

92

And then the silhouette appeared again, this time darting between a slim gap in the metal shelves, and it waved an agile limb over one of the pair, like casting a spell with an invisible wand, and then it disappeared for a second time and the second guard twirled in a sick pirouette, hands flying to his throat, arterial blood spurting from the long thin line drawn across his neck. He made eye contact with the green-eyed man holding Slater, and his eyes said, *No fucking way,* and then he died gruesomely, his pupils rolling up into his sockets, exposing two milky whites, and blood ran from his mouth and nose and he pitched forward and face planted the ground, already a corpse.

At which point the green-eyed man tensed up, still holding the Beretta tight against Slater's head, but with all his concentration fixed on the third guy, who seemed destined to succumb to a horrific death seconds from now. It was the next inevitable course of action, obviously. It was as if they were both watching a twisted theatre performance play out in front of them. Slater watched the guard too, suddenly all alone a dozen feet away from them, surrounded by shelves and shadows. He seemed to sense the same thing, and he spun three hundred and sixty degrees, far too fast to see anything, rattled to the core.

Slater tensed up.

The green-eyed man tensed up.

And then the silhouette came out of the corner, a couple of yards to Slater's right. He flinched and squeezed his eyes shut, aware there was nothing he could do with the green-eyed man holding him in a vice like grip, and his entire right side fundamentally useless in a combat situation. He shifted on his left foot, stamping it into the concrete, and waited to die.

Blood hit him across the upper back, hot and powerful, like a jet.

That's it.

Here comes the pain.

You're dead.

But it wasn't his blood.

The grip around his throat slackened, and the Beretta's aim wandered a few inches downward and Slater thrust his chin back, a violent purposeful motion that brought him a few millimetres out of the line of fire when the green-eyed man yanked on the trigger in his death throes and fired. The gun went off right in his face, ruining what little hearing he had left, and then the rest of the incident played out like some kind of bizarre silent film from the twentieth century.

Slater accidentally put weight on his broken foot and the nausea sent him toppling to the concrete, and the corpse of the green-eyed man collapsed on top of him, blood streaming from his cut throat. The final guard spotted the silhouette and turned to adopt a firing position, and the small figure pitched their arm back and hurled the knife through the air. The blade tumbled end over end and entered messily, nothing like the clean kills you see in the movies. It struck in a downward sweeping motion, tearing a line down the guard's face. It didn't end up embedded in his forehead — instead it fell to the floor between his feet, leaving him disfigured and bleeding and forgetting about his weapon entirely.

At which point the silhouette leapt over Slater and pounced on the guard, taking him down with a dexterity that was instantly recognisable.

Slater spotted full amber eyes staring down at the last guard, who was bleeding and whimpering.

She put him out of his misery, fetching the knife from where it had fallen and plunging it through the top of his head.

She crawled off the body, cat-like.

Slater said, 'Was all that really necessary?'

'Remember,' Ruby Nazarian said. 'I grew up here. I know what these guards do when no one's looking.'

'Christ.'

Slater lay back, in a world of agony, and squeezed his eyes shut.

Hoping it was all a bad dream.

Then Shien came sprinting out of the shadows and put her hands on his chest.

93

She whimpered.

He opened his eyes, and smiled through bloody lips. 'Hey.'

'Hey.'

'You okay?'

Shien frowned. 'I'm fine. Look at you.'

Slater turned his eyes to Ruby, completely at her mercy.

She wasn't at a hundred percent capacity. Nowhere close. Slater eyed her twisted nose, pointing in the wrong direction, freshly broken. And she seemed to be hunched over, tender around the mid-section. He wondered if he'd broken any of her ribs after all. Perhaps she was made of steel. Then again, it was entirely possible. Adrenalin was a miraculous thing. She could crash at any second, the stress chemicals replaced by the awareness of the damage inside her. But for now, she was holding up okay. And that was all that mattered. It seemed she hadn't needed functioning ribs or the ability to breathe through her nose in order to kill the four men around them.

Slater held his hands up. Palms out. Fingers splayed. Same gesture.

Vulnerable to anything.

She studied them both with a keen interest, her glowing eyes analysing and computing and figuring things out, and then she removed the knife from the last guard's head, and she wiped it on her tracksuit and slotted it into a special holster at her waist.

She said, 'You two do what you need to do. I've given Shien the garage code.'

And she walked straight past them, heading for the stairs.

'Wait,' Slater mumbled through bloody lips.

She turned.

Impatient.

Eyebrows raised.

She said, 'Yes?'

'Don't you ... want to talk ... about all this?'

She shrugged. 'What is there to talk about?'

'I mean ... you had a change of heart ... shouldn't we at least discuss what happens now?'

'Nothing happens now. Take the girl, and get the hell out of here. Isn't that what you always wanted?'

'What are you going to do?'

Ruby put her hands behind her back, and bowed her head, and locked those amber eyes onto his. Cat-like. 'This isn't your fight, my friend. This isn't your story. You don't get all the answers.'

'How did you get in here?'

'There's a narrow window, only a few inches above ground level, up the back. It's not big enough for a man to fit through. But I got in okay.'

'That's what I thought about,' Shien muttered. 'When I

said there might be another way out. But it was banked up with snow the last time I checked. She ... must have cleared it. Before she did all this.'

Shien lifted her gaze to the bloodbath all around them.

'Don't look at them,' Slater said. 'Look at me.'

'I've seen dead men before.'

'I know, but...'

'I'll be okay.'

'This isn't what I wanted you to see.'

'I'll be okay,' she repeated.

He coughed, nearly hacking up blood, and she put a tiny hand behind his head to support him.

He said, 'This isn't a world for a nine year old.'

'Well, that's good then. Because I'm ten.'

He looked at her. And managed a weak half-smile. 'Happy birthday.'

'Thanks. You're a month late.'

'I would have got here sooner ... if I'd known.'

Over Shien's shoulder, Slater noticed Ruby shrinking into the shadows, creeping toward the staircase.

'I know why you did it,' he called.

Ruby turned, and cocked her head. 'Do you?'

Like Mother had.

'I have an idea.'

'You might scratch the surface. But you'll never really get a grip on all of it. Living in a place like this for most of your teenage life and being taught day and night that it's the best thing, the right thing, the only thing. And then going out in the world and putting everything you learnt into practice and learning that there's others, people like you, people who seem to have an off-switch. And suddenly realising that maybe spending your whole childhood around this particular set-up might have scrambled your wires. That's just a sliver of what I'm dealing with.'

'I didn't kill you in that parking lot,' Slater said. 'That's what tipped you over the edge.'

She shrugged. 'Maybe.'

'Where are you going?'

'You left a man by a tree. I passed him by on the way to the lodge. I left him there too. He's not going anywhere. I think I'm going to pay him a visit. I think I'm going to have a one-on-one chat about all the things he did to me. The choices he made for me. I'm starting to realise a lot.'

'If you need to talk...'

She smirked, the amber blazing hot. 'You're just as screwed up as I am, Will. Maybe even more so. Because you chose this life all on your own. You weren't manipulated into it like I was. No ... talking's not going to do it. But I'll deal with the man who thought it was a good idea to put me here, and then I'm gone. Maybe back to Colombia. Or somewhere even more remote. I can support myself. It's time to try and carve some kind of a life out of these circumstances. A normal one.'

Silence.

She said, 'I know what you're thinking. Maybe I don't deserve it. Maybe I deserve a bodybag. After all the people I've killed. But that's just something I'll have to deal with. And if that's really what you're thinking, then you're on no pedestal yourself.'

'Actually,' Slater said. 'I'm not thinking anything at all. I don't know what to think.'

She nodded. 'Good call.'

'What about the rest of the kids?'

'I'll take care of them. Until the clean up crew arrives.

They'll probably have a few senior figureheads with them. I'll have a talk to them about the program.'

'You think you'll change their minds?'

'I doubt it. But I'll try. They had to know it would lead to something like this eventually. All roads pointed to a blood-bath. Sooner or later.'

'Watch out for yourself,' he said. 'I wouldn't trust anyone in Command. It's a sociopathic career choice. In every sense of the word.'

'I've always kept my wits about me.'

'Just be careful.'

'I will.'

'Can you promise me one thing?'

Ruby shrugged. 'I guess.'

'Stall them for long enough to let us get away. I've made an enemy of an entire country. At least, the only part of it that matters. The covert section. I'm dead to them, perhaps even worse than I used to be. I need a head start.'

'I can give you that.'

'And then get out of here. Don't play around with them. You know as well as I do how they function.'

'It's a dangerous world.'

'One last thing.'

She said, 'What?'

'Are you going to visit your family?'

She pursed her lips. 'Seems like you already did that for me.'

'They deserved to know.'

'Let me put it this way,' Ruby said. 'I'm intent on getting as far away as humanly possible from that part of my life. I'll cross half the world if I need to.'

'You still hate them?'

'I never hated them. Now I realise I never deserved them in the first place.'

'They'd want to see you.'

She smiled a sad smile, her broken nose twisting upward. 'Not like this. Not what I am now.'

'You don't know that.'

'Are your parents around?'

'No,' Slater said.

'If they were ... would you ever tell them the things you've done?'

He looked around at all the blood. 'No.'

'Well, I don't want to lie to them. So I should never see them again. They deserve my life to be an eternal "what-if." Because anything they imagine is better than the reality.'

'Okay,' Slater said. 'I hope you make peace with yourself.'

'You too. Seems like that's not your style, though.'

Slater shrugged. 'Maybe I need to change my ways.'

Ruby paused, a long poignant quiet. She stared at Shien, her gaze intense. She didn't blink.

She said, 'No. Don't. Your ways are fine. You've saved one life, at least.'

'Maybe two,' Slater said.

Staring at her.

Ruby stared back.

Then she nodded, slow and controlled, and it said everything that needed to be said.

She turned her back on them and disappeared up the stairs.

Never to be seen again.

94

S later managed to pull it together long enough to feed Shien instructions.

She retrieved a first aid kit from one of the shelves up the back of the room, and did her best work to stop the bleeding in his shoulder. Her hands shook as he pulled his jacket off sleeve by sleeve, and he reassured her as best he could, even though the crimson pooling around him on the concrete left ample room for worry. He couldn't confirm whether the chill in the air was really as severe as he thought it was. The mind conjured all kinds of cheap tricks when it was depleted.

He sat hunched over and warned her the results would be grisly.

She shook her head, as if there was nothing more ludicrous.

She peeled his stained undershirt up and gasped at the sight of the ragged flesh.

'Told you,' Slater said.

'What do I do?'

'Can you push the skin together and wrap the gauze around it tight?'

'Is that good enough?'

'It'll do for now.'

'Until what?'

'Until I get myself to a doctor.'

'What will you do with me?'

'I'll figure that out on the road. For now, all we need to focus on is getting away from here.'

She took a deep breath, suddenly pale in the weak light, and did her best to follow his commands. She jammed the skin together and looped the gauze bandage around it once, twice, three times, and Slater stared deep into the shadows and did everything he could to take his mind off the wound. Shien cut off a small piece of medical tape and sealed the bandage.

He lowered and raised his arm.

Good enough.

It wouldn't fall off for the next few days, at least.

He wiped sweat off his brow, despite the chill, and put a hand on Shien's shoulder.

'Sorry,' he said. 'I need to lean some of my weight on you.'

He clambered to his feet. There was none of the athletic energy he'd utilised before — the threats were neutralised, and the danger had passed. His body had already dipped uneasily into the reserve bank, searching for something to latch onto, coming away with nothing.

He tried not to look at his foot.

'Where's the garage?' he muttered, lucid.

'Do you need food and water?' Shien said.

Slater nodded, smacking his lips. 'That'd be good. Garage first, though.'

She nodded too.

'Do you need to go upstairs for food and water?'

She nodded again.

'Then don't worry about it.'

'Why? There's no-one left. Just the other kids.'

'That woman who just saved us is a complicated puzzle that I don't want you running into again, even by chance. There's no guarantee she'll feel the same five minutes from now.'

'Who is she?'

'She grew up here.'

'I don't want to turn out like her, Will.'

'You won't,' Slater said. 'Not anymore.'

Shien stood smaller than usual, her shoulders hunched.

She'd seen a hell of a lot for a kid.

But the shock would set in all the same.

Slater aimed to be in a vehicle and on the open road by then.

He hopped along the basement floor, heading for a darkened stretch of the room. Shien guided him by the hand, taking a considerable amount of his weight — far more than he ever expected.

He grimaced and said, 'You're strong.'

'Mother makes us exercise. Push ups and sit ups and running. So much of it. I was so sore, all the time. Then I got used to it.'

'You get used to everything.'

'Why did they make us do it?'

'They wanted you strong. Suits the job they had in mind for you.'

'What were they training us for, Will? Mother never said. She never explained. Some of the older girls knew, but they'd been told not to talk about it. I hate not knowing things.'

'Maybe it's best you never know.'

'To be like you?'

Slater nodded. 'Something like that. Close enough.'

'Is this how you became what you are? You're a good guy, but I don't like this.'

'It's not supposed to be fun.'

'Did you start as young as I am?'

'No. I was an adult.'

'Oh.'

'That's why I came. To get you out.'

'Oh.'

'If you want to be like me, that's a choice you'll have to make. But not for a long time.'

'Thank you, Will.'

'Where's the garage?'

'Right here.'

Shien let go of his arm and darted over to a barely visible cutout in the wall, just large enough for a doorframe. He eyed a sleek metallic keypad, and her finger hovered over the buttons.

She screwed up her face.

'How many digits was it?' Slater said.

'Eight.'

'How many times did she tell you the code?'

'Once.'

He couldn't let her panic. Not now. Not with everything riding on this. If the government showed up, he was as good as dead, and she was reserved for a fate perhaps even worse. Because anyone would be reactionary showing up at a scene like this. If Ruby changed her allegiance and decided to disappear instead of putting the Lynx program on blast, they might never realise the consequences.

'It's okay,' he said. 'You'll get it.'

She stabbed at the keypad, eight consecutive times.

A green light.

The door popped open, accompanied by a brief electronic buzzer.

Smart kid, Slater thought.

They hustled into the garage.

95

There were four vehicles spread across the open concrete space, roughly the same size as the basement beside it. Three ATVs, painted black — one for each guard booth, he assumed — and a huge Toyota Land Cruiser with a jacked-up suspension and tinted windows. All the buggies had fresh snow on the tyres, yet to melt. It was freezing down here. The guards must have used them for a morning patrol. Maybe part of the routine. Each booth moving out separately, always leaving four guards at a time at the facility. In case of intruders.

In the end it hadn't mattered anyway.

'The big one,' Slater muttered, and Shien ran for the Toyota.

It was a fairly new construction, a world away from the rundown rust-buckets he'd made use of in Yemen. Out there, in the hot oppressive desert, nine out of ten vehicles were Toyota Land Cruisers. A big pick-up truck in such a state of disrepair might attract attention in the North Maine Woods, but this particular Toyota was shiny and sleek and seemingly brand new. Unlikely to have been utilised much at all. Slater used the massive hood to work his way around to the driver's seat, and he clambered up into the cabin.

'Key's on the wall,' he called out into the empty chamber.

Shien jogged over and fetched the fob off a hook set a few feet off the floor. She threw it across the garage, and Slater caught it and fired the truck to life. He worked the controls on the door and manoeuvred the seat as high as it would go, letting his broken foot dangle out in empty space. A whole lot more preferable to resting it against the footwell. Otherwise every bump and pothole and rut would send pain spearing through his ripped muscles, and that was all but a guarantee out here.

He tested the accelerator and brake with his left foot, unaccustomed to using his other leg to drive. It seemed to work simply enough.

Shien climbed up into the passenger seat and sat in the middle of the leather, her tiny frame nearly swallowed up.

She said, 'Mother has the door remote.'

They stared out through the windshield at an enormous garage door made of something resembling plexiglass. It took up an entire wall, and blurry daylight trickled in through the translucent material.

'Put your seatbelt on, Shien,' Slater said.

She obliged.

'Close your eyes.'

'Why?'

'If the windshield breaks, I don't want you catching one of the splinters in the eye.'

'Why don't you use one of the buggies to weaken the door first? Those big tyres can do a lot of damage.'

Smart kid, Slater thought again.

He said, 'We're running on a limited window of time

here. I don't want to alarm you, but I'm about to pass out. I'd prefer that happened with some distance between us and this place.'

'Oh.'

'Eyes closed?'

'Yes.'

'Good.'

He shifted in his seat, turning his left foot horizontal, and stamped it on both pedals in unison. The engine roared and whined and protested, and Slater gave it a few seconds, and then he let go with his heel. The Toyota shot off the mark and covered the gap in a couple of seconds flat, and it hit the door with a shuddering impact that transferred through the seat, into his legs, down his calves, and then all the broken bones and torn muscles in his foot rattled in place, and he gasped and scrunched up his nose and fought through the whirlwind of agony, and suddenly they were out in the open, the door smashing upward along its tracks instead of bending to distribute the weight, which Slater gave thanks for.

They rocketed out onto a path no wider than a single vehicle, carved through the snow by repeated tyre tracks over the same ground, leading away from the lodge and into a narrow gap between the pine trees. The daylight reflected off the snow, no matter how cloudy it was overhead, and Slater squinted as his eyes adjusted to the new conditions. He saw Shien doing the same out of the corner of his eye.

He braced himself for a war, touching a hand to the HK416 he'd deposited cautiously on the centre console.

Natural instinct.

From repeated experience.

But this was North Maine. There was no urgent response, no matter how secretive the program was, no matter what level of clearance it involved. There was simply no feasible way to muster troops who had access to this kind of knowledge. Not in a hurry. The response would come later, and the upper echelon, or Command, or whatever the hell they went by, would sneak into the clearing under cover of darkness and sanitise all the buildings at once.

And then rebuild…

Slater hit the brakes, hard, and the Toyota jackknifed and slid to a stop in the lee of the lodge. The log building loomed up behind them, overbearing, beckoning them back.

Shien turned, wide eyed, and said, 'What are you doing?'

They'd almost reached the tree line.

Freedom was right there. A mile or so on an off-road trail, and then a short journey across a bridge, and then back on State Route 161 and onward, to wherever the hell they wanted…

But Slater said, 'If Ruby changes her mind, then these kids won't have anyone looking after them.'

'There's food in the house. There's water. Mother was training us to kill people. They can feed and wash and clothe themselves. They're not idiots.'

'Who's the oldest?'

'Rachel. She's seventeen.'

Slater nodded. 'Good enough for me.'

He stamped back on the accelerator, and they took off again.

'You're not trying to save them?' Shien said.

'I can't,' Slater said. 'Not all of them. But I have a feeling Ruby's about to bring the whole program down. And if she doesn't, I will.'

'How?'

'Anonymous op-ed.'

'What?'

'That's a conversation for another time.'

He mounted the trail, reuniting with the gloom as the tree canopy passed over their heads. Relatively close to a state of delirium, Slater leant forward and looked past Shien, out through the passenger window, searching for a particular tree not far off the trail where he'd left a man he'd thought he could trust.

He spotted a glimpse of ... something. The Toyota was travelling at thirty miles an hour, so it was nothing more than a fleeting image, like a still frame in a moving picture, but it was enough. He saw Russell Williams seated with his back to the trunk, his head drooped and his shoulders slumped, his eyes open but unfocused. And he saw a slender hand around his throat, connected to a lithe frame and a pair of eyes that burned brighter than anything else Slater had seen before. Ruby Nazarian was speaking to him, her tongue darting in and out of her mouth, her nostrils flared, anger and rage and pain in her eyes.

Williams sat there, listening.

And then it all disappeared as they rumbled past, and for a moment Slater thought he'd glimpsed a switchblade in Ruby's other hand — he couldn't be certain, but he thought he'd seen the flash of steel. He would never know for sure. He was now a sworn enemy of the United States government, directly responsible for sabotaging a confidential program designed to neutralise enemies of the state. Even if Williams died along with his pet project, their cross-country trip had been captured on every surveillance camera from here to New York. An investigation was hardly necessary.

They would know it was Slater.

He was excommunicated, all over again.

'I missed this,' he whispered to himself.

Shien stared at him. 'What?'

'Nothing.'

'You said something.'

'Ruby said it best. This isn't my fight. This isn't my story. It's none of my business what happens to Lynx. I can't save everyone.'

'Then why did you come?'

'Because I can at least save you.'

'Thank you. You don't know what it means to me.'

'Yes, I do. And I'm sorry. For not doing my due diligence. For handing you over to Williams without careful consideration.'

'You don't need to be sorry.'

He smiled through tears. 'Actually, that's the only thing I need to be sorry for in the whole world.'

96

They drove for hours on I-95, back the way Slater had come hours earlier, out of Maine. The snow receded and the woods shrank away, replaced by dull drab terrain. With nothing on the outside of the vehicle worth looking at, eventually Shien's attention turned inward, as Slater knew it would, and the strange silence gave way to deep thought, and then questions, and then the urgent need for answers.

She seemed to come to her own conclusions.

Conclusions he'd reached well before he'd rescued her.

She said, 'I can't stay with you, can I?'

He shook his head. 'No.'

'That was never in the plan, was it?'

'No.'

'You think your life is too dangerous.'

'I can rescue you. But I can't raise you.'

'I can't survive on my own, Will.'

'I know.'

'What's your plan?'

'I have an idea.'

'Can you tell me?'

'Not yet.'

'Will,' she said.

And something about her tone made him turn.

Her eyes brimmed with tears, but she didn't sob. She sat there, silently furious, staring him down.

She said, 'I'm not some thing to be discarded. I have a life and I have feelings and emotions and right now I'm doing what you seem so good at doing. I'm pretending they don't exist. I'm stuffing them deep down inside and trying to convince myself that I didn't just see people die and bodies everywhere and blood and ... things I shouldn't see. I'm ten years old. And it seems like you don't care about any of that. I can put up with it for a while but ... I need someone, Will. My parents are gone and that lodge was the furthest thing from a home and I need someone in my life who's going to take care of me and it sounds like ... you're just going to toss me away again...'

He didn't respond. Not for a beat. Because there was a titan in his chest ready to burst out, and he only needed to give himself permission to release it.

And it did.

And it all came pouring out.

'Shien,' he said, his voice low and cold. 'My foot is torn off the bone. I've lost somewhere close to a pint of blood. I can barely see straight. And I have eight hours of driving ahead of me, and the entire government at my heels, and the bare foundations of a plan, and no experience of being a father, and no future prospects, and no family, and no friends, and no one that gives a shit about me. There was one man who cared about me, and he saved my life in the

Russian Far East, and he's the closest I came to looking in the mirror without actually staring at my reflection. But Jason King is gone, and he wants nothing to do with me, or this life, and I can't have a normal existence because it isn't in my DNA. If I sit still for any amount of time I feel set to explode, but that's hard to put into words because not many people understand what that's like. I need chaos and carnage because otherwise I feel like I'm wasting my existence for purely selfish purposes. If I gave it all up to raise you there'd be a hundred or a thousand men and women out there who wouldn't get their warm ending. They'd die miserable and alone and in horrendous pain in captivity somewhere, all because I made the decision to give up my talent and refuse to go out looking for them. So all these thoughts are constantly jumbled up inside my head, and if I ever let them out or truly think about them, long and hard, I'd arrive at a pretty miserable conclusion no matter what. Which is that I'm destined to break bones and tear muscle and get shot and stabbed until my body finally falls apart from the continuous stress. That's why I might appear so cold all the time. I care about you more than I've cared about anyone in my entire life, and that's why I made an enemy of the government again. Because that's the last goddamn thing I wanted to do. I just sacrificed my own future for yours. And I'd do it every single time. So don't sit there and talk about my lack of emotions. You're the most important thing in my life right now, and I can't exactly say why, but every single part of me is trying my absolute hardest to come up with the best future for you that I possibly can. And that's a lot to deal with. Okay?'

The silence elongated, the cabin supercharged with raw emotion, and finally Shien threw herself over the centre console and hugged him tight and cried into his chest.

'I'm sorry,' she said. 'Thank you for what you did.'

He rested a palm on the top of her head, and fought back his own tears, and focused on the road ahead.

Heading for New York.

97

Five hours later, after stopping for gas and food and drink and several cups of hot black coffee, and more medical supplies, and a few pain pills, Slater drove into the outskirts of New York with enough confidence in his ability to see this through to the end.

Whatever that constituted.

'Can you please talk to me?' Shien finally said. 'You've been so quiet.'

'You want the truth?'

'Of course.'

'I don't want to give you to anyone. I screwed it up the first time and now there's a voice telling me no matter what I do, I'll screw it up again. And on top of that, I care about you. I want you to stay with me. But at the same time, the most important thing is that you have a normal upbringing, which is all I ever wanted for you in the first place before Russell Williams ruined everything. And you deserve that a hell of a lot more than I deserve a companion.'

'I don't want you to give me up.'

'The feeling's mutual.'

'So why do you need to?'

'Did you hear what I told you about my life?'

'Yes. But isn't that just chance? We've only met when bad things are happening around us. But there have to be normal parts of your life, right? It can't all be like this.'

'You'd be surprised.'

'Why don't you stop?'

'That requires a long and complicated answer, Shien. I'm not in the mood right now.'

'Where are you taking me?'

'Not far.'

'How long do we have left?'

'Maybe thirty minutes.'

'Then try and put it into words. Because won't this be the last I'll see of you?'

'I'll try to drop in. From time to time.'

'No,' Shien said, her voice low.

Slater had never heard her sound like that.

He looked across. 'You mean that?'

'Why wouldn't I? You don't get to swing around whenever you feel like it. You either choose to look after me or choose not to. It has to be black and white for something like this.'

'You don't talk like you're ten years old, you know?'

'Yeah,' Shien muttered. 'Life experience, I guess. I've grown up fast.'

'I'm sorry I have to be like this.'

'You don't have to.'

'That's part of the long and complicated answer.'

'Give me some of it.'

'Have you ever had an itch you can't scratch? In the middle of your back, or somewhere similar?'

'Yes.'

'When I sit down and do nothing, that's what I feel.'

'Is that so bad?'

'Think of it like an itch on my mind.'

'Why do you get it?'

'Since I was eighteen, all I've known is working out and training and drilling combinations on bags and putting in time at the shooting range, and a million other similar exercises. I've probably put more time into my body and mind than most people put into their careers, because I had a multi-million dollar pool of government money behind me. You following?'

'I'm following.'

'All this happened because I was born with a genetic predisposition.'

'A what?'

'I react incredibly quick in combat situations.'

'I've seen it.'

'How would you describe it?'

'Like you're punching at the same speed as the other guy but you look at them like they're stupid for even trying to win. It's like you're built different. I don't know how to describe it.'

'I'm built the same, but my mind isn't. Whenever something happens in front of you, there's always a delay of milliseconds until the brain processes it. It has to travel through the eyes and down the proper pathways and then it gets translated into information and the brain commands the body to respond. I've got some crazy statistic in that field. Someone goes to throw a punch and I see all their muscles tensing and running along a chain in their body, so I know a right hook is coming and I can sidestep it, and it's almost lazy. You following?'

'I'm following.'

'Or I can register three people in front of me and shift my aim from body to body before they even realise what's happening. None of it's planned. It's some animal instinct, from millions of years ago. Mine's just faster than most.'

'It's a talent.'

'Yes, it is. And if I sit around and do nothing, then it's a talent that's wasted. And it's a talent that happens to be able to help almost anyone that's stuck in a bad situation. That's the best way I can break it down. When I sit down and try to concentrate on myself, and stay in one place for too long, I see people dying in my head, all across the country, all across the world. And I'm letting it happen by sitting still.'

'You shouldn't think that way.'

'I shouldn't have done a lot of things.'

'Like rescue me?'

Slater looked at her. 'No. That's something I'll never regret.'

'Can you tell me where we're going now?'

'I can show you.'

He hit the brakes, and they screeched to a stop in a quiet Brooklyn residential neighbourhood, in front of a house with a neat manicured lawn and a white picket fence.

98

S later put the car in park, and said, 'Wait here.'

It was now mid-afternoon, and he made sure to sweep the street up and down with his gaze a couple of times before hobbling out of the driver's seat. He touched down on the opposite kerb with his good foot, and used the fully automatic assault rifle on the centre console as a rudimentary walking stick.

Shien hissed, 'Are you sure that's a good idea?'

'I don't see any alternative,' Slater said. 'And I only need to make it to the front door.'

'Let me help you.'

'Wait here,' he repeated. 'There's a conversation I need to have first.'

'With who?'

'Wait here.'

He hopped across the road, each step sending a bolt of agony through his right foot, even though it never touched the ground. He jammed the barrel of the HK416 against the asphalt and gripped the stock and made it to the other side of the street in a few massive leaps.

Bone-crushing agony came along with it.

What's new? Slater thought.

He moved on autopilot. He thought on autopilot. There was little other choice. He'd been driving for nigh on eighteen hours straight, with a short pit stop in the Allagash Wilderness to take a bullet to his shoulder and get his foot mangled beyond all repair. Sleep deprived, drained of blood, with the broken bone and torn muscle in his foot grinding in place, he knew he belonged in the ICU.

But he had a job to do, and he was damned if he wasn't going to see it through to the end.

He struggled up the short path to the front porch, head bowed, breathing hard.

He stopped a foot away from the stairs up to the landing, and regarded them with unashamed irritation.

There were only two steps, but he'd maxed out his energy reserves ten hours ago, and he was running on empty.

He sat down on the first step, slid the rifle out of sight underneath one of the deck chairs, and banged hard on the wood panelled floor of the porch.

Half a second later, the screen door burst open.

Frank Nazarian rushed out carrying a suitcase, with his wife and his daughter trailing along behind.

Slater said, 'Going somewhere?'

99

Nazarian peered down at him, noting his sorry state. Then his eyes wandered to the rifle under the chair.

He said, 'Slater, this is my wife Anastasia, and my daughter Abigail.'

They peered down at him too.

Slater said, 'Pleasure to meet you both.'

He raised a hand to wave, before realising it was crusted in blood and dirt.

Then he sighed and slumped against the nearest post. He half-closed his eyes. He said, 'Sorry everyone. It's been a real long day.'

He tried to make out Anastasia and Abigail's features, but he was seeing double. He managed to work out Anastasia had blonde hair, and Abigail had brown hair, and they were both regarding him like he was something that had come out of a swamp and dropped itself on their doorstep.

With abject disgust.

He couldn't disagree with them.

He said, 'How's this for a first impression?'

He thought he saw Anastasia smile.

She said, 'Thank you for what you did for my husband.'

'He told you?'

'I caught him with two unconscious men in his trunk. He had a lot of explaining to do.'

'I take it that's the first time that's happened.'

'Shame,' Nazarian said. 'I was thinking of making a hobby of it.'

'Who the hell is he?' Abigail whispered to her parents.

'Put the bags in the car,' Nazarian said. 'I need to talk to him alone for a minute.'

'Maybe a couple of minutes,' Slater said.

'Why?'

'I have a proposal to make.'

100

Nazarian sat down on the step next to him, only a few inches away, but Slater needed him close, because now he could barely utter a word in anything above a whisper.

'We need to take you to a hospital,' the man said.

Slater shook his head slowly, eyes closed, a wry smile on his face. 'That's not a good idea right now.'

'What did you do?'

'A hell of a lot.'

'Did the Whelans do this to you?'

Slater smacked his lips together, and squinted. 'The Whelans...?'

'I told you not to go after them.'

'Oh,' Slater said. 'The Whelans.'

It seemed like months since he'd dealt with them. It hadn't even happened twenty four hours ago.

'You see,' Nazarian hissed, low, under his breath, just in case Anastasia and Abigail could hear from their position, milling around the plain sedan in the driveway. 'This is what I warned you about. You weren't as tough as you thought you were, and now you show up on my doorstep like this at a time where my family are already scared half to death. Me included.'

'Where are you three going?'

'Anywhere. We're getting off the grid for a couple of weeks. Maybe a month. In fact we might stay on the road. Sell the house. I've got enough tucked away to take care of us, and Abigail's built up a small fortune herself, despite her age. I'm sure you can understand why she got a phone call telling her not to come back to work.'

'When did she get that?'

'Yesterday. Before you showed up.'

'She can call back. She can get her job back. Just like that.'

'If you're going to sit there and feed me bullshit, you can go. I don't care how hurt you are. I'll send you away.'

'But why?'

'Stop talking crap.'

'The Whelans didn't do this to me,' Slater said with a small smile. 'You should pay them a visit and see how they're healing up.'

'Do you really believe your own delusions?'

'I beat the shit out of every Whelan I got my hands on, and then I stirred up enough trouble and planted a certain name in enough places to draw an old colleague out of his covert lair, and then I took that same man all the way up the East Coast in one of the Whelans' vehicles, and then I saved a little girl from the same program that man put your daughter in.'

Nazarian didn't respond.

Slater said, 'You think I made all that up?'

'I don't know what to think.'

'She's in the car.'

'Who's in the car? Which car?'

'That one,' Slater said, and pointed to the Land Cruiser across the street, but the windows were tinted to the maximum, and Shien appeared as nothing but a dark silhouette behind a dark sheet of glass. 'She means everything to me.'

'Who is she?'

'The girl I tried to tell you about when I first visited you.'

'I said I didn't want to hear your reasons because I believed in you. I didn't want you to bring your baggage here.'

'She's not my baggage.'

'I can't take her.'

Slater waved a hand up and down, gesturing to his body. 'This is my life, Frank. This is all I am. I destroyed the Whelans and I destroyed the Lynx program and now I'm going to heal up and go searching for the next thing.'

'You don't have to.'

'I do.'

'Why?'

'I just had that conversation.'

'With who?'

'Shien.'

'That's her name?'

'That's her name.'

'What's she like?'

'She's the sweetest little girl you'll ever meet.'

'So do your job and raise her.'

'I'm not fit to raise anyone.'

'You could try.'

'I'd fail. And not just that. I'd get her killed.'

'You don't know that.'

'I do.'

'Tell me about her.'

'I pulled her out of a sex trafficking ring in Macau. In the depths of one of the largest casinos in the province.'

'Jesus. Did they...?'

'No. They'd only just taken her. But they were about to start preparing her for the industry. I got involved just in time.'

'Does she know what would have happened to her if you didn't save her?'

'I don't think so. And I'd like to keep it that way.'

'What happened after that?'

'I gave her to Russell Williams.'

Nazarian said nothing. There was nothing that needed to be said.

Slater said, 'I didn't know.'

'I can't see how you could have.'

'I trusted him.'

'So did I. Back when we were friends.'

'I thought he would do right by her.'

'And he didn't?'

'He sent her to North Maine.'

'What's in North Maine?'

'A lodge.'

'You're not telling me much.'

'Best we leave it to implode on its own.'

Silence.

Slater said, 'It's where your daughter grew up.'

Nazarian's gaze drifted to the step between his feet. He picked at the wood with a nail, fighting back emotions Slater had no concept of. He couldn't even begin to decipher the intricacies of a situation like this. So he sat back and let the pain wash over him and waited for a response.

Nazarian said, 'Did you see her again?'

'I did.'

'How's she doing?'

'She tried to kill me.'

'Jesus Christ. I'm so sorry.'

'And then she changed her mind. I think it all hit her. And I mean all of it. I don't know what triggered it. Maybe the doubt was already there. But something tipped her over the edge. She saved my life. Directly afterwards.'

'Where is she now?'

'I don't know.'

'Does she want to see me?'

'No.'

Nazarian broke his nail on the wooden step. Blood dripped from his finger. He stared at it absent-mindedly. Not really there. Somewhere far away. Thinking.

Slater said, 'It's not what you think.'

Now the tears came. Nazarian said, 'I tried so hard to raise her. But I didn't know how. I didn't think I did that bad of a job...'

'You didn't. She recognises that. She's ashamed — as far as I could tell. She said you might not want her back the way she is.'

'That's not true.'

'It's how she feels. It might be for the best.'

'How dare you fucking—'

'Frank,' Slater said, his voice cold. 'I don't say that lightly.'

A pause.

A long pause.

Nazarian said, 'What's she like?'

'She's something else. A childhood like the one she had will do that.'

'Does she have decency in her heart?'

'I think her emotions aren't anything we could conceive. I think her mind is a mess that'll take her years to dissect.'

'Do you think she'll be able to do it?'

'I've never met a stronger woman.'

'You're not just saying that?'

'She'll be okay. That's my gut instinct. And I always go with my gut.'

'I hope she finds me. I hope she finds us.'

'She might. Some day. But it can't be soon. She's too volatile right now. Anyone would be, in her position.'

'Maybe it's best we're hitting the road, then.'

'You don't have to. I was telling the truth about the Whelans. They won't bother you anymore.'

'What the hell did you do to them?'

'What I do best.'

'Was it enough?'

Slater recalled the punishment he'd dished out. 'They won't touch you. They'll be too busy looking over their shoulders for the rest of their lives.'

'Why did you do it?'

'To get to Williams.'

'I see.'

'But I probably would have done it anyway. For you.'

'You mean that?'

'I only say things I mean.'

'But, I mean, truly?'

'Truly.'

'You saved my life when you showed up at my door yesterday.'

'I know.'

'I'll take the girl.'

'Don't do it for me,' Slater said. 'And don't you dare put a half-hearted effort into it.'

'I would never.'

'I've done this once before, and I fucked it up about as bad as anyone can fuck anything up. I couldn't stand to make the same mistake twice.'

'Do I look like Russell Williams?'

'No. You don't.'

'What happened to him, if I might ask?'

Slater recalled the glimpse of Ruby in the woods.

'I don't know,' he said.

'Is that the truth?'

'If I had to guess, I'd say he's dead.'

'But you can't be sure?'

'I left him in the hands of your daughter.'

'Right.'

'This must be a lot to deal with.'

'I've had a strange life for as long as I can remember. I'll cope.'

'If your daughter doesn't end the program, I'll make sure to.'

'How?'

'I know things.'

'They'd better be relevant.'

'They will be.'

'And then what?'

'And then nothing. I go back to being a ghost. The U.S. government wants my head. I'll run into trouble until it kills me. Same old stuff.'

'Sounds grim.'

'It's my life.'

'Do you enjoy your life?'

'Enjoy isn't the right word.'

'Do you find meaning in it?'

'More than you could imagine.'

'Then keep doing what you're doing. Tell me more about the girl.'

'Her name's Shien. She doesn't know her mother. Her father's dead. She was put through a situation in Macau she should have never been a part of. She's seen things she never should have seen. She deserves a normal life with a normal family.'

'I wouldn't class us as normal.'

Slater turned his gaze to Abigail, and then to Anastasia, and then to Frank.

'You're kind people,' he said.

'We try to be.'

'You're a tight-knit family.'

'We try to be.'

'You'd love her and care for her like a daughter.'

'We'd try to.'

'Then that's probably the closest thing to normal she's ever experienced.'

'Is she okay with this?'

'She knows it's the only way.'

'Does she know who you are? Deep down inside?'

'All the way through to the core. I told her. On the way here.'

'Does she like it?'

'She doesn't like it. She accepts it.'

'Will the government be looking for her?'

'She was already off-the-record. Ruby will take care of the remnants of what's left in North Maine. And like I said, if she doesn't, I will.'

'She might not want to talk to you again.'

'She said she can't see me again. If I do this.'

'And you're still okay with giving her away?'

'This isn't a fairytale. I can't do it all. I couldn't even

come close. My life is such a trainwreck, it's almost laugh-
able. But you're a good man. You have a good family. You
had a daughter you didn't get along with — but I'd say that's
the same in almost every household in the United States. I'd
wager a bet most kids run away, too. Even if it's only for an
hour. We've all spat the dummy in our childhood. Neither
you or I have any idea how manipulative Williams was. It's
possible he picked her up within minutes of her storming
out. We'll never know for sure. But you should never blame
yourself for that. You befriended a manipulator, and you
paid for it through no fault of your own. I know who you
are. You raised a beautiful, successful daughter in Abigail,
and you would have done the same with Ruby if she hadn't
been thrust into a world she knew nothing about against
her own free will. Now you and Anastasia can do what you
know how to do. You can raise an amazing kid. But not with
Ruby. With Shien. You lost a girl to Lynx, and you gained
one too. Think of it as poetic.'

'What about school? What about...?'

'Frank,' Slater muttered. 'I'd love to sit and chat about
the administrative details, but I need a firm yes or no
answer. Because right now my situation is dire. To put it
mildly. I'll have the whole government on my heels for a
while at least, and I need to lay low and recuperate.'

'Holy shit,' Nazarian whispered. 'Your foot.'

'You just noticed?'

'It's a swollen pumpkin.'

'It's even worse on the inside, trust me.'

'How are you going to fix that yourself?'

'I'm not. I'm a man of improvisation.'

'What does that mean?'

'It means I'll probably catch a doctor walking out of a
hospital after his shift is over and offer him five grand to

patch me back up with the best medical instruments and painkillers on offer. Off the record, of course.'

'You do that often?'

'I've been improvising most of my life.'

'You've got that kind of money?'

'It's a long story.'

'Let me meet the girl,' Nazarian said. 'Then I'll decide.'

'I thought you already promised.'

'I need to see her to know for sure. I don't know why. It's instinct. A fatherly thing.'

'How will you let me know?'

'I'll nod.'

'And if it's not right?'

'I don't know. But don't force this on me. It's a commitment you know nothing about, if we're going to be honest. I need to make the choice on my own. I can't stress how important that is.'

'I understand.'

'So where is she?'

Slater lifted a hand up, in full view of the Land Cruiser, and beckoned.

S he stepped out of the passenger seat. Small and gentle, with her wide eyes locked onto Frank Nazarian. Seeming to understand that this was more than likely her new father.

Nazarian turned to Slater, and he nodded a confirmation.

It couldn't have been more than a couple of seconds.

Shien had that effect on people.

She made it across the street, casting a shy glance in the direction of Abigail and Anastasia, and then she stepped up to the pair of them.

'Hi,' she said.

'Hi, Shien,' Nazarian said. 'It's a pleasure to meet you.'

'You too.'

Nazarian pushed himself to an upright position.

'I'll be right back,' he said to Slater. 'I need to talk this over with my wife. She needs to be on board, obviously. But I'll explain what you told me. Every word of it.'

'You two share everything with each other?'

'Of course. I love her.'

Slater smiled.

Nazarian sauntered away, and then it was just the two of them.

'You're not looking good,' Shien said.

'Thanks.'

'I mean it.'

'I couldn't agree more.'

'You need to fix yourself up.'

'I happen to be very good at that.'

'Is this goodbye forever?'

'If you want it to be.'

'I don't want it to be. But if it's goodbye for now, then it needs to be goodbye forever.'

'You sure?'

'You told me I'm only ten. But I can make up my mind with something like that. I can do the right thing.'

'You're the toughest ten year old I've ever met.'

'Have you met many?'

'I've seen them around. Most of them seem like pests.'

She smiled. 'You going to be okay without me?'

'Almost certainly not.'

'But it's in your DNA, right?'

'Right.'

'I just wanted to say that you've done more for me than anyone else would, and I don't know why. I don't know if I'll ever work it out. But I can't put into words how thankful I am, Will. Thank you so much. For everything. That's two times in a row you've put me on a new path. I don't really want to know where those paths would have led without you. It scares me. I can't lie about it. It keeps me awake at night and it gives me bad dreams. But that's better than actually living it.'

'There won't be a third,' Slater said. 'Not with these

people. They'll protect you. They'll look after you. They'll give you what I wanted you to have all along. I'm so sorry for what Williams did. I can't put that into words either.'

'Maybe words aren't the best for a situation like this.'

'Maybe not.'

'We could talk for hours and we wouldn't scratch the surface.'

'I agree.'

She hugged him, nestling into his barrel chest, and transferred all the emotion she wanted to put into words, but couldn't. And he did the same, and then they parted, and Frank and Anastasia Nazarian approached with warm smiles on their faces and open arms, and Slater figured it couldn't get much better than that.

So he stood up and nodded to each of them and used the rifle to hop back to the Land Cruiser, where he sat motionless in the driver's seat, in a world of pain but feeling none of it, watching each of the Nazarians hug Shien in turn through the tinted glass. He watched them pile into the family sedan and back out of the driveway and take off down the quiet suburban street, until they disappeared from sight, leaving him alone.

He lowered his forehead to the steering wheel, and he breathed a sigh of relief quite unlike any sensation he'd ever experienced, and he cried tears of joy for the first time in his life.

Then he put the truck into gear and accelerated, because his life was nothing without momentum.

And he smiled.

MORE WILL SLATER THRILLERS COMING SOON...

Visit amazon.com/author/mattrogers23 and press **"Follow"** to be automatically notified of my future releases.

If you enjoyed the hard-hitting adventure, make sure to leave a review! Your feedback means everything to me, and encourages me to deliver more novels as soon as I can.

Stay tuned.

Join the Reader's Group and get a free 200-page book by Matt Rogers!

Sign up for a free copy of '**HARD IMPACT**'.
Meet Jason King — another member of Black Force.

Experience King's most dangerous mission — action-packed insanity in the heart of the Amazon Rainforest.

No spam guaranteed.

Just click here.

BOOKS BY MATT ROGERS

THE JASON KING SERIES

Isolated (Book 1)

Imprisoned (Book 2)

Reloaded (Book 3)

Betrayed (Book 4)

Corrupted (Book 5)

Hunted (Book 6)

THE JASON KING FILES

Cartel (Book 1)

Warrior (Book 2)

Savages (Book 3)

THE WILL SLATER SERIES

Wolf (Book 1)

Lion (Book 2)

Bear (Book 3)

Lynx (Book 4)

BLACK FORCE SHORTS

The Victor (Book 1)

The Chimera (Book 2)

The Tribe (Book 3)

ABOUT THE AUTHOR

Matt Rogers grew up in Melbourne, Australia as a voracious reader, relentlessly devouring thrillers and mysteries in his spare time. Now, he writes full-time. His novels are action-packed and fast-paced. Dive into the Jason King Series to get started with his collection.

Visit his website:

www.mattrogersbooks.com

Visit his Amazon page:

amazon.com/author/mattrogers23

.

Printed in Great Britain
by Amazon